27m

BITTERSWEET

COLLEEN McCULLOUGH

Simon & Schuster
New York   London   Toronto   Sydney   New Delhi

Simon & Schuster
1230 Avenue of the Americas
New York, NY 10020

This Simon & Schuster export edition August 2014

Originally published in Australia in 2013 by HarperCollinsPublishers Pty Limited.

SIMON & SCHUSTER and colophon are registered trademarks of Simon & Schuster, Inc.

For information about special discounts for bulk purchases, please contact Simon & Schuster Special Sales at 1-800-268-3216 or CustomerService@simonandschuster.ca.

The Simon & Schuster Speakers Bureau can bring authors to your live event. For more information or to book an event, contact the Simon & Schuster Speakers Bureau at 1-866-248-3049 or visit our website at www.simonspeakers.com.

Interior design by Aline C. Pace
Jacket design by Jackie Seow
Jacket photographs: (woman) © Bettmann/Corbis;
(landscape) Bethune Carmichael/Lonely Planet Images/Getty Images

Manufactured in the United States of America

10 9 8 7 6 5 4 3 2 1

Library of Congress Cataloging-in-Publication Data
McCullough, Colleen.
 Bittersweet : a novel / Colleen McCullough.
    pages   cm
1. Sisters—Fiction. 2. Twins—Fiction. 3. Nurses—Fiction. 4. Choice (Psychology)—Fiction. 5. Self-actualization (Psychology) in women—Fiction. 6. Self-realization in women—Fiction. 7. Australia—Fiction. 8. Psychological fiction. I. Title.
 PR9619.3M32B58 2014
 823'.914—c23   2014001475

ISBN 978-1-4767-6768-0
ISBN 978-1-4767-6769-7 (ebook)

For Val and Alex Martinez
with
much love and many thanks
for all the kindnesses
through the long years

BITTERSWEET

PART ONE

❧

FOUR NEW-STYLE NURSES

E dda and Grace, Tufts and Kitty. Two sets of twins, the daughters of the Reverend Thomas Latimer, Rector of St. Mark's Church of England in the Shire & City of Corunda, New South Wales.

They were sitting on four slender chairs in front of the vast maw of the fireplace, where no fire burned. The very large drawing room was filled with chattering women invited by the Rector's wife, Maude, to celebrate the event looming in less than a week: the Rector's four daughters were quitting the Rectory to commence training as nurses at the Corunda Base Hospital.

Less than a week to go, less than a week to go! Edda kept saying to herself as she endured the embarrassment of being on display, her eyes roaming about because she preferred not to look at her stepmother, Maude, dominating the talk as usual, natter, natter, natter.

There was a hole in the wooden floor to the side of Edda's chair, the last in the row of four; a movement inside it caught her attention and she stiffened, grinning deep within herself. A big rat! A rat was about to invade Mama's party! Just an inch more, she thought as she watched the head, then I'll emit a loud gasp and screech "*Rat!*" at the top of my voice. What fun!

But before Edda could find her voice she actually saw the head, and froze. A polished black wedge with vibrating tongue—huge for what it was!—followed by a polished black body as thick as a woman's arm—a black body, yes, but beneath it a red belly. And the thing kept on coming and coming, seven feet of red-bellied black snake, lethally venomous. How had it found its way in here?

It was still emerging, ready the moment the tip of its tail was free to make a bolt in some unpredictable direction. The fire tools were on the far side of the hearth, with the oblivious Tufts, Grace, and Kitty in between; she'd never reach them.

Her chair had a padded seat but no arms, and its frail legs tapered to fine round points no bigger than a lipstick tube; Edda drew in a great breath, lifted herself and the chair a few inches, and brought the left front leg down on the middle of the snake's head. Then she sat, hard and heavy, hands clenched grimly around the sides of the chair seat, determined to ride out the tempest as if she were Jack Thurlow breaking in a horse.

The leg pierced its skull between the eyes and the snake, all seven feet of it, reared high into the air. Someone gave a shrill scream and other screams followed, while Edda Latimer sat and fought to keep the chair leg embedded in the snake's head. Its body whipped, pounded, crashed around and against her, dealing her blows more savage and punishing than a man's fist, raining on her so thick and fast that she seemed surrounded by a whirling blur, a threshing shadow.

Women were running everywhere, still screaming, eyes filled with the sight of Edda and the old man snake, unable to get past their panic to help her.

Except for Kitty—pretty Kitty, gritty Kitty—who leaped across the hearth wielding the tomahawk used for last-minute splitting of over-chunky kindling. Wading through the lashing snake's blows, she severed head from spine in two hacks.

"You can take your weight off the chair now, Eds," Kitty said to her sister as she dropped the hatchet. "What a monster! You'll be black and blue from bruises."

"You're mad!" sobbed Grace, running tears of shock.

"Fools!" said Tufts fiercely to Edda and Kitty both. The white-faced Reverend Thomas Latimer was too occupied in dealing with his second wife, in rigid hysterics, to do what he longed to do—comfort his wonderfully brave daughters.

The screams and cries were dying down now, and the terror had diminished sufficiently for some of the more intrepid women to cluster around the snake and inspect its mortality for themselves—an enormous thing! And for all that Mrs. Enid Treadby and Mrs. Henrietta Burdum assisted the Rector in soothing Maude, no one except the four twins remembered the original purpose of this ruined gathering. What mattered was that that strange creature Edda Latimer had killed a lethally venomous old man snake, and it was time to run home, there to perpetuate Corunda's main feminine activity—Gossip and her attendants, Rumour and Speculation.

The four girls moved to an abandoned trolley of goodies, poured tea into frail cups and plundered the cucumber sandwiches.

"Aren't women fools?" Tufts asked, waving the teapot. "You would swear the sky was going to fall in! Typical you, though, Edda. What did you plan to do if the chair leg didn't succeed?"

"Then, Tufts, I would have appealed to you for an idea."

"Huh! You didn't need to appeal to me because our other brilliant thinker and schemer, Kitty, came to your rescue." Tufts looked around. "Stone the crows, they're all going home! Tuck in, girls, we can eat the lot."

"Mama will take two days to recover from this," Grace said cheerfully, holding out her cup for more tea. "Rather beats the shock of losing her four unpaid Rectory housemaids."

Kitty blew a rude noise. "Rubbish, Grace! The shock of losing her unpaid housemaids looms far larger in Mama's mind than the death of a snake, no matter how big or poisonous."

"What's more," said Tufts, "the first thing Mama will do when she has recovered is serve Edda a sermon on how to kill snakes with decorum and discretion. You created a rumpus."

"Dear me, yes, so I did," Edda said placidly, smearing rich red jam and a pile of whipped cream on top of a scone. "Yum! If I hadn't made a rumpus, the four of us would never have managed to get a scone. All Mama's cronies would have gobbled them." She laughed. "Next Monday, girls! Next Monday we start lives of our own. No more Mama. And you know I don't mean that against you and Tufts, Kitty."

"I know it well," said Kitty gruffly.

⑤

It wasn't that Maude Latimer was *consciously* awful; according to her own lights she was a saint among stepmothers as well as mothers. Grace and Edda had the same father as her own Tufts and Kitty, and there was no discrimination anywhere on the remotest horizon, Maude was quick to tell even the least interested observer of Rectory life. How could four such gorgeous children be irksome to one who adored being a mother? And it might have worked out in reality as it had within Maude's mind, were it not for a physical accident of destiny. Namely that the junior of Maude's twins, Kitty, had a degree of beauty beyond her lovely sisters, whom she surpassed as the sun dims the brilliance of the moon.

From Kitty's infancy all the way to today's leaving home party, Maude dinned Kitty's perfections in every ear that came into hearing distance. People's private opinions were identical to Maude's public ones, but oh, how *tired* everybody got when Maude hove into view, Kitty's hand firmly in hers, and the three other twins walking a pace behind. The consensus of Corunda opinion was that all Maude was really doing was making three implacable enemies for Kitty out of her sisters—how Edda, Grace, and Tufts must hate Kitty! People also concluded that Kitty must be unpleasant, spoiled, and insufferably conceited.

But it didn't happen that way, though the why was a mystery to everyone save the Rector. *He* interpreted the love between his girls as solid, tangible evidence of how much God loved them. Of course Maude usurped the praise her husband gave to God as more fairly due to her, and her alone.

The Latimer girls pitied Maude quite as much as they disliked her, and loved her only in the way that bonds females of the same family, whether there be a blood tie or not. And what had united the four girls in their unshakable alliance against Maude was not the plight of the three on the outer perimeter of Maude's affections, but the plight of Kitty, upon whom all Maude's affections were concentrated.

Kitty should have been a brash and demanding child; instead she was shy, quiet, retiring. Twenty months older, Edda and Grace noticed well before Tufts did, but once all three saw, they became very concerned about what they recognized as their mother's effect on Kitty. Just how the conspiracy among them to shield Kitty from Maude gradually began was lost in the fog of infancy, save that as time went on, the conspiracy became stronger.

It was always dominant Edda who took the brunt of the major upheavals, a pattern set when the twelve-year-old Edda caught Kitty attacking her face with a cheese grater, took it from ten-year-old Kitty, and hied her to see Daddy, who was the sweetest and kindest man in the world. And he had dealt with the crisis wonderfully, approaching the problem in the only way he knew, by persuading the little girl that in trying to maim herself, she was insulting God, Who had made her beautiful for some mysterious reason of His own, a reason that one day she would understand.

This held Kitty until the beginning of her last year of school, at the Corunda Ladies' College, a Church of England institution. By postponing the start of his elder twins' education and advancing that of his younger, all four girls went through primary and secondary school in the same class, and matriculated together. The headmistress, a dour Scot, welcomed the eleven girls who stayed at school into their final year with a speech designed to depress their expectations from life rather than encourage them.

"Your parents have permitted you to enjoy the fruits of two to four extra years of education by keeping you at C.L.C. until you matriculate," said she in the rounded tones of one educated at Oxford, "which you will do at the end of this Year of Our Lord 1924. By the time that you matriculate, your education will be superb—as far as education for women goes. You will have university-entrance grounding in English, mathematics, ancient and modern history, geography, basic science, Latin, and Greek." She paused significantly, then reached her conclusion. "However, the most desirable career available to you will be a suitable marriage. If you choose to remain single and must support yourself, there are two careers open to you: teaching in primary school and some few secondary schools, or secretarial work."

To which speech Maude Latimer added a postscript over lunch at the Rectory on the next Sunday.

"What drivel!" said Maude with a snort. "Oh, not the suitable marriage! Naturally, girls, you will all achieve *that*. But no daughter of the Rector of St. Mark's needs to soil her hands by working for a living. You will live at home and help me keep house until you marry."

In September 1925, when Edda and Grace were nineteen and Tufts and Kitty eighteen, Kitty went to the Rectory stables and found a length of rope. Having fashioned a loop in one end and flung the rope over a beam, Kitty put her head through the loop and climbed onto an empty oil drum. When Edda found her, she had already kicked the drum over and hung, pathetically quiescent, to rid herself of life. Never able to understand afterward where she found the strength, Edda got Kitty free of the choking rope before any real harm was done.

This time she didn't take Kitty to the Rector at once. "Oh, dearest baby sister, you can't, you can't!" she cried, cheek on the silky mop of hair. "Nothing can be this bad!"

But when Kitty was able to croak answers, Edda knew it was even worse.

"I loathe being beautiful, Edda, I abominate it! If only Mama would shut up, give me some peace! But she doesn't. To anyone who'll listen, I'm Helen of Troy. And she—she won't let me dress down, or not make up my face— Edda, if she could, I *swear* she'd marry me to the Prince of Wales!"

Edda tried being lighthearted. "Even Mama must have realized you're not His Royal Highness's type, Kits. He likes them married, and much older than you are."

It did get a watery chuckle, but Edda had to talk for far longer and with every ounce of persuasion she owned before Kitty consented to take her problems to her father.

"Kitty, you're not alone," Edda argued. "Look at me! I'd sell my soul to the Devil—and I mean that!—for the chance to be a doctor. It's all I've ever wanted, a degree in medicine. But I can't have it. For one thing, there isn't the money, and there never will be the money. For another, Daddy doesn't in his heart of hearts approve—oh, not because he's against women in the professions, but because of the terrible time everyone gives women in medicine. He doesn't think it would make me happy. I know he's wrong, but he refuses to be convinced."

She took Kitty's arm and squashed it between strong, slender fingers. "What makes you think you're the only unhappy one, eh, tell me that? Don't you think I haven't considered hanging myself? Well, I have! Not once, but time and time again."

So by the time that Edda broke the news to Thomas Latimer that Kitty had tried to hang herself, Kitty was malleable clay.

"Oh, my dear, my dear!" he whispered, tears running down his long, handsome face. "For the crime of self-murder, God has a special Hell—no pit of fire, no company in the suffering. Those who commit self-murder wander the vastnesses of eternity forever alone. They never see another face, hear another voice, taste agony *or* ecstasy! Swear to me, Katherine, that you will never again try to harm yourself in any way!"

She had sworn, and adhered to her oath, though all three of her sisters kept a special eye on Kitty.

And the attempted suicide turned out to have happened at exactly the proper time, thanks to the fact that the Rector of St. Mark's was a member of the Corunda Base Hospital Board. The week after Kitty's crisis, the Hospital Board met, and among its business was a mention of the fact that in 1926 the New South Wales Department of Health was introducing a new kind of nurse: a properly trained, educated, *registered* nurse. This, saw the Rector at once, was a career fit for a girl brought up as a lady. What imbued the Rector with greatest enthusiasm was that the new, properly trained nurses would be required to live in the hospital grounds so that they were on a moment's call if needed. The pay after deducting board, uniforms, and books was a pittance, but his girls each had a modest dowry of £500, and the pittance meant they wouldn't need to touch it; Maude was already complaining that four extra mouths at the Rectory were too many to do the housework. Therefore, said the Rector to himself as he sped home in his Model T Ford, why not dangle a nursing career under the noses of his girls? Fit for a lady, living at the hospital, paid a pittance—and (though he was too loyal to voice it, even in his mind) freedom from Maude the Destroyer.

He tackled Edda first, and of course she was madly, wildly enthusiastic; so even Grace, the most reluctant, was relatively easy to enlist. If the thought of being free of Maude worked more powerfully with Grace and Kitty than the prospect of the work itself, did that really matter?

Far harder for the Rector was the single-handed battle he fought on the Hospital Board to persuade his twelve fellow members that Corunda Base should be among the pioneer New Nurse hospitals. Somewhere inside Thomas Latimer's gracefully gangling gazelle of a body there lurked, so forgotten it was positively moth-eaten, a lion. And for the first time in Corunda's memory, the lion roared. Teeth bared, claws unsheathed, the lion was a manifestation of the Reverend Latimer that people like Frank Campbell, the Corunda Base Hospital Superintendent, didn't know how to deal with. So that, highly delighted at what leonine aggression could do, the Reverend Latimer found himself victor on the field.

Sated if not quite glutted, the four Latimer twins looked at each other in quiet triumph. The drawing room was deserted and what tea was left in the pots was stewed, but in each young breast there beat a happy heart.

"Next Monday, no more Maude," said Kitty.

"Kitty! You can't call her that, she's your genuine mother," said Grace, scandalized.

"I can so too if I want."

"Shut up, Grace, she's only celebrating her emancipation," Edda said, grinning.

Tufts, who was the practical one, stared at the corpse of the snake. "The party's over," she said getting up. "Cleanup time, girls."

Eyes encountering the snake, now surrounded by blood, Grace shuddered. "I don't mind getting the tea leaves out of the pots, but I am not cleaning *that* up!"

"Since all you did when the snake arrived was screech and snivel, Grace, you most certainly are cleaning it up," said Edda.

Tufts chuckled. "Think that's a mess, Grace? Wait until you're on the hospital wards!"

Generous mouth turned down ungenerously, Grace folded her arms and glared at her sisters. "I'll start when I have to, not a minute before," she said. "Kitty, you created all that blood by chopping off its head, so you do it." Her mood changed, she giggled. "Oh, girls, fancy! Our days as unpaid housemaids are over! Corunda Base Hospital, here we come!"

"Messes and all," said Edda.

The Reverend Thomas Latimer, who had some Treadby blood but was not a native of Corunda, had been appointed the Rector of St. Mark's Church of England in Corunda twenty-two years earlier. It was that dash of Treadby had made him acceptable to the largely Church of England populace despite his youth and his relative lack of experience; neither of these latter qualities was felt to be a major handicap, as Corunda liked shaping raw clay to its own ends. His wife, Adelaide, was from a good family and was very well liked, which was more than most could say about the Rectory housekeeper, Maude Treadby Scobie, a childless widow with the right blood and an insufferable idea of her own importance.

Thomas and Adelaide settled down to become increasingly loved, for the Rector, extremely handsome in a scholarly way, was a gentle and trusting soul, and Adelaide even more so. Pregnancy followed after a decent interval, and on 13th November 1905, Adelaide gave birth to twin girls, Edda and Grace. A horrific bleed drained her; Adelaide died.

With the efficient Maude Scobie already well versed in all Rectory matters, the Governors of St. Mark's thought that the broken-hearted Thomas Latimer should retain Mrs. Scobie's services, especially given the presence of newborn babies. Maude was six years older than the Rector and on the wrong side of thirty into the bargain. Awesomely genteel and remarkably pretty, she was delighted to continue as housekeeper. Her job was not a

11

sinecure, but it was a comfortable one; the Governors were happy to fund nurserymaids as well as scrubwomen.

The entire congregation understood when, a year after his first wife's death, the Rector took a second wife, Maude Scobie. Who fell pregnant immediately and bore slightly premature twin girls on 1st August 1907. They were christened Heather and Katherine, but later became known as Tufts and Kitty.

However, Maude had no intention of dying; her intention was to out-live the Rector and, if possible, even her own children. Now she was the Rector's wife she became far better known within the community, which—with some exceptions—loathed her as pushy, shallow, and social-climbing. Corunda decided that Thomas Latimer had been tricked into marrying a designing harpy. A verdict that ought to have crushed Maude, but didn't even dent her conceit, for Maude was the sort of person whose self-satis-faction is so great, so ingrained, that she had no idea whatsoever that she was detested. Sarcasm and irony rolled off her like water off feathers, and snubs were things she administered to other people. With all this came an incomparable luck: disillusioned very early in their marriage, her husband regarded matrimony as a sacred and lifelong contract never to be broken or sullied. No matter how unsuitable a wife Maude was, Thomas Latimer hewed to her. So he dealt with her patiently, humored her in some things and maneuvered her out of others, bore her tantrums and whims, and never once contemplated even the mental breaking of his vows to her. And if, sometimes, a tiny wisp of a thought popped into his mind that it would be wonderful if Maude fell in love with someone else, he banished the thought even as it formed, horrified.

Neither pair of twins was quite identical, which led to fierce debates as to what exactly constituted "identical" in twins. Edda and Grace had their mother's height and slenderness as well as their father's ability to move beautifully. Both lovely to look at, their facial features, hands, and feet were identical; each had hair so dark it was called black, highly arched brows, long thick lashes, and pale grey eyes. Yet there were differences. Grace's eyes were widely opened and held a natural sadness she exploited, whereas Edda's were deeper set, hooded by sleepy lids, and held an element of strangeness. Time demonstrated that Edda was highly intelligent, self-willed, and a little inflexible, while Grace was neither a reader nor a seeker after knowledge, and irritated everybody by her tendency to complain—and, worse, to moan. With the result that by the time they started to train as nurses, most people didn't see how like each other Grace and Edda were; their dispositions had stamped their faces with quite different expressions, and their eyes looked at dissimilar things.

Maude had never really liked them, but hid her antipathy with subtle cunning. On the surface, all four girls were kept equally neat and clean, clothed with equal expense, and disciplined fairly. If somehow the colors she chose for her own twins were more flattering than those bestowed on Adelaide's, well . . . It couldn't—and didn't—last any longer than mid-teens, when the girls appealed to Daddy to choose their own styles and colors. Lucky for Edda and Grace, then, that after this adolescent fashion revolution was over, Maude's selective deafness allowed her to ignore the general opinion that Edda and Grace had far better taste in clothes than Maude did.

Tufts and Kitty (Tufts was born first) were simultaneously more and less identical than the senior set. They took after their mother, a pocket Venus of a woman: short, with plump and shapely breasts, tiny waists, swelling hips, and excellent legs. Owning the perfect kind of beauty for girl children, they were genuinely ravishing almost from the time of birth, and it thrilled people to realize that in the case of Tufts and Kitty Latimer, God had used the mold twice. Dimples, curls, enchanting smiles, and enormous round eyes gave them the bewitching, melting charm of a kitten, complete to domed forehead, pointed chin, and a faintly Mona Lisa curve of the lips. They had the same thin, short, straight noses, the same full-lipped mouths, the same high cheekbones and delicately arched brows.

What Tufts and Kitty didn't share was coloring, and that was the difference between Kitty's sun and Tufts's dim moon. Tufts was honey-hued from the amber-gold of her hair to the peach glow of her skin, and had calm, dispassionate, yellow eyes; she toned in a series of the same basic color, like an artist with a severely limited palette. Ah, but Kitty! Where Tufts blended, she contrasted. Most remarkable was her skin, a rich pale brown some called "café au lait" and others, less charitably inclined, whispered that it showed Maude's family had a touch of the tar-brush somewhere. Her hair, brows, and lashes were crystal-fair, a flaxen blonde with hardly any warmth in it; against the dark skin they were spectacular; only time scotched the rumors that Maude bleached Kitty's hair with hydrogen peroxide. To cap Kitty's uniqueness, her eyes were a vivid blue shot with lavender stripes that came and went according to her mood. When she thought no one was watching her, Kitty gazed on her world with none of her twin's tranquillity; the light in her eyes was bewildered, even a little terrified, and when things got beyond her ability to reason or control, she turned the light off and retreated into a private world she spoke of to no one, and only her three sisters understood existed.

People literally stopped and openly stared at first sight of Kitty. As if that weren't bad enough, her mother constantly raved about her beauty to anyone she encountered, including those she encountered every day: a shrilly simpering spate of exclamations that took no notice of the fact that their object, Kitty, was usually within hearing distance, as were the other three girls.

"Did you ever see such a beautiful child?"

"When she grows up, she'll marry a rich man!"

The kind of remarks that had led to a cheese grater, a rope, and the decision Edda made that all four of them would join the new trainee nursing scheme at Corunda Base Hospital at the beginning of April 1926. For, her sisters agreed, if they didn't get Kitty out from under Maude, the day would come when Edda might not be on hand to foil a suicide attempt.

Because the only world children know is the one they inhabit, it never occurred to any of the four Latimer girls to question Maude Latimer's behavior, or stop to wonder if all mothers were the same; they simply assumed that if anyone were as ravishing (Maude's word) as Kitty, she would be subjected to the same remorseless torrent of attention. It didn't occur to them that Maude too was unique in her own way, or dawn on them that perhaps a child with a different nature than Kitty's would have relished the attention. All things being as they were, the Latimer girls understood that it was the main task of three of them to protect the vulnerable fourth from what Edda called "parental idiocies." And as they grew and matured, the instinct and the drive to protect Kitty never faded, never diminished, never seemed less urgent.

All four girls were clever, though Edda always took the academic laurels because her mind grasped mathematics as easily as it did historical events or English composition. The quality of Tufts's mentality was very similar, though it lacked Edda's fierce fire. Tufts had a practical, down-to-earth streak that oddly dampened her undeniable good looks; through their adolescent years she displayed scant interest in boys, whom she thought stupid and oafish. Whatever the essence was that boys emanated to waft under the noses of girls and attract them utterly failed to stir Tufts.

There was a male equivalent of Corunda Ladies' College: the Corunda Grammar School, and all four Latimer girls associated with the boys in the matter of balls, parties, sporting, and other events. They were admired— even lusted after, in schoolboy fashion—kissed as much or as little as each desired, but things like breasts and thighs were unplundered.

Rules that were no hardship for Tufts, Kitty, and Edda, were irksome for the more adventurous, less bookish Grace. Perpetually submerged in gossip and women's magazines about film stars, stage actors, fashion, and the world of royalty as represented by the Windsor family who ruled the British Empire, Grace was not above local gossip, either. Her brain was self-centered but acute, she was an expert at wriggling out of trouble or work she disliked, but Grace had one inappropriate passion: she adored the steam locomotives of the railways. If she disappeared, everyone in the Rectory knew where to find her—down in the shunting yards watching the steam locomotives. In spite of her many undesirable characteristics, however, she was naturally kind, immensely loving, and devoted to her sisters, who put up with her tendency to moan as her nature.

Kitty was the one with the romantic imagination, but was saved from a spiritual beauty the equal of her physical by a tongue that could be caustic, or salty, or both. It was her defense against all those rhapsodies of praise, for it took people aback and made them think there must surely be more to her than just a beautiful face. The bouts of depression (though they called it "Kitty's dumps") that assailed her whenever Maude pierced her defenses were an ordeal helped only by her sisters, who knew all the reasons why, and rallied themselves behind her until the crisis was over. In school examinations she did well until mathematics reared its ugly hydra heads; she it was who took the essay prizes, and expressed herself extremely well on paper.

Maude loathed Edda, always the ringleader in opposition to her plans for her girls, especially Kitty. Not that Edda cared. By the time she was ten years old she was taller than her stepmother, and, when fully grown, towered over Maude in a way that complacent lady found as uncomfortable as menacing. The pale eyes stared like a white wolf's, and on the rare occasions when Maude suffered a nightmare, her dream tormentor was always Edda. It had given Maude great pleasure to talk the Rector out of making the monetary sacrifices that would have let Edda do medicine, and she counted it her most satisfying triumph; every time she thought of denying Edda her life's ambition, inside herself she purred. Had Edda only known who exactly had cast the deciding vote in her parents' debate on her medical career, things would have gone harder for Maude, but Edda didn't know. Caught between the irresistibly iron pressures of a wife and his own conviction that, in denying Edda, he was sparing her a life of pain, Thomas Latimer never breathed a word to anyone. As far as Edda knew, there simply had not been the money.

Edda and Grace, Tufts and Kitty, all four packed the single suitcase each was allowed to take with her into this hospital world, and at the beginning of April 1926 reported for duty at the Corunda Base Hospital.

"Typical!" said Grace mournfully. "It's April Fools' Day."

The Shire & City of Corunda was a kinder and richer rural area than most in Australia, sitting as it did on the southern tablelands three hours by express train from Sydney. It produced fat lambs, potatoes, cherries, and pigeon's blood rubies, though the Treadby rubies, found on cave floors and the like, had run out, leaving the Burdum deposits without rival world-wide.

At this altitude summer gathered her bounty and departed for other climes at the end of March; April was the beginning of a rather English-flavored autumn, complete with imported deciduous shrubs and trees as well as a passion for gardening in all styles from Anne Hathaway to Capability Brown. So April Fools' Day saw the first nip in the air, and the leaves of the native evergreens had that tired, dusty look beseeching rain. The Rector dropped his daughters off outside the main entrance of Corunda Base Hospital and let them carry their suitcases inside unaided, his grey eyes full of tears. How *empty* the Rectory would be!

Though the Latimer sisters were not to know it, Matron Gertrude Newdigate had only been in her job for a week when they arrived, and she was not amused. When she took the Corunda post there had been no mention of new-style nursing trainees, a big reason why she had decided in Corunda's favor. Now—! Sydney had been in turmoil over the radical change in nursing, and Matron Newdigate wanted no part of it. Now—!

A glacial figure in white from head to toes, she sat behind her office desk looking at the four young women standing to face her. Expensively and fashionably dressed, all wearing Clara Bow lipstick, powder and mascara, their hair bobbed short, pure silk stockings, kid shoes, purses and gloves, an English inflection in their voices that spoke of a private school . . .

"I have no suitable accommodation for you," Matron said coldly, the starch in her uniform so dense that it creaked when she breathed deeply, "so you will have to go into the disused sisters' cottage the Superintendent, Dr. Campbell, has been forced to refurbish at considerable cost. Your chaperone will be Sister Marjorie Bainbridge, who will live with you but in some degree of privacy."

Her head, encased in a starched white organdy veil that stood out like an Egyptian headdress, moved just enough to cause the silver-and-enamel badge pinned at her uniform throat to flash: the insignia saying Miss Gertrude Newdigate was a fully registered nurse in the State of New South Wales. Could the girls have identified them, they would have noted that other badges said she was a registered midwife, a registered children's nurse, and a graduate of the School of Nursing at the world's second-oldest hospital, St. Bartholomew's in London. Corunda Base had got itself a very prestigious nurse.

"Officially registered nurses," Matron said, "are called sisters. The title has nothing to do with nuns, though it came into being centuries ago when nuns did nurse. However, with the dissolution of the monastic and conventual orders under Henry VIII, nursing was relegated to a very different kind of woman—the prostitute. Miss Florence Nightingale and her companions had to surmount incredible obstacles to gain our modern profession its due, and we must never forget that we are her heirs. For three and more centuries nursing lay in disrepute, the province of criminals and prostitutes, and there are still *men* in authority who think of nurses that way. It is far cheaper to employ a prostitute than it is a lady." The pale blue eyes shot icy rays of terror. "As Matron of this hospital, I am your ultimate superior, and I give you warning that I will not tolerate any misbehavior of any kind. Is that understood?"

"Yes, Matron," they chorused in awed whispers, even Edda.

"Blood relationship and names," the voice went on, growing crisper.

"I have decided that you will keep your blood ties among yourselves. Your nursing companions in this hospital have neither your money nor your privileges nor your education. One of the things I personally detest most about you is your upper-class appearance and accent. Your—er—air of superiority. I do suggest you tone it down. Names . . . As hospitals cannot permit confusion, you will all nurse under different surnames. Miss Edda Latimer, you will become Nurse Latimer. Miss Grace Latimer, you will become Nurse Faulding, your mother's maiden name. Miss Heather Latimer, you will become Nurse Scobie, your mother's first married name. Miss Katherine Latimer, you will become Nurse Treadby, your mother's maiden name."

The starch creaked as Matron drew a long breath. "Formal instruction in the sciences and theories of nursing will not commence until July, which means you will have three months to grow accustomed to the duties and routines of nursing before you open a textbook. Sister Bainbridge is your immediate superior, responsible for your day-to-day instruction."

A light knock sounded on the door; in bounced a cheerful-looking woman in her late thirties whose face was devoid of lipstick or powder; she looked at Matron like a half-starved, fawning dog.

"Ah, in good time!" said Matron. "Sister Bainbridge, please meet your charges—Nurse Latimer, Nurse Faulding, Nurse Scobie, and Nurse Treadby. Kindly go with Sister, girls."

Given no opportunity to get their breath back, the four girls followed Sister Bainbridge out.

Sister Marjorie Bainbridge wore the same stiffly starched Egyptian head-dress veil of white organdy as Matron did, but thereafter bore no likeness. Her uniform was a long-sleeved dress done high to the throat with detachable celluloid cuffs and collar; her ample waist was encircled by a rubberized dark green belt that sprouted lengths of white tape ending inside her pockets; to these, they would learn in time, were attached her bandage scissors, a mouth gag in case of epileptic fits, and a tiny tool kit inside a change purse. Her starched uniform was of narrow green and white stripes, her beige stockings were thick lisle, and her shoes black lace-ups with two-inch block heels. An outfit that added no charms to her square figure, or made the sight of her huge bottom any smaller as it moved like a soldier's on parade, up-left, down-right, up-right, down-left, not the slightest suggestion of femininity about it. In time the girls would grow so used to the look of a disciplined nurse's bottom that they acquired it themselves, but on that brisk, chilly April morning it was a novelty.

A five-hundred-yard walk brought them to a sad, dilapidated wooden house that had a verandah across its front. Matron's use of the word "cottage" had led them to expect something small and dainty, but this looked more like a barn squashed to one story by a steam hammer. And if Superintendent Campbell had incurred "considerable cost" in refurbishing it, then even Edda's eagle eye failed to see where. To compound the building's unsuitability, it had been partitioned off in sections that gave it the interior of a block of flats, and the four new-style trainee nurses were not plentifully endowed with space—or comfort.

"Latimer and Faulding, you'll share this bedroom. Scobie and Treadby share that one. The two rooms you can access are this bathroom and that kitchen. My quarters are through that locked door cutting off the rest of the hall. Once I'm in them, I am not to be disturbed. I'll leave you to unpack your cases."

And off she went, through the locked hall door.

"Well, starve the lizards!" said Kitty feebly.

"Pretty austere," said Tufts, sighing. They were standing in the kitchen, a small apartment serviced by a gas stove but nothing else labor-saving.

Grace was priming herself for a bout of tears, gazing wet-eyed at the small wooden table and four hard wooden chairs around it. "I don't believe it!" she whimpered. "No common room except four hard chairs in a kitchen!"

"If you cry, Grace, I'll personally feed you to the dogs," said Tufts, running a gloved fingertip along the top margin of the stove. She grimaced. "I could forgive the lack of a new coat of paint, but no one has *cleaned* our quarters properly."

"Then that's our first job," said Edda, sounding remarkably happy. "Just think, girls! They don't want us here."

Three pairs of eyes flew to Kitty, the fragile one—how would she take this news she had to know, and the sooner the better?

"Bugger the lot of them, then!" Kitty said in a strong voice. "I'm darned if a Latimer is going to be beaten by a parcel of over-complacent female dogs!"

"Bitches, you mean," said Edda.

Kitty giggled. "What they don't know is that they're in the amateur league when it comes to bitches. We've had a lifetime of Mama, who could teach Matron lessons in bitchery."

Tears dried, Grace stared at Kitty in wonder. "You're not down in the dumps?" she asked.

"Not so far," Kitty said, grinning. "I'm too dazzled at the thought that I'm finally leading a life of my own."

"What do you think of Matron, Edda?" Tufts asked.

Grace answered. "A battleship in full sail, so she's accustomed to firing salvos at things so far away she can't even see them on the horizon."

"I'd rather say that to her, we mean extra work," from Tufts. "According to Mrs. Enid Treadby, Matron took this job to round off her career in a place where she could afford to retire."

"Why save that gem to tell us now?" Edda asked. "It's vital information, Tufts!"

"I never think of repeating gossip—I can't help it, Eds, honestly! You *know* that."

"Yes, I do, and I'm sorry for flying at you—Grace, stop bawling like a motherless calf!"

"Matron is a detestable woman, and so is Sister Bainbridge," Grace said through sobs, tears running down her face. "Oh, why didn't Daddy send us to a Sydney hospital to train?"

"Because in Corunda Daddy is someone important, so he can keep an eye on us," Tufts said. "Sore bums from hard chairs, girls, and no common room. I wonder if there's a hot water heater hiding anywhere? This is a hospital, after all."

"No hot water in this kitchen," said Edda, grimacing.

Kitty came out of the bedroom she was to share with Tufts, holding up a green and white-striped object so starched that it resembled a sheet of cardboard. Clenching her right fist, she began to punch its two layers apart. A laugh escaped. "This is as bad as punching the hide off a slaughtered lamb." Putting the dress down, she produced a sheet of white cardboard. "I think when this is punched apart it will be the apron." She laid into it with her fist. "Oh, look! It must wrap right around and over the uniform—only the sleeves will show. But I realize why our stockings are homely, knitted black wool."

In the midst of repairing her lipstick and powder, Grace looked up. "What do you mean?" she asked.

"Oh, Grace, don't be so thick! Why do you think Matron delivered us that sermon on nuns and chastity and prostitutes? She was really saying that for the next three years we have no sex, even if statistically we are female. No flirting with any of the doctors, Grace, whatever else you do. Matron Newdigate would forgive your killing a patient far ahead of your conducting yourself like a whore. That's why we're going to be wearing ugly uniforms and thick, knitted black stockings. I'd be willing to bet that no touch of lipstick or powder will be allowed either."

"Cry again, Grace, and you're dead!" Edda snapped.

"I want to go home!"

"No, you don't!"

"I loathe cleaning up messes." Then Grace brightened. "Still, by the time I'm twenty-one I'll be registered, and able to do all sorts of things without permission. Such as marry whoever I want, and vote in the elections."

"I suspect the hardest thing we'll have to do is learn to get along with the other nurses," Edda said thoughtfully. "I mean, who are they? None of us has ever been in hospital, nor do our parents mix with hospital people. I found Matron's instructions to tone ourselves down ominous. I inferred that she meant we are a distinct cut above the other nurses socially and ed-ucationally. The last thing in the world we've ever been is snobby—Daddy would be appalled, especially with Mama as an example." She sighed. "But unfortunately people tend to judge books by their covers."

Tufts aired her knowledge of local facts yet again. "The nurses are all from the West End, and rough as bags," she said.

"Well, we start by removing phrases like 'rough as bags' from our speech," said Edda. Oh, Tufts could be exasperating! The trouble was that she wasn't a talker, so none of the others expected her silence to conceal information.

"I always thought using a dinner napkin added dreadfully to the laundry," Kitty said cheerfully. "I mean, you can wipe your mouth with your hand, and if your nose is runny, you have your sleeve to wipe it on."

"Very true," said Edda gravely. "We'd better get in training to wipe mouths and noses as well as wounds, for I very much doubt there will be dinner napkins. Men's handkerchiefs, too, girls. No wisp of lace." She huffed. "Fool things anyway, women's hankies."

Kitty cleared her throat loudly. "I know I get down in the dumps, girls, but I'm not a coward. No amount of West End nastiness is going to defeat me. Nursing doesn't attract me the way it does you, Edda, because for you it's the next-best thing to medicine. But I think I can *grow* to love it."

"Good girl, Kitty!" Edda cried, applauding the little speech. In front of her very eyes Kitty was unloading the cargo of childhood. She's going to get *properly* better, thought Edda, I know it in my bones. So frank about Maude, so aware of the dangers lurking anywhere in Maude's vicinity. After Maude, West Enders were nothings.

"I'm long past my grief at not being able to do medicine," Edda said now to Kitty, worried that her plight was being exaggerated in Kitty's mind. "Nursing is more sensible, and our new-style training means we won't be ignoramuses who know how to bandage, but not why. Think of me as an old warhorse—the slightest whiff of ether has me whinnying and stamping the ground. In a hospital I'm *alive!*"

"Speaking of whinnying and stamping the ground, does Jack Thurlow know you're going nursing?" Tufts asked slyly.

The shaft went wide; Edda grinned. "Of course he does. And his heart isn't broken any more than mine is. The hardest part will be keeping Fatima exercised up to Jack's expectations. I daresay I'll be riding more on my own in future."

"If you still had Thumbelina, it would be easier," said Grace. "Daddy wouldn't be under an obligation to Jack Thurlow, who doesn't even come to church."

Kitty leaped in ahead of the storm clouds gathering on Edda's face. "Shut up, Grace, that's not up for discussion! My perpetual question, Eds, is why you like riding."

"When I'm on top of a horse's back, I'm a minimum of five feet clear of the ground," Edda said, her voice serious. "To me, that's all the thrill of riding. Being taller than a man."

"I wish I were tall!" Kitty said with a sigh.

The hall door rattled, flew open. Sister Bainbridge stood and glared at her charges in outrage.

"What is the meaning of this, nurses? You haven't even begun to unpack your suitcases!"

orunda Base Hospital was the largest rural hospital in New South Wales, having 160 beds in its general section, eighty beds in its mental asylum, and thirty beds in a convalescent/aged home out Doobar way, where the air and the elevation were felt more beneficial. Unlike the sandstone magnificence of some other hospitals, its appearance charmed no one, for it looked like army barracks. Built of wood atop limestone piers and foundations, it was a series of long rectangular structures saved from being called sheds by the presence of a broad, covered verandah down either long side. Men's One and Two were double-length, as were Women's One and Two; Children's, Outpatients, X-ray-cum-Pathology, the Operating Theatre, Kitchens and Stores were single in size, while Administration, fronting onto Victoria Street, rejoiced in a building made entirely from limestone blocks. The amount of land was acres in extent, and dotted with outbuildings that ranged from Matron's storybook cottage to houses put up for the duration of the Great War, when it had also been an army hospital. One overall fact made the site workable: down to the last square foot of the last acre, it was level. And this in turn had led to the struts and strands that linked the buildings together like the Brooklyn Bridge or a spider's web— roofed walkways that everybody called ramps. Most ramps held some protection from the elements beyond roofing in the form of four-foot-high sides, though the last two hundred yards to the Latimer house consisted only of a floor and a roof. Where Men's straddled the ramp to either side, it had been completely enclosed to form a waiting room; Women's had been similarly dealt with. Those who waited to visit children used Men's or Women's. Midwifery was lucky; it was inside the administration building, as were the Casualty station and a small Operating Theatre.

The shocks fell thick and fast upon the Latimer girls, though if Matron's reading of their characters had been right, not one of them would have lasted longer than that first day at Corunda Base. They had been carefully brought up as ladies and had never wanted for a material thing, but Gertrude Newdigate's youth had passed beyond her recollection, and she had forgotten to take strength of purpose and character into account at all.

The first and greatest shock was not personal; it was the realization that a hospital was a place to which you, a patient, were admitted in order to die. Fully one-third of the patients left a hospital through its morgue, and a second third returned home to die. A statistic given to them by a doleful hospital porter named Harry, who thus became a teaching authority for the four new nurses weeks before they met their instructor, Dr. Liam Finucan.

"It's in the patient's eyes!" cried Tufts, horrified. "I feel more a minister to death than a healer—how can the other nurses be so cheerful?"

"They're inured and resigned," said Grace, stemming tears.

"Rubbish," Kitty said. "They're experienced, they know the best way to treat death is to persuade the patients that they are not going to die. I watch them, I don't care how nasty they are to me. How they treat us isn't important. *Watch them!*"

"Kitty's right," Edda said, her indignation saved for things like cut-up newspapers for toilet paper and towels too worn to dry wet skin—weren't hospitals properly funded? "Grace, you've already exhausted today's allowance of tears—don't *dare* cry!"

"That Nurse Wilson slopped a bowl of vomit on me!"

"You copped the vomit because you let Nurse Wilson see how revolted you were by it. Govern your disgust, and it won't happen."

"I want to go home!"

"That's not on the cards, Miss Piglet," said Edda, hiding her sympathy.

"Now go and change your apron before the vomit soaks into your dress. Pew! You do stink!"

Yet somehow their first week passed; at the end of it they could clothe themselves faultlessly in their starched "cardboard," even fold the absurdly complex pleated parts of their caps that looked like a pair of wings. The other nurses wore more sensible uniforms and aprons, including short sleeves, while the Latimers, as new-style trainees, were done up in more wrapping than parcels.

The food, they discovered, was appalling for patients and staff alike, but they worked so hard that they ate everything from watery cabbage to lumpy gravy swimming in fat; the kitchen in their quarters, Sister Bainbridge informed them, was for making cups of tea, coffee, or cocoa.

"Nothing else, even toast," said she, looming.

The Rector had sheltered his girls from the more horrible and sordid aspects of his religious calling, and excluded the words incest, syphilis and perversion from their vocabulary. Due to climate and no refrigeration, the dead were buried in a closed coffin within twenty-four hours. So when, on their second morning, Sister Bainbridge showed them how to lay out a corpse, it was the first time they had seen or touched a dead body.

"A syphilitic who raped his sister," Bainbridge said, joking.

Their response to this explanation was a blank look.

"Keep your pride!" said Edda in a furious whisper as soon as Bainbridge moved away, laughing at their ignorance. "Remember that we are Latimers. What upsets us today will be old hat tomorrow—don't let them beat us! No tears, and no down in the dumps."

They were perpetually tired in a way entirely new and very hard to bear; their feet ached, their backs ached, their joints ached. Everything taught to them by dainty Maude had to be abandoned; there was neither room nor time for daintiness in Corunda Base, whose superintendent was an arch-miser unwilling to pander to the needs of any and all entities save money, to which he was fused like a leech to a piece of vein-riddled flesh.

April, May, and June vanished in a thick fog of exhaustion that actually worked in the hospital's favor. Not even Grace had the energy to think of quitting; the very notion of creating such a fuss reared as high as Everest, unattainable. They just endured.

Edda held them together, convinced in her soul that things were bound to change, as things did from sheer familiarity. Perhaps the only thing that kept them quietly resigned was the one thing they would lose if they returned to the Rectory: heated rooms. With winter upon them, it was so *beautiful* to live in warmth, no matter how enormous the indignities and insults of their nursing life might be. And, Edda was sure, once they proved themselves to the cruel women who ruled them, the rewards would come: like chairs with soft seats, the chance to make toasted sandwiches, a little kindness. For at the end of their first three months instruction would begin, they would be called upon to do something with their brains as well as their hands and voices. April, May, and June had seen them no different from the West Enders.

Their tutor was Dr. Liam Finucan, the staff pathologist (and also Chief Coroner of the Shire & City of Corunda). He had agreed to take on tutorial duty for two reasons: the first, that he regarded nursing brainpower as wasted; and the second, that he had noted the quality of the four new-style trainees as they were shuttled around the hospital on some kind of speedy orientation program.

A Protestant Ulsterman, Liam Finucan had taken his medical degree at St. Bartholomew's in London when Matron Gertrude Newdigate was there, so they were old acquaintances; his love for pathology had led him to the great Sir Bernard Spilsbury, and his qualifications were such that he could have headed the pathology department of any hospital in Sydney or Melbourne. That he had chosen a minor post at Corunda Base was due to his wife, Eris, a Corunda girl he met and married in London. In 1926, when the Latimer girls commenced nursing, he had been in Corunda for fifteen years.

Typical of many pathologists, he was quiet and shy, owned no bedside manner, and found the dead more interesting than the living. However, by the middle of July, after two weeks of instructing the new nursing trainees, Liam Finucan developed a side to his personality hitherto undetected by anyone who knew him, and that included himself. Out of a mental stable came a warhorse, and out of a cobwebbed cupboard came a suit of armor; mounting the one and donning the other, Liam tilted his lance and rode off to make war. His quarry wasn't that miserable skinflint Dr. Frank Campbell; it was Matron Newdigate.

"You've given these four girls absolutely no kind of help or support, Gertie, and it has to stop," Liam said, his softly lilting voice steely, foreign. "You ought to be ashamed of yourself! When one of the old-style nurses starts here, she's taken into the West End fold, overwhelmed with advice and many kindnesses. Whereas these four young women have no one to turn to at all. I don't care how new you were to your own job when they started, you had a duty to them that you shamelessly ignored because their presence upset the West End majority. D'you think I've forgotten how much you grizzled to me during your first week at the thought that you were going to be lumbered with the new trainees after all? Here it is, the middle of July, and you've acted as if they don't exist. You saddled them with a quarter of a dilapidated house, gave that fat and lazy crawler Marje Bainbridge charge of them, and rewarded her with *half* of the same house!" His eyes had gone the same dark grey as a stormy sea, and pinned her contemptuously.

"Your new-style trainees are even more tired than they should be," he went on. "Their accommodation is pure Frank Campbell—hard chairs and two-foot-three beds, a kitchen they're forbidden to use. By the sheerest accident their house is on the steam line, so at least they've been warm, but they have to chop wood and feed it to their boiler to have hot water, and that's unconscionable! Hear me? *Criminal!* In spite of their privileges they've been brought up to think of themselves with humility—it's just your good luck that their mother is a selfish bitch."

He leaned forward to put the palms of his hands flat on her immaculate desk, and glared at her. "I'm off to see Frank Campbell next, but I'm warning you, Gertie, that I expect your wholehearted support in this. Since the girls are required to live in, they will each have a bedroom. You will provide a common room with easy chairs, and desks and bookshelves for studying. The kitchen will be at their command for light meals as well as liquids, and see they have an ice chest before spring. Get off your pampered bottom and see to their welfare! Use Marje Bainbridge as a chaperone, by all means, but not in the lap of luxury. I hear that there will be money to build a new home for nurses, but until it's finished, I want my trainees adequately accommodated."

Gertrude Newdigate had listened, but wasn't prepared to take the blame for Frank Campbell's parsimony. "Fight your own battles with that awful man!" she said coldly. "My hands are tied."

"Rot! I've known you for twenty years, and you don't scare me. Nor does Frank. Gertie, *think*! Those four young women are so good, that's the real tragedy of it! Why on earth are you risking four potential matrons just to please a gang of petty West End nurses who don't know sodium from potassium? Who wouldn't know a Latin or a Greek medical root if it bit them on the bum? Devote your energy with the West Enders to convincing them that in future medicine will demand educated nurses, so look to their daughters. Don't be so in tune with yesterday!"

Her natural detachment was returning; she could see what Liam meant, though she hadn't intended it to happen. The trouble was that she was too new to Corunda Base, and hadn't understood how dismal the quality of West End nursing was when it came to science and theory. Still, she had one dagger she could slip in.

"How is your wife?" she asked sweetly.

He didn't bite, he spurned the bait. "Philandering, quite as usual. Some things never change."

"You should divorce her."

"Why? I've no mind to take another wife."

The Latimer girls loved Dr. Liam Finucan, a solitary ray of light in a densely black tunnel. Having discovered how bright and well prepared they were, he applied himself with vigor and enthusiasm to the task of tutoring them, thrilled to find that their knowledge of mathematics and physical phenomena already enabled them to understand things like the gas laws and electricity. They were as competent as men in the early years of a medical degree. When it came to subjects new and strange, they seized upon knowledge eagerly. Even Grace, he was learning, had more than enough brains to cope with the theory; what slowed her down was lack of true interest. To Matron he had said "four matrons," but three was more correct. Whatever Grace burned for, it was not to become a registered nurse.

His favorite among the four was Tufts, whom he always called Heather. Edda was the more gifted and intelligent, but the pathologist in Liam admired order, method, logic, and in those areas Tufts reigned supreme. Edda was the flashy surgeon, Tufts was the plodding pathologist, no doubt about it. His liking for her was reciprocated; neither the monocled handsomeness of the surgeon Max Herzen nor the bubbling charm of the senior obstetrician Ned Mason held anything like as much attraction for Tufts as Dr. Finucan did, with his white-winged black hair, long and finely featured face, ship's grey-blue eyes. Not that the unromantic Tufts mooned over Dr. Finucan, or dreamed of him when asleep; simply, she liked him enormously as a person and loved being in his company. Understanding her nature, her sisters never made the mistake of teasing her about men, especially Dr. Liam Finucan. Though nothing about her was nunlike, Tufts did bear some resemblance to a monk.

The fire Liam lit under Matron was a little like a torch, in that Matron lit a fire under Sister Bainbridge, who kindled one under the leader of the West End nurses, Lena Corrigan, and she felt the flames enough to set the whole West End nursing coterie ablaze. The afterburns went on for weeks.

Suddenly the nurses' house was opened up and ruthlessly scoured: the four girls each had a private bedroom; four easy chairs and desk sets appeared in a common room, which even held a wireless set; the kitchen could be used for light meals; there were two bathrooms, and hot water was laid on at the bottom of a hastily dug trench. Harry the porter picked up their uniforms for laundering every single day, and the kitchen cupboards held hard biscuits, tins of jam, bottles of sauce, plenty of tea, Camp Essence of Coffee & Chicory, cocoa powder, saline powder for cool drinks, and blackcurrant cordial. All of which paled before the vision of the ice chest, big enough to hold a large block of ice and keep the eggs, bacon, butter, and sausages cool.

"I've died and gone to heaven," said Grace with a sigh.

Out of the blue, totally unexpected, Sister Bainbridge was moved to a small house next door on the same ramp. But before she went she introduced the girls to the magic of Epsom salts; dissolved in hot water in a tub or basin, they cured aching bodies and aching feet. How had they ever survived without the bliss of Epsom salts?

"It's my turn to die and go to heaven," said Edda. "My feet are human again."

And though the West End nurses took many months to admit that the stuck-up new-style trainees were every bit as good at old-style care as they were themselves, the malice died out of West End persecution. What was the use of malice, when its targets always managed to survive it?

"It dates back to the middle of July," said Edda as September expired in a tossing yellow sea of daffodils. "*Someone* had the kindness to intervene— but who?"

Their guesses were many, and varied from Deputy Matron Anne Harding to the least offensive West Ender, Nurse Nancy Wilson; but no one, even Tufts, suspected the hand of Dr. Liam Finucan. Who sat back contentedly and watched his four protegées flourish in this happier, more rewarding atmosphere.

"The Great War brought many advances in surgery," he said in his soft voice to his class of four, "but did far less for physical medicine. The great killers are still killing in huge numbers—pneumonia, heart disease, and vascular disease. You young women represent the greatest advance in pneumonia treatment in the history of the world to date." His brows flew up, his eyes danced. "What? Can't see it? Because, ladies, the Powers-That-Be now understand that a properly trained and educated nurse tackles the nursing of pneumonia *intelligently*. Grounded in anatomy and physiology, she doesn't limit her care to emptying the patient's sputum mug, bed pan, and urine bottle, and making his bed. No, she badgers him into constantly exercising even when confined to his bed, she makes him believe he can get better, she explains to him in simple language what the doctors never do—the nature of his ailment—and she never leaves him alone to languish like a stuffed dummy without attention, no matter how busy she is. Only one thing saves the pneumonia patient—relentless, informed nursing care."

They listened avidly, and assimilated what Liam Finucan was not allowed to say: that only knowledge of the underlying science could push a nurse to the extra work Liam Finucan's kind of care demanded.

"It's what's wrong with the West Enders," Edda said to her sisters over sausage sandwiches in their warm kitchen. "They live at home, have all those cares and worries on their shoulders as well as here, can hardly read or write beyond the basics, and know only what medicine they can pick up on the wards. Some of them are very good nurses, but to most of them it's just a job. If a pneumonia case needs pummelling, moving around, to be forced to cough, and have his bed changed, it depends on how busy the nurses are, what the Sister-in-Charge is like, and which West Enders are on duty. There's no underlying foundation of knowledge."

Grace sniffled. "That's not likely to happen to us," she said mournfully. "My head aches from all the terms and diseases."

"Go on, Grace, your head aches because it's got something to do with itself apart from swooning over Rudolph Valentino."

"I love the instruction," said Tufts, nose in *Gray's Anatomy.*

"If you drip sausage fat on that page, Tufty, you'll be in hot water," said Edda, face menacing.

"When have I ever lost a drop of sausage fat?"

Their instruction went on; Dr. Finucan never flagged.

"There are no medicines or pharmaceutical techniques worth a pinch of pepper," he said, "for any of the major killers. We know what germs are and can destroy them in our surroundings, but not once they're inside our bodies. A bacillus infecting tissue, like pneumonia in the lungs, is untreatable. We can look at the thing under a microscope, but nothing we can administer by mouth or skin or hypodermic injection can kill it."

For some reason his eyes went to Tufts—a perfect matron!

"As I am Corunda's Coroner, I conduct autopsies, which are surgical dissections of the dead. The other name for autopsy is post mortem. You'll learn your anatomy and physiology standing around the morgue table. If the dead person is an itinerant without family or friends, I'll carve the corpse minutely to show a particular system—lymphatic, vascular, digestive, for example. We'll have to hope that I get enough indigents, but usually I do."

He gazed at them sternly. "Remember this, nurses, always! Our subject under the knife is one of God's creatures, no matter how humble. What you see, what you hear, what you touch and handle is, or was, a living human being and a part of God's grand scheme, whatever that may be. Everyone is worthy of respect, including after death. Nurse Latimer, you must remember that the patient's wishes count as well as your own. Nurse Treadby, that not all children are angels in character or inclination, Nurse Scobie, that there are times when your most cherished systems will not work, and Nurse Faulding, that even the foulest mess a patient can produce has its place in God's plan." He grinned. "No, I am not religious like your father, ladies, for the God I speak of is the sum total of everything that was, or is, or will be."

A fine man, was Edda's verdict, echoed by Tufts; to Kitty he was a little bit of a spoilsport, but to Grace he was the Voice of Doom reiterating the background chorus of her nursing life—messes, messes, and more messes.

Of one thing they were very glad: though Matron, Dr. Campbell, and Dr. Finucan knew they were twinned sisters, no one else did. A whole world existed between St. Mark's Rectory and Corunda Base Hospital.

n Edda's opinion, no man could hold a candle to Jack Thurlow, whom she had met on the bridle path along the Corunda River when she had been all of seventeen. Then as now, he was riding a tall thoroughbred of dappled grey with a blackish mane and tail, the kind of horse Edda, astride fat old Thumbelina, would have given much to own, and knew she never could.

Still she could remember the day: Winter coming, and the long, graceful canes of weeping willows were flying yellow leaves like a blizzard of slender darts. The river water was as clear as glass, freshly shed along the crest of the Great Divide whose rounded old mountains hunched against Corunda's eastern rim. A magic world of sharply tangy winds, the far-off breath of snow, pungently redolent soil, a streaming mackerel sky . . .

He was cantering down the bridle path, so she first saw him through the rain of frozen willow tears. Sitting his horse so well, his brown, sinewy arms loose across his mount's neck, barely holding the reins. Horse and rider were old friends, she thought, pulling Thumbelina off the path and waiting to see if he would just thunder by without acknowledging her presence, or stop to greet a fellow rider.

The overcast day meant he wore no hat; slowing, he lifted his hand to his brow, fingers curled as if they gripped a brim that wasn't there. No film star, he, but to Edda he was better than one of those artificial gentlemen, with their pancake makeup, mascaraed lashes, and lipsticked mouths. A true Corunda landsman, and beautiful in Edda's adolescent eyes. Display-

35

ing good manners, he halted, dismounted, then helped Edda down, for all she didn't need helping.

"This old lady needs turning out to pasture," he said after introducing himself, patting Thumbelina's nose.

"Yes, but now Daddy has a motor car, she's the last horse left in the Rectory stables."

"I'll trade you."

The hooded pale eyes widened. "Trade me?"

"The Rector, really. My home paddock is too small for a good young horse, but it would suit your old lady just right. I'll take her in exchange for a four-year-old mare named Fatima, provided you keep her exercised," said Jack, rolling a cigarette.

"If Daddy says yes, it's a bargain!" Edda cried, feeling as if in a dream. A horse worth riding as well as a lush little paddock for Thumbelina! Oh, pray Daddy said yes!

At the time Jack Thurlow was just thirty years old, tall and well built without seeming clumsy or lumbering; his thick, waving hair was streaked between golden and flaxen, his face was handsome in a masculine mold, and his eyes were a stern blue. A Burdum to the core, Edda thought, from hair to eyes.

"I'm old Tom Burdum's heir," he said gloomily.

Her breath caught; Edda laughed. "You're *complaining*?"

"Darned right I am! What would I do with all that money and power?" he demanded, as if money and power were disgusting things. "I've managed Corundoobar for old Tom since I was eighteen, and Corundoobar is all I want. The fat lambs bring in a steady income, and the Arab horses I breed for lady's hacks are beginning to win me prizes at some important country shows. Anything more would swamp me."

A man with finite ambitions, thought Edda, fresh at that moment with the heartbreak of learning she couldn't do medicine. If old Tom Burdum gave me £5,000 to do medicine, he wouldn't even notice a pinprick in his wealth, while his heir is of a mind to renounce everything except a pinprick. Corundoobar is 5,000 acres of magnificent land, but it's not even the biggest or the best of old Tom's properties. What circles we run in!

☖

That had been the start of a curious friendship limited to rides along the Corunda River, a friendship that Edda was surprised to find her father did not oppose in any way, from Fatima the gift horse to the unchaperoned nature of his daughter's contacts with Jack.

For which, blame Maude. The ready-reckoner in her mind began to hum and then to click as the indignant Rector informed her of Jack Thurlow's cheek in scraping an acquaintance with his virgin child, and there would be no Fatima in exchange for Thumbelina, and definitely no more rides for Edda along the bridle path . . .

"What utter piffle!" snapped Maude, astonished at the Rector's stupidity. "You will drive me out to Corundoobar this evening, Thomas, and thank Jack Thurlow very prettily for his kindness in giving Edda a decent hack. Oh, what fools men can be! The man is very comfortably off, a Burdum by blood, and at the moment old Tom Burdum's only heir. You ought to be down on your knees at the high altar thanking God for throwing Edda in Jack Thurlow's direction! With any luck as well as plenty of good management, she'll be his wife within three years."

A tirade that all four girls overheard, and discussed many times over those three years. The object of it, Edda, took it better than her sisters, as success meant Fatima and a new friend. The one who cringed and flinched at such naked determination was poor Kitty; if Maude could behave like that over Edda, about whom she didn't care, what would she be like when Kitty's turn came?

Friendship was all it could be, of course. Virginity was highly prized, and the Rector's daughters brought up to believe that a decent man expected his wife to be a virgin on her wedding night; pregnancy out of wedlock was the worst sin imaginable.

There were reasons, of course, and the Rector, as religious instructor to his daughters, made sure they understood that this was not a caprice, but a logical law. "A man has only one proof that he is the father of his wife's children," said the Reverend Latimer in his most serious voice to his fifteen-year-old girls, "and that is his wife's virginity on her wedding day, coupled to her fidelity during the marriage. Why should a man give food and shelter to children who are not his? Both Old and New Testaments condemn unchastity and infidelity."

From time to time Thomas Latimer repeated this sermon, though without understanding that his greatest help in assuring the innocence of his girls was the fact that none of them was tempted to throw her cap over the windmill, including Edda.

For all his attractions, Jack Thurlow didn't tug at Edda's heart. Nor had any other man, for that matter. Knowing herself capable of fascinating men, Edda waited for the tug at her heart that never came. Because it is human nature to blame the self, she ended in deciding that she lacked profound emotions. I am a cold person, she said to herself; I can't feel as others feel. Not one of the boys and men who have kissed me since the C.L.C. ball in 1921 has provoked a deep response. A bit of a pash-up in a dark corner that I inevitably remember as ending in my slapping sweaty male hands away from my breasts—what on earth gets them so *excited*?

Despite such fancies, she continued to encounter Jack Thurlow on the bridle path, grateful because he never tried to embrace her or kiss her. Oh, there was a definite physical attraction between them, but clearly he disliked its ruling him as much as she disliked its ruling her.

Then in January of 1926, she kissed him.

The moment he saw her he kicked the grey gelding to a hasty meeting, slid off its back, and yanked her from Fatima with trembling hands.

He was shaking and openly weeping, which didn't stop his lifting her off the ground and twirling her in a crazy, stepless dance—a kind of fool's caper.

"A new Burdum heir has crawled out of the woodwork!" he said, putting her down. "Edda, I'm let off old Tom's chain! At ten this morning I became the legal owner of Corundoobar free and clear, and signed a paper renouncing any other claims on old Tom's estate. Free, Edda! I'm free!"

She couldn't help it; she kissed him on the lips, a warm and loving message of congratulations that went on for long enough to hover perilously on the brink of becoming something more serious, more intense. Then he broke away, face wet with tears, and took her hands in one of his.

"I am so happy for you," she said huskily, smiling.

"Edda, it's my dream!" He groped for his handkerchief to mop his eyes. "Corundoobar is a prime property of just the right size, and there's not a ruby anywhere near it, so money and power will pass me by." Grinning, he ruffled her bobbed hair, something she hated. "With you going nursing in three months and our rides at least curtailed, I didn't know what I was going to do. I even thought of going out west to merino country. Now this!"

"We can still ride on my days off," she said seriously.

"I know, and it's a factor."

Old Tom Burdum, apparently, had finally found a suitable heir, and the entire district naturally expected the new heir to appear off the Sydney or Melbourne train. But he never did, and old Tom refused to say why.

When news of the heir did come, it consisted of miserable little snippets devoid of hard facts, and never sufficient to sate the greedier among the Corunda gossips.

The most enterprising of them was Maude, who, blessed with a tree of early apples, most considerately took a basket of them out to old Tom and old Hannah Burdum. There she applied the instruments of gossip torture with unsurpassed skill, but to very small effect. However, she learned just enough to whet her appetite and stimulate her to new heights of information gathering.

From old Tom and old Hannah she learned that the new heir's name was Charles Henry Burdum, that he was an Englishman born and bred, was thirty-two years old, and still lived in England. Even old Tom's massive estate was as nothing to him, he was so wealthy in his own right; he dabbled, said old Tom with awe, in the money markets of the City of London, financial capital of the world!

Armed with these facts, Maude was on the sleety station at 3 A.M. to board the night express from Melbourne to Sydney, where she arrived at 6 A.M., had breakfast in the Central Railway restaurant, and was waiting at the doors of the public library when they opened. And there, in the reading room, she found out all about Charles Henry Burdum. A woman of resource, Maude Latimer.

A money man he might be, but Charles Burdum had an altruistic streak, too: he was a medical doctor, a graduate of Guy's, and actually held a job as a deputy superintendent at the Manchester Royal Infirmary—very prestigious! Of course his money wouldn't slow his medical career down, would it? Maude looked up biographical dictionaries (Eton, Balliol, Guy's), ponderous broadsheet newspapers, yellow-journalist tabloid newspapers, society magazines, less fussy magazines, and the notorious, rather ratbaggy journals that skated on the thin ice of the libel laws. They all yielded grist for her mill; Dr. Charles Burdum was news.

In 1925 he became engaged to the only daughter of a duke. The sensational, scandalous affair had been headlines in tabloids on both sides of the Atlantic, for Dr. Burdum, despite his wealth and the ownership of some thousands of acres of Lancashire, was not good enough according to the lights of the duke. When his daughter, Sybil, made the front page of the *News of the World* dancing a mad Charleston with Charles Burdum at a shady party, the Duke stepped in and removed Sybil from Charles Burdum's life. Enthralled, Maude discovered that Sybil was a mere seventeen, well and truly under her father's authority. It was obviously a blazing love affair; the couple ran away, were caught, and Sybil vanished from the face of the earth. A prowling French photographer took a picture of the girl sitting mournfully on the loggia of a Riviera villa; in the next photograph she was clad as a bride and marrying the Duke's choice of husband for her—a fellow who went back to William the Conqueror on his distaff side, was six feet four inches tall, owned most of Northumberland and Cumberland, and was related to the old House of Hanover on his father's side.

What she couldn't obtain was a decent photograph of this remarkable chap, half money, half medicine. The black-and-white pictures of him didn't even answer the vexed question as to whether he was ugly or handsome: a mouth, a nose, two eyes and a mop of what seemed fair hair. However, snaps of him in a group of men said that he wasn't overly tall. That's good, thought Maude; too tall a man would never suit Kitty.

Though she was happy to disseminate the gossip, Maude spoke of her plans for Kitty to no one. Sooner or later Charles Burdum would visit his colonial inheritance, and the intensity of his foiled attempt to marry a duke's daughter said that the wound to his pride would not heal quickly. His visit would occur while he was still a bachelor. And in the meantime, Kitty would be fully occupied by her nursing training, popped into storage on a shelf unawakened. Things were going so well! Edda would marry Jack Thurlow, Grace would marry some shiftless no-hoper who worked with his hands for a living, and Tufts would become that vital necessity, the maiden aunt, shuttled from sister to sister as their children needed her.

That all would go as she planned Maude had no doubt; even God conspired in her schemes, for the simplest of reasons: He was a sensible fellow, otherwise He wouldn't have created any Maudes.

The first six months of anything new and strange are always the worst to endure: a mantra that ruled the lives of the Latimer sisters until the very end of 1926, when, to their amazement, they discovered they had survived, even Grace the Unwilling.

The pity of it, thought Tufts, is that we haven't really expanded our human horizons. From nurses' dining room to accommodation, everything is stratified; we're not allowed to mix with doctors or menials, and the sisters make sure that the West Enders know we are a cut above them, harbingers of a new nursing order. I can't befriend Harry or Ernie the porters, I can't sit amid the West End nurses in the dining room, and if a doctor appears on the ward, I am immediately sent to sort the dirty laundry or scrub bed pans in the sluice room. I sit on a level above or below which I dare not go. How can there be *esprit de corps* or camaraderie among the various kinds of people staffing a hospital if they are not allowed to communicate with each other as friends? Yet our bitterest opponents, if not outright enemies, are exactly the people who would benefit the most. I yearn to offer to teach Lena Corrigan, Nancy Wilson, and Maureen O'Brien the rudiments of chemistry and physics, make them see that water has three states of being, and that iodine is an element. But they don't want to know because they would see confessing to their ignorance as admitting defeat in this senseless battle they wage. How do I get it through their heads that knowledge is the only road that leads out of penury and subservience?

"The West Enders are convinced that if we have no company save our own, we'll fall apart at the seams," said Edda. "When do you think they'll wake up?"

Christmas was coming and they were dressing for church, the first Sunday since they had started nursing that all four were off duty together. After service they were going to the Rectory for a celebratory lunch; Tufts and Kitty had turned nineteen in August, and Edda and Grace twenty-one in November, but without birthday dinners. Today was very special.

Having checked that the seams of her sheer silk stockings were straight, Grace looked up. "The West Enders don't know we're sisters," she said, "and they do a lot of wondering about how bad our rows and quarrels are."

Beautiful! she was thinking as she gazed at Edda—why can't I look like that? It's the way she moves, sinuous and slinky, the way she holds her head, that tiny, enigmatic smile. Red was definitely her color, no matter what its exact shade; today she wore Chinese red, a dress of heavy crepe that hung loose yet suggested how superb her body was. On her head she wore a ruched-up pancake of red crepe tilted over her left eye, and black kid shoes, bag, and gloves.

"You look wonderful, Grace," Edda said unexpectedly—or do twins read minds? "I wish I had the patience to work embroidery like that! It turns your cream crepe into a butterfly's wing with a black skeleton. Aubrey Beardsley to a tee."

Pulling on long black kid gloves, Grace glowed. "My hat? Is it all right, Eds?"

"Perfect. Like folded black-edged wings."

A group of West End nurses saw the four girls walk down the ramp to Victoria Street; Lena Corrigan frowned. It beggared understanding that after eight months of inflexible isolation from all avenues of hospital friendship, these four females were still on speaking terms with each other. Looking like a million dollars, they passed along the ramp laughing and joking with each other, so obviously, inexplicably happy.

"Can posh accents and education do that?" Lena asked.

"Do what?"

"I dunno, Nance, but they've got *something*." Lena sighed. "Trouble is, the longer I know them, the better I like them. Most specially Latimer. A queen to look at, but not stuck-up."

"No, they ain't none of them stuck-up," Maureen said. "Even Treadby the bottle-blonde is nice."

Nurse Corrigan turned away. "Know what, girls? I'm fed up with war. They're hardly twenty yet, but before we know it they'll have state registration. I think it's time we thought about fighting the old man for some of his beer money to see our daughters matriculate. And yeah, you're right—that's not my idea. It was something Scobie said."

Life on the wards was a challenge for Edda, Tufts, and Kitty, but for Grace it was an ordeal. Every last one of Corunda's sisters was an import and an official public servant. Unofficial West End nurses were at liberty to be married because they were described as "casual workers" without benefits, like the porters, wardsmaids, kitchen staff, typists, and the rest. Female public servants could not be married, so there were no married nursing sisters. Widows were employable; so, technically, were divorcees, save that a divorcee would never get as far as a face-to-face interview. What divorcees there were pretended to be widows, and took fine care never to be seen in the regular company of men. A lot of sisters "lived out" in rented premises, usually shared with a fellow sister, but Corunda Base, like some other hospitals, did offer on-site accommodation for a number of sisters. Frank Campbell preferred to see a little rent coming in from the Great War housing than keep it empty, and sisters were ideal tenants, being spinsters—no children, no beer-swilling husbands.

What no one save the sisters themselves thought about were the intangibles of holding down a professional career: the unborn babies, the empty other side of the bed, the lack of stimulus in eternally female company, the worry of indigent old age. So they buried themselves in their work, tried to find congenial housemates, had occasional affairs with men, or made do with each other. None of which made them easy bosses. It was, however, a rigidly level playing field; if there had been such a person as a female judge, she too would be a spinster if she took a government salary.

The day was divided into three shifts—six in the morning until two in the afternoon, two in the afternoon until ten at night, and ten at night until six in the morning. Each ward required a minimum of one sister on duty at all times; the double wards, Men's and Women's, demanded two, as did Children's. With the result that there were a total of fifty nursing sisters, including those at the mental asylum and convalescent/aged home.

Some, like Sister Una Robertson of Men's and Sister Meg Moulton of Children's, were known within a day of starting to work anywhere in the hospital, while others, like Deputy Matron Anne Harding, remained anonymous for months. It was a question of personality. Sister Moulton was an absolute dear, whereas Sister Robertson was the dragon to end all dragons. Both were middle-aged women just beginning to sprout whiskers on their chins, thickened midriffs, and leathery skins, but there the similarities ended. All Sister Robertson's love was given to her men patients, who were as terrified of her as were the doctors. To Grace, the Devil was a far easier adversary.

"Faulding, you are running," Sister Robertson snarled at a frantic Grace. "Kindly desist this minute! There are only two reasons a nurse runs—fire or hemorrhage."

But how, asked Grace of herself, is the work to get finished if I'm not allowed to run? And why does every man have to be shaved every day? *Fifty shaves a day, even if they're dying!* A sentiment many of the men shared with Grace.

"You could do with a shave yerself, Sister," said one angry man in Grace's hearing. "Gimme yer veil and take me place under the bloody razor—yer worse than Kaiser Bill!"

"Poor chap!" said Grace to Kitty later on, wiping tears of mirth from her eyes. "He got a *rabid* suppository rammed up his arse by Sister in person not five minutes later, and spent a terrible morning on the toilet. Luckily he could walk."

There were many funny moments, but there were also moments so wrenchingly sad that it took all that year of 1926 for the Latimers to learn to cope with the sorrow. Some people, they discovered, were so brave! Others flinched and started squealing before they were touched. No one stayed in hospital any longer than possible, not entirely because it was hospital policy. The notorious stinginess of the Superintendent, Frank Campbell, affected the patients as much as the staff. Lumpy old mattresses, sheets worn so thin they were darned, towels devoid of their nap, homemade and hideously caustic soap, cut-up newspapers for wiping bottoms, and the worst food shearers' cooks could provide.

What baffled the Latimers was how their father could be a member of the Hospital Board and stroll through the wards every day without seeing what Frank Campbell had done and was doing. No, Daddy drifted on his saintly way, smiling, comforting the patients spiritually while ignoring their acute physical misery as if it did not exist. For hospital wasn't *free*. Even the poorest patient received a bill, which made the Almoner's job the hardest in all of Corunda Base; she had to find a reason not to charge for services, and that was very often impossible. The consulting specialist doctors were a decent bunch, but Frank Campbell charged for every square of cut-up newspaper.

Kitty bloomed, especially after she was sent to Children's, where many of the little patients had bone problems: broken limbs in the main, an occasional congenital displacement of the hips, infected fractures, diseases of bone density, and too much rickets among the poor. Whatever was wrong, they tended to be cheerful children inured to pain and bed, or a perilous nuisance once they were allowed out of bed. To Kitty it didn't matter; she loved every child, every obstacle, every moment.

Boys and girls were nursed together until they turned six, after which the ward was split into Boys and Girls. At fourteen they were admitted to the adult wards. Winter saw more broken bones, summer more enteric or gastric diseases, but all year round the fifty beds were filled, as child patients tended to need longer hospitalization. Here alone had the Reverend Thomas Latimer made an effort to ease the suffering; there were plenty of toys and books, and the steam radiators were kept functioning, which wasn't always the case elsewhere. Frank Campbell's budget provided for just one plumber, whose perpetually unfulfilled dream was to have a plumber's mate.

The moment when Kitty realized that her depression had gone for good was so buried under the demands of her work that she was never able to pinpoint it. Perhaps it had been too stealthy, too gradual, but certainly after she went to Children's it never reared its head. Children's nursing wrapped a blanket of well-being around her that comforted, nourished, calmed, and satisfied her every desire. The world, she understood, was stuffed with people whose needs and insults made her own seem laughable, ridiculous. From nineteen years of being the center of the world, Kitty saw herself relegated to its outermost margins—a nobody, a nothing. And she loved it so much that she forgot she was beautiful, even forgot Maude and life in the Rectory. Not the naughtiest or nastiest child had the power to dent her newfound confidence, the tranquil peace she concluded with herself. Finally, Kitty flew free.

What she didn't understand was that her awakening had only served to increase her beauty. In desperation to remove her from the gaze of as many men as possible, Matron had sent her to Children's as a last resort.

"The trouble is that Treadby is such a good nurse I can't afford to lose her," Matron said to Liam Finucan, "and I can't say she's stuck-up or conscious of her looks, because she's not. But she makes men as silly as wheels, and women patients hate her as much for the sweetness of her nature as they do for her face."

"Luckily," said Liam with a grin, "Corunda Base has no Paris to tempt our Helen of Troy."

"Why are you impervious to her, Liam?"

He shoved at his hair, which had a tendency to fall over his brow and part-blind him. "I have no idea. Perhaps I dislike bottle blondes?"

"That hair is not out of a bottle! I wish it were—a black root might disillusion some of our junior doctors."

"Children's will suffice for Treadby," he soothed.

"Yes, but she can't stay on Children's forever."

"True. Just keep her adult nursing down to the minimum."

"Meg Moulton adores the girl—that's a relief! I'm told that Treadby is a perfect children's nurse. The ward's a happier place on her shifts, and she works like a navvy."

"No human being is perfect, Gertie."

Bouncing through the ward with smiles, dances, and skips that had the children in giggles, Kitty continued on her voyage of discovery, wondering at her own blindness. Until she started nursing, but especially children's nursing, everyone except her sisters and her father had discounted her as a productive member of society. Now, she had a purpose.

Not that Children's permitted time for internal reflections. If Jimmy Collins hadn't picked the top off an unready scab or Ginny Giacometti fallen out of bed trying to play a joke, then Alf Smithers had eaten a whole packet of pastel chalks because the meals never filled his bottomless belly.

"The effect of his multihued smile might have been quite charming," Kitty said to Sister Moulton, "except that he ate the black pair last—revolting!"

Came a wail from Barry Simpson that made them spin around.

"Nursie, nursie! I done poohs in me bed!"

"And bang goes Frank Campbell's bottom sheet," Kitty said. "Barry's poohs are formidable."

Even on Children's, though, there were men to bother Kitty. The most persistent nuisance was the resident, Dr. Neil Cranshaw; he had the weight of medical authority to bolster his pursuit. Kitty loathed him, but his rank insisted that he be treated with fawning respect.

"Dinner at the Parthenon?" he asked, supervising Nurse Treadby as she dealt with Jimmy's scab.

"Sorry, sir, I'm busy."

"You can't possibly be busy every night, Nurse."

"I am until June of 1929."

"What happens then?" he asked, wondering which of several expressions would work best on her—what a little beauty she was! He assumed a look of admiration quite spoiled by the lust seething inside his brain.

"I graduate as a registered nurse," she said demurely, "and will be free to accept dinner invitations. Until then, I'm forced to study in all my free time."

He might have argued, but Sister Moulton was bearing down on them with her fifteen-inch guns loaded. Dr. Cranshaw vanished.

"Ta, Sister," said Kitty.

"Unmarried doctors," she said later to the other three, "are a pain in the bum."

"Tell me something I haven't learned for myself," said Edda.

"Neil Cranshaw bothering you?" Tufts asked, and doubled up with laughter. "He asked me to dinner at the Parthenon the other day—caught me on the ramps doing a message for Sister Smith. So I stood there and stared at him, slowly sucked my lips together like a fish, and crossed my eyes. He ran away."

"Mind you," Edda said, "Corunda Base doesn't get the cream of the Sydney Med School crop. They go to Vinnie's and RPA and North Shore in Sydney. We don't get the worst, but they're pretty awful."

"Where else would a Stan Laurel like Cranshaw be called the hospital heartthrob?" Tufts asked.

"He does have that woebegone Stan Laurel look," Kitty agreed.

"He always reeks of cheap cigars," said Grace, "and I can't stand red hair on a man. In fact, girls, there's not a doctor here I fancy. They all think they poop ice cream."

Happily for Dr. Neil Cranshaw, he wasn't privy to these remarks, nor was he aware that Nurse Treadby, who looked like a Botticelli angel, possessed a tongue salty enough to rival the Dead Sea. So he continued to make a nuisance of himself on the Children's ward, free to plague Kitty because he was rotating through Dr. Dennis Faraday's service at the moment; Dr. Faraday was Corunda's child specialist, loved and respected.

The ward was just emerging from a frenzied battle against an epidemic of diphtheria that had been imperilled by insufficient stocks of specially modified rubber tubing used to assist a child to breathe. A typical Frank Campbell false economy; Deputy Matron Harding had to take the morning express to Sydney, pay far too much for stocks from a medical supplier, then return on the night train to find that Liam Finucan had rigged replacements out of ordinary tubing that worked well enough to avoid what would have been two negligent deaths. As with all infectious children's diseases, only the worst cases were hospitalized—over a hundred patients between two and twelve years of age with laryngeal diphtheria: a malignant membrane in the swollen throat expanded to block the airway, which this modified piece of rubber tubing kept open. It was a serious epidemic that saw seventeen children die and four require some months of hospital care due to heart complications.

There were always two empty but absolutely ready wards at the end of a special ramp to serve as an isolation area for epidemics, but the last time they had been used so intensively was in the three years following the Great

War, when influenza killed more people than the war had. It always seemed too that very lethal epidemics attacked children or younger adults; perhaps, thought Edda, if a body had survived everything to reach old age, it was tougher, far harder to kill.

Kitty hadn't nursed in the diphtheria wards. Sister Meg Moulton had preferred to keep her in Children's proper, though Grace, Edda, and Tufts all did duty on diphtheria. For Kitty it was double shifts and cancelled days off, but the crisis in available nurses was acute. Only a number of volunteers, retired West Enders, saw Corunda Base survive.

In a private, unpublicized way, the diphtheria epidemic marked a victory for Kitty, a triumph she shared only with her sisters.

"Dinner at the Parthenon any night you care to name?" asked Dr. Neil Cranshaw of Kitty while she was making beds.

And suddenly it was all too much. If there hadn't been a diphtheria epidemic—if the hospital owned a decent sheet—if Cranshaw didn't have such a sloppy mouth!

"Oh, for Crissake, you dopey moron, shove your invitations up your flaming arse! Now piss off and leave me alone!"

He would have been less surprised if a butterfly had savaged him during a walk in the garden; certainly he never thought of fighting back. A blaze of violet from those usually blue eyes had him scuttling out of the ward like a mouse evading a straw broom.

B y the time that June of 1927 rolled around, the Latimer sisters had been nursing for fourteen months, entering their second winter under Frank Campbell's administration, and had conquered all their foes and bogeys. How Grace had lasted the other three didn't know, save that her streak of cunning stood her in good stead, and her nursing, now that she was more or less inured to messes, passed muster; it had come as a refreshing surprise to learn that not every day brought messes.

They had rotated once through all the wards. When June dawned Kitty was back in Children's, together with Tufts. Edda had been convinced someone would spot the likeness between the twins, but not even Sister Meg Moulton did; the uniforms concealed their bodies and the differently colored eyes dominated their faces. It also helped that Kitty liked caring for boys, whereas Tufts preferred girls, so they were usually seen as individuals.

"Report to me in my office, nurses, as soon as you return from lunch," said Sister Moulton with unusual curtness.

"What on earth is the matter?" Tufts asked Kitty over ham sandwiches in their house. "However, *my* conscience is clear."

"That was said with a smirk, Nurse Sanctimonious. Since I know Moulton far better than you do, I'm going to guess that we are about to be handed some sort of special job."

The correct guess, as they found out half an hour later in Sister

Moulton's office. Dr. Dennis Faraday was there, too, both of them looking grave.

"Because the case you will be nursing will also be a brief one, Matron has suggested that the four new-style trainees be assigned to it," Dr. Faraday said in his deep, pleasant voice. A very big man who had been a famous rugby player in his youth, he reminded those who met him of a benign, friendly brown bear—brown skin, brown hair, brown eyes—and possessed an indefinable magic in handling children.

"Under ordinary circumstances," he went on, "dying children are nursed on the ward as far as possible. However, the child you will be nursing cannot be subjected to curious eyes. Corunda is a hotbed of gossip, and child patients have many visitors. Your patient will be nursed in isolation, away from outsiders. The child's name is Michael Vesper, but he responds to Mikey. He's riddled with metastatic sarcoma and suffers terribly. A tiny dose of opiate liberates the most wonderful little boy—so cheerful and so grateful! He knows he's dying, and he's a hero."

The doctor's eyes shone with tears; Sister Moulton sent a glare at Kitty and Tufts that warned them not to discuss Doctor's emotions. "When I can, nurses, I'll give you the police reports, the Almoner's notes, everything I can find about Mikey." Dr. Faraday blinked, drew a breath. "Mikey is two years old, but looks no older than twelve months. Until today, he has been undiagnosed and untreated. Were it not for the curiosity of our District Nurse, he would never have been noticed or rescued. I give him about two or three weeks to live, but I am determined that those paltry few days will be the happiest and most comfortable of all Mikey's life."

Dr. Faraday moved to the door. "Sister, further explanations are in your hands." And with a smile, he disappeared.

The ensuing silence seemed to last for hours; in reality, a few minutes that saw Grace and Edda arrive, learn what was about to happen. In fourteen months they had never served together as a quartet, nor would they nursing Mikey Vesper, though he was their only patient. Kitty and Tufts elected to do 6 A.M. until 10 P.M. together, Grace did the night shift, and Edda was spell nurse.

"Matron chose you," said Sister Moulton, "chiefly because you won't gossip to *anyone*. Why she's so confident I have no idea, but I accept her judgment. What I personally want to say is that you retain some measure of detachment. Mikey Vesper is a heartbreaking case, but if you let him break your hearts, you'll never achieve registration."

"We will survive, Sister," said Edda.

But Sister Moulton wasn't finished. "How much of Mikey's malnutrition is due to cancer metastases and how much to sheer neglect we don't know, except that both have contributed. Worst of all is that Mikey has never mattered enough to anyone to develop an identity. He's no more and no less than a nuisance underfoot. His mother is forced to work harder than most slaves—Vesper sells her services as a laundress. District Nurse doesn't know if she's mentally dull or the victim of a language barrier—the family is German, and has only been in Corunda eighteen months. Children are something the poor woman gestates, bears, and suckles until they're old enough to eat and drink. There are three boys between thirteen and sixteen, then a gap followed by three girls between six and nine. And Mikey, aged two."

"Why the gaps, Sister?" Tufts asked. "Was Vesper serving prison sentences?"

Meg Moulton's blue eyes grew round. "That's a clever deduction, Scobie. Sergeant Cameron could make police enquiries."

"Are the boys in school?" Kitty asked.

"No, definitely not." Sister Moulton sighed. "Well, you have to know, and you've been nursing long enough not to be shocked. The headmaster of the Corbi school has lodged a complaint with Sergeant Cameron. The three little Vesper girls have all been interfered with by their father and their brothers."

"The youngest is only six," Edda said, mouth dry, "and none has reached puberty."

"So Vesper must be aware that trouble is coming from all directions," said Grace, who had grown enough not to cry. "He ought to be hanged!"

"They won't do that," said Tufts, "but he will go back to jail for a long time."

Junior Sister poked her head around the door. "Michael Vesper is here," she said.

Room One was too tiny to have contained a full-sized bed, but Mikey Vesper was in a cot that accommodated him spaciously. Though Kitty knew his age, he did indeed look no more than half of it, and the abdominal distension that went with malnutrition gave a false impression of substance. He had a fine fair skin and curly brown hair; immense dark eyes set in an oddly elderly face told his story, for they were stern, intelligent, composed. Not a beautiful child, save for the eyes. A highly experienced nurse, Meg Moulton knew Mikey was one of those children with the power to haunt even waking dreams.

Overlooked and underfoot in his own home Mikey might have been, but his sarcomatosis had thus far spared his brain, as Tufts and Kitty, sharing a long double shift, soon discovered. Both of them understood that Mikey was one patient who would be given as much opiate as he wanted to stem the intractable pain; addiction was not a consideration for a dying patient. And he was so *grateful* for a tiny drop of opiate! What must his agony have been like, month after month as the cancer spread, without anyone attempting to ease his torments? Morphine had him beaming—thank God he wasn't one of those it nauseated! Not that he begged for more opiate; he saved the injections for real need, explaining to Grace in the middle of a wakeful night that if he was sedated all the time, he wouldn't know all his lovely nurses the way he did. Kitty danced the Charleston for him while he laughed and clapped, Tufts danced the seven veils with Frank Campbell's darned sheets, and Edda played tunes on metal bowls and basins, singing nonsensical songs. Whatever his nurses did for him, Mikey loved.

His only visitor was Maria, the middle Vesper girl, who would appear like a ghost out of nowhere to stand at the foot of Mikey's cot and listen as he breathlessly regaled her with all the wonderful things his nurses were doing for him, from the needle pricks that eased his pain to the craziest Kitty song and dance. Not that Maria visited every day; perhaps one day in five. What she couldn't possibly have mistaken was Mikey's devotion to Kitty. Though he loved all four, Kitty held pride of place in his heart. What transpired between the two Vesper children remained private; the nurse on duty was almost inevitably Kitty, who respected their family ties by leaving them alone for fifteen minutes if Mikey was well enough; Maria's visits always saw his condition improve.

ᔥ

Sergeant Jim Cameron of the New South Wales Police Force had grown very interested in the Vespers, between Mikey's neglect, the schoolteacher's complaints that Bill Vesper and his sons were sexually molesting the Vesper girls, and his rooted conviction that Vesper was rustling fat lambs. Head of the Corunda branch of the police, Cameron had a feeling he ought to call in the experts from Sydney, but his streak of Scots stubbornness kept saying no to outsiders. The Vespers were *his* problem, and he could solve it.

Pauline Duncan, the District Nurse, had been a kind of catalyst for Sergeant Cameron, who knew her well. On the day Mikey Vesper was admitted to the hospital, Sister Duncan had been called out before dawn to help with the mopping up of a brawl in the gypsy camp under the West Corunda River railway bridge. Having dealt with bruises and stitched up a couple of knife slashes, she climbed into her Model T and headed back into town. The old house in which the Vespers lived was on her way, and the niggling doubt she sometimes felt about Bill Vesper caused her to slow down, then stop. Why not? she asked herself. I'm actually here, so why not take a peep inside? The male Vespers won't be here at this hour, maybe I can talk to that poor woman.

Mrs. Vesper was boiling sheets in a copper outside the back door, and the three daughters, home from school with black eyes, were helping her. A tiny boy hobbled between their legs, weeping silently, and from time to time one of the females would brush him aside. A single glance was enough. Pauline Duncan rushed forward, scooped the boy up, and ran to her car. With the child on the passenger seat next to her, she drove straight to Dr. Faraday's rooms. An hour later, Mikey Vesper was in Corunda Base, and Sergeant Cameron was having a fuse lit under him by Dr. Faraday.

As for Mikey's nurses, warned not to become haunted, it was far too late.

"How could anyone treat a little child so cruelly?" Kitty asked.

"A man like Bill Vesper doesn't even know what cruel means," said Grace, wiping her eyes. "If people don't want children, then they shouldn't have them."

"Huh!" snorted Edda. "There's no way to prevent having them."

"Then I'll make sure I marry a man who can support them," said Kitty, chin up.

"Don't tempt fate, Kits," Edda said. "If any of us could see into the future, fortune tellers wouldn't enjoy fat incomes. Look at the film stars Grace is always blathering about. They all consult clairvoyants. Yet, when you think about it, what can possibly worry a film star?"

Tufts grinned. "An unwanted baby?"

Under the influence of so much love and care, Mikey's dying slowed. If his days weren't always free of pain, Dr. Faraday kept that pain as bearable as possible without causing coma. Mikey's favorite treat was to be towed up and down a disused section of ramp in a wooden pony cart painted bright yellow, with his nurse playing a whinnying, stamping pony. Only Grace never experienced the joy of being Mikey's pony, but Grace knew Mikey had some very bad nights, and that they were his time to talk.

Pain and deprivation had pushed his brain into a precocious maturity, but anyone expecting enlightened wisdom from his lips would have listened in vain. His thoughts, albeit a trifle advanced for his years, were still very much the thoughts of a toddling boy. What earned him love was the sweetness of his disposition, and what earned him admiration was his bravery.

"Or perhaps," said Grace to Edda, changing shifts, "what really makes Mikey so lovably memorable is his refusal to complain. And I should know!" Her face puckered. "How terrible, to be taught that lesson by a two-year-old!"

Wisely, Edda did not reply.

As the milestone of one month loomed for Mikey, his pain grew suddenly even worse, which meant the pricks of opiate grew more frequent. He couldn't manage to eat any more, subsisting on chocolate-flavored milk shakes and barley sugar or butterscotch toffees.

"Tired, Kitty," the child said just after he passed one month as a patient, "terribly tired."

"Then sleep, darling."

"Don't want to sleep. Soon I won't wake up."

"Oh, tiddly-pooh to that, Mikey! There's always a waking up."

"Not for me. Too tired."

When Maria came on her visit, Sister Moulton told her to give her mother and father the message that Mikey would not last out another twenty-four hours; the little girl nodded and left. That afternoon a drunken Bill Vesper and his three drunken sons arrived at the hospital demanding to take Mikey home. Frank Campbell's response was to summon the police, who, led by Sergeant Cameron, threw all four Vespers in the cells to sober up. Next morning, hung over but *compos mentis*, nothing was said about Mikey or his removal from the hospital; the Vespers climbed into their ancient utility truck and drove away.

At dawn of that same day Mikey endured a sudden shift in his spine, where the primary growth was, and began to scream. The shattered Kitty summoned Meg Moulton, who summoned Dr. Faraday from a sound sleep at home.

Finally the screaming stopped; Kitty was holding Mikey in her arms while Dr. Faraday prepared his injection. The child's eyes opened and he smiled at Kitty, let out a breath as if to start saying something. Smiling back, Kitty waited to hear what he would say, but no breath came.

"Put your syringe away, sir," she said to Dr. Faraday. "Mikey has passed from life."

"Thank you. You know what to do, Nurse," Dr. Faraday said, and left the ward.

She laid Mikey out, wrenchingly aware how quickly such a tiny body cooled. By the time she had prepared him for his final rest, Mikey's flesh was cold, cold, cold . . .

No one saw Kitty slip away, down the ramp to her private bolt-hole, where she had taken to retreating after Mikey arrived. It wasn't raining yet, but the winter sky was lowering with dense grey cloud, a bitter wind was blowing, and the ramps were deserted. Her place was an old tree stump under a section of ramp bridged to let a streamlet trickle away. Groping blindly for the stump, Kitty sat down on it with hands clenched, and felt the tears pour hot down her face. Mikey, Mikey! Why put you on this earth at all if your only purpose was to endure two years of pain, pain you've done not one thing to deserve? How I hope there is a heaven full of yellow pony carts and chocolate milk shakes!

The convulsion of grief didn't last long. Finished with it, Kitty returned to Children's, there to report to Sister Moulton that Michael Vesper had peacefully passed away. Dr. Faraday hadn't done so, and that she had known somewhere deep down.

The Shire & City of Corunda paid for Mikey's funeral, to which no member of the Vesper family came; Bill Vesper had been heard in his pub declaring that if the government had the power to abduct a man's flesh and blood, then the government could pay to bury a man's flesh and blood. The Reverend Latimer conducted a graveside ceremony attended by quite a few of the staff of Corunda Base. Enough money was donated to make sure that when the ground above Mikey Vesper had settled, he would have a memorial monument of grey granite carved with gilt letters. Somehow it was important that Mikey Vesper should go into a decent grave.

The story of Mikey Vesper got around Corunda after the little boy died, and contributed to the general loathing for Bill Vesper and his boys. Since Sergeant Cameron couldn't persuade any one of the girls to lay charges of sexual molestation against her father and brothers, the situation continued to fester, yet at the same time slipped from the forefront of Corunda's memory.

The fierce winter storm that had been threatening to break over Corunda's head for three weeks eventually made up its mind to unleash its full fury at the end of June, and after dark had fallen.

Tufts was the only one of the four Latimers on duty, working Men's One, the most neglected of all the wards.

Even Matron had been drawn into the strife between Dr. Frank Campbell and those members of Corunda Base's staff who had anything to do with Men's One; Men's Two, smaller, suffered less in winter than Men's One. Horrified that the steam line lost too much pressure to heat Men's One, Matron had installed two coke-burning heaters in the long ward, only to find that Campbell, tricked into buying the stoves because coke was so cheap, refused to buy enough coke to make the purchase worthwhile. And on the gale nights, like this one, both coke heaters had to be supplemented by steam, feasible if the left-hand radiators were shut off and all steam pressure sent to the right bank.

Matron arrived in the ward at nine to find no coke in the big scuttles and no fires in the heaters.

"Scobie," she said to Tufts, her uniform screeching starch, "go to Dr. Campbell's house, get him out of bed, and down here to me at once! Don't just stand gawping—*do it!*"

Tufts did it. Amazing, she thought as she hustled Dr. Campbell along the ramp, the lengths a resourceful nurse will go to when she's ordered to *do it!*

"Matron's gone mad, you say?" the Superintendent asked.

"Stark raving, sir. Oh, *please* hurry!"

And indeed when Tufts and the Super reached Men's One, Matron did look insane. The starch had given up and wilted, her veil was on the floor, and the fleshy fingers of both hands were curled into claws. "Miser! Skinflint! Despot!" she roared, grabbed Frank Campbell's dressing-gown collar and lifted him off the floor. A skinny little man who had been a despot for twenty-five years, Campbell hung from Matron's fist like a carcass in a butcher's shop, paralyzed with fear. This grizzle-haired scarecrow was a maniac!

"I have warned you before, Dr. Campbell, that I will not see men die of pneumonia because you refuse to heat the wards properly! If coke is not provided and steam pressure kept up, I am going to see the Minister for Health in Sydney and tell him exactly what goes on in Corunda Base Hospital! It has taken me nearly eighteen months to get an appointment, but I finally have one, and when I see the honorable gentleman, I will produce filing cabinets full of your sins against humanity—men, women, and children who are sick!"

There was more. Every man and nurse in Men's One forgot why they were there, the patients sitting up in bed with eyes shining and their hearts, if not their bodies, warmed by Matron's diatribe.

"Oh, it was wonderful!" said Tufts after waking her sisters up to tell them this glorious news. "Matron shook Frank like a terrier a rat—most of the time his feet were clean off the ground."

"Matron has won the Battle of Men's One," said Edda, "but the big question is, has she won the war?"

Perhaps not, but there was a definite improvement in heating the wards, and the plumber got his plumber's mate at last. Matron cancelled her appointment with the Minister for Health, wise enough to know that men will stick together. If she did nothing more for Corunda Base than ensure its inmates were warmer, she hadn't spent her time there in vain. And she did one other thing, on the theory that at worst it could change nothing, but at best it could change everything. She bought a curse from an old gypsy crone the next time the gypsies arrived under the railway bridge. Oh, not a death curse! Just a curse that would see Frank Campbell pack his traps and move elsewhere. Hell would be lovely, but unnecessary; Darwin or Bullamakanka would suffice.

That winter saw the last of the Vespers. When District Nurse Pauline Duncan drove out Corbi way in October of 1927, she found the dilapidated old house empty. Bill Vesper and his family were gone; where to, no one knew. All that remained was the grey granite memorial stone in St. Mark's burial ground, with its bold, bright gilt letters saying this was the final resting place of Michael Vesper, aged two years. No one knew his birthday; none of the Vesper children was registered.

PART TWO

※

ONE DOWN, THREE TO GO

race was always in trouble. The longer her nursing career became, the more irritating things there were to remember, until eventually even the most basic precepts of nursing refused to be recollected.

"Explain the fluid balance chart to me, Nurse Faulding," Matron commanded, brought in as a last resort.

"The fluid balance chart is kept to make sure that the intake of fluids is sufficient to balance output," said Grace, rattling it off in that tone tells any teacher that the student is a parrot.

"To what does the fluid balance chart pertain?"

Grace looked blank. "The balance of fluids, Matron."

"Even a blind man can see that, Faulding. What I mean is, to whom does the fluid balance chart belong?"

Grace looked blanker. "To the hospital, Matron."

"Of whom is it a property?" Matron labored.

"The hospital?" Grace asked doubtfully.

The mouth thinned to a lipless gash. "Given the quality of your three sisters, Faulding, I refuse to believe that you are thicker than two planks, but you certainly make my faith hard work! The fluid balance chart is a property of something called a patient, and is indeed a record of how much fluid the patient to whom it belongs drinks as well as how much fluid he or she produces as, in the main, urine, but may also include—?"

"Uh—feces?" Grace asked hopefully.

"Not if formed, Faulding. Fluids are liquids, not so? The chart should also include measurements of vomitus, blood, sputum, and saliva, if in measurable quantities," said Matron, who wasn't enjoying herself. What Corunda Base needed was a Sister Tutor—badly! "Why is it necessary to keep a fluid balance chart?"

"Oh, that's easy!" said Grace artlessly. "Dropsy!"

The starch in Matron's uniform creaked dangerously. "Dropsy is part of the symptoms referred to as incipient kidney failure, Faulding—it's just one aspect. You have not told me why it is necessary to keep a fluid balance chart, only that it may be an indication of kidney disease. What about liver disease? Ulcers? What do you do when a fluid balance chart says the patient vomits more than he or she urinates? Go back to the library and read, then write me a five-page essay on the fluid balance chart, Nurse."

Dismay flooded into Grace's expression; she swallowed. "Yes, Matron. I apologize, Matron."

"Your apology is perfunctory, it has no meaning in the terms of this interview." Matron's short but well-manicured nails sat as belfries atop her steepled fingers. "It has not escaped me that most of your routine duties are sloppily performed. Where are you, Nurse Faulding? I cannot tolerate a wandering mind, and yours is as directionless as a cow's tail in a plague of flies—here, there, everywhere. It has to stop, do you hear me? For instance, do you *like* nursing? Or is nursing just something you endure so that you can continue to be with your sisters?"

And there it was, the question she had yearned to be asked, sure that when she was, all her doubts and problems would come pouring out. But *Matron* was doing the asking, and how could a lowly worm find words to tell such an exalted personage all about her petty woes? Grace swallowed convulsively, clenched her hands together, and looked down at them resolutely.

"Of course I like nursing, Matron," she lied. "As you say, what I lack is the ability to rule my mind. It—wanders."

"Then find that ability, Nurse. You are dismissed."

It could have been worse, thought Grace, speeding down the ramps toward their house. Today was the commencement of three days off—bliss! The essay Matron had set her loomed; Grace gave a sniff. No, she wouldn't spend her precious leisure in writing a punishment! It could be done on duty days—after all, no completion date had been mentioned.

With the first twelve months behind them, their house could now lay some claim to cottagey looks, as all four girls had strong, if different, homemaker tendencies. So they painted walls, hung pictures, "tarted up the outside," as Kitty put it, and created a cottage garden. Living in her private premises next door, Sister Marjorie Bainbridge certainly couldn't complain that they thought of their accommodation with contempt. They lived a happy life.

Not that Grace was staying in this afternoon. Humming under her breath, she unearthed the shabby rust-red clothes she wore to pursue her hobby, watching steam locomotives. The yards were too dirty for her to wear good things, and besides, she didn't want to stand out; she wanted to blend in as much as a woman could under such odd circumstances. Ever since she had discovered steam trains at ten years of age, they had enchanted her; so much so, indeed, that her sisters' teasing had no power to discourage her.

Dressed, hatted, gloved, Grace let herself out through the stipulated side gate into the park and made her way westward along Victoria Street. As she walked her mind dwelled upon its other preoccupation, the fashionable occult as alluringly portrayed in the magazines, whose famous clairvoyants predicted disasters that actually came true, and coincidentally threw out broad hints as to what the private lives of film stars were like. Not all her thoughts were wafty; Grace rather suspected that adulation and wealth, coming as it had to young and beautiful people, had pushed some into hedonistic excesses their fan clubs wouldn't like.

Just beyond the last of Corunda's row of public buildings on Victoria Street was a fence of iron spears that led to the shunting yards; twisting her slim body through a makeshift turnstile, Grace hurried on into the shunting yards themselves.

No one saw her. Each double line of standard-gauge track was concealed by rows upon rows of freight cars: coal trucks that brought gasworks coal and powerhouse coal from Wollongong, the slatted covered wagons that held tiers of fat lambs on their way to abbatoirs in Sydney or Melbourne, flat cars for machinery, ore trucks, every kind of rolling stock.

Grace loved the smells: rust, oil, coaly smoke, dried lamb droppings, hemp from sacking, metals, eucalyptus, tired grass.

The locomotive sheds loomed. She slowed down, looking for the best place today's arrangement of freight wagons offered her, and found an ideal spot on a high shelf at the end of a slatted car. Scrambling up to sit on it wasn't difficult; comfortably ensconced, Grace settled to enjoy the view in seclusion.

She was there to watch the locomotives, the great steam-powered engines that hauled every piece of rolling stock in and out of the yards, all over the rail network of New South Wales. Today there were five locomotives, an average number; Corunda was the peak of the southern line, so here an extra engine was attached to a train for the long haul uphill, or detached because the long haul was over. The other end of the peak and the other locomotive terminus was fifty miles closer to Sydney, but here in Corunda were the workshops and the permanent sheds, a thriving industry.

Exactly why the sight of a C-36 or C-38 steam locomotive so moved her, Grace had no very good idea. Simply that since her tenth birthday, when first she stood next to one, the sight of these vast iron mules, enveloped in smoke and steam, thrilled her. She would sit for hours just watching them, revelling in the power that pushed the drive rods to make the wheels go around—wheels taller than she was herself, capable of reducing her to mincemeat. The roars, clanks, hisses, and sliding flurries of puffs elated her, and when she watched one thump its way down the line giving off staccato bursts of inky black smoke, she yearned to be at one with it, feel its huge internal thrust.

Today, she soon realized, was going to offer her a special treat. Corunda had a turntable, a massive rotating iron wheel with a diameter longer even than a C-38 locomotive and tender, its single set of rails communicating with rails to either side of its circle. Running on rails set a rigid distance apart meant that a locomotive had a limited ability to turn itself; a gentle curve over several miles could see its direction change significantly, but the only way to change its direction without consuming miles was the turntable. The locomotive and tender were positioned on the turntable, which did the rotating.

Someone jumped up beside her; Grace twisted slightly to see a man in a three-piece suit, then, deciding he was there for the same reason she was, she forgot all about him in the excitement of watching an experienced train driver lock a gigantic locomotive exactly to the turntable rails.

"I wanted to be him when I was a little codger," said the man on the shelf alongside her.

"Then why aren't you?" she asked in a dampening tone as the turntable began to rotate.

"No union contacts in the railways."

"Oh."

Conversation died; they were too absorbed in the engines and their turntable gyrations. But finally it was over. Grace leaped down before the man could help her.

"That was bonzer," he said, balancing on a rail and running his hat through his fingers by its brim. "Thanks for the company."

"I could say the same. Sharing makes it more exciting."

"Unusual thing for a young lady to enjoy."

"I know. My sisters tease me perpetually."

He laughed. "Can I ask a favor, Miss?"

"You *may* ask," she said with delicate emphasis on "may."

Whoever he was, he hadn't received a proper education.

"Can I look at your face?"

Her turn to laugh. "You *may*," she said, confronting him.

"No, I mean without that silly hat." Surprised, a little flustered, she pulled the cloche from her head, her own eyes taking in the young man's countenance: quite presentable but unusually fair, as if he'd been dipped in a bucket of frost, though his skin was tanned rather than a freckle-marred pink. As if, thought the fanciful Grace, his northern sun shone in cloudless skies and so demanded his ancestors have a more pigmented epidermis. *I have learned something!* she cried to herself. Some of the nursing instruction has soaked in after all.

"You're lovely," he was saying. "Where are you going? Can I walk with you? Swagmen lurk around the railway yards." No one had ever called her lovely before, just "grouse" or a "humdinger." He may not be educated, but he had finer feelings. In fact, thought Grace complacently, I doubt Kitty or Edda is called lovely. Sensing no danger in him, Grace smiled and nodded.

"Thank you, Mister—?"

"Björn Olsen. But you can call me Bear. Everybody does. Björn is Swedish for bear. What's your name?"

"Grace Latimer. I'm a nurse at the hospital, where my name is Faulding to avoid confusion. There are four of us with the surname of Latimer, you see."

Her feet felt light, as if the ground they trod were soft cloud; pleased to note that he was considerably taller than her own five feet seven inches, Grace entirely forgot reality. All she was conscious of was walking with Bear Olsen, of wanting to discover everything about him. And her heart floated in time with her feet, only differently, warm and glowing. How old was he? What did he do? He thought she was lovely, and his bright blue eyes caressed.

At the turnstile they passed into the back reaches of the park and found a seat in a deserted corner. Nobody was about on a Tuesday, it felt as if the whole world belonged to them, as if they were the sole people in it.

"You don't mind if we sit here?" she asked anxiously.

"I'd rather take you somewhere I can buy you a cuppa tea and a scone," he said, white teeth in a smile that revealed a chipped incisor. So endearing! "Isn't there a hospital cafeteria?"

The eyes she turned on him were horrified, terrified. "No! Oh, no! You can't come onto hospital property with me, it's against the rules. I'd get into terrible trouble, and I always seem to be in trouble. I'm a trainee nurse of the new type, and the rules are iron. Iron!"

Slightly winded, he stared at her. The poor little beggar! "Sounds more like a jail than a job," he said.

"It's complicated," she said miserably.

"Will you get into trouble if we meet at the Parthenon or the Olympus?" he asked.

"Oh, no, not at all," she said, relieved. "Provided we don't break the law, Matron doesn't mind what we do when we're out of uniform and off hospital property."

"A convent, not a jail," said Bear.

She giggled. "To some extent, yes, but no prayers."

"Are you a Catholic?"

"No, my father is the Rector of St. Mark's Church of England—staunchly Protestant, but rather High than Low."

He looked blank. "Really?" he asked vaguely.

Only the lengthening shadows recalled Grace to the world; after agreeing to meet Bear for lunch at noon the next day in the tried-and-true environment of the Parthenon café she bolted, her hat still in one gloved hand, and her heart singing.

Bear Olsen! Several cuts beneath her, she was well aware of that, and didn't care a fig. Bear had told her he was one of a type of man notorious for multiple girlfriends and even, in worst cases, bigamous wives. Yes, Bear was that seedy individual, a commercial traveller! Infidelity was easy when the job involved moving from place to place on a very large circuit that did repeat itself, but not quickly. Commercial travellers talked well, were always charming to women, and commonly held to be able to sell flames in Hell. Daddy would hit the roof if he knew about Bear, but Grace had no intention of telling him, let alone Stepmama. In her sisters she could put perfect faith: they'd never breathe a word, no matter what they privately thought. Edda for one would deem Bear not good enough. None of it mattered, however: Grace knew her fate. In a single afternoon she had fallen in love with Bear Olsen, and would marry him. Oh, not immediately, and not without opposition from her parents. But marry him she would!

He was a Perkins Man, which had to count for *something*. No lounge lizard with patent leather hair and a toothbrush moustache, out to sell a dozen pairs of silk stockings to an Outback farmer's wife, Bear Olsen! Perkins manufactured and marketed balms, tonics, liniments, ointments, lotions, emollients, aperients, antiseptics, elixirs, emetics, little blue liver pills and little mauve kidney pills, soaps, and a fizzy saline drink that either brought it all up or settled it all down. Everyone bought from the Perkins Man. Perkins products weren't sold in shops but from door to door, so city and country knew the Perkins Man. Perkins horse liniment and Perkins ointment were bywords, and every house had a tin of Perkins saline powder. Children actually liked Perkins laxative liquor; as the alternative was castor oil, it was *very* popular. Grannies swore by the little mauve pills, poppas by the little blue pills, while everybody swore by the tonic, loaded with alcohol and creosote. After so long nursing, even Grace knew how momentous calling the doctor was. When people felt poorly, they dosed themselves, usually with something bearing a Perkins label. It was cheaper than the doctor, and nearly always just as effective.

Bear had told her that he came from Sydney's western suburbs at a place called Clyde, where the railway workshops were; he had spent his childhood listening to the huffs, whistles, and howls of steam locomotives, but his father, a hopeless drunkard, had not courted the railway workers' unions, so his tribe of sons became unskilled laborers far from railways. Bear, the youngest, was determined to get out of Sydney, and had answered a newspaper advertisement for a commercial traveller with Perkins Products.

The deputy manager who interviewed him was as shrewd as he was experienced; what he saw, Grace divined as Bear went on with his story, interested him above and despite educational limitations. For Bear had a naturally honest face, bore no hint of the exotic foreigner to frighten a woman at home on her own, a certain self-confidence, and a streak of generosity that might lead him to offer to chop the lady a bit of wood for her cooking stove. Most heartening of all to that deputy manager had been Bear's skill with a car, allied to a knack for fixing cars. The result? Bear got the job.

To hear Bear talk, he had never looked back. For one thing, he discovered that he loved the act of selling. Nor did he ruin things for himself by overspending on his living allowance. Steadily he rose to better and even better circuits, was given the first new car in a batch, an increased expense allowance, and raises in pay. After five years he was the top Perkins Man in New South Wales, and in the four years since then, he had kept his edge over every other Perkins Man in Australia *and* New Zealand. At thirty, he told Grace jubilantly, he was in good shape—he had a secure career and money in the bank.

That he was very attracted to her was obvious, especially given that they shared this strange obsession for steam engines. He too had done a little fishing into her life-stream, and been delighted to find her several cuts above him. It meant she was an ideal wife, her children domestically educated to be ladies and gentlemen, her aspirations for their education high. Only how was he going to persuade Grace's family that he was the right, the *only* husband for her?

ᔕ

He lost no time in discussing everything with her as soon as they slid into a back booth at the Parthenon; she ordered curried egg sandwiches and he a steak with fried potatoes, tomatoes, and field mushrooms. What bliss! Absolutely no one noticed them! Con Decopoulos, the proprietor, was serving lunch himself, no waitresses to sticky-beak.

"I know I'm not your equal, Grace," Bear said earnestly over a pot of tea and an ice-cream sundae, "but I'm going to marry you. There's no other woman for me, I knew it when you gave that screech at the streamlining on the C-38 that hauls the *Spirit of Progress*. Then I saw your face—lovely! It's got to be marriage, and I won't take no for an answer." He clasped her hand. "The sooner the better, dear. I love you."

Her eyes darkened by emotions new and strange to her, Grace gazed into Bear's frost-fair face hardly able to believe what he was saying. Marriage?

Nor had he finished; as he talked his thumb caressed the back of her hand. "I can sell anything, dear. I'll never be out of a job. I love selling Perkins products because they're so good, I can be honest. Honest selling's as important to me as my life is. I've got two thousand pounds in the bank, and that's enough to buy a decent house in Corunda with plenty left over—oh, not as ritzy as the sort of home you're used to, and we couldn't afford more than a scrubwoman, but I'll rise higher, Grace, I will! One day you'll live in the lap of luxury."

She returned his clasp with trembling fingers. "Oh, Bear! As if I could ever call any time spent with you hard! I must have known, too, because ever since I met you yesterday, my mind can't think of anyone or anything except you."

His face, she decided now, drowning in the ardor blazing from his eyes, is strongly handsome. Yesterday I found his extreme fairness off-putting, too strange, but today it's inside me, a part of me forever. His brows look frozen, his lashes sparkle like crystal—where does that tanned skin come from? And I have never seen eyes so blue, so enthralling . . . His nose is like Edda's and mine; we will have fine-featured children, and they will be tall. Oh, *please* not twins! Just a pigeon-pair, a son and then a daughter.

"Will you marry me?" Bear was pressing.

"Yes, dearest Bear, of course I will," said Grace.

71

Face alight, he visibly swelled. "Back to our seat in the park, woman! I want to kiss you."

He hurried her, but Grace scarcely noticed the pace, her mind whirling, her heart singing. For the first time in her life she was idyllically happy, and dreaded that it might end. Bear loved her, Bear wanted to marry her! The joy was so great it was almost a pain, and the future loomed before her like a huge, roseate sunrise too glorious to assimilate. I will never be alone again—I am loved, and I love. What more can there be to life than that?

There was no one in sight. They sank onto the bench half-turned toward each other; Bear took Grace's head between shaking fingers, staring down into her smiling, uncertain eyes.

Then his face was too close to see; Grace closed her eyes and waited for the touch of his lips—cool, sleek, light as a feather. After the first little shock she moved her own lips, beginning to savor the incredible sensations in a kiss given by someone loving and loved; for it was as if she had never been kissed before, this was so different, so reciprocated. Nor did he force her mouth open before she was ready, or use any of the techniques other young men seemed convinced girls craved. When the kiss did deepen and become passionate, it was with Grace's heartfelt participation, and the touch of his hands over her breasts, clothed though they were, was electric.

"Only we're not going any further until my wedding ring is on your finger," he said, pushing her away a few minutes later. "Nothing is too good for you, Grace, and I'll not dishonor you."

By an odd chance all three of her sisters were in the common room when Grace walked in; no one was on afternoon shift at present. Edda looked up and stiffened. "The wind is in your tail, Grace," she said.

It was a saying they had picked up from an early nanny; as far as they could translate it, it meant existing in a state of sheer confusion, the way animals became when the wind blew the scents of all their enemies over them at one and the same moment.

Grace blurted her news out. "I'm going to be married!"

Even Tufts lifted her head from the books; Edda and Kitty gaped, astounded. "Rubbish!" said Tufts with a snort.

"No, no, it's true!"

"Who is the lucky fella?" Edda asked, half joking.

"His name is Bear Olsen, and I met him yesterday while I was watching the locomotive turntable rotating engines," said Grace, her elation beginning to die, quite why she didn't know.

"*Yesterday?*" Kitty asked with awful emphasis.

"Yes, yesterday! It was love at first sight," said Grace.

The other three groaned.

"Grace, Grace, it doesn't happen like that!" Edda cried.

"When he's the only one, it can," Grace maintained. "He *is* the only one, Edda, and I'm going to marry him as fast as I possibly can!"

"How about finishing nursing first?" Tufts asked. "You'd have something to fall back on in times of need, Grace."

"I *hate* nursing! I just want to marry Bear!"

"Mama will never let you marry anyone she doesn't approve of," Kitty said, "and your behavior *screams* the fact that this chap is unsuitable."

"I am twenty-one," Grace said defiantly, "so how can anyone stop me marrying whomever I choose?"

"You don't have the steel," said Edda clinically.

"This time I do!" Grace declared in ringing tones. "I have met my *soul mate*, Edda! We share enthusiasms and ideals; I have nailed my colors to the mast of his ship of destiny! I tell you straight, I *will* marry Bear Olsen, no matter who opposes me!"

"What's his name?" Tufts asked.

"Björn Olsen. His family is Swedish. Björn means bear, so everybody calls him Bear. He's a Perkins Man, the leading salesman in the company, and while he may not be my social equal, he's going places." Grace thrust out her chin and looked, for Grace, singularly unbendable. "I *will* marry him!"

"Not before you give your sisters a chance to inspect him," Kitty said, sounding affectionate. "Come, Grace, give us—and this Bear Olsen!—a chance, please. I can understand why you think Mama won't approve, though perhaps you judge Father too harshly. He's not a snob, Grace, and if he likes your man, he'll be a valuable ally. But you must bring Bear to afternoon tea here tomorrow, while all four of us aren't working the second day shift."

"We can't invite him here!" said Tufts, startled.

"Oh, can't we?" Edda asked, getting to her feet. "I'm off to see Matron."

"Edda, no!" Grace wailed.

Too late: Edda was gone, and lucky enough to find Matron with time to see her.

"Yes, Latimer?"

"May I have permission to invite a young man to afternoon tea in our cottage common room tomorrow, ma'am? All four of us will be present to meet him."

No explosion of wrath greeted this request: instead, Matron indicated the supplicant's chair with an expressionless face. "I think you had better sit down, Latimer, and explain this rather extraordinary request."

"It's about my sister Faulding, ma'am."

"You are aware she isn't happy nursing?"

Edda sighed, hunched her shoulders. "Yes, I am."

"Is she in another scrape?"

"Not yet, but if she isn't handled properly she could get into a very serious one. By handled properly, I mean her sisters need to move closer to her in her present dilemma," said Edda, struggling to leave so much unsaid, as it had to be. "Our stepmother has very fixed ideas—laudable, naturally!— and a situation has blown up that we sisters need to know more about before Stepmama is informed." Her hands went out, appealing. "You see, Grace has met a young man she wants to marry, but unfortunately he isn't from Corunda—in fact, he's an itinerant, a commercial traveller. A Perkins Man, respectable, but we need to meet this young man and find out more about him. Afternoon tea in our quarters would be ideal."

"Permission granted," said Matron, foreseeing an answer to her difficulties with Grace. "I will inform Sister Bainbridge."

"What an eminently sensible young woman Latimer is!" said Matron to Sister Bainbridge over dinner in her house. "She came to me, which is exactly what she should have done. To keep the nurses terrified of us is vital, but it is so refreshing to find that some nurses can see under the veneer. A clever young woman, too. Not one word of criticism did Latimer pass against Maude Latimer, but I was able to plumb all the currents. The young man is socially suspect according to Maude's lights, clearly. We must do what we can to help, Marjorie, including with the Rector, if it comes to that. Can our cook manage scones, jam, and cream?"

Two hours with Bear Olsen reconciled Grace's sisters to this stunningly sudden change in Grace's life and future welfare. That he loved her was plain, but—equally important—he wasn't a shiftless ne'er-do-well of a commercial traveller. He was a genuine Perkins Man, the best in the Antipodes, with a promising career, two thousand pounds in the bank, and friends in high management. He was not a drinker and he would be a good husband to Grace; her three sisters came away from the interview fully convinced of that.

"I'll be on this circuit for at least another five years," he explained, having done justice to the sisters' cook's scones with jam and cream—a mark of Matron's generosity and approval that staggered its recipients. Perhaps beneath the iceberg lay a human being? An appalling thought of an alien kind. "For that reason," said Bear, "I wouldn't want to uproot Grace from Corunda and her family yet. I've found a decent house on Trelawney Way, which means it's on the city water and sewer. I can get it for eleven hundred pounds, cash."

"That's a good price for city water and sewer," Edda said.

"Well built, Edda, honest! The roof's properly lined with tar paper, the interior walls are plastered, and the toilet's in a separate room from the bathroom. The floors are karri and the windows are all properly flashed— they can be easily fitted with mesh to keep out flies and mosquitoes."

"That's all very good," Edda conceded. "What about furniture? How many bedrooms are there?"

"Three, and I'll have enough left after buying the house to let Grace pick what furniture she likes," Bear said, uncomfortably aware that he had to win this encounter if he were to succeed in marrying his dearest Grace. She sat anxiously listening, yet said not one word—utter terror, he suspected. Grace's sisters had a tendency to bully her, he had noted. "Trelawney Way is on the iceman's run, another good thing—Grace can have an ice chest. That's real important for the kiddies."

Kiddies? Three pairs of eyes bored into him.

"I hope you intend to limit the size of your family to the number of children you can afford to educate properly," said Tufts with a growl in her voice.

"Believe me, my children will be educated," Bear vowed.

Grace saw him off the premises, leaving the other three to deal with the realities.

"Mama will never bless this union," Kitty said desolately.

"Nonsense!" Edda countered briskly. "We just have to handle Maude the right way. Which means we go through Daddy. It's the social come-down will get Maude's goat, so we have to make a strong case for a top Perkins Man as distinct from shady purveyors of quack remedies and vulgar women's undies. In other words, we enlist Daddy's help to untar Bear from the commercial traveller brush. At least he's not a foreigner in looks or name! He's very respectable from appearance to actions, he drives a new Model T, and our bank manager won't sneer at him. Personally, I think Grace has done extremely well for herself."

"I agree," said Kitty, "and I'll harp on it to Mama."

"Me, too," said Tufts. "Bear is exactly right for Grace. I mean, they met in the shunting yards oohing and aahing over steam engines. How odd is that?" She giggled. "Their babies will dine on coal rather than milk, and hoot rather than cry."

"So what's wrong with that?" demanded Grace, entering.

"Nothing, dear, nothing," said Kitty. "How are we going to prise a wedding out of Mama?"

"I don't want a wedding," Grace said flatly. "I don't mean I won't wear a white dress and carry a bouquet of flowers, just no fusses like breakfasts and speeches. Bear doesn't have any family or close friends to fill one side of a church, and I'll not have him embarrassed. So I want Daddy to marry us quietly, then I'll go on his circuit with Bear instead of a formal honeymoon."

Her cup was full to overflowing; not even the prospect of Maude Latimer's umbrage had the power to dent Grace's happiness.

The four agreed that it would be Edda to broach the subject of Grace's marriage to the Reverend Thomas Latimer and his wife, and that she would do it at the start of her next days off.

If Maude and the Rector were surprised to see their senior daughter, they put a good face on it and asked her to lunch.

"I fail to understand what the fascination of nursing is," said Maude, whose sense of self-preservation was keen enough to tell her that Edda nowadays was impervious to the slights and sarcastic comments of other times. A self-possessed young woman with an unshakable knowledge of her own worth; Maude felt a trifle shrivelled as she realized the girls, in embracing nursing, had somehow outstripped her in character, resolution, admirability. All sensations Maude didn't like.

"Nursing endows those who like it with real purpose," said Edda, thoroughly enjoying Rectory cooking after the nurses' dining room. "How does Cook manage to make her shepherd's pie so tasty, Stepmama? The hospital cooks ruin it."

"I have no idea," said Maude loftily. "All I have to do with it is set the menus each week."

"That's all Home Sister does, too, but the results are far different." Edda's strange eyes sought her father's, and pinned them. "Grace, however, hasn't taken to nursing."

Maude snorted. "Huh! Why doesn't that astonish me? Your twin sister, Edda, is a genuine no-hoper."

Edda laughed. "That shaft went wide of the mark, if its mark was me. It certainly indicates that you won't mind if Grace resigns from nursing to marry another no-hoper."

Maude went rigid. "I beg your pardon?"

"You heard me, Stepmama. Grace is about to marry a Perkins Man—a nice young chap, very much in love with her. They are ideally suited, Daddy."

"Grace will do no such thing!" Maude turned to the Rector, who thus far had made no comment on Grace's conduct, nor indeed given his private thoughts away on his face. "Tom, you can't just sit there without a word! Grace is *not* marrying a no-hoper!"

"I rather gathered that from what Edda has told us," said the Rector placidly, wiping his lips with his napkin. "You are too hard on people, especially those nearest and dearest to you, Maude, and I confess it perturbs me. I am quite sure that a Perkins Man is not a no-hoper—your own pantry is full of Perkins products, including that new face cream you're so enthusiastic about." He smiled at Edda, openly grinning. "You, of course, are the advance guard, Edda?"

"Yes, Daddy. Grace's fiancé is properly named Björn Olsen, but we call him Bear. Money in the bank, Perkins's top salesman, and quite besotted over Grace. He wants to meet you as soon as possible because they don't want a long engagement."

"She's expecting!" cried Maude, grinding her teeth.

"No, she isn't! What a foul mind you have, Stepmama!"

Down went the Rector's knife and fork on his plate with a loud clatter; the mild grey eyes flashed. "Cease and desist, Maude! If you can't say something kind, then say nothing! Why must you be so uncharitable?"

Fascinated, Edda looked from her father to her stepmother and back again. The sharpness in Daddy's voice was utterly new to her—was living alone with Maude such a trial, then?

"I'll see my prospective son-in-law at noon tomorrow," the Rector said to Edda, "and Grace can come to the Rectory at half past. Maude, I want a special lunch."

"She isn't expecting, Daddy, but I predict there will be grandchildren to hold in respectable swiftness," Edda said, eyes dancing. "I'm happy for her because Bear will never let her down and will always look after her."

Hardly able to credit the Rector's snub—in front of Edda!—Maude Latimer sat through the rest of lunch in silence, resolved of one thing: Grace would pay. In fact, they'd all pay.

Nurse Grace Faulding-Latimer had lasted fifteen months as a new-style trainee, and left in order to marry.

It was a small, very hospitable wedding, for the groom's contingent, all Perkins Men, numbered but three, and the bride's was kept to family and a very few friends. Married at the beginning of July 1927, which was midwinter, the happy couple had an odd but educational honeymoon; Grace accompanied Bear on his Perkins circuit in southwestern New South Wales. By the end of it, she did not envy Bear his lot. Thrilled at being in a home of her own, she moved into the house Bear had bought in the Trelawneys. Though only Bear knew it, she was pregnant.

Never having been parted from Grace in all their twenty-two years, Edda had no premonition how much separation from her sister was going to hurt. Leaving their physical similarities out of it, they were not alike temperamentally or spiritually, or indeed in any other way commonly attributed to identical twins. Many and many were the times, Edda reflected now, when she had cursed Grace for tagging along—for not being, it had seemed to a busy, pushy child like Edda, more fun, more joy, a better teammate. No, it was always Edda obliged to lead, Grace compelled to follow. And now that Grace was gone, Edda found herself unreasonably devastated.

"I hope I've never thought of Grace as an inoperable and malignant tumor," she said to Tufts, to whom she related better than to Kitty, "but I can't deny that in many ways being Grace's twin felt like hosting a tumor. Now Hymen Goddess of Marriage has separated me from my tumor like the most ruthless surgeon."

"Well, dear, you're rudderless," said Tufts tenderly. "It will take a long time to get used to being without Grace."

"You don't understand!" Edda cried. "I always thought I'd be ecstatic at losing Grace."

"Yes, the way I'm sure I'll feel when I shed Kitty, except that common sense says I'll mourn her going dreadfully. Like me, Edda, you have common sense. How could it not be a colossal wrench to lose one's other half?"

Edda heaved a sigh. "How, indeed?"

"At least Kitty and I understand, remember that."

Edda tried to, but witnessing their united front every day only served to emphasize her own loss. Not that there weren't compensations. The most important to Edda was her father's sudden spurt of independence from Maude, so noticeable that all sorts of people were a little startled. Not that he treated his second wife with less respect, just that the henpecked deference was missing. Too superficial to search her own conduct, Maude blamed the Rector's new attitude on her fading looks and promptly went to spend three months in a sanatorium in the Blue Mountains, there to diet, exercise, and pour her heart out to people known as "alienists." She couldn't have made a worse move, for it took her out of the Rector's life just at the moment when the first daughter's marriage reminded him that he too was growing old. Life without Maude, he discovered, was very pleasant: he could have whatever he wanted for breakfast, pick his own hymns for the choir, compose his own sermons, and visit his impoverished and therefore unimportant parishioners as often as he liked. Habits that, when Maude returned from her health treatment, he refused to give up; his ears, it seemed, had grown awfully deaf.

"It serves my stepmother right," said Edda jubilantly to Jack Thurlow when they met on the bridle path and dismounted to "have a decent yarn," as Jack put it.

They didn't meet very often; nursing had cut a huge swath through the old freedoms of leisure, when the four girls had done little for their keep beyond housework for Maude, a flexible business. Nursing meant a physical exhaustion that made going to the pictures or, in Edda's case, riding, too much an effort.

Amused by the discovery, Edda learned that Jack Thurlow did not appreciate his demotion to, as he put it:

"A convenience you stick in a cupboard and only bring out when the fancy takes you. I don't know why I oblige you."

Internal mirth became open laughter; Edda roared with it. "Oh, Jack, grow up! You're eleven years older than me, but you act like a little boy whose big sister has pinched your favorite toy. I work for a living these days, and work is the significant word. Nothing pleases me more than a ride with you, but I don't have the time or the energy often—is that clear enough?"

"When you started to nurse you were full of the idea that regular rides would help you cope, but you've been nursing now for an eternity and the rides keep dwindling. Your father uses Fatima in a pony cart for Maude, just to give the poor creature exercise."

Her face fell, but she nodded. "Daddy's right, but I know you don't approve of hacks being harnessed, and I'm sorry." Her face assumed its most seductive look. "The trouble is that I love to ride her when I have the chance, and if she goes back to you, all my chances will vanish. Is it really so damaging for Fatima to tow Maude around in a lightweight cart? I know why you gave me Fatima—she's a very stupid but simultaneously placid horse. Maude's even trained her to pull the clippings to the compost heap."

His grin was reluctant, but gradually broadened. "A pity you're a woman, Edda. There's a master politician inside you."

"Then I'll marry a master politician," she said lightly.

"Ride up to the house with me, have a cuppa and a scone," he wheedled. "More comfortable than the river bank."

She rose to her feet at once. "And less public," she said, mounting Fatima, which really was a perfect horse-of-all-trades, yet contrived to master all of them. Stupidity was a help.

"Any news of the Burdum heir?" she asked over buttered cheese scones still hot from the oven—a superb scone baker, Jack!

"The Pommy bloke? Old Tom doesn't say much, but I don't think the new heir has any plans to come to Australia any time soon. He has lots of irons in Pommy fires, especially London."

"Why do we call the English Pommies?"

"I never met anybody who knows," said Jack, shrugging. "The new heir won't even know he's a Pommy until he gets here. Old Tom says he's a doctor."

"Maude said that, but I confess we took no notice of her." Edda pulled a face. "According to her, he's a tycoon as well."

"Impossible. They're opposites—altruistic *and* exploitative. Like being a saint and a demon rolled in one," said Jack.

"Oh, I know dozens of people just like that." Edda smirked. "Look at those with knees shiny from praying—awful villains!"

"That's why I like you. You see what's hidden."

"My profession helps. You can't learn much about human nature from fat lambs, Jack, but you can from sick people."

"Maybe that's why the Burdum heir became a doctor. Money is no teacher of what makes human beings tick either." Jack took her cup and plate. "Come on, I'll drive you back to the hospital."

Heart singing as it had not since the loss of Grace, Edda returned to the hospital in Jack's battered old utility truck. Why has it come as such a shock to realize that Jack Thurlow is the man for me? I've always been drawn to him, and the intimacy of our friendship says what I feel. And yet it was during the two hours of easy talk in his kitchen, drinking tea and eating scones, that it had dawned on me: *a part of me loves him!* How had that happened? Why had it happened? I don't want to marry him, and I pray he doesn't want to marry me, but the bond is there, and it's strong, very strong.

I want to travel, I want to shake free of Corunda once I've completed my nursing, but Jack shows me how lovely it would be to travel in the company of a beloved someone else. There to cover each other's exposed weaknesses, while there is still enough freedom left to feel at liberty. I have the right amount of love for Jack, but has he the right amount of love for me? And that, I do not know. He hasn't transmitted the right signals yet. So I keep holding back, and he keeps holding back. Trust? Oh, trust! It doesn't exist.

Kitty noticed her happiness when she walked in. "You're getting over Grace at last, Edda."

"Yes, I am," said Edda, pulling off boots and jodhpurs. It was on the tip of her tongue to mention Jack, but she didn't—leave well enough alone. "Did you listen to Maude prattling about the Burdum heir?" she asked instead.

"Only that he's a doctor. Where does he consult, I wonder?"

"I have no idea," Edda answered. "Just that he's a Burdum heir who outranks Jack Thurlow."

Tufts erupted into the common room. "Edda, the duty roster has been changed. You're to have your days off, but then you're going to the operating theatre." Her pretty face twisted. "Half your luck! I was hoping I'd be the first."

"Dr. Finucan won't let you go until you've finished whatever it is you're doing for him," Kitty said unsympathetically. "You can't have all the treats, Tufts."

"I know, just as I know that my turn will come."

But why did I say nothing to them about Jack? Edda asked herself as she headed for the bathroom, there to eliminate the aroma of horse. They are my *sisters*! But he's made no overture to me beyond friendship, and what if he should fall in love with Kitty? No, I won't let that happen! Great though my love for Kitty is, I won't stand by and let her ruin my life.

A thought that, one day later, Edda found uncanny; by sheer accident she and Jack chanced upon Kitty walking the bridle path. Jack made all the correct responses, so did Kitty, but the horses were in a mood to canter, and Kitty, afoot, disliked being in such close proximity to huge animals.

"Pretty girl," said Jack after they sat on their log.

"The prettiest in the world," Edda said sincerely.

Jack grinned. "If you like the type, I daresay. But dumpy azalea bushes don't thrill me. I like sophisticated poplars."

Her turn to laugh. "Do you know what sophisticated means?"

"There's a lot about me you don't know," he said enigmatically.

Corunda Base Hospital's Casualty department held a small operating theatre adequate for stemming a hemorrhage or immobilizing broken bones until the patient could be transferred for more major procedures to the hospital's one full-sized and fully equipped theatre, which lay down-ramp from the junction of the Men's and Women's wards. Two surgeons attended the hospital, both also having private practices in rooms nearby: Dr. Ian Gordon was the general and abdominal man, Dr. Erich Herzen the orthopedic man, and both were considered good surgeons. The anesthetist was Dr. Tony Watson, skilled in the administration of chloroform, ether, nitrous oxide, and local injections; he also had a good instinct for when it was necessary to give the patient a whiff of oxygen to lighten the gas-induced coma up a little.

When Edda stepped through the double doors she found herself at the start of a series of chambers, only one of which was the operating theatre proper: there was a scrub room, a gassing room, a sterilizing room where all the instruments were stored as well as sterilized, a changing room for the men and another for the women, a room for storing bulky things that might be needed, and six single rooms where the recovering patients were put until the surgeons considered them fit to go back to their wards. Maternity, she had discovered long ago, was pursued elsewhere—unless the expectant mother needed a caesarean section, which was done in this main theatre. The obstetrician, Dr. Ned Mason, was a Corunda institution; anyone under forty born in Corunda had been delivered by Ned Mason, who had no intention of retiring.

Theatre Sister was a martinet named Dorothy Marshall; under her command she had ten nurses and two junior sisters. All the nurses were West Enders permanently seconded to Theatre, but Edda's arrival heralded the beginning of a change that would steadily grow in size as the years went on. Consequently Theatre Sister was not pleased to see her. However, she understood that her ability to transmit her knowledge to a passing parade of trainee nurses would radically affect her own future welfare. Therefore she was determined to make a good theatre nurse out of Latimer.

Edda would commence, she learned, in Theatre itself, working as the "dirty nurse"—a clean and scrubbed but not sterile servant to those whose sterility had to be maintained. She was there to remove the used instruments, scrub and wash them clear of every particle of tissue and blood, then put them into the sterilizer to boil for twenty minutes before removing them with sterile forceps and laying them out on sterile, cloth-covered trays that went then to a steam autoclave. It was dangerous and uncomfortable work, between the burns, scalds, and heat that dogged every phase of antisepsis. Because of its perils, the job of dirty nurse was a rigidly fixed length of time. Before fatigue set in, a nurse came off dirty nursing and was given sedentary duties for the rest of her shift.

Theatre Sister herself acted as chief surgical assistant and often closed the incision; if the procedure were extremely taxing, another qualified doctor would join the surgeon, who was prone to grumble because Theatre Sister knew more and operated better. She did not, unfortunately, have a medical degree, so the rich, having the knowledge and ability to sue, were actually worse off than the poor, who got Theatre Sister no matter what. Many the chuckles Edda enjoyed as her nursing career went on and she saw for herself that the privileges of rank and wealth did not always guarantee the best medical care. Nor did it pay to be an obnoxious patient; a nurse made to suffer by a patient for no reason beyond malice had all kinds of revenges at her fingertips, from frightful laxatives to itching rashes. Nurses too were human!

Instrument nurse, Edda learned, passed the sterile instruments either to the surgeon or to Theatre Sister, and dropped the used ones in a dish for the dirty nurse to collect and clean. One of the several around the table, usually Swab Sister in Sister Marshall's establishment, was responsible for counting the number of swabs placed inside an incision. If it were an abdominal operation, swabs might be the size of women's handkerchiefs, and be stuffed into the cavity by what seemed like the dozen. Yet every swab had to be recovered before a gaping abdominal incision could be closed. Should a swab remain inside, death could ensue.

One nurse hovered by the anesthetist's shoulder to assist him, and had no other duty than whatever he demanded of her. In fact, each gowned and masked body clustered around the operating table had specific duties and could be pardoned nothing. Theatre Sister, a junior Sister, and five nurses made up the team, with a second team ready to take over the moment Theatre Sister ordered it. That was usually at the end of an operation, but if the procedure were very long and difficult, the team might change in midstream. Not that the second team sat idly by; there were recovering patients to nurse, many things to do.

To her intense gratification, Edda found that watching an operation held neither nausea nor revulsion for her; it was just too interesting. The steady gloved hands sopping up beads of blood, applying a metal tube to suck up a stronger bleed, the deft snapping shut of a pair of artery forceps on a stubborn bleeder, the neat way a whole group of these hemostats, as they were called, was gathered together and confined with a tie to keep them out of the way—fascinating! Admittedly the crunch of cutters through thick bone came as a shock—so much for that romantic twaddle about the delicate hands of a surgeon! Surgeons needed hands like engine mechanics.

Dr. Gordon was glad to have a new audience, it seemed, for he cheerfully talked his way through an appendectomy, just to instruct her and annoy Junior Sister.

"You'll note, nurse, that we don't simply dive into the middle of the abdominal contents—too dangerous. But you can see the colon clearly, lying across the thinner entrails, can't you? Yes? Good! Note that the interior of the abdominal cavity is a vivid pink—first indication of coming sepsis, but we're here in time, he won't develop peritonitis. The operation is simple enough because the cecum lies close to the ventral surface, and the vermiform appendix juts off it. Nuisances that are always infecting! Things get stuck inside with nowhere to go, like hard little fecal pellets."

Was she supposed to ask questions? "Constipation, sir?"

He guffawed. "Wrong end of the colon for that, nurse."

"Do you open the bowel itself, sir?"

"I wish! No, the bowels contain fecal matter that teems with germs. Open the bowel, let any fecal matter spill into the abdomen, and you've caused peritonitis, sepsis, death. You see, we don't have any medicines that can kill the germs. So if I do a Billroth I or Billroth II to remove part of the stomach or the pylorus for ulcers or cancer, it's of paramount importance to clamp the ends of the remaining tissue so that no contents can escape before you anastomose them together. You can try the same if removing bowel for cancer with a view to an end-to-end anastomosis, but it's very risky. Gall bladders are easier," said Dr. Gordon. "What we have to do is find a way to kill germs by mouth or injection. Come on, nurse, ask questions!"

But the one question Edda burned to ask, she did not dare: why were so many surgeons of Scottish ancestry? If they weren't surgeons, they seemed to be engineers, and there *was* a connection.

Dr. Herzen was a German born and bred, and Corunda knew itself extremely lucky to have acquired a bone specialist of his distinction; patients came from Sydney to see him. The most mortifying incident in Dr. Herzen's history had occurred during the Great War, when, despite Corunda's screams of outrage, the jingoistic federal government had interned him as an enemy alien and denied him the right to practice. As his medical degree was from Sydney University, it made no more sense than did his two-year detention. His devotion to Corunda was understandable, given the town's staunch fight to free him, but Corunda had known what it was doing. A natural denizen of Macquarie Street, Sydney, chose to continue practicing in Corunda, which had also obtained him a British passport.

Herzen's days in Theatre were inevitably busy, whereas Dr. Gordon's intake varied. Both surgeons saw their share of work in the Casualty department, and they could, if necessary, pinch hit for each other.

Edda's most extraordinary experience came after she had been promoted to instrument nurse. Theatre Sister had decided to like her, which meant she would receive the full gamut of Theatre's jobs apart from Sister's own, and even that would be touched on.

Gordon and Herzen operated together, with Herzen taking the lead, and no anesthetic.

"The patient is comatose and has been fitting," said Sister Marshall as they scrubbed. "Dr. Herzen is going to try to remove a subdural hematoma—a blood clot that has formed over the outer surface of the brain and is pressing down on it. Such clots keep on absorbing fluids and swelling. Because the cranium is a bony box, swollen contents have no room to expand. So even though the brain itself isn't injured by the external clot, it becomes injured as a result of being squashed. Unless the pressure is released, the squashing will progress to death. And our surgeons are going to try to stop the squashing by removing the clot."

"How do you know the patient has a subdural hematoma?" Edda asked. "There's no test to show it up, is there?"

"The coma, the epileptic seizures on one side of the body only, and one pupil bigger than the other—this last is the classical sign of a subdural hematoma," said Theatre Sister. "No X-ray shows the clot, but Dr. Herzen is sure he'll find a huge clot over the left fronto-temporal cortex. The patient had developed a specific speech loss indicating this area, and Dr. Gordon agrees."

"Wouldn't you rather have Nurse Trimble on instruments?"

"Frankly, no. Some of the instruments had to be borrowed from Sydney and Trimble wouldn't know them, whereas you've had tutoring on unusual instruments, even if only from books. With any luck, none of them will be needed, but—"

The goddess had spoken. Edda climbed up to stand on her stool just to one side of Theatre Sister, her training vindicated.

Having made a small incision in the scalp and laid bare the bone, Dr. Herzen picked up what looked exactly like an ordinary bit-and-brace. The bit was circular, hollow, and toothed, with a spike in its center; it was about the size of a ha'penny or a quarter. When the surgeon turned the handle on the brace wheel, the bit gouged its way into the bone, with Dr. Gordon carefully scraping up the moist granules of bone dust as the bit bored downward.

"I've reached the table—watch out," Herzen warned. A moment later, and the bit withdrew holding a ha'penny coin of bone. The surgeons huddled to look; Edda couldn't see.

"It's black from blood under the dura, Erich—you're right on the nose!" said Dr. Gordon delightedly.

"Sucker ready?"

"Yes."

"I'm going to snip the dura—Sister, are your nurses set to deal with our patient if he comes to and panics?"

"Yes, sir."

Dr. Herzen made a minute pair of snips, cross-shaped, with small, curved, pointed scissors; blackish jelly welled into sight immediately, and Dr. Gordon went to work with the sucker tube.

Still comatose, the patient didn't rouse as the pressure on his brain was relieved, so the two surgeons waited to see whether the bleeding was still going on, or the right kind of clot had formed underneath the malignant one. Finally Dr. Herzen sighed.

"I think we can close up, Ian."

The disc of bone was gently pushed back into place and the bone shavings patted around it; four scalp sutures, and the craniotomy was over. The patient began to stir.

"Why didn't you use a trephine, Erich?" Dr. Gordon asked.

"Don't like 'em," was the reply. "It's too easy to go too far once you reach the table. Well and good for the Sydney boys who do this sort of thing all the time, but how often do I ever drill burr holes in a skull? Sure means not sorry. A bit-and-brace I find easier to control."

"Understood, and filed for future reference."

When the patient went home a week later none the worse for his head injury, Edda regarded it as a minor miracle; one day, she vowed, she would see the real neurosurgeons operate at Queen's Square in London. Perhaps by then the ghost of Victor Horsley wouldn't be pedalling his bicycle around Bloomsbury, but there were others, and that part of London abounded in famous hospitals.

After two years of nursing, the three remaining Latimer sisters were well ensconced in their niche; their faces under the silly winged caps were well known to everyone from Matron Newdigate and Superintendent Campbell through West Ender nurses to wardsmaids and porters, and each had discovered a preference for one kind of nursing above all others, though none liked mental asylum nursing.

For Edda, the Operating Theatre and Casualty nursing reigned supreme. The reasons why were glaringly obvious: the drama and air of urgency and peril that accompanied every patient beyond the walking wounded. Would the procedures go smoothly, or would the patient produce some unexpected, occasionally shocking, factor that turned the surgery into a race for life? Impossible to tell. Since the horrors of the Great War, surgery had gone ahead rapidly, but there were still so many problems it could not, as yet, even begin to tackle. Once her nursing training was over and she was registered, Edda decided that the life of a theatre sister was for her.

Her trim, tall form attracted attention from men that could not be misinterpreted, for she drew men; yet Latimer was not a man-eater, never seemed to notice the glances, passed off the comments with a shrug, and gave a terse refusal to those who had plucked up the courage to ask her out. Except, that is, for Jack Thurlow, with whom she maintained a genuine friendship. For though she loved him, she had no intention of putting his demands on her emotions ahead of her nursing. No, Jack Thurlow would have to wait a little longer before she made any move in his direction. Even then, a part of her was unsure about marriage. A lifetime of Maude had soured her regard for wedlock, she supposed, or perhaps it was more truthful to say that something in her just plain rebelled against taking the subordinate role in life that marriage demanded of a woman.

"It's logical," she said to Tufts and Kitty one evening after they had all come off duty, "that women have to be subordinate in a marriage, I suppose. They bear and raise the babies, who do better in the care of their mothers than they do in the care of minders or even nannies. But it doesn't seem fair all the same."

"Then don't marry," said Tufts, grinning. "I won't."

"Oh, poop to the both of you!" Kitty cried. "A career is well and good, but what about love and companionship?"

"What's love got to do with companionship?" Edda asked.

"Everything! Oh, you're deliberately baiting me! Surely you can see that love without liking is doomed to failure? Love *and* liking must both be present."

"The men who've inspired the one in me certainly haven't inspired the other," said Edda, eyes gleaming.

"Oh, yes, and of course you're so experienced! You, Edda Latimer, are a fraud," Kitty said, disgusted.

It was on the tip of Edda's tongue to mention Jack Thurlow, but she didn't. Somehow Jack was her secret, hers and only hers. Especially now they were meeting regularly. Oh, just as friends, good friends in that slightly remote way she had set as their style very early on. For Edda had great pride; she had no intention of showing any man, even Jack Thurlow, her vulnerabilities. He must believe that she cared little for love and less for casual dalliance; that, to her, his male sex was a simple accident of fate, of no importance to their relationship. No come-hither glances or fiery invitations from *her* eyes!

"You're determined to travel once you're registered," Kitty said to Edda in accusing tones.

"Yes, naturally. Oh, come, Kitty, don't tell me you're going to endure three years of this just to get a job in Corunda Base as a junior sister!" said Edda, astonished.

"I *love* Corunda!" Kitty protested. "Why travel to see yet more human misery than we have here?"

"Don't talk like that, Kitty," said Tufts sharply.

"No, no, I don't mean it in a down-in-the-dumps way, Tufty, honestly! But I do love Corunda, and I want to marry a man I love *and* like, preferably right here in Corunda."

"More fool you," said Edda, pouring tea.

"I understand," said Tufts more kindly, and smiled at her twin. "However, like Edda I mean to travel, do different sorts of nursing."

"We've never been apart," said Kitty on a sniffle.

"Nor had Edda and Grace, but growing into legal adults says we're bound to split up. Edda is a nurse, but Grace prefers being a wife. You and I are exactly the same. I'm the nurse, you're the wife," said Tufts.

"Oh, enough!" Edda shouted, thumping the table.

The next time Edda met Jack Thurlow on the bridle path, she did something she never afterward understood, even years later, when time and distance lent her thoughts detachment: she asked him if he would like to meet her twin sister, Grace.

They were sitting companionably on their log and he was rolling a cigarette, his square brown hands entrancing Edda as the bones empowering them moved under the smooth skin; not the hands of a manual laborer, for all that he said he worked on the land. His were the boss's hands, neither cracked nor crabbed.

The fingers stopped moving; he glanced at her from under his brows in that keen, searching look he sometimes gave her when she surprised him. "Meet your sister Grace?" he repeated.

"Yes, but only if you'd like to," she said quickly. "I do occasionally realize that I never make any of the expected social overtures to you." She shrugged offhandedly. "Feel free to say no, Jack, and I do mean that." She produced a bored expression. "It wouldn't be very exciting. Grace is expecting a baby in about three months, and rather full—" she chuckled, "good pun!—of her cleverness at doing such a unique, amazing thing."

His laughter was hearty but ironic. "Poor Edda! You're asking me because you want company. Your visit must be overdue."

"How well you know me! Will you come? Say no!"

"I'd like to meet your twin, though the mind boggles at two Eddas. You're identical?"

"At birth, yes, but living rather lessens the likeness. My twin looks like me, but she's a far different sort of person, and less overpowering. *Not* another Edda!"

"That's a colossal relief."

"Nonsense! Since when have I overpowered you?"

"Never, I admit it. Sometimes I wish you did."

"Grace's house is on Trelawney Way," Edda said, changing the subject. "Number ten. Shall we meet there—when?"

He lit his cigarette. "When's your next afternoon off?"

"Tuesday."

"I'll pick you up in front of the hospital at three."

"No, make it the Town Hall for pickup." And that was that. Instead of accompanying her, Jack remounted, tipped his hat in her direction, and cantered off.

Edda stared after his retreating form in dismay. Fool! To alter anything in a relationship was dangerous, yet she had to go and do it! Why? For the same reason, she thought, riding back to the Rectory stables, that once made me put my chair leg on top of a snake's head. To see if I could. What is it about me, that I can't leave well enough alone? Is it alive, or dead? All others will run, but Edda will stay to investigate, experiment.

Jack Thurlow rode away wondering why he had agreed to meet Grace Olsen née Latimer, though in his bones he had an uncomfortable sense that it was because Edda Latimer fascinated him. Did she not, he wouldn't bother with these fool gallops he didn't need, in the saddle every day and longing to be out of it. He had a huge physical lust for her, but he was a man who knew how to control his passions, and he had no intention of giving in to Edda. Elegant, sophisticated, aware of sex, she gave off powerful emanations of a carnality his experience told him was rare in one so carefully brought up. A true virgin, but by choice; she hadn't met anyone good enough yet, the little snob. He realized that she was attracted to him, too, but he had dismissed it as a symptom of her boredom. This was a young woman who hankered for a bigger, wider life than Corunda offered.

For the moment marriage wasn't on her agenda, and it was never on his; a good reason not to start anything—anythings could wind up in pregnancies. So perhaps, he thought exultantly as he turned off the bridle path in the direction of his home, his acceptance of Edda's invitation was the best way to reduce the girl to ordinariness: an unimpregnated sister with a pregnant sister, part and parcel of the Corunda he hated most.

When old Tom Burdum had given him Corundoobar for his own, deeded it outright, Jack Thurlow's world had completed itself, and he was happy. The son of old Tom's daughter, he had endured a stormy childhood of financial and social ups and downs that still bewildered him, they had been so many and so different. Its chief result, in Jack's mind anyway, was his ongoing horror of the Evil Twins—Money and Power. A horror that had led him to refuse to be old Tom's principal heir, and set the old man off in search of a new heir, the Pommy doctor. Well, good luck to old Tom!

At five thousand acres, Corundoobar wasn't the largest of the Burdum properties; this was rich country, a man didn't need many thousands of acres to do well as a pastoralist or as a farmer. The soil was deep and nutritious, the rainfall higher and more reliable than in most Australian places, and the district's plateau elevation gave it a kinder climate, at least during the six months of summer.

Jack had worked Corundoobar since returning from boarding school in Sydney at eighteen; his education had been excellent as far as it went, but he chose not to advertise the fact, preferring the image of inarticulate pastoralist engaged in producing fat lambs and, more recently, the breeding of Arab saddle horses. Arabs were too small for many male riders, but ideal lady's mounts, and everybody knew women were the horse-mad sex. Old Tom had derided the venture, but had to swallow his scorn when Jack's Arabs did amazingly well right from the start. Nowadays Jack was entering his Arabs in the big rural shows across the state; his ambition was to exhibit them at the Royal Easter Show in Sydney, the biggest and most important venue for livestock in the whole of Australia.

Corundoobar homestead sat athwart a cone-shaped hill, rolling down all its flanks to an enviable three-quarter-circle frontage on the Corunda

River where it never dried up into a string of water holes; windpower gave him enough pressure to pump to his paddock troughs, while the home gardens were so enclosed by the stream that watering them was a tank tower and gravity feed. For drinking water, there were underground storage tanks to hold rain runoff from roofs.

The original Burdum house, it was built of limestone blocks on a square pattern with a hip-roof of corrugated iron and a wide verandah all the way around it. The gardens were lush, green, and a mosaic of flowers from September to April; at the present moment, high spring, everything producing bloom was in luxuriant flower. Each time he rounded the hill on the Doobar Road and saw the homestead come into sight Jack felt his breath catch, his heart leap in his chest as it never had for a woman. The loveliest place in the world, and legally, irrevocably his!

Though it lacked a woman's touch, this bachelor's house was neat and clean. Like many another man, Jack Thurlow could cook, sew on buttons, take up a hem, darn socks, scrub a floor, and produce whiter-than-white washing; as a child there had often been no one else to do these things, so they had fallen to him and he was proud of his domestic skills. Like the education, they were part of his secret: he was a man to whom duty called more powerfully than any other human condition, for he was a man who had done what he did out of duty, not out of love, and he knew duty for a cruel mistress. To Jack Thurlow, nothing was worse than to be exploited as a duty, and never to see a scrap of love in return. So he hid his secrets, praying he could live like this for the rest of his days, responsible to no one, owing no one a duty of any kind. That was what appealed about Edda Latimer; she would never be his duty, no matter what her life might do to her. Whereas her twin, he shrewdly suspected, was a duty to everybody she knew. He laughed. "Edda's duty, never mine," he said.

When Jack pulled up outside the Corunda Town Hall at the wheel of a Daimler, Edda blinked in astonishment.

"Nice," she said, allowing him to open her door.

"Tom lends it to me when I need it."

"We could have walked, it's not far."

BITTERSWEET

He grimaced. "Ungentlemanly, Edda. Why wouldn't you let me pick you up outside the hospital?"

"And set all the tongues wagging? No, thank you!"

He was dressed, she noted, in the obligatory three-piece suit, and looked strangely unapproachable. Of course she had been regretting her invitation ever since tendering it; now the sight of him in his suit threw her completely off balance, so she said nothing at all until they turned into Trelawney Way, which ran uphill from George Street in a fairly good part of town. The West End was two miles away.

"That cream and green cottage there," she said. Silence fell again; she let him extricate her from the car, horribly aware that curtains were furtively being drawn back in every window of every house in the vicinity. Oh, neighbors! Then Jack opened the gate in the picket fence and escorted her up the path to the front door, set in a verandah. Someone, she noticed, had been working in the garden, which wasn't up to Corunda standards; the roses weren't blooming as they should, had red spider as well as black spot. But then, Grace had never been a gardener. I am selfish, Edda thought, I should donate an occasional day off to helping her. Bear isn't a gardener either, even when he's home. Where are the azaleas and rhododendrons? The pansies and lobelias?

Then Grace was at the open door, ushering them inside, her surprise written clearly on her face. "Edda did explain she was bringing someone, but I confess I never expected you, dear Mr. Thurlow," Grace gushed in best Maude mode. "Sit down, please."

Oh, poor young woman! Jack Thurlow was thinking as he sat rather awkwardly in the wrong sort of chair. So like Edda, yet so unlike her! Very attractive, especially with her pregnant bloom suffusing her skin, yet no vitality, no zest for life. "Call me Jack," he said, smiling at her.

The ice was broken; soon Grace and Jack were laughing, her big grey eyes shining as he put her at her ease, carefully hiding his pity as she, no doubt terribly lonely stuck here all day, expanded under his very ordinary brand of attention.

While the pair talked, Edda was free to assess the house as she never had before, always too immersed in Grace to spare a moment. *But the house had changed!* How long since her last visit here? A month? No, Edda, it's

95

at least three months. I always buy her lunch at the Parthenon to free her from her domestic jail, I hate coming to the Trelawneys. Now look at this! Oh, God, why haven't I kept a more vigilant eye on Grace and her house?

The place was furnished like a rich man's mansion! That huge Persian rug on the floor in her lounge room. That gorgeous coromandel screen. Genuine tapestry seats on the dining chairs. Grace, Grace, what have you done?

"Jack, content yourself with your own company," she said as soon as seemed natural, "while Grace and I fetch tea."

The moment the kitchen door was closed Edda grasped her twin by the shoulder a little cruelly and shook her. "Grace, when did you buy all this furniture?"

Grace glowed. "Isn't it lovely, Eds? I ran into Maude and Mrs. Enid Treadby about four months ago, and they took me to this wonderful shop way out on the Melbourne road—such stunning bits and pieces! People come from Canberra to shop there."

The rage died; Edda gazed at her sister in despair. "Oh, Grace, you— you *idiot*! Well, there's nothing else for it, you have to return the lot. You can't live without *some* money in the bank, and you spent more than your own five hundred pounds, didn't you? Don't say Bear let you spend all his money, too!"

"Of course he let me, I'm his wife," said Grace in wounded tones. "This is *real* furniture, it appreciates with time!"

"There's an old proverb, twin, that you have to cut your coat to suit your cloth," Edda said tiredly. "You're imitating Mrs. Enid Treadby, who's rich enough to buy furniture that will appreciate. Oh, you fool! Stepmama led you into this, I know she did, the bitch! It wasn't Mrs. Treadby, it was Maude."

By this, Grace was weeping. "I can't return it, Edda, I *bought* it!" she wailed. "I love it, and Bear loves it, too. He says I have the best taste in the world."

"Put the kettle on your fancy new gas stove, Grace, or we'll look as if we're neglecting our guest," Edda said on a sigh. "In future, Grace, you come to me before you spend a single penny on anything that doesn't belong in a pantry or ice chest, hear me?"

Somehow the visit got itself over and done with; Edda sat in the Daimler's front passenger seat and said not a word.

"Something's up," Jack said.

"Indeed it is."

"I'm a good listener."

"I know, but it's family trouble, Jack. Let's just say that I forgot how absolutely stupid Grace can be, all right?"

"Ah, poor little Grace! I daresay she is stupid, Edda. It's her nature, don't you agree? The trouble with being smart and clever and efficient is that so many people aren't smart and clever and efficient—or even one of those. But she's a loving little thing just the same. I bet she gives her husband a lot of headaches, but he probably thinks the love she gives him is worth every pang. That's the difficulty women like you always have, Edda. For every ounce of cleverness in your brain, you've had to give up at least an ounce of love."

The pain! It lanced through her like a needle of cold fire, but Edda Latimer would have died rather than show this Lord of Creation that his words hurt. "That is utter nonsense," she said crushingly. "You sound like a women's magazine."

"I'd rather call it an exercise in accounting. The debits have to equal the credits, it's a law of nature. Grace's credits are measured in love, whereas yours are measured in intellect. Oh, not entirely," he added, his own eyes twinkling at the anger in hers, "but love would never be enough for you. Its rewards are far too ephemeral, like trying to see water evaporate."

"And would love be enough for you?" she asked icily.

"No, unfortunately it wouldn't. However, today has solved one puzzle I've always wrestled about twins."

For a moment Edda contemplated not rising to his bait, then admitted that if she didn't, he wouldn't tell her. Ever. "And what puzzle has been so baffling?"

"Why twins at all?" he said. "There's too much to pack inside one person, but spread over two, the mixture's thin and lumpy."

"So a twin is a lesser kind of human being?"

"More different than lesser."

"You think Grace got all the love and I the brains?"

"Not exactly. Just that she needs some of your good sense and you need some of her compassion."

"I'm not sorry I got the brain. Grace is going to suffer."

"Not if she has a good husband."

Bear's frost-fair face rose before Edda's internal gaze; she smiled, squeezed Jack's hand as it lay on the steering wheel. "Then she'll be all right. Bear Olsen is a very good man who will always look after her." Doubt crept into her voice. "If, that is, he can stop her spending money. How odd! I never realized that she's a spendthrift until now, when I saw all that expensive furniture. She left not a penny in the bank."

"I don't suppose she's ever had the freedom to spend."

"With our stepmother in control, true words. Yet it was our stepmother encouraged her to buy the furniture." The Town Hall loomed, the car stopped. "Let me drop you at the hospital," he pleaded. But Edda was already out of the car, and smiling brilliantly.

"No, thank you. I'll see you on a ride, no doubt?"

His laughter sounded exciting. "No more rides for a while, Edda. You and I are going to spend our spare time at Grace's, doing things in the garden. Grace is getting too swollen to tend it, and Bear's on the road. It's the least we can do. When are you off duty?"

"Tomorrow," she said numbly.

"Then I'll see you here at eleven tomorrow morning. I'd be earlier, except that I have to beg, borrow, or steal cuttings and plants from Hannah, Enid, and whoever else to fill those vacant beds. A house in Corunda without rhododendrons and azaleas? A prunus or two? Daffodils under the grass?"

He was still talking as he drove away, leaving Edda standing to stare after him as at a vanishing genie.

Finally she turned and began to plod toward the hospital side gate, mind whirling. Looking back over the events, she had no idea what she had expected might happen beyond a friendly cup of tea with her twin, about whom Jack had indeed wondered from time to time. If Edda had fretted over an introduction, it was in the belief that Jack might fall for the softer sister. Instead he seemed to pity Grace—why was that more annoying?

Then Edda grasped her unruly emotions firmly, brought them under control, and conjured up an image of Grace as she had been this afternoon. Remarkably pretty, as pregnant women tended to be, showing a seven-months tummy but not yet unwieldy, her big grey eyes filled with love for—oh, everybody! How extraordinary, that a man as unversed as Jack Thurlow had felt it, too, Grace's voracious appetite for love. She hadn't tried in the least to captivate him, but he wasn't proof against Grace's brand of charm, against her air of helpless incompetence. Owning no incompetence herself, Edda despised it, and had assumed Jack would, too. To find that he didn't came as an unpleasant shock.

Tufts was sitting in the common room surrounded by books, but of Kitty there was no sign—yes, on duty in Children's, as per usual. Odd, that. Kitty thirsted for duty on Children's, and Matron, it seemed, was prepared to indulge her.

"Tufts!" Edda rapped, lighting the gas under the kettle. "Do you ever get tired of being the capable and intelligent twin?"

"A cuppa? Oh, yes, please!" Tufts looked up, her sherry-colored eyes brightening. "The strong twin, I think you really mean," she said.

"Do I?" Edda stared at her half sister, frowning. Tufts was extremely pretty, too, if one saw her without Kitty there to eclipse her. The same sweet face, straight nose, enormous eyes, domed forehead. Her coloring was more uniform, less striking than Kitty's, and her dimples rarely showed, but minus Kitty she was a stunning girl. Why does the world never see it?

"Well, you can't honestly mean Grace and Kitty are stupid or incapable," Tufts said, puzzled, "because they're not. They just burn for different things than you and I do."

"Things like love," said Edda, giving "love" an unpalatable inflection. "Love! Knuckling under to some man, is what it is."

"I can understand why you dismiss it as that, Eds, but if nursing has taught you anything, it is surely that women and men are as differently constructed mentally as they are physically. I grow very tired of egalitarian generalizations—all men are not equal, nor are all women. Individualism should be prized."

"Bravo, Tufts!" Edda cried, laughing. "Getting back to love, I'd sooner die than become a slave to it."

"Harken back to your experiences nursing, please! Habit is what enslaves,

Edda, and that can include love after it becomes a habit." Tufts poured boiling water into the teapot. "Habits can be almost impossible to break."

"Oh, Tufts, you're much wiser than I am! Dr. Finucan talks about hormones. Maybe you and I have a different concentration of them from Grace and Kitty? Or our brains developed in some different way? And what's a habit, in a brain?"

Edda poured milk, Tufts stirred the teapot to speed up the infusion process. Then, cups brimming with steaming tea, they sat to enjoy this panacea for all woes.

"What brought this on?" Tufts asked, sipping.

"I took Jack Thurlow to see Grace today—what an insane idea! He made his fishing for an introduction sound like sheer curiosity, so I thought once he'd met her, he'd forget her." Edda gave a wry laugh. "Wrong! Now instead of meeting Jack for a lovely ride on my days off, I'm doomed to go with him to Grace's house and act as an unpaid gardener and skivvy."

"That's not why you're so angry, Edda."

"Have you seen Grace's house?"

"Yes. Very tasteful. It surprised me."

"Didn't it occur to you that she must have spent every penny Bear has in the bank as well as her own five hundred? Maude bamboozled her into furnishing her house in a style she plain can't afford!"

"I never thought . . . My mother is an awful woman," Tufts said quietly, "we both know that. What was she out to do?"

"Get Grace into trouble with Bear, I imagine. Whenever she splurges on furniture for the Rectory, our gentle father grows less gentle, and makes it impossible for her to keep the item—she's obliged to return it. She assumed that Bear, a lower class than Father, would make Grace's life very unhappy if she overspent." Edda shrugged. "Well, Maude miscalculated. Bear would forgive Grace anything."

"And thank God for it!" said Tufts roundly. "Her influence on Kitty has waned, of course, so she's thirsting for revenge as well as other avenues of mischief-making. Grace and Bear is just a practice run, I think. Beware, Edda, you're Mama's main target, I'm convinced of it."

"I'm inclined to agree, sweetheart, except that I've thrown off Maude's authority over my life, such as it was. How can she hurt me, Tufts?"

"Once Grace tells her about Jack Thurlow, through him, is my guess. She'll try to smear you."

Edda laughed. "Well, if they start talking about me and Jack, they'll stop gossiping about you and the doctors."

Poor Edda! Tufts thought as she made her way down the ramp to Pathology, one of the larger shedlike buildings because it also housed the library and the new X-ray facility, a huge piece of equipment so heavy that it had had to be installed on specially strong foundations. As the more ordinary half of her set of twins, Heather/Tufts had escaped much that Kitty had suffered, and the same could be said for Grace in relation to Edda, who killed snakes with a chair leg and dared anything as well as being both glamorous and alluring. Yet it was Grace had found love, Tufts reflected: genuine love, the kind that lasted, the kind that forgave all sins, contained no condemnation. No matter how many mistakes poor, silly Grace made, Bear would be there to pick up the pieces. Now, it seemed, when Bear wasn't there to pick up the pieces, other men would volunteer, for the purest of reasons. Hooked on Edda's line Jack Thurlow might be, but his alacrity in going to Grace's rescue told Tufts that he wished Edda had need of him, wished Edda were just a little helpless.

Of course Edda didn't see that; she didn't want to see it. Edda prized her independence, her ability to take care of herself. Which ought not to make her less deserving of love, yet did. Some women were far more difficult to love. Poor Edda!

Only the night lights were on as Tufts let herself in to walk down the long internal hallway with doors opening off it to the left and right; all the way to the far end, where the hall finished at a red-painted door leading to Dr. Liam Finucan's lair, his office. It too was dark; the pathologist had gone home for the night, the experiments were all hers. Well, not actually experiments . . . Tissue culture dishes, a lump of mammary tissue embedded in paraffin for sectioning, various histological stains to prepare. The routine stuff like urinalysis had been done by Liam's one technician; that he managed to exist without a second technician was due to her, Tufts Scobie, who loved the exactitude of this kind of work and did it far better than the young man officially employed for the purpose.

Without turning on the lights she let herself through a side door in the office and emerged into the laboratory, where she threw some switches and blazed the room into glaring yellow relief. They had an automatic microtome blade sharpener, very precious, and the blade on it was ready for use; Tufts went about the task of fixing the chunk of paraffin in place on the microtome base, prepared her stains, and settled to slicing, sliding, and mounting the transparent sections of what had once been a woman's breast, so absorbed that she neither saw nor heard anything in her vicinity.

"Thanks for that, Heather," said Dr. Finucan's voice.

She jumped, then beamed at him. "They'll be ready on time."

"I'd be willing to bet it's a carcinoma," he said.

"Oh, poor woman! She can't be much past thirty, her children aren't at school yet."

Tufts slid off the tall stool and went back to the office, there to wait until the pathologist locked up the lab.

Like his surgeon confreres, Liam Finucan was a genuine asset to Corunda Base; like them, he could easily have carved a Sydney or Melbourne career with great success. However, his wife was a Corunda girl, and he had loved the place at first sight: its Old Country feel, the green of its grass, its rich European shrubs and flowers. Born and bred in Ulster of Protestant stock, he had taken medical degrees in London sufficiently good to earn him a post as a pathologist anywhere. He had worked with Sir Bernard Spilsbury! For someone who'd grown up in the religious wars of Ulster, Corunda was paradise.

It was probably the only good turn Eris had ever done him, to push Liam Finucan into choosing Corunda, but, he remembered, she'd been young and homesick, poor Eris. A beautiful girl, a beautiful woman, Eris had always been discontented. His area of specialization did not demand long hours away or great inroads on his personal time; in a way, he wished it had, for if it had, he could have remained blind to Eris's dabblings in men. And the whole of Corunda knew.

Mostly he had coped by ignoring her affairs, only discussing them whenever she decided it was time to ask for a divorce. His refusals were not on account of religion, but grounded in compassion. If such were her nature, let Eris dabble in men, but it was not in her nature to suffer public humiliation, no matter how she begged for divorce. The scandal would wreck her. There was, besides, another aspect to Eris: the man she was wildly in love with this year would be dust and ashes the next. If he, Liam, deserted her, too, she would perish in a world she was not equipped to inhabit. If she had had children, things would have been different, but she was barren; the number of men and her contraceptive ignorance proved it to a pathologist's mind. Her philandering, thought Liam, was actually a desperate quest in search of a child.

At the moment things were worse than they had ever been. Corunda was not a bottomless pit of men, and Eris had run through those she fancied. A month ago she had secretly packed her bags and gone to Sydney, too rapidly for Liam to follow her. A technical desertion that gave him inarguable grounds for divorce. His private detective located her living with a man who ran a dairy farm at Liverpool, and Liam finally gave up the struggle.

"I saw Don Treadby today," he said to Tufts.

"Shall I make us a cup of tea?"

"What liquor is to most houses, strong tea is to a house of healing," he said with one of his rare smiles.

"It's the caffeine and other whatsits in tea, especially as strong as we drink it. Sit down, close your eyes and count. I'll be back in one shake of a dead lamb's tail."

"An apt metaphor for Corunda," he called after her.

"Better alive than dead," floated her voice.

She was back quickly, bearing the tea tray.

"What did Don Treadby have to say?" she asked, pouring.

"That it's high time I bit the bullet and divorced Eris."

"Well, unless you do the divorcing, it's terribly sticky. You're the injured party. Seems odd to me," said Tufts, blowing on her tea to cool it, "that either marital partner can't sue."

Ordinarily fairly straight, his black brows flew into peaks. "Heather! You'd allow an *adulteress* to sue for divorce?"

"What a lot of tosh men do talk!" Tufts said crossly. "You say 'adulteress' as if adultery were on a par with murder—for a woman! I see it as an indication that the marital partner just turned out to be a terrible disappointment. In my opinion, your wife is sick. And if you were the adulterer, as a man the crime would be minor, have extenuating circumstances." She leaned into him, eyes gone more golden in the dim light, and gleaming wickedly. "I mean, here you are, well after the dinner hour, closeted alone in your office with a twenty-one-year-old nurse! What do you think the gossip mills of Corunda would make of that?"

He laughed, teeth surprisingly white because his skin was darkish. "Cast not pearls before swine," he said.

"Shouldn't they be rubies?"

"And silk purses, not to say sow's ears?"

They laughed together, minds attuned.

"You think I should divorce Eris, Heather, don't you?"

"Yes, Liam, I do. You can afford to make her an allowance of some kind—perhaps not as much as she'd like, but under the law you don't have to give her anything, do you, since she's the guilty one? It's still a man's world."

"But *you* are my friend?" he asked, suddenly serious.

"Yes, you fool of a man! It's why we call each other by our Christian names—frowned on, except between good friends."

The door opened and Matron strode in; both heads turned to gaze at her in, Matron saw at once, complete innocence.

"Working late, Dr. Finucan?"

"Actually, Matron, no. I did come to do some late work, only to find that Nurse Scobie had already done it."

"Scobie is an excellent nurse as well as a superb path technician, Dr. Finucan, but she is on duty at six tomorrow morning in Women's. I suggest you get some sleep, nurse, so I'll bid you goodnight."

Tufts rose at once. "Yes, Matron. Goodnight, sir."

Nothing else was said until after Tufts was gone, then Liam Finucan spoke. "That was unkind, Gertie," he said.

"Sometimes one has to be cruel to be kind, as well you know, Liam. Don Treadby says you came to see him this morning."

"Jesus, is nothing sacred?"

"In Corunda? Absolutely nothing." Matron fished in her immaculately starched pocket and produced cigarettes and lighter, selected a cork-tip and proceeded to kindle it. "Given this new situation, Liam, you can't afford to entertain trainee nurses in your office at all hours. If Eris's solicitor got a whiff of it, you'd be in the soup—and so would Nurse Scobie."

"I never thought," he said dully.

She eyed him with some sympathy. "Yes, well, men tend not to think in certain circumstances, I find. Certainly I refuse to let your thoughtlessness ruin a wonderful nurse's chances of a brilliant career. In future, Liam, you are never to be seen alone with Nurse Scobie, or have her do special work for you."

"I never thought," he repeated.

"Least said, soonest mended, old friend. Get your divorce from Eris, that's first and foremost. You ought to have done it years ago, when you were a younger man and might have been an eligible mate for someone like Heather Scobie-Latimer. As it is, you're forty-three years old and a bit frayed around the edges." She stubbed out her cigarette and rose. "I may rely on your good sense, Liam?"

"Of course."

After she had closed the door behind her, an image of Tufts appeared before Liam Finucan's eyes; he closed them on the first real pain he had felt in many, many years. "God rot you, Gertie Newdigate!" he said aloud. "You've ruined something before it occurred to me to dream of it."

Forty-three and a bit frayed around the edges—not the kind of lover for bewitching little Heather Scobie, so much was definitely sure.

Several weeks of working in Grace's garden had reconciled Edda to the change in her relationship with Jack Thurlow, but not to the missed horse rides. In most ways the gardening was too similar to the physical tolls of nursing either to relax or refresh; the spine took the brunt, and all the crouching down exacerbated it. Nor, as digging hundreds of holes for daffodil bulbs proved, could gardening offer delight to the soul—no vista to thrill the eyes, no freedom for the soul. It was, besides, Grace's garden, over which, swollen to toad proportions, she presided like, as Edda put it to herself, Lady Muck of Dunghill Hall.

Jack entered into the spirit of his good deed with energy and enthusiasm, apparently oblivious to Edda's feelings or needs. A mere two visits saw Grace expecting them every time Edda had days off; worse, Jack assumed Grace was their only activity. So it was goodbye to Fatima, her friendship with Jack, those wonderful gallops, and a large measure of her privacy. It turned out too that Grace was a gossip and Jack enjoyed hearing it. Peace! cried Edda silently. Give me a little peace!

On the rare occasions when Bear was home, the atmosphere was lighthearted; Jack and Bear yarned together in that masculine world men seemed to prize so much—machines malfunctioning, a crop not prospering, finding decent work dogs, the unfairness of some judges at the stock shows—Corunda land subjects that Bear, with his extensive travels, was eminently qualified to discuss.

In fact, Bear was about as happy as a recently married man could be, and awaited the birth of his first child with a mixture of awe and a delightful dread.

"I honestly don't care if it's a boy or a girl," he told Jack and the sisters-in-law over dinner, "because we're going to have some of both. If my preferences are for a boy first, it's to help Grace with the heavy work around the place."

"They have to grow a little first," said Kitty, who liked Bear very much.

"Oh, they do *that* overnight! I was chopping kindling and lighting the stove for my mum when I wasn't much more than one year old," Bear said cheerfully.

"Yes, but you won't subject your children to the same kind of tyranny as your father did you," said Tufts.

"I should hope not! That's why I signed the Pledge early on—the drink really is a demon. But still, it doesn't hurt children in a big family to help pitch in with the work. I reckon it's better for them than too much pampering."

"That," said Grace, rising clumsily, "they won't get, Bear my love. I'm too hopeless as a housekeeper."

Edda looked up swiftly, but Grace had turned, removing her face from Edda's probing glance. Oh, Grace, what are you doing now? She got to her feet and followed Grace to the kitchen.

"Why are you a hopeless housekeeper, Grace?"

"My word, Edda, you do pick up on every little thing!" Grace said defensively. "It's nothing—just that I saw some gorgeous material for the lounge room curtains, and rather overspent my housekeeping allowance. Bear is so generous, too."

Horrified to hear herself yet unable to restrain herself, Edda imitated Maude Latimer and ground her teeth. "Oh, Grace! You can't do that! Especially with a child due shortly, surely you can see that? Your house is finished, inside it's far too nice for the neighborhood, and there was nothing wrong with the old lounge room curtains. If your spending gets Bear into debt, he'll have to put one of those awful little notices in the *Post* that Mr. Björn Olsen will no longer be responsible for his wife's debts. Because if you keep spending money you don't have, you leave Bear with only two alternatives—disavowing your debts or being declared bankrupt. And if Bear were declared bankrupt, every scrap of your precious furniture would go on the auction block, together with this house. Don't you remember what Mrs. Geordie Menzies did to Geordie last year?"

The tears were rolling down Grace's face. "I can't see how it matters this once," she said, digging for her handkerchief and mopping her eyes. "The lounge room *needed* new curtains!"

"Grace, you're the one needs to change," said Edda in a hard voice. "No more spending—and no running to Bear about this conversation of ours, either. Cut your coat to suit your cloth, I keep telling you." A thought occurred. "Have you been entertaining Maude?"

"Sometimes," Grace whispered.

"Then don't. Refer her to me, I'll put a flea in her ear!"

I must, thought Edda as she left in Jack's car with Tufts and Kitty, scotch this relationship between my gullible sister and our frightful stepmother. She's trying to break Grace and Bear up by pushing Grace into profligate spending.

Of course Jack had noticed something amiss; curious, that he, no blood relation, is the one who sees clearly. After Kitty and Tufts scrambled out of the back seat, he made no attempt to evict Edda. "Go on in, girls," he said to them, "while I take Edda down to the river for a bit of a cuddle."

"A cuddle!" she said in disgust, as they drove to the river and parked. "Still, it did the trick. How did I know things would change if I introduced you to Grace?"

"Not right now, Edda. Look at the night, you Philistine!"

And he had wanted to share it, wanted *her* to share it with him. Edda, you *are* a fool! The smell and sound as well as the sight of summer washed over her as she went and sat with Jack on a log, looking. The night was stunning, the light of the stars bled out of the sky by an immense round silver moon that poured invisible radiance across the rolling hills and struck the entire world to a glowing indigo.

"Feel better now you've seen this?" he asked, making a cigarette.

"Yes, and I thank you. You're a funny blighter, Jack, I never know what makes you tick. But I did think your meeting Grace would change things, and I was right," she said, wondering why cigarettes had come to bore her.

"Grace is such a helpless sort, though I didn't realize until she married Bear that in our Rectory days I used to manipulate her like a puppeteer. But at least then she wasn't in trouble, now she's never out of it. You're a part of keeping Grace on the rails, too. She used to spend her free time in the railway shunting yards. She met Bear there, they fell in love over steam locomotives. Silly, isn't it? Anyway, Grace runs on rails. She can't turn herself around unaided. And for reasons I can't fathom, our stepmother is busy inserting herself into Grace's life with disastrous effect."

"What disastrous effect?" he asked, framing the moon in a diaphanous smoke ring.

"Oh, do stop doing that!" Edda snapped. "The last thing a perfect world needs is a man-made smoke ring! Have you no real appreciation for beauty?"

The smoke ring had been his overture to taking her in his arms and kissing her out of this obsession with Grace, but her reaction stopped him cold, desire shrivelled to nothing. Medusa the Gorgon snake lady, that was what they called her, and rightly so. Because Jack listened to gossip he heard all the tales of men patients falling in love with Kitty or Tufts, whereas they never fell in love with Edda. No one nursed better, could make a man feel more comfortable and special, yet she couldn't inspire love of the man–woman sort. His own feelings for her were intensely physical as well as more cerebral, but he couldn't even begin to convince himself that she cherished womanly feelings for him. Edda was like a glorious statue on a pedestal, and he suspected that she preferred her life that way.

"What disastrous effect?" he repeated.

"She has no money sense, she gets herself into debt."

"Oh, I see. And your stepmother?"

"Is encouraging her tendencies. I have to stop it!"

They walked back to the car. "No doubt you will, Edda."

She said nothing until the side gate of the hospital loomed, then gabbled. "Don't play the gentleman, Jack, I can get out by myself. Are you going back to Grace's tomorrow?"

"I'd planned to, since Bear is still in town. He and I are going to tackle that tree."

She slid out of the car. "Good luck with it. I won't be there, I've had enough of Grace for the time being, and Fatima is getting very fat from lack of exercise in Daddy's stables. It's back to the rides for me, they promote my health. Good night."

And she was gone.

For a long five minutes he waited at the curb, sure that she would change her mind, return to say she'd see him at Grace's. But it was Liam Finucan who leaned into the car.

"Could you drop me home, Jack?"

"Hop in. Now you've filed for divorce, what happens to the house? It's too big anyway."

"I'm selling it. There's a nice wee house in the hospital grounds will do me. I'll long-term lease it and do it up."

"Sensible. Besides, I know you," Jack said, smiling. "You want a little money to give Eris an allowance."

The long face looked wry. "Och, poor soul! She can't help her nature, Jack, and I've enough for my needs."

"She put the hard word on me once, Liam. I said no."

"She put the hard word on everyone with a penis, Jack."

"And you're well out of it."

The one who suffered most from Dr. Finucan's divorce was Tufts, who had no idea what had passed between Matron and Liam after she had been dismissed on that memorable night. When, on her next period in the pathology lab, she turned up eager to learn a new analytical technique he had promised to teach her, she found him seated behind his desk, and had to stand before him. *Carpeted?*

No, not that. He wasn't looking well, which worried her. The floppy hair hadn't seen a brush and was at least partially blinding him, the gunmetal eyes were shadowed, and the sag of his cheeks cried fatigue. What on earth was the matter? Where was the crease that always lurked in the right corner of his mouth, made it so good humored? Not there today. Nor was a certain softness Tufts had grown used to in his smile. Today, no smile.

"Sit down, Nurse Scobie," he said, sounding wooden.

Puzzled, she sat, hands folded in her lap, eyes on him.

"This is very awkward," he said after a pause, "and most likely not what Matron wants me to do, but I fail to see how I can cut off private instruction to a nurse as bright and eager to learn as you without an adequate explanation. Please believe that Matron is acting with your best interests at heart."

The deep, Ulster-inflected voice ran down, though his eyes never left hers; he swallowed, collected himself, ploughed on. "I've told you that I am suing my wife for divorce on the grounds of her constant adultery. This means I am the wronged party and will receive favorable treatment in court. However, my wife's solicitors will try their hardest to drag me down to her level. If she can prove adultery against me, then her advantages in court will be the same as mine. Since I have never committed adultery, it behooves me to—er—keep my nose clean, Nurse."

He ran down again, staring at Tufts painfully.

I must help him, thought Tufts. Otherwise he'll pass out.

"You mean, Dr. Finucan, that you and I must never be alone together in circumstances that might make it possible for Mrs. Finucan to allege misconduct on our parts?" Tufts asked, voice steady and detached.

"That is Matron's contention."

"I agree with Matron." Tufts began to get up from the chair. "From now on we must never be alone together, or call each other by our Christian names." Her face became stern. "From now on I suggest that young Bill participate in your teaching sessions alongside me. You've fought against that because he's not as quick on the uptake as I am, but perhaps that's cruel to Bill, given his position on the staff. Whatever instruction you give me must be given to others at the same session."

His eyes flared, looked suddenly fierce. "I am sorry, my dear—very sorry."

"Pooh, nonsense!" she said lightly. "How long will it be?"

"Two years, apparently. The divorce courts are heavily oversubscribed, I have to wait my turn."

"Oh, that is too bad! I had hoped we might return to normal before I qualify, but we won't," Tufts said sadly.

"I am afraid not, no."

"May I go now, sir?"

"Yes, of course. I'll block out a new roster for you and Bill, and one for the nurses."

That awful woman! thought Tufts, marching down the ramp with an unapproachable look on her face. Playing up on such a decent chap, then destroying what little bit of innocent pleasure he has. For he *liked* our sessions together, I know he did!

An eternity of formal correctness is looming, and I am wild with rage at the very idea of it. No more cups of tea in the middle of the night, no more wordlessly understanding glances. I am being sent into an exile of the spirit. Oh, I know why Matron stepped in, and I'm glad she did. Otherwise Liam would be ruined, I would be ruined, and we'd both have to go. Liam and I have harmed no one, but now we are cut apart as finally as a butcher halves a hunk of meat. But there is one thing I am going to do, out in the open of his office or his lab—brush Liam's hair. That Mason Pearson hairbrush cost me money, and I bought it to cure Liam's blinding flop of hair. It will—if the brushing is twice daily and ruthlessly hard on his scalp. I have to bully those follicles into growing backward, not forward. And divorce or no divorce, I am going to do it!

Edda hadn't gone to Maude about her encouraging Grace to spend money she didn't have; she went to her father, a shrewder move.

After his daughters went nursing, the Reverend Thomas Latimer had gradually fallen upon more emancipated times. Alone in the big Rectory with Maude after she had returned from her visit to the Blue Mountains, he began to sever those of his ties to her that he had never much liked, from her dominance over his daughters to his choice of hymns and sermons. And though he wasn't wealthy, from his Treadby mother he had inherited sufficient to live on very comfortably. By nature he was a careful manager of money; Maude, for example, had only limited access to it. While he loved this second wife well enough, he was not blind to her faults. Maude's interference in Grace's financial affairs he interpreted, quite correctly, as a devious way of achieving what she had wanted for herself but was denied the funds to do so. Every time she went to Grace's house she gazed around and congratulated herself on her power to tamper with those she disliked, even severely damage them.

But when an awesomely angry Rector put his foot down, Maude had no choice other than to obey; in her future dealings with Grace, she was informed icily, she would actively discourage the spending of money. Otherwise her own allowance would suffer.

Edda had a more difficult time persuading her father that he must not replace Bear's £900 and Grace's £500.

"Please, Daddy, don't," she begged. "Bear is too soft with Grace to hide the return of the money from her, so, knowing it's there, she'll spend it all over again. To be spendthrift is in Grace's nature, so leave her husband to deal with it. If you want to help the Olsen family, then pay for their children to be well educated at a decent school. Look at what it did for us."

And so the matter had been left.

A part of her disgusted that Grace had utterly ruined her relationship with Jack Thurlow, Edda visited Grace less and less as her pregnancy drew toward full term. Though, truth to tell, the fault lay with Jack, not with Grace. In succumbing to Grace's wiles Jack was baring a secret self whom Edda found soft and weak; he was not at all the kind of man Edda had always thought him. Grr!

When Grace went into labor at the beginning of April 1928, she was huge and, according to obstetrical calculations, overdue. Trying to time his arrival to that of the baby, Bear was already in Corunda; it was the baby ignoring human schedules.

Because Maternity wasn't busy, nor expected to be busy, Dr. Ned Mason had brought Grace in before her labor pangs even began. Her admission to Maternity acted like a cattle goad: no sooner had Grace unpacked her little suitcase and sat experimentally on the edge of her bed to test its comfort than her water broke. Aware of her identity and aware too that all her sisters were on duty elsewhere, Maternity Sister soothed Grace's injured feelings as tenderly as competently. The water was cleaned up, a pretty nightgown found, and the company of a sweet West Ender nurse was designated to help her walk around.

"But I don't want to walk, I want to go to bed!" she protested to Edda when Edda appeared in Theatre travelling scrubs, two masks around her neck. "Why won't they let me go to bed?"

"Dr. Mason thinks you're in for a long labor, Grace, which means hours and hours in bed. Now, while you still can, *walk!*"

Kitty and Tufts came in to hug, kiss, explain the walking all over again because Grace was being recalcitrant and refused to believe it helped. Edda muffled a sigh.

"Grace, you were a nurse yourself," Kitty pointed out.

"Yes, but never on Maternity! Ow, ow, ow, it hurts!"

"Of course it hurts," Tufts said, pushing Grace inexorably ahead of her. "You did do some anatomy and physiology, Grace, so you must remember Dr. Finucan's explaining how a woman's whole pelvis has to open up to let something as huge as a baby out—it's amazing how much you open up, so yes, it hurts badly. You have to do a day's work, darling, in really beastly circumstances, before you can expel a baby. Just remember that it's the best work you'll ever do because the end result is so wonderful—a healthy, full-term baby."

"It's got to be a boy!" Grace panted to Kitty hours later.

"Rubbish," Kitty crooned, wiping Grace's face. "What's so special about having a boy?"

"All men want a son. Girls are a letdown."

"Don't wives' wishes count? After all, they do the hard part."

Grace made a contemptuous noise. "Who in her right mind would want a girl? Restrained, confined, sat on? If Edda had been a boy, Daddy would have beggared himself to send her up to university and let her do medicine. But Edda was a girl, so . . ."

"Yes, well, unfortunately we don't have any choice in the sex matter, darling. Whatever emerges, boy or girl, is yours. Here, have a sip of water. You need more fluid."

Bear had driven Grace to the hospital, and was allowed to see his weeping, tormented wife briefly once she was settled in. Then he was exiled to the father's waiting room, where a prospective father paced, chain-smoked, tried to think of something other than the fate of his wife and child. If he had had company it would have been easier, but Grace's baby came long after the September rush of babies conceived during the end/beginning of the year, when too much alcohol was drunk and too few precautions taken. Bear had to wait alone save for flying visits from Grace's father and sisters.

Twenty-seven hours after labor had started, Bear learned that he was the proud father of a nine-pound baby boy in the absolute pink of health.

Grace was exhausted, but none the worse for her travail apart from stitches in a torn perineum. A boy! A boy with snow-white hair, brows, and lashes, and a long, strong body.

"Well, Grace, that's the hardest day's work you'll ever do," said Aunt Tufts, expertly holding the baby. "A very nice little chap, too! What are you going to call him, Bear?"

"Brian," said Bear so quickly that Grace's opinion was lost.

"Brian? I like it, Bear, but you've never mentioned it."

"He was my favorite brother. Died in a pub brawl."

If Aunt Tufts, the only family present, thought it macabre to name a child after someone killed in a pub brawl, she gave no indication of it. Smiling, she handed the bundle to Bear. "It is a fine name, manly and not open to playground persecution."

"Exactly," said Bear, gazing down at his progeny with awe and humility. "Grace's names were all airy-fairy, but I'll not have my boy saddled with a sissy name. Brian Olsen sounds good."

"Oh, Bear!" cried Grace reproachfully. "I wanted something that sounds right with a knighthood. Sir Maximilian Olsen!"

"Maximilian is sissy," said Edda, entering. "Brian? Ideal! Thank God there's one member of the Olsen family with sense."

To be the grandfather of a male child delighted the Rector, who had worked out how to help Grace without putting money in her purse. He paid for a scrubwoman to clean the house on Trelawney Way once a week, and come three times a week to do the worst job of all—wash the dozens and dozens of big terry-cloth "nappies," as baby napkins or diapers were called. All Grace did was hose the solids from the dirty nappies, then dump them in the copper. The scrubwoman boiled them, rinsed them, and hung them out to dry on the clotheslines that now criss-crossed the backyard and turned it into a flapping jungle. The laundry was now a shed in proximity to the back door; what had been the laundry was a nappy-soak area.

Bear, Edda noticed now, was less eager to go out on the road than of yore. Part of that was due to his enchantment with his son, but a larger part of it was rooted in worry for Grace, who, despite so much house and laundering help, couldn't seem to cope with her son's advent. She was so well endowed with milk that she leaked it, and within a week of Brian's birth was so revolted that she put him on a bottle, enduring milk withdrawal as the lesser evil. Dr. Mason roared in outrage, so did District Nurse, but Grace turned deaf ears. Changing his nappies revolted her, too, so she did it less often than she should have; the result was nappy rash so severe that all three of her sisters were forced to bully and badger her into the proper care. And in the end Grace got what she wanted from the Rector: full-time nursery help.

"Somehow," said Edda wrathfully to Kitty and Tufts one day when baby Brian was three months old, "our artful sister has managed to wriggle out of every task she finds unpalatable. But this is the bitter end! It's daylight robbery, I tell you! A full-time maid to make sure that Brian is clean and dry enough not to break out in not rashes, but sores! I am ropeable!"

"It just goes to show how much Grace must have hated nursing the sick," said Kitty, eyes bright with tears. "Maude likes a dainty house, and passed that on to us. She's not a nice person, but she never really treated any of us like a Cinderella. Maude's tortures were all of the mind. And she got to Grace."

"What Grace's maternal conduct proves," said Tufts firmly, "is that she hates messes, and that was there in her nursing, too. That she never neglected her patients the way she's neglecting Brian was due to her fear of the ward sisters—she was more afraid of them than of cleaning up the messes. Now she has a baby incapable of producing anything but messes, and no one to terrorize her into cleaning them up."

"Don't forget the confusion," Kitty said. "We've always known that Grace couldn't organize a booze-up in a brewery, but with Mama and we three for sisters, she never had to organize anything. Now she's responsible for running a home and a baby, and she's too confused to know how to go about it. Father has stepped up to the breach, which was the worst thing could have happened—what about later on, when she has no father or sisters to help her?"

"Disaster," Edda said hollowly.

"Too pessimistic," said Tufts. "Someone will always step up to the breach to save Grace."

"Why should they?" Edda asked, unable to see it.

"She's every man's dream woman—incapable of existing without a man to lean on." Tufts snorted. "Come on, Edda, you know what I mean! Grace transforms herself into property that has to be managed by a superior being—a man. Everything she does tells men that she can't look after herself. And they love that! Or a certain kind of man does, anyway. The Bears of this world."

"Well, rather Bear than me!" said Edda savagely. "Why can't she understand how comfortable her life would be if she organized it better? No one likes cleaning shit off baby wraps, but as it has to be done, *just bloody do it*! All that expensive furniture, yet her house smells like a cesspit!"

"Why so violent, Edda?" Kitty asked.

"Grace is pregnant again. When the new one is born, they'll be fourteen months apart."

Lavender-blue eyes collided with amber-gold ones: Kitty and Tufts exchanged a look of silent commiseration. Of course it hurt Edda more! She was Grace's full twin. And, greatest misfortune of all, as controlled as Grace was disorganized. The flaws of a Grace lay very far from Edda's heart.

If Kitty and Tufts had known the significance of one Jack Thurlow, what Edda was suffering would have made even more sense.

PART THREE

THE NEW SUPERINTENDENT

I n April 1929, the three years of nurse training finished. Edda Latimer, Heather Scobie-Latimer and Katherine Treadby-Latimer found themselves certificated junior sisters. Edda had won several prizes, and all three qualified with distinction.

By this time there was nothing about Corunda Base Hospital they didn't know, nowhere in Corunda Base Hospital they hadn't worked. The mental hospital was a nightmare best forgotten, mostly because nothing could be done for the poor creatures save to shut them up in padded cells or a dormitory—the asylum was a place of screams, raves, drifting ghosts, murderous maniacs.

No new trainees had appeared in 1927 or 1928, but this year, 1929, would see eight trainees, all matriculated, and all from the West End. With Edda in the lead, the three had talked, argued, pushed, shoved, and campaigned to convince the West Enders that they must, must, *must* take advantage of the new system, that the old one was dead. The future of nursing lay with training and registration; those nursing unregistered would be reduced to poorly paid skivvies stripped of every atom of interesting work: there to wash, clean up messes, lift and turn patients, serve the meals—all under the supervision of a formal trainee. Lena Corrigan, always leader of the West Enders and at first an obdurate enemy, had come around first, too, and added her voice to the three. With 1929's eight trainees the result, a grant was secured from the Department of Health to build a proper nurses' home incorporating flats for sisters. To Edda, Tufts, and Kitty, that battle was the one most worth winning, for it offered girls from underprivileged backgrounds the chance to espouse a proper career without the masculine complications that schoolteaching brought with it, or the servility of secretarying. Nurses had a certain power; anyone thrust into the live-or-die maw of a hospital came out with a profound respect for them, whether they roared like dragons or floated like exquisite angels above the sickbed. Real or imagined, nurses were *remembered*.

Three new sisters meant difficulties, of course. How could a district hospital employ all three? That the task was easier than it had been in 1926 was purely due to attrition: seven of the most experienced West End nurses from the old system had retired. Unfortunately, their wages were not the equal of registered nurses' salaries. The hospital was, besides, thrown into an instantaneous chaos early in June—an utterly unexpected, unpredictable cataclysm.

The General Medical Superintendent, Dr. Francis Campbell, had been superintendent for twenty-five years when 1929 arrived, and fully anticipated continuing in his post for another decade. Then, at precisely the same moment as the three junior sisters received their certificates by mail, Frank Campbell died of a heart attack while seated at his desk, an item of furniture to which hospital people firmly believed he was welded, since he was never seen anywhere else on hospital territory. For Frank Campbell, Corunda Base Hospital *was* his desk. The horrors his kind of superintending generated took place elsewhere, so he didn't see them. No one knew whether he had felt his heart attack, as he had been alone when it came on, and there was no system of internal communication that he might have used to summon help. He had refused to install one as too expensive. For him, it certainly was.

Hospitals existed under the umbrella of the particular state's Department of Health, but to most intents and purposes they ruled themselves, especially the non-teaching rural ones. The Hospital Board was empowered to decide things, including filling its staff vacancies from highest to lowest, setting its policies, and administering its funds. Corunda Base Hospital had a huge endowment, safely banked under the control of its Board—moneys that had come from three-quarters of a century of bequests plus astonishing savings.

Decisions about what to do with three junior sisters were deferred until after a new superintendent was appointed, leaving the Latimers in a temporary stasis, entitled to wear the starched organdy veil but not yet permitted to doff their nurse's aprons. Edda stayed as close to Theatre as she could, working Casualty or Men's; Kitty stayed on Children's; and Tufts oscillated between Maternity and Night Sister, the latter wandering the ramps and wards armed with a hurricane lamp. Frank Campbell was too mean to buy batteries!

Then, most unexpectedly, Matron sent for Tufts, who appeared wearing both her sister's veil and her nurse's apron.

"I think the apron can go, Sister Scobie."

"Not yet, ma'am. It can come in handy. Our duties aren't so defined that we can be sure we won't encounter a mess."

"As you wish." The smooth, rather bland face wore its usual air of unemotional interest. "Though your future careers cannot be decided as yet, Sister Scobie, I feel confident enough of the direction yours should take to be able to speak to you about it even at this distressing time."

"Yes, Matron."

"With no less than eight trainees due to begin nursing in about another ten weeks, it behooves me as head of the nursing staff to take immediate steps about their education. The plans Dr. Campbell had formulated I considered wrong in all respects, and make no bones about telling you, Sister, that with his death I have scrapped them to start again. After three years in this establishment, I imagine that I don't need to tell you my reasons for scrapping his plans?"

"No, Matron, you don't. I understand, and am delighted."

"Good!" Matron eased a little in her chair. "Would you be interested in the position of Sister Tutor?"

Tufts swallowed. "That would depend, ma'am."

"Upon what?" The voice was icy.

"Upon the amount of authority the position carries. If I can carve out a training system that satisfies the Nursing Council yet incorporates various aspects that stem from my own deductions, then I am interested. I would also block out an entirely new educational syllabus that goes beyond Nursing Council ideas of what a nurse needs to know. Naturally I would present all my work to you and the new superintendent before submitting it to Sydney, but what I couldn't undertake is to be an automaton who obeys someone else's schemes." The wide gold eyes held an obdurate look. "You see, ma'am, I have my own schemes."

For a moment Matron Newdigate didn't answer, the starch of her dress creaking a little more than usual—a sign that she was breathing hard. Finally the words came, measured and detached. "I think, Sister Scobie, that if you didn't have your own ideas, I would not be offering you this position. It is a senior one carrying a deputy matron's rank, so I could justify the importation of a Sister Tutor from Sydney or Melbourne. However, a person from Corunda is preferable if a suitable one can be found, and I believe you are eminently suitable. I agree to your terms."

"Then I accept the post." Tufts rose to her feet smoothly. "Thank you, Matron. Er—there is one other thing."

"Pray enlighten me, Sister."

"I will need to confer privately with Dr. Liam Finucan a very great deal. Unless, of course, you plan to use a different medical man to give the lectures and do some teaching?"

"It will be Dr. Finucan, and I have no objection whatsoever to your being closeted alone with him. These days he's a perfectly respectable single man—and your colleague," said Matron, secretly loving this clever, slightly dangerous young woman.

"Good," said Tufts, and departed.

She found the other two junior sisters in the cottage, drinking tea with Lena Corrigan. Though Sister Marjorie Bainbridge had been given the title of Home Sister and moved into a flat in the newly built nurses' home, no one from Matron down had bothered to move the Latimers out of their original housing. They now possessed the whole of it, and a degree of comfort that the denizens of the new nurses' home would never know. The reward of the pioneers.

"I have a definite new job," Tufts said, accepting a cup.

They all looked interested, but Kitty got in first. "What?"

"Sister Tutor, with deputy matron's status."

"Stiffen the snakes!" Lena said on a gasp. "That's the absolute and utter grouse, Tufts. Glorious!"

Amid hugs and choruses of congratulations, Tufts told the tale of her interview, with a smiling Edda the quietest—oh, not from anger or disappointment, they all knew; it came from an extra joy. Rank and importance for women meant much to Edda.

"Lena, I know the Rectory Anzacs are tastier than arrowroot bikkies, but you're not drinking tea with us just to dunk an Anzac or see what color Edda's lipstick is today—you have news, too," Tufts said, on her second cup of tea and third Anzac biscuit.

"Correct as always, Miss Myrna Loy. She's the film star Men's has decided you resemble, Edda, by the way. Kitty is always Marion Davies, but you wobble around a bit."

"Get on with your news, Lena," said Tufts with a growl.

Lena's hands flew up in surrender. "All right, all right! I saw Matron, too, and I've got a promotion, too. After nearly twenty years classified as nursing help—"

"I hope Frank Campbell is burning in Hell!" Kitty snarled.

"Matron has managed to what she called 'grandfather me in' as an officially registered nurse. I'm Sister Corrigan, and I'm going where my heart lies—the Asylum, as deputy matron in charge."

That provoked a fresh outburst of triumphant joy; yet one more victory for women, and so well deserved! This time, however, their descent from the heights was tempered with dismay, though all of the Latimers knew their concern was wasted.

"Lena, after three years I *know* how much you love nursing in the Asylum, but now you're officially registered, and with your fund of knowledge, you can pick your kind of patient," Edda said, eyes gone dark grey with anxiety. "Are you sure that being there a thousand percent of your time won't drive you around the bend, too? There's nothing can be done for mental cases, and psychiatrists are no help. All they do is observe and catalogue the forms dementia takes. Mental nursing is physically dangerous, but it's far more dangerous to the spirit. Think of the frustration!"

A wiry woman in her mid-thirties, Lena Corrigan had a mop of dark red, curly hair, and eyes of much the same color; she was the widow of a man who had been fonder of the bottle than his wife, and had no children. More than that bare outline the Latimers did not know; she was proud and embittered, Lena Corrigan.

"Lord bless you, Edda, I know the pitfalls," Lena said, her patience intact because she knew Edda's protest was genuinely felt. "Loonies fascinate me, I suppose that's the crux of it, and now Frank Campbell's gone, the asylum stands a chance of a psychiatrist and some treatment. Mental nursing won't always be a lost cause. I know it attracts some people who are definitely loonier than the patients, but it's not an irrefutable law. If I can't do anything else, I'm going to keep detailed notes on every single case— one day observations like mine will be seen as important." The fiery eyes glowed redly. "I'm in on the ground floor, just as I have been as a nurse who scraped an education. And I thank you for the help, especially from Edda and Tufts. You girls can *teach*."

"Deputy matron in charge," said Kitty. "Many congratulations, Lena, and at least you'll be paid well at last." Suddenly she jumped. "Oh! Listen, girls! Mama told me a rumor yesterday."

"About what?" Edda asked, sounding bored.

"Our new superintendent."

"Of course! Daddy's on the Hospital Board!" Tufts cried.

"Who? What? Where? When? Why? And how?" Lena asked.

"I knew you'd all prick up your ears at that!" Kitty said on a chuckle. "No, he's not Jack Thurlow, Edda."

"Take a running jump, Kits. *Who?*"

"Maude says he bears a famous Corunda name, and it is not Treadby. His name is Dr. Charles Henry Burdum, he's thirty-three years old, and until this job came up he was the superintendent of a large sector of the Manchester Royal Infirmary," said Kitty.

"Stone the bloody crows!" said Edda on a gasp, then frowned. "That's rot, Kitty. 'Superintendent of a large sector' indeed! You mean he was one of half a dozen deputy supers swanning around one of Europe's most prestigious hospitals." She gurgled in her throat. "Superintendent of bedpans and urine bottles!"

"Mama said he was 'high up'—whatever that means."

Lena waved her hands about. "Oh, Edda, shut up! What I want to know is, which Burdum is he? A Corunda Burdum, or some ring-in from the Old Country with the same name? As far as I know, old Tom Burdum has no heirs except Grace's Good Samaritan and Edda's riding companion, Jack Thurlow." She emphasized "riding."

Kitty gave a shiver of delicious anticipation and settled to tell the rest of her tale secure in the knowledge that she had hooked her audience completely. "He's the son of old Tom's son, would you believe? I mean, the whole of Corunda knows Tom and son Henry had a shocking quarrel sixty years ago, and that Henry left not only Corunda, but also New South Wales, as it was then—no Commonwealth of Australia sixty years ago! Henry went to England, and never communicated with old Tom. About twenty years ago old Tom was notified that Henry had been killed when two trains collided in Scotland—dozens of people died, it seems. The letter to old Tom said Henry was a bachelor with no issue."

"Yes, and all Corunda knows that was what soured old Tom on the world, especially after Jack Thurlow let him down," Lena said.

"Well," said Kitty triumphantly, "the letter from Scotland was wrong! Not long after he had arrived in England, Henry married a well-off widow and didn't need old Tom's money. He founded a successful insurance underwriting company, while his wife's family made big bikkies milling cotton textiles. A son, Charles, was born thirty-three years ago. The wife died in labor with him, and Henry went quite crazy in a harmless way. It was left to the mother's family to care for the boy, Charles."

"But surely old Tom wouldn't have been misled about Henry's death? That's ridiculous," Edda said.

"I gather the train accident was a shambles, and while the authorities found identification on Henry's body, they found no evidence of a wife or son. With the wife dead and her family estranged from Henry, no one suspected he was on the train. The boy's name of Burdum didn't arise during his minority, at least in a way that was noticed. Simply, after some stipulated waiting period produced no answers about Henry, the authorities assumed that old Tom in Corunda was his next-of-kin, and notified him. In the meantime, Henry's son, Charles, lived and prospered in Lancashire. He went to Eton and Balliol College at Oxford, then took a medical degree at Guy's." Kitty looked rather naughty. "It turns out that Mama already knew most of the story—she did quite a lot of research on Dr. Charles Burdum when she first heard of him a couple of years ago."

"Piffle!" said Tufts. "Maude would have spread the story."

"No, she decided to sit on her knowledge—guess why?"

"Too easy," said Edda with a sneer. "Maude earmarked the rich doctor as your future husband, Kits."

"If there was a prize for instinct, Edda, you'd win it," Kitty said, sighing. "You're undoubtedly right." She brightened. "Anyway, we have plenty of time. Cables may fly the ether in an hour, but it still takes six weeks to sail from Southampton to the east coast of Australia, and first the Board has to offer the job to a Pommy—that wouldn't be popular, were his name not Burdum."

Grace's reaction was similar when Edda called the next day; for the moment she was standing by for Theatre, which wasn't busy, and Grace was on the telephone party line into the Trelawneys, so could be visited. As a new mother, Grace craved company—why was it her lot to conceive if Bear so much as took his trousers off?

The side of Edda that loved her twin utterly was very happy to know that Grace's impulsive marriage had worked so well; they were as content a couple as one could find, devoted to each other, fretting when they were apart, wrapped in their two sons, Brian and John. Brian had been born on 2nd April 1928, and John fourteen months later on 31st May 1929. Though Grace hadn't managed to produce twins, she had produced her two children close enough together in age to suggest that they would enjoy an unusual bond of affection as they grew up. Certainly Brian, a frost-fair mite who walked and talked early, was passionately attached to his wee brother, now two months old, equally fair and equally forward. Of course there were those who predicted that this closeness in age would lead to lifelong brotherly hatred, but that was people.

Corunda had replaced district nurse Pauline Duncan with a fearsome dragon, Sister Monica Herd, who combined visits to the district's housebound invalids with visits to new mothers. An import from Sydney who revelled in driving miles to see the sick, Sister Herd was exactly who Grace needed, just as the ward sisters had been in her nursing days. In other words, Sister Herd frightened the living daylights out of Grace, who cleaned up baby messes at once and didn't allow the nappy situation to deteriorate as it had during Brian's diaper days. The prize Sister Herd dangled was a fully toilet-trained child at nine months: Grace worked with feverish zeal to achieve this freedom, terrified of Sister Herd's visits—oh, that tongue! A whiplash soaked in acid.

"Bear's due for another raise in pay," said Grace over tea and thin, delicate crumpets called pikelets, served with jam and whipped cream. "Honestly, I'm so lucky! My boys are well ahead of anybody else's the same age, I live in a nice house, and I have a good, teetotal husband—oh, how most husbands drink! The housekeeping money goes in beery urine."

Edda nodded absently, used to this patter. But she was never proof against her nephews—pray that at least one of them has a bit of Edda in him to stiffen all that sweetness and light! Bear and Grace are fine as long as things are fine, but how would they cope if disaster struck? Then she shook herself and admitted that the other part of her love for Grace rather purred at the prospect of a very small and transient misfortune for them. That was the part of Edda that didn't love her sister wholeheartedly; it loved, yes, but with qualifications and quantifications that grew every time she realized afresh how incompetent Grace was, how *stupid*. And how weak Bear was with her, the fool.

Even to having children, for heaven's sake! Bear had told her, man-to-man (and what does that say about you, Edda?) that he feared he and Grace were the kind who made a baby nearly every time they—well, did it.

"So I'm not going to do it until we can afford another one, and especially until Grace has had a good rest. That means," said Bear earnestly, "being abstemious while little John grows a whole lot more. When he's two, we'll go back to it."

"Have you discussed this with Grace?" Edda asked, winded.

"She'll like it. Oh, she loves me and—um—*it*. But a few minutes of pleasure can be followed by two years of mess and upheaval, and, well, Grace doesn't thrive in chaos."

"Most of the chaos," Edda said tartly, "she causes herself! But you do whatever you think you must, Bear."

She had left the subject severely alone thereafter, but if Bear and Grace truly were living without *it*, the chaos was no less. Grace just plain couldn't organize herself.

"What are you going to be when you grow up, Brian?" Edda asked the child, perched on her knee.

"A train driver," he said solemnly, eating his pikelet with jam and cream. "Big locomotives, but."

She burst out laughing. "Now why doesn't that surprise me?"

"Bear and I take them both down to the shunting yards when he's home," said Grace. Her glance slewed sideways, grey and cunning. "What about you and Jack?" she asked.

"What about us?" Edda countered, making Grace work for it.

"Well, you're an item, you have been for years. But you never seem to push things along, do you?"

"I don't want to—push things, as you phrase it, Grace. I don't want a husband or children."

"Well, you jolly well should!" said Grace crossly. "Don't you realize how awkward you're making life for me?"

Edda's eyes were always a little strange, but sometimes they could grow uncomfortably dangerous, as they did now while she stared at her twin. "How have I made your life awkward, dear?" she cooed dulcetly.

Grace shivered, but a lifetime of Edda made it possible for her to stick to her guns long enough to fire the round she had always intended to fire. "People gossip about Jack Thurlow and me," she said grittily, "and I dislike it. There's nothing going on between us because he's your friend, not mine. Now people are saying I made up the romance between you and Jack to hide my own involvement with him. That you and Jack are *my lie*!"

With a kiss for Brian's cheek, Edda put the child down and rose to her feet. "Hard cack, Grace!" she snapped. "If you think for one moment that I'm going to marry Jack Thurlow just to make *your* life more endurable, then you've got another think coming! Try looking after yourself, then you won't need Jack."

At the corner of Trelawney Way and Wallace Street an irate Edda, not looking, stepped into the road amid squealing brakes.

"Jesus, Edda, I nearly hit you!" Jack Thurlow was saying, his face white. "Get in, woman."

"Going to see Grace?" Edda asked, strangely unshaken.

"I was, but I'd rather see you. Busy?"

"I have to be near a phone, so how about my hospital home?" She laughed. "When I think of how Matron went on about men on the premises when we started training over three years ago! Now that we've turned into sisters, she can't say a thing."

They had been lovers for a year, and it had been good for Edda, who had done a copious amount of research before setting off down her primrose path to Sin. From Polynesian, Indian, Chinese, and various other sources she had worked out her personal "safe" period for sexual intercourse, and adhered to it inflexibly. Luckily her menstrual cycle was clockwork regular, so the safe segment ought to be sufficient. Thus far it had worked, which gave her additional faith in it, but no amount of physical desire in the world, she vowed, would see her break that schedule. She had also armed herself with a dose of ergotamine tartrate to dislodge an early fetus, and more than that she couldn't do.

"I'm chuffed," she said, putting the kettle on.

He gave her that wonderful smile. "Why, exactly?"

"Why do you suppose we drink so much strong tea?"

"Habit. It's a drug within the bounds of the law."

"Very true!"

"Why are you so chuffed, Edda?"

"We've managed to throw so much dust in Corunda's eyes that the whole town is convinced you're sleeping with Grace."

"Shit!" He sat up straight, face suddenly angry. "I might have known! *Grace?* Grace is a duty, not a thrill!"

Finished making the tea, Edda sat down. "What I've never really worked out," she said as she poured, "is why Grace became your duty. She's not your relative."

"It's impossible to explain to someone as efficient and well organized as you, Edda," he said, clearly at a loss. "Grace is one of those people who can't manage—"

"Oh, well do I know it!" Edda interrupted, voice bitter. "Yet before she went nursing, when we lived at the Rectory, Grace *was* organized. She always knew what she wanted and how to get it—even Father noticed that, and it foiled Maude on more than one occasion. Underneath all that woolly thoughtlessness there's a Grace quite capable of organization and method. It's just that she gets what she wants by being helpless, so the old Rectory efficiency has been buried. How deeply? I don't know. Except that it's there, Jack. Believe me, it's there." She shrugged. "Grace has bamboozled you into thinking you owe her a duty, but the truth is that you owe her nothing. You toil on her behalf, and she never pays. In other words, you give her charity. In which case, go to it, my friend."

"Yes, a charity duty," he said, nodding. "That fits. But I can't have Corunda thinking the worse of her."

"I have a partial answer," she said.

"You wouldn't be Edda if you didn't. Tell me!"

"We have to become less furtive about our relationship, is first and foremost. If you're known to be sleeping with me, Corunda will have to revise its theories about you and Grace. Yes, I know it's scandalous to be sleeping together, but for no other reason than the act. We're both unattached, free to love."

"What I call 'pristine scandal'—virtuous enough within itself," Jack said, laughter creeping into his eyes, "but all too easily tainted by exposure to the heat of human attention."

"Sometimes I suspect you got high marks at school, Jack. I'll have to leave your name and number with the hospital switchboard." His laughter spilled over. "That will definitely set the gossip ball rolling!"

Jack would be an ideal lover, the seventeen-year-old Edda had told herself, though it was toward the end of 1928 before she learned the fact as a fact, and then she had only her tastes to tell her. No matter that she couldn't compare: Jack knew how to please her.

It had happened suddenly, unexpectedly, in the glaring daylight by the river—anyone might have come along and found them! But no one had, and that set the pattern of their luck as this new phase in their old relationship flowered to full perfection.

Simply, they had been sitting side by side on the grass, the horses tethered to a tree, when he reached for her and kissed her with an experimental lightness that she ardently returned as soon as she got her breath back. The kiss deepened; an alien desire spread through her that prompted her to remove his shirt as fast as he was removing hers. No protests, no pretexts, no pretenses, no hesitation. Edda thought the feel of Jack's naked body against her own skin the most glorious sensation imaginable, something far beyond the blind groping of an ignorant brain. It reminded her of being lashed by that snake; she was sophisticated enough to know that the snake/man metaphor was very popular in psychiatric circles. But that didn't detract at all from the colossal wrench of utter pleasure invading her, or the feel of those muscles.

And her luck had held: no pregnancy, because his impulse had occurred during her safe period. After those first frenzied couplings that had come almost without pause, Jack lay so exhausted that Edda, invigorated rather than fatigued, was able to explain her system of birth control, all worked out, but with no place to go until this day. Her energy and logic took him aback, but he listened, and, wanting no babies himself, he readily agreed to limit their sexual activity to her safe times. In fact, it had been a shock to find her a virgin; she gave a flawless imitation of an experienced woman of the world, and she was twenty-three. The little fraud! But at least she had prepared for this day, which made her a rare virgin indeed.

Now, of course, Jack knew Edda well enough to obey orders; if Grace needed their affair to be made public, then so be it. The worst repercussions would fall on Edda, who surely knew what she was unleashing. His own reputation would be enhanced. Thus Jack cooperated willingly in letting Corunda know which Latimer girl he was entertaining in a biblical way.

Edda broke the news to Grace personally on her next visit, and, hurting because she was wounded, spoke extremely frankly.

Quite what reaction she had expected Edda hadn't known, save that she thought Grace would be very pleased, and loved her enough to feel glad she, too, had some masculine company.

What Edda saw was a stiffening of Grace's body, an expression of blazing anger on that pinched little face—why was it pinched? Had the person inside it shrunk? And why did Grace's eyes blaze?

"You—you snake in the grass!"

A confounded Edda drew back. "I beg your pardon?"

"You bitch! You traitor! You selfish, selfish cow!" Grace cried, beside herself. "Why did you have to steal Jack, of all men? Aren't there enough others in Corunda for you?"

Edda tried, hanging desperately onto her temper. "The last time I saw you, you complained to me that Corunda deemed Jack Thurlow your lover, and you asked me to help allay that. I have obeyed your request. Corunda knows which woman Jack Thurlow is really involved with, and it isn't you."

"Bitch! You stole him from me!"

"Bullshit I did, you stupid ninny!" said Edda, temper going. "Jack belonged to me, not to you, always! I introduced him to you, remember? How could I steal from you what you've never, never owned? You have a husband, a really decent one at that—why should you need any part of *my* lover?"

"Bitch! Thief! Jack is my friend! *My friend!* My husband approves, and if he approves, what business is it of anyone else's? Leave Jack Thurlow alone, you—you snake!"

Little Brian was standing, arms wrapped around his baby brother, looking from his mother to his beloved aunt in complete bewilderment, his clear blue eyes full of unshed tears. Neither Grace nor Edda noticed him.

"I see," said Edda, drawing on a pair of red kid gloves. She was looking particularly attractive in one of the newer styles, waisted and longer, in the same stunning red. Nor was she wearing a hat, preferring to let the world see her black hair immaculately waved in the new fashion, curling at its ends. The outfit had struck Grace like a hammer, made her feel dowdy, parochial, the housewife-mother-of-two, stuck in a dreary rut.

Edda's bag was black patent leather with a big red kid bow across its front; she clipped it under her arm and turned on one fashionable black patent heel. "A ridiculous conversation, Grace, that I am hereby terminating. Your trouble, sister, is that you're spoiled and indulged by two men, to one of whom you have no legal claim. If they didn't run after you, you'd be much better off."

Grace opened her mouth, burst into tears, and howled; so did Brian, equally noisily. Edda stalked to the door.

"Another thing," she said, opening the door. "Choose your audience. The only thing this bout of waterworks does for me is make me want to smack you—hard!" And she was out, she was gone.

At the front gate she began to tremble, but there were too many curtains pulled partway back to emulate Grace. Chin in the air, Edda walked down the street looking as if she owned it, only then remembering that she hadn't told Grace about Dr. Charles Burdum, who Corunda gossip said was taking over the hospital.

Only Tufts weathered those confused, uncertain weeks between the death of Dr. Francis Campbell and the appointment of the new General Superintendent, for she floated above an opalescent haze of happiness nothing had prepared her for. On the surface, her new position as Sister Tutor wasn't very demanding, as she would have a mere eight trainees under her wing, but she also saw that she could train the West Enders left until time eliminated them; some at least would repay the effort. That Matron had given her leeway to implement her ideas was wonderful, for there were yet other areas where a Sister Tutor's hand could make vast differences. No one could work at Corunda Base for three years and be unaware how indifferent the domestic and culinary staff were to the purposes of a hospital. Tufts wanted to change that, too, make the wardsmaids understand what a germ was and where it lurked, make the cooks and kitchen staff proud to serve tasty meals that earned them praise from all who ate them. Domestic and Culinary came under the care of a deputy matron of retirement age, Anne Harding, one of those relics of a bygone era all institutions seem to harbor in dark and dusty corners. Well, all of it had to change. No more feeding everybody for sixpence a day. Only how was she going to go about dragging Domestic and Culinary into the twentieth century?

If a secret glow of warmth cocooned her heart, that was because she was back on the old terms with Liam Finucan, who had suffered the sixteen months of his divorce suit as unobtrusively as possible, and emerged at its end legally severed from his faithless wife and under no obligation to pay her something known as alimony. That in spite of the judicial ruling he did pay Eris a small allowance was not symptomatic of weakness but of compassion; he couldn't live with the thought that a partner of fifteen years left the union without the prospect of living any better than her man-friend-of-the-moment decided.

"I'm glad you pay her something," Tufts said as she bustled around the pathologist's office. "Oh, Liam, what a mess you've let this place become! You didn't used to be so untidy."

"I missed my chief assistant, even if she was never official. I could have murdered Gertie Newdigate," he said, watching her.

Tufts giggled. "Gertie! The name doesn't suit her one bit."

"No, but it probably pushed her into an early dragonhood."

"What's the lab like?"

"In fine form. After you left I buckled down and taught Billy to be a much better technician than he was. Now I have a second technician, Allen, who's better trained and qualified."

"So all I have to do is sort out your office."

"Yes." The dark grey eyes gleamed. "I saved it for you."

"Big of you. Well, come on, man, chop-chop! Sort all these files into alphabetical order and then we'll look at them, decide if the labels are the right ones, and *then* file them."

"You're a lot bossier, Heather."

"Tufts, not Heather. And as I'm now a sister, of course I'm bossier. You and I have to produce training schedules of all sorts, but we can't do that until your office is in order."

He hadn't changed a bit, she concluded as the shambles disappeared before a formidable new organization—far more profound than any he had ever practiced before. Necessary, if either of them was to be able to put an unerring finger on a file or book or paper without hesitation. The hospital carpenter, who had a lot of free time, suddenly found himself busier than he had been in years; Tufts commissioned him to make proper drawer units for all Liam's assortment of records. Since the job appealed to him and he liked Dr. Finucan, the carpenter unfurled the wings of a talented cabinetmaker, and dowered Liam's office with quite beautiful cabinetry, all stained a matching pale mahogany.

"Which means," said Tufts with huge enthusiasm, "that when I'm finished with your office, it will look far spiffier than the Superintendent's. I like that, so you're going to cough up for a Persian carpet on the floor and some prestigious etchings on the walls. I'm sending your books to a good binder—they'll look spiffy leather-bound and gilt-lettered."

As each directive was issued he nodded mutely, then obeyed it; she had that effect, Sister Tutor.

Who doted publicly on Liam Finucan, with curious consequences. Even including the sixteen-month hiatus of a divorce that severely curtailed their personal relationship, Liam and Tufts had been such good friends and colleagues for so long that the entire staff of Corunda Base *knew* there was nothing shady going on between them. "The Experiment" was a good example. Tufts had found two other men on the staff whose hair flopped in their eyes and blinded them, and bought each one a Mason Pearson hairbrush. Then every morning she attacked the floppy lock, assaulting the scalp and its follicles so ruthlessly that, as the days turned into weeks and the weeks into months, the hair began to grow in the opposite direction. Each man's lock was measured with calipers on the first of the month and the measurements entered in a journal, together with photographs. And by winter of 1929, The Experiment had succeeded—each man's lock of hair no longer blinded him. Her two other guinea pigs were given Sister Tutor's blessing and dismissed, but Liam never was. Tufts got a kick out of the project, and saved her most difficult problems or questions for hairbrush time. People viewed it as an intrinsic part of a very special, completely Platonic friendship.

Interestingly, the one name never mentioned on the gossip grapevine was Tufts Scobie's. Given that she was quite stunningly pretty, her Diana-the-Goddess image puzzled people on early contact, but longer acquaintance showed them it was part of her mystique.

The man who understood Tufts's nature best was Liam Finucan, who loved her with every particle of his being, and never thought of her as Tufts. Perhaps it was his forties endowed Liam with the wisdom never to declare his love, or perhaps it had all to do with a unique sensitivity of the soul; whatever the root cause was, he loved in the complete silence that doesn't give itself away even by a fleeting look or a tiny yet betraying gesture. Liam and Heather were absolute best friends.

The winter months of 1929 saw Corunda Base Hospital in a worse state of flux than anyone remembered, for the Board was engaged in a storm of cables with Manchester and Dr. Charles Burdum. No new superintendent was contemplated for the moment.

The junior sisters—even Tufts, with a firm job offer—were in a state of Limbo, a name given it by Edda because it was good and blessed, but had no God; the Superintendent was hospital God.

Uncertainty over their futures hovered perpetually—would the new Super be another Frank, or his opposite? It began to seem to Edda that she would be leaving for parts unknown, especially given the shattering quarrel with Grace, who was behaving like someone Edda had never met—indeed, Grace *refused* to meet! Oh, to think that my *twin* sister damns me as a trollop! Unconscionable! She's turned into a fishwife who'd burn me as a witch!

Superintendent Francis Campbell had been a conservative stick-in-the-mud whose sole venture into nursing training, the Latimers, had been virtually forced upon him; repercussions, like the West Enders now starting to train and register in the new way, had annoyed him greatly. What he visualized was a grossly increasing budget for nurse wages and salaries in years to come. Yes, as trainees they were paid a pittance, but they had to be housed, fed, taught, and supervised, and when they achieved their registrations they cost far more than old-style West Enders. Almost his last thought before dying was that the eight trainees beginning were all West Enders: his cheap nursing asset was no more. How *dared* West Enders do this? Good-for-nothing trollops! He might have gone on in this vein, had he not died instead.

Dr. Campbell's tenure of the chief hospital position far predated the Great War, and many of the new techniques and treatments had passed him by; those that had not been forced upon him by his two senior surgeons, three senior physicians, his anesthetist, and that perennial nuisance, Ned Mason the obstetrician, were not adopted. Such as the appointment of a radiologist whose job would have been to run a proper X-ray department containing the very latest X-ray equipment, and a psychiatrist for the asylum. As far as Dr. Frank Campbell was concerned, the main function of his hospital was to keep its costs right down and incur no new expenses in the name of medical progress. Pah! Hospitals were places to die in. If you didn't die, you were lucky. Treatment only slowed the dying down.

To compound the woes of the new junior sisters, Matron and her two deputies spent the rest of that winter of 1929, until September, in getting their records and arguments into an order that would impress the new superintendent; he would see the nursing department as a collection of disciplined individuals able to spare him much time and energy when it came to every aspect of nursing's nature. The hospital Secretary, Walter Paulet, was similarly closeted with his accounts department; rumor had it tearing their scant hair out by its roots over the lack of system in Frank Campbell's paperwork. Somehow when they were reduced to black figures on white paper, Dr. Campbell's machinations to feed everyone for sixpence a day looked—well, rather appalling.

But, as luckily is the way with most institutions, Corunda Base Hospital itself continued to function on doctors, nurses, domestic staff, food preparers, and ancillary staff in the same old way, so that the patients lived (or died) in relative ignorance of the drama going on at an executive level. Indeed, it was a rare patient even knew that a hospital had executives.

Informed that she was on three days off, Kitty Latimer promptly packed a suitcase, waved her sisters a merry farewell, and set off for Sydney. There she occupied a room at the Country Women's Club and plunged into a happy frenzy of shopping, seeing films, and going to every play and exhibition Sydney was offering. Talking pictures were just coming in, and she wasn't sure if she liked them very much—now that the mouths were uttering words rather than miming dramatic phrases echoed on a fancy blackboard, the actors seemed too stagey, too artificial, even too amusing—and did the men really have to wear so much feminine-looking makeup? If talking pictures were to survive, thought Kitty, the whole technique of making them would have to change.

However, at the end of her three days she installed herself in a first-class compartment on the Melbourne day train, as all through expresses had to stop in Corunda to drop their second locomotive; on a through express it was a three-hour journey that she loved, especially given the fact that she usually managed to keep the whole six-passenger compartment to herself.

But not, alas, today. Having settled in her window seat and suggestively pulled the corridor blinds down to semaphore a message that the compartment was full, Kitty kicked off her new pink kid shoes—they were pinching at the heels—and opened the romance novel she was reading with half her mind, thus leaving the other half free to wander in more unconscious realms. The last thing a nurse needed was grim reality in a book. Where

Kitty was wiser than most was in understanding that her romance author undoubtedly, in her real life, knew all about grim reality.

The sliding door onto the corridor opened, a head poked in, then the door opened fully to admit a man.

"Oh, good!" he said, making for the other window seat.

Kitty lifted her head. "This is a nonsmoking compartment," she said in freezing tones.

"I can read," he said, pointing, then looked at her and stared in open rudeness. "Marion Davies!" he exclaimed.

"Piss off, you presumptuous little twerp!" Kitty snapped. "If you insist on coming in here, don't you dare sit opposite me! Take a seat at the corridor end, keep your remarks to yourself, and leave me a little privacy. Otherwise I'll call the conductor."

A shrug; he threw his case up onto the overhead rack and sat down at the corridor end, but facing her. Deprived of a window, he looked at the NSWGR antimacassars shielding the velvet squabs.

Kitty returned to her book. Underneath her icy composure she was seething. How dared he! A dapper little chap, not above five feet four inches tall, wearing a pin-striped navy blue suit complete with waistcoat, gold watch, fob, and chain; a magnificent cabochon ruby ring adorned his left hand, another ruby was stuck in what looked like an old school tie, and his cuff links each bore a ruby. His feet, she noted in tickled delight, were sheathed in handmade shoes that bore distinct heels—he was extremely conscious of his diminutive size, then. I'll bet he struts like a bantam rooster, she thought, assimilating all this with her unusually acute peripheral vision, the gift of three years as a nurse trained to see almost around corners. He has a Napoleon complex, or so the alienists are calling it, and *doesn't* he love to strut, the little poseur?

His hair was thick, wiry, and curling, a genuine guinea-gold color also present in his brows and lashes, though as yet Kitty had no idea what color his eyes were, beyond some shade around tawny. Darkish skin that was already tanned, an extremely close shave, and a face she was obliged to admit she thought fascinating, though not because it awed or attracted her. Simply, it didn't seem to know whether it was ugly or handsome, and changed while you looked at it. One visage had film star properties, as beautiful as the extras who adorned a film's background crowds and eclipsed the leading man. Had he been taller and owned this face alone, he might have been a king or a president or the leader of a religious sect. As it was, his second visage negated any hope of being freely gifted with the world. This face belonged to a gargoyle or perhaps a castrated satyr; ugly and twisted, it had the power to turn the film star features into a sinister map as hard as heartless.

Whoever this man is, he frightens me, Kitty thought, her book unable to compete with such an authentic out-of-the-pages-of-history character. Yes, he was going to matter, if for no other reason than he'd die in the trying. Judging by the rubies, the gold, and the hand tailoring, a rich man—he'd be getting off in Corunda because those were Corunda pigeon's-blood rubies, the world's most coveted and expensive. And with that dipped-in-a-crucible-of-gold look to him, he's a Burdum.

The penny dropped; with a great effort Kitty kept her eyes on her book and her breathing regular. Unless she was mistaken, this was Dr. Charles Henry Burdum, late of the Manchester Royal Infirmary, and going to Corunda to become superintendent of the hospital. Small fry! He could go to Bart's or the Middlesex or Guy's, so what has brought him to a place he doesn't know from a bar of soap? He's a Pommy, not an Australian, and I never saw a man less suited for Australian life. A wee bantam rooster . . .

After that initial exchange the three hours passed without a word; as was his wont, Sid the conductor arrived with five minutes to spare, took Kitty's suitcase down and carried it along the corridor to the carriage door, where he waited, yarning to Kitty, whom he knew from many train trips. The dapper stranger was forced to carry his own bag and stand behind them as the two big locomotives pulled in, groaning and clanking, to stop at the station. Edda was there to meet her, talking to old Tom Burdum.

"Where did you get that dress?" Edda demanded, with no eyes for the man as Tom Burdum left her to hobble forward.

"Mark Foy's. I found a gorgeous one for you, snake lady." Kitty tucked a hand through her sister's arm and led her away. "Turn back and take a squizzy at the chap old Tom is meeting."

"Jeeeeesus! What a Little Lord Fauntleroy!"

"Bang on, Edda. I can't be absolutely sure, but I'm willing to place a hefty bet that he's Dr. Charles Burdum, therefore the new superintendent."

"Corunda hasn't been told a new one's been appointed yet."

"Then perhaps he's come to inspect the place, with a view to declining." Kitty skipped. "We shared a compartment and I had to put him in his place."

"Oh! Did he actually put the hard word on you, Kits?"

"No. He called me Marion Davies."

"That's worse. Your reply was salty—or worse."

"Just as salty as the Dead Sea. Pickled in brine! I told him to piss off. We rode the rest of the way in frigid silence."

Edda had turned and was blatantly staring at the newcomer. "Well, he's a Burdum, and he's more conceited than Lucifer. What a face! Like Janus."

"Yes, poor chap."

"You feel sorry for him?" Edda asked incredulously.

"Very. Look at his handmade shoes, dear. Two-inch heels. He's a living, breathing Napoleon complex. Gifted with everything except the height no man can bear to be without."

"Yes, I see what you mean." Edda brightened. "Still, if he does decide to take the job, he'll probably settle down after the worst is over. So he doesn't know you're a nurse?"

"He has no idea."

"What fun when he finds out!"

If Charles Burdum had been a shock to Kitty, it was as nothing compared to his effect on old Tom Burdum, who had been waiting ninety-five years for the appearance of a permanent heir. He had gone to the station expecting to meet someone who looked like Jack Thurlow; instead, he found a lordly midget whose suit had been tailored in Savile Row and shirt made by Turnbull & Asser. With a Balliol tie, no less! Though that Tom only discovered because he asked, expecting a joking answer. But not from this fellow, who oozed self-confidence, walked as if he had a poker rammed up his arse (so Tom told Jack later), and was very put out because the train conductor hadn't lifted down and carried his suitcase.

"In Australia, conductors don't," said Tom, not knowing how else to disillusion him. "In Australia, no one waits on you."

"He was quick enough to carry the little madam's case!" Charles Burdum said in a clipped, not quite pear-shaped accent.

"Who, Kitty Latimer?" Old Tom chuckled. "A man would have to be dead not to want to carry Kitty's case."

"She told me to piss off—not the language of a lady."

"Tch! I'm sure you deserved it, Charlie."

"Don't call me Charlie, my name is Charles."

"If you stay in Corunda, it'll be Charlie. Or Chikker."

"*What?*"

"No airs and graces in this part of the world, grandson. I speak because someone has to, and I'd rather it were me than, for instance, your cousin Jack Thurlow. He's my other heir, except that he doesn't want to be the heir. You'll inherit the title of leading light in Corunda—if you go about it the right way," old Tom said, bidding a man load three suitcases into the back of his Daimler. "Do you have more luggage in the guard's van? Yes? Then give the tickets to Merv here and he'll collect and deliver them for you." He waited while Charles found his luggage tags and handed them over, together with a five-pound note that had the man gobbling. "Tch!" said old Tom. "That was silly, Charlie! Never tip a man earning wages. I pay Merv well enough not to need tips. Now you've made him discontented with a very fair wage, all because where you come from, he wouldn't earn a very fair wage, and would depend on tips to eke it out. Lesson number one."

They settled in the open Daimler Tonneau, its canopy folded. "As Hannah, my wife, is also in her nineties, we haven't put you up at our property, *Burdumbo.* You're at the Grand Hotel on Ferguson Street—a hop, skip, and jump from the hospital as well as George Street, which isn't a bad shopping center—even has a department store. Though be warned! If you want a really decent feed, go to the Olympus or the Parthenon. They're both run by Greeks, and there's nothing in it for quality—superb steaks!"

Old Tom rambled on as the big car, buffeted by a sharp wind, drove through a landscape that resembled an extremely untidy rural England—no neat barnyard complexes but plenty of tumbledown sheds, no stone fences but barbed wire strung between ugly posts, rounded hills crowned not with coppices but clumps of granite boulders. It was not the scorching semi-desert of his imaginings, but it wasn't Europe either, even Greece or Majorca.

People were staring at him, though not in admiration. Some grinned openly, most just looked interested, the way they would at a zebra or giraffe. His great intelligence informed him this was chiefly because of his dress. A few locals did wear three-piece suits, but shabby and years out of date. Most, including old Tom, favored moleskin trousers, a shirt and tweed jacket, elastic-sided riding boots, and low-crowned, broad-brimmed felt hat. The women wore ghastly early-twenties, unfashionable clothes, while some, he noted in horrified fascination, actually strolled around town in men's riding gear, right down to the elastic-sided boots and the broad-brimmed hat—*and nobody seemed to think them peculiar!* So where were the women like that ravishing girl on the train and the girl who met her? They had been dressed in the height of the mode! But his extensive tour revealed no women like them. Well, they had not been figments of his imagination, they did exist in this benighted town somewhere.

He was being shown everything, and had now reached the public buildings on Victoria Street, which ran parallel to George one block over. Town hall, municipal services, the hospital, St. Mark's Church of England and Rectory—oh, would it never end?

Then his hotel finally appeared, one of those frightful Bournemouth or Bognor establishments constructed for the lower middle class who had saved all year to enjoy a week's seaside holiday. Inside the Grand were rather inexpertly painted red columns, plush red wallpaper, wooden floors that echoed around immensely high ceilings, a dining room wherein he'd bet all soups tasted of potato and all meats of old fowl. Dear God! 11,000 miles for *this*?

Well, he knew why, but old Tom Burdum didn't—nor would he. Of course he had no idea that Corunda contained people of Maude's caliber, so thought the sly grins everyone gave him were due to his hand-tailored, dandified clothes. If he had been aware that all Corunda knew of Sybil the duke's daughter before he arrived, he would have fled screaming, and Corunda would never have known him.

Toward the end of August 1929, when he did arrive in Corunda, Charles Burdum still hurt so badly that he was convinced no worse pain would ever be visited upon him. Though his smiles were broad and his manner cheerful, they hid a damaged soul. His old ambitions were dead; all he had salvaged were material possessions.

His love for Sybil had been genuine, as was her love for him. It hadn't occurred to either of them that the duke might think a Charles Burdum wasn't good enough to marry his daughter, but when Charles applied for her hand in marriage, so it turned out. Sybil would go to a husband with ancestors worthy of an eighth duke's line; money and brains were insufficient, especially in a man so appallingly short in stature. The interview with the duke over, Charles was hideously conscious that of all the hurts it had produced, the one about his height had galled the most. Naturally, he knew the identity of Sybil's ducally approved husband—six feet three inches tall—and blamed his failure on his lack of stature. If one found the right genealogical researchers, one could prove descent from William the Conqueror *and* Harold Godwineson.

His self-image shattered, his ego so mauled that he couldn't bear to see all those smirking faces, Charles buried himself in Manchester's illnesses. When that didn't work, he bit the bullet and spent time in the City of London dealing with his fortune, then fled England. Not good enough, eh? Well, there was another place where he could make a splash—admittedly a smaller puddle, but he'd be a much bigger frog, and that appealed strongly to a very small man. Prime Minister—now that was a prize worth going after, even if it were only a colonial prime ministership. Canada hadn't beckoned; his French was nonexistent, and Canada was so *cold*. Whereas in New South Wales he owned land, mineral wealth, family—why, he'd be Prime Minister of Australia in no time!

Upstairs in his hotel room, a gloomy cavern of browns and beiges and a horrible mustard yellow, he ran a bath and pulled on a robe. Of course there was no room service, but a word with the duty manager secured a pot of execrable coffee and a plate of ham sandwiches. The food was surprisingly good; the bread was home-baked, the ham sugar-cured and juicy. He ate hungrily, thinking, scheming, and all revolving around his observations of Corunda as well as old Tom's comments.

In future, no Savile Row suits, no ruby accessories; instead, soft shirts complete with collars and cuffs. A diminished English accent, easy for a natural mimic like Charles; he'd find a voice that didn't grate on idiotically oversensitive Australian ears! This afternoon he'd go to the shops and buy the right kind of apparel, then tomorrow he'd skulk around the town anonymously to do some research. If his plans were to succeed, he would have to know a great deal more about Corunda, its importance in the Australian scheme of things, its importance in its own eyes, and what its inhabitants expected of the men who led them, both publicly and politically.

He had automatically assumed that this massive ex-colony of Australia would differ little from England; to discover enormous differences was coming as a series of shocks that showed no sign of diminishing. This was a far different place that had evolved down very strange roads. People called Corunda "very English," but to the very English Charles it was ugly, ramshackle, tasteless, and vulgar. How was he ever going to survive here if he took the superintendent's position?

By the time that Tom and Hannah picked him up to go to dinner at the Parthenon—*a Greek café!*—he had made his preliminary decisions, the first of which was not to wear black tie. By now he was wondering whether there was ever a black tie dinner in Corunda. He was beginning to doubt it. However, the Greek café more than made up for the limitations of its food menu by serving Tom and his party a magnificent dry white wine and an even better red—*Australian* wines! But they were world class!

"Have the steak and chips, everyone does," Hannah advised.

"I'm afraid I'm not in the habit of eating steak," Charles said charmingly. "It's considered crass in England. However, Grandmother, when in Rome I shall be a Roman, and try to acquire a taste for it. I suspect its lack of popularity in England is due to its astronomical price."

"Then have the lamb cutlets, they're local," said Tom.

So Charles opted for the lamb cutlets, which would have been delicious had they not been so thoroughly cooked. The steak Tom and Hannah were eating with gusto, he noted, was also thoroughly cooked. Underdone was not on the menu.

Superb meat cooked to death, and deep-fried potatoes with everything. No sauces that take three days to make—even, I'll bet, in Sydney's top restaurants. Fried or grilled anything, but not real haute cuisine.

"Tell me about that ravishingly pretty girl on the train," he said, having declined dessert, which consisted of an ice-cream sundae or a banana split. The coffee, he found, was drinkable if he ordered it Greek-style, brewed with the grounds in a small copper pot. How to get decent coffee? Though his meal with the Burdums told him that no one in Corunda drank coffee; they drank tea so strong it looked black, and this, apparently, the Parthenon made exactly the way the natives liked it. I am now marooned in an ocean of coal-tar tea, a substance I hate!

"Kitty Latimer," said old Tom thoughtfully. "There are four Latimer girls, the daughters of our Church of England minister, Tom Latimer. Corunda, incidentally, is full of Toms. Down the road in Bardoo they're mostly Daves, while out Doobar way they're Bills. Corbi is solid Bobs. I've no idea why."

"Kitty?" Charles prompted gently.

"Oh yes, Kitty. The Rector's had two wives. His first one died giving birth to twin girls, Edda and Grace. That was Edda met Kitty at the station—tall, slinky girl. Maude Scobie was the second wife—she'd been Rectory housekeeper." A dry chuckle escaped. "When Adelaide died, Maude married Tom Latimer quick as a wink. *She* gave birth to a second set of twins, Heather and Kitty. Odd, isn't it? Off to the races only twice, but four fine fillies not even two years apart."

"Is it a wealthy family?"

"Not really, though Kitty has more than the other three, thanks to Maude's intrigues over a will."

"Sounds a trifle unfair," Charles ventured, tone casual.

"Oh, it was! Maude dotes on Kitty, but doesn't care for the others the way a mother should. I'm not being malicious—it's general knowledge from the West End to Catholic Hill."

"The other three must loathe Kitty," Charles said.

"Oh, no!" Hannah cried, and laughed. "You'll never meet four sisters as devoted to each other as the Latimers. Why, I have no idea, but Kitty seems to be the one the others love and protect the most. They adore Kitty, absolutely."

Time to ingratiate himself a little. "Grandfather, sir, you won't be getting any bills from the Grand, for all you instructed them to send my expenses to you. I'm quite rich enough to pay my own way, and have told the Grand I'll be paying." He paused, shot old Tom a keen look out of eyes that were a muddy mixture of grey, green, and gold-brown. "One thing you could do for me is recommend a bank. I have a letter of credit on my London bank, but if

I should take the Superintendency, I'll need to transfer more funds and establish a solid financial reputation here. I hope, incidentally, that the local banks are modern enough to cable funds, even very large amounts?"

"We'll see Les Kimball at the Rural Bank tomorrow afternoon," Tom said warmly. "You may as well bank with the Rural, all the Burdums do— or have. It's a modern establishment, the bank of the New South Wales Government. Is that what you want?"

"Thank you, yes."

"I was under the impression that my son, Henry, remained a no-hoper after he left New South Wales," old Tom said as he broached his third cup of tea.

Charles shrugged. "It would appear not, Grandfather. He founded an insurance company, became one of Lloyd's underwriters, and married into the Lancashire plutocracy. As an only child, I inherited a fortune when he died—but, as you probably know, by then he had become what the English call eccentric, denied his wealth and family, and chose to live like a funded itinerant."

"And your mother too is dead, I understand?"

"When I was born," Charles said in a tone of voice that indicated he didn't wish to talk about her. As if to soften this, he gave an irresistible smile and said, "Who will give me an honest assessment of the Corunda Base Hospital? I mean someone who knows the place inside out, has seniority yet no desire to be its superintendent, and isn't afraid of treading on a few medical toes when he gives his opinions?"

"Liam Finucan," said old Hannah instantly.

Old Tom nodded. "Yes, Charlie, he's your man. I might be on the verge of ninety-six and long past serving on the Hospital Board, but I swear Liam is the only senior medical man situated to help you—and he will help you. He's staff, a true pathologist with no private practice. Add, a Protestant Ulsterman who qualified in London—too good for Corunda, which got him because of his marriage to a Corunda girl. She was a trollop and they're now divorced, but by nature he's really a bachelor. I can arrange for you to see him tomorrow." He frowned. "Can you afford a car?"

"I have a Packard in the process of being delivered to me from Sydney. It's due to arrive early in the morning."

"An American car rather than an English one?"

"I note your car is German, sir." The face, such an intriguing blend of beauty and ugliness, creased up impishly. "I bought it due to its color—maroon, not the inevitable black."

"I thought all cars had to be black!" said old Hannah, shocked.

"For which, blame Henry Ford." Charles finished the last of his Hunter Valley claret and politely stifled a yawn. Time for bed.

When Charles met Dr. Liam Finucan the following afternoon, it would have been difficult for Kitty Latimer to have identified him as the same man were it not for his height. He was wearing moleskin trousers of the sort could double for riding breeches, a soft-collared white shirt with Balliol tie, a tweed jacket, elastic-sided boots (with built-up heels—cunning!), and a broad-brimmed felt hat. Only the tendency to strut hadn't vanished, though he was trying to lessen it; these rude Colonials didn't bother hiding their amusement at any kind of affectation, especially in a man, and they were as unkind as ruthless. The concept of masculinity, he was learning, was forged in hardened steel.

Dr. Liam Finucan, who had been in Corunda for eighteen years, fancied that Dr. Charles Burdum looked like a Burdum without the erosion of barbed wire and Solvol soap—a soft fellow, as the English were if their class was elevated enough. And he wore a ruby ring on his left little finger, a very strange, effeminate conceit in this part of the world. His eyes were the color of a British soldier's Great War uniform, a coppery khaki more rust than green, and he was quite as ugly as he was handsome. However, Liam found him curiously likable, and had no axes to grind about the vacant superintendency, so cherished no preconceived resentments.

"If I'm to consider taking the job," Charles said in the Grand lounge over drinks with Liam, "I need an unbiased report from someone who knows all the ins and outs. My grandparents say you're my best bet, so here I am. What do you consider the allurements of this job as it's being offered to me?"

"The run-down nature of the place," Liam said without a moment's hesitation. "Frank Campbell was a penny-pinching Scot who scrimped and cut corners on everything. All that's carried Corunda Base through twenty-five years of his administration are the quality of the medicine and the nursing, both achieved against the odds. At the root of the trouble was the Hospital Board's love of old Frank's parsimony—*wicked*! It rejoiced in the fact that he fed the patients and staff alike on sixpence a day and made the nurses darn the linen on duty. For me, the pathologist, it meant a chronic shortage of reagents, chemicals, glassware, stains, equipment—you name it! I've found it much easier to get major apparatus because any man of enterprise can coax a willing donor into buying an automatic microtome blade sharpener or an imposing microscope. No, where the place has hurt the most has been in basic supplies, from toilet paper to scrubbing brushes and high-watt light bulbs. Do you know that babies are nursed on newspaper? Antimony is *toxic*! All to save the linen, not to mention the expense of laundering! While the Board members cheer Frank on! Weasels? I'd call them cockroaches!"

"Do they know the grisly details, or just the figures?"

"Just the figures, of course. The Reverend Latimer would've been horrified if he'd known the details. But he could have found out."

"If it means extra effort, Liam, people won't exert themselves."

"The food is terrible, really terrible, yet out at Bardoo is a hospital farm and convalescent home that should be producing milk, cream, eggs, pork, and some vegetables in season. The convalescent side Frank turned into a boardinghouse, and the edibles that should have gone to the hospital kitchens he sold to local shops or suppliers. Digusting! *Wicked!*" The softly accented voice, modified by so long in Australia, had not so much risen, as hardened. "I tell you, Charlie, that man should rot in a worse hell than Lucifer could devise. He made a profit out of sickness and death."

"By Jove!" Charles exclaimed, having no idea what phrase an Australian would use. "Is there State Government money as well?"

"Yes, of course, but I'd be willing to wager more was saved than ever spent. Frank was brilliant at fiddling the books, though he never took a farthing for himself. There have been dozens and dozens of bequests to the hospital—it's a favorite charity. But nothing has ever been spent unless on a specifically named item."

"This is wonderful!" Charles cried. "I'd envisioned years of fighting the faceless slugs of a civil service for the funds to make Corunda Base as modern as the Mayo Clinic, but now you tell me there's actually money in the bank? How much? Six figures?"

"Seven figures," Liam said with angry emphasis. "There are four million pounds residing in the Corunda branches of several big Australian banks. That's why Frank Campbell was so hated—he was sitting on a fortune he refused to spend."

Charles was gaping. "Four million? That's impossible!"

"Not when you think about it," Liam said flatly. "Take the Treadby ruby bequest. The patch ran out in 1923, but the bequest came into being in 1898—the first £100,000 in each year were to go to Corunda Base, and did. Not a single penny of it was ever spent, including the miserable interest the banks pay. All the result of a blazing row between Walter Treadby and his sons. Walter changed his will and died two days later, an after-effect of apoplectic tendencies that dumped the Treadby rubies in Frank Campbell's undeserving lap for twenty-five years. Had Walter lived a further two days, he would have removed the new codicil from his will."

The laughter broke through; Charles roared with it. "Never underestimate a tendency to apoplexy! Tell me of the Hospital Board."

"The Board's as bad as Frank was. Well, they're Frank's own creatures, he hand-picked them to obey his every dictate, and they did. For example, the nurses, always recruited from poor families—girls without any education or hope of registering later on, but splendid nurses he paid virtually nothing. The land is tax- and rate-free, the electrical power supply negotiated down to next to nothing, and the gas dirt cheap."

"No wonder the Board never opposed him," said Charles, tone tinged with admiration. "The man was a genius of sorts." He looked suddenly cunning. "I don't suppose you'd like to be the Deputy Super?" he asked.

"No, thank you!" Liam snapped. "I'll gladly help you all I possibly can, Charles, but my ambitions are confined to having the best pathology department in the state, from analytical equipment to the breadth of its functions and facilities. I also want a radiologist in a separate radiology department, a staff appointment rather than a private practitioner. I have been used as the radiologist when I have neither the time nor the talent—I can see a break, but hairline fractures? I cringe. Erich Herzen is better, but he's not trained, either. We need a true radiologist capable of more complex techniques, and we need an X-ray technician."

"I see X-ray is a sore point, Liam, but I give you my word that when the dust settles, radiology will be a department of its own having nothing to do with pathology," Charles said, smiling. "It also doesn't escape me that this hospital has an excellent pathologist. Now tell me about the cheap nurses."

This interview plus several more endowed Charles Burdum with a knowledge of Corunda Base Hospital that most of the men involved in the selection of a new Superintendent never expected or suspected. Charles acquired a reputation for uncanny shrewdness, and also took the job. The day after he was officially informed of his success, he started work; no pussyfooting around for the new Superintendent!

Between his arrival on the Melbourne day express and the notice of his appointment in the *Corunda Post*, three weeks had elapsed. During them, old Tom Burdum gifted his grandson with Burdum House, the mansion Henry Burdum, the founder of the family, had built on the heights atop Catholic Hill, which was Corunda's best residential district. Charles staffed it at once from maids to groundsmen, pulled the dustcovers off the furniture, and then laid plans for a two-acre garden in the style of Inigo Jones. His maroon Packard had arrived together with two small flivvers for running around in when the big car was too ostentatious; and a carrier from Sydney delivered some ten huge trunks packed with belongings from England that apparently Charles could not live without. His ten thousand books, he told his grandparents, were crated and warehoused in London, but would not make the six-week sea journey until he converted one of Burdum House's larger rooms into a proper library.

"I confess," said old Tom Burdum to the Reverend Tom Latimer, "that my grandson Charlie is a bigger bite than I can comfortably chew. I've hung on grimly to reach this age in the hope that I'd live to set eyes on my Pommy grandson, who wasn't in a hurry to come out. What I hoped was that he'd be more satisfactory than Jack Thurlow. Well, he is—but does he have to be so *Pommy*?"

"Tom, he *is* a Pommy," said the Rector, "and he has no idea what that means. They have to arrive here before they understand Pommyness. Yet I don't despair for him. He's not as thick about the phenomenon of Pommyness as most Pommies are. In fact, I think when Charlie is told not to come the superior Pom over colonials, he will actually pipe down."

"That's perceptive of you, Rector." Old Tom leaned back in his chair, a steaming cup of tea at his elbow and one of Maude's butterfly cream cakes on a plate—delicious! "At first I didn't think I could like him, but it turned out to be easy. He's no slouch, my grandson Charlie! Jack looks and behaves right for Corunda, yet now I'm starting to get a feeling that Charlie may be righter in the long run." The creased, incredibly old face broke into a wide grin. "The Pommyness means he has some ratbaggy notions that will have to be pounded out of him, but he doesn't have any ironbound conviction that he's better than the colonials just because he's a Pommy. In fact, his background and education say he'd behave the same to Pommies as he does to us colonials."

"You're getting muddled, Tom, but I know what you mean," said the Rector. "Eton, Balliol, and Guy's put him a long way out in the forefront of society, even Pommy society. After all, he has the money to be a Prince of Wales playboy—Mayfair parties, horse races at Ascot, sunshine on the Côte d'Azur, skiing at Kitzbühl, et cetera. Yet he qualified in medicine and hasn't known an idle day since his time at Balliol. I think your grandson Charles has a streak of the altruist in his nature. So, incidentally, does your other grandson, Jack, though in a different way." A fierce frown descended on the Rector's brow. "One thing they share in common is a reluctance to come to church."

Old Tom burst out laughing. "Jack's a lost cause, Rector, as well you know. However, I'm sure that when the novelty of his appearance in Corunda wears off, Charles will grace the Burdum pew in St. Mark's. If he attended at the moment, he'd stir up a near riot—the whole town is dying to inspect him at close quarters, and where else than in the Burdum pew can the poor chap be imprisoned? Ask three of your own four daughters."

Which left the Reverend Mr. Latimer without a word to say.

Of course every member of the Corunda Base Hospital staff was agog to meet the new Superintendent, who hadn't worn the first set of creases into his starched long white coat or heated the leather seat of his office chair before he was in action, marching up and down the ramps, sidling into wards waving an airy hand to signal that he wasn't really there at all, invading Matron's sacrosanct areas and privileges, demanding the account books, bank books, and property portfolios from Secretary Walter Paulet, and even going so far as to sample the patients' frightful meals.

"He's a busy boy," said Tufts to Kitty and Edda over hot bacon sandwiches in their cottage.

"Having little heart-to-hearts with your favorite medical man, Liam Finucan," said Edda, chewing blissfully. "Oh, there is nothing like crisp bacon rashers on fresh white bread!"

"I freely admit that Liam is my favorite medical man," said Tufts without resentment, "but since Kitty's bantam rooster took over the coop, I scarcely see Liam. As you say, Edda, constant heart-to-hearts with the new Super."

"I wonder when the spiffy new broom is going to get around to deciding what to do with his four newly registered sisters?" Kitty asked, basking in the distinction of having told the Great Man to piss off and leave her in peace. She'd also told him he was a presumptuous twerp! Since she had relayed the story to several nursing friends as well as to her sisters, it had become general gossip, though thus far Kitty had not been offered the opportunity to meet him in her hospital guise. In fact, his way of insinuating himself into hospital business without ever once introducing himself to his subordinates was seen as unorthodox and rude—but then, he was a Pommy and they were mere colonials!

Tufts was speaking; Kitty emerged from her brown study. "I imagine that we four junior sisters are pretty low on his totem pole," Tufts said, licking her fingers. "Liam says he's a master planner and formulating a new character for Corunda Base, which is why he's to be found poking into forgotten corners. In fact, according to Liam, the man's a powerhouse dynamo capable of rare analytical detachment and logical construction."

"I knew a bacon sandwich would get more out of you than a whole syringe full of truth serum," Kitty said smugly. "So the bantam cock is counting every feather in the henhouse?"

Edda smiled. "Matron must be foaming at the mouth."

"Oh, he conquered Matron during their first five-minute talk," Tufts contributed, enjoying her position as oracle even more than the lunch. "Apparently they see eye-to-eye about nursing and nurses, *and* matters domestic and culinary."

"I heard a rumor that the fur is flying out at the convalescent home," Kitty said.

"My darling sisters," said Tufts, "there is so much fur flying in so many directions from so many pelts that the air is thick with it." She dropped her choicest item. "We are to see Dr. Burdum himself at eight tomorrow morning. Lena, too."

"Out of Limbo at last!" Edda cried.

"Yes, but up to Heaven, or down to Hell?" asked Kitty, face falling into a grimace. "I have an odd feeling about Dr. Burdum."

"Well, it's going to be difficult for you—how do you get back into his good books after telling him to piss off?"

The eyes flashed a sudden burst of violet. "Huh! He asked for it, the miserable little worm! If he offends me again, I'll do worse than tell him to piss off."

The four new Sisters, veiled yet still in aprons, presented their starched persons to Dr. Charles Burdum's outer office at one minute before eight the next morning; they were apprehensive, but not frightened. Lena Corrigan suffered least, but no one envied her. To volunteer, especially once certified, to nurse mental patients was so extraordinary that there was little chance an enlightened hospital chief would refuse to employ her. The days of Frank Campbell were gone; Dr. Charles Burdum, even on such short notice, was proving himself a sensible and sensitive chief.

Cynthia Norman, who had been an assistant secretary with nostrils just above the level of the typists' pool, and was now Dr. Burdum's personally chosen private secretary, sent all four in together. The new Superintendent didn't rise to greet them, nor bid them sit down; three stood facing his desk (which, noted Edda, had had its legs cut down), while the fourth turned her back on him to examine the titles of his many medical tomes. That it didn't appear insolent was due to the crowded room.

Seated, he looked quite tall, a common trait in small men, whose trunks tended to be average in length; they lost height in their legs. Disproportionate, thought Edda, the tallest of them. How glad I am that I'm wearing two-inch heels on my shoes! Blocky heels on stodgy work shoes, but heels for all that, ha ha. Now why does he provoke that attitude in me? Not because he's a Pommy, no. More because he's so bloody sure of himself.

"Thank you for being so punctual, Sisters," he said from his chair, "and forgive my not bidding you be seated. You won't be here long." A charming smile turned his face from gargoyle to film star. "Three out of four beginning nurse-trainees attained registration, and one superlatively good long-term nurse has been grandfathered in as registered, not before time." Came a dazzling smile. "Don't give me your names, I'll work from my list. Sister Lena Corrigan?"

"That's me," said Lena. "I'm the grandfather."

"A very youthful one. It says here that you want to nurse in the mental asylum—is that correct?"

"Yes, sir."

"Excellent, excellent!" he exclaimed, as if it really were. "You carry twenty years of general nursing with you, Sister, an incomparable asset for one who will assume command in the asylum just in time to ready the place as much as possible for the new psychiatrist I intend to appoint. There's not much can be done for chronic epileptics, congenital dementias, and the like, but I do believe we'll learn to treat things like mania and depression successfully in years to come. You will be the top-ranking deputy matron, but your title within the asylum will be Matron. Work on building the necessary additions to the asylum will start immediately, and the psychiatrist will arrive in the New Year. Is that satisfactory, Matron Corrigan?"

"I'm walking on air, sir. Thank you, thank you!"

"Then I'll see you at two this afternoon for another talk."

Face transfigured, Lena went out.

"Sister Edda Latimer?"

"Yes, sir."

No film star for her! The gargoyle went on leering, forked tongue out. "I see that your preference is for Theatre work, but of course you know there are no vacancies at present," Dr. Burdum said, sounding sorry for it.

"Yes, sir."

"I haven't been in the district long enough to gain any real impressions about the hospital's adequacies as well as its more obvious inadequacies, so I can't give you any idea as to whether I think there should be a second theatre, only that thus far things seem to say one theatre is plenty. With Sydney only three hours away, more complex forms of surgery are probably better done there apart from true emergencies." The eyes, she saw, had changed from bright gold to a dull khaki; the gargoyle retracted his tongue and looked wry. "I can offer you work, Sister Latimer, but not theatre. The six until two shift on Men's Two needs a second sister, so does the same shift on Maternity. Any preferences?"

"Thank you, sir, I'll take Men's Two," said Edda, turned smartly, and walked out.

"Sister Heather Scobie?"

"Yes, sir."

"Basically," he said chattily, "you're already sorted out as Sister Tutor, and have been doing sterling work in Domestic and Culinary as well. What I plan is to put Domestic permanently under a deputy matron who will also be responsible for nurses' aides and porters. However, wardsmaids, porters, and aides from now on will be obliged to attend a course of instruction in hygiene and basic cleaning, will also be shown how to do their duties, and once a year attend another course. Sister Tutor will have charge of all instruction."

"That's a terrific idea," said Tufts, beaming.

"Culinary is a different problem," Dr. Burdum went on, "with some of the same elements. They too will need instruction in hygiene, for example. As everybody must know by now, feeding people is going to cost more than sixpence a day, but over and above that is the problem of decent cooking. Matron and I intend that Culinary will have its own deputy matron responsible for nothing else, but where should I start?"

"With an axe, sir," said Tufts. "Matron Newdigate is a city person who wouldn't know a shearers' cook if she fell over him, but Dr. Campbell has always run Corunda Base on shearers' cooks. Shearers, sir, work extremely long hours of extremely hard labor, and they'd eat *anything*. Sick people, on the other hand, find it hard to eat the tastiest food." She shrugged. "I leave it up to your imagination, sir. Sack the cooks and get decent ones."

"I will indeed. It goes without saying, Sister Scobie, that you are Sister Tutor and in charge of *all* hospital education."

"Thank you, sir," said Tufts, smiled at him, and left.

Three down, one to go, she who was still studying his books.

"Sister Katherine Treadby?"

She turned in a near pirouette, stripping his face of all ability to be either gargoyle or film star; it had been ironed free from all expression save amazement. "You!" he gasped.

"That depends who 'you' is, sir. However, I am certainly the 'you' belonging to Sister Katherine Treadby."

"But your name is Kitty Latimer, you're the Rector's girl!"

"Yes, I'm that, too," she said, thoroughly enjoying herself. "My legal name is Latimer, but since all four trainees who started nursing here in April of 1926 were blood sisters with the same surname—Latimer—three of us were given new surnames. Edda kept Latimer. Grace, who left to marry, became Faulding. Tufts—oops, I mean Heather—took Scobie, while I, the youngest by some minutes, became Treadby."

He got to his feet and came around the desk, smiling at her in a way that left her feeling breathless, for the smile reached inside his eyes, an extraordinary rusty-khaki color that, she suspected, could dissolve and change the way a chameleon lizard changed the color of its skin. The shock of such an unexpected meeting with this woman who had haunted him, waking and sleeping, ever since he boarded that train weeks ago was profound; every vestige of good sense in Charles Burdum ceased to exist. All he could do was extend his hand and smile fatuously, lovestruck.

"Sister Treadby, then, if such be your name," he said, and inched too close to her. "There is only one position I'd offer you—that of my wife. From the moment you snubbed me on that train, I've thought of nothing and no one else! I mean, look at us!" he cried, carving up the air with his left hand. "You're the right size for me, you divine creature, and no word of Marion Davies will e'er pass my lips e'er again, I vow it on Guinevere's grave! I adore you! I worship the ground you float above! I am your slave, your prisoner of love!"

Transfixed, Kitty stood listening in utter disbelief until he finished, when he, too, stood apparently transfixed, though by very different emotions. Her lips twitched, trembled; she fought to keep control of herself, but without success—it was the look on his face, which reminded her of Francis X. Bushman trying to convey undying passion in silence, waiting for the blackboard to appear on the film and tell his audience the words Dr. Charles Burdum was actually speaking.

She burst into peals of joyous laughter. "Go on, sport, pull the other one! I've never heard such a heap of tripe in all my born days—don't tell me that Pommy women actually fall for that stuff! It's so syrupy I want to puke!"

Mortification dyed his face a purplish crimson; for a few heart-pounding seconds he was literally powerless, had no idea what to do. He could reel off the names of a dozen women who'd melted into compliant puddles when he said such things to them—they were sincerely meant! And he had even proposed *marriage*! But this young woman derided him for being— being what? She was a woman, and women loved lavish compliments!

He retreated, but not unintelligently; finding a laugh in him somewhere, he gave it, stepped back in an easy way, and took hold of a chair. "Sit down, Sister," he said. "Having crushed me so savagely, it's the least you can do."

"All right," she said, and sat.

"To what did you object in my declaration?" he asked, his rump perched on the edge of his desk, which had been lowered, she noted. Oh, poor chap! The colonies aren't doing well by you.

"Your question is a good example—so grammatically prim and proper! To an Australian ear it sounds stilted, false. Like the poetical declaration of love. It sounded hysterically funny to me."

"Barbaric," he muttered.

"Probably an apt description. Australia must be a shock."

"How does one speak of love in Corunda, then?"

"Noah may have waxed lyrical around the time of the Ark, but not since in Corunda. You could experiment on a Toorak girl, she might nibble at your romantic bait, but few Australian women would. I mean, not out of the blue, sir! In a staff interview? It makes you look a dinkum ratbag! There's not a woman born on the face of the globe doesn't know that all men consider themselves her superior in every way, so when a man mouths syrupy, pukey rubbish to a woman, his sincerity is of the moment. Give him what he wants, and he'll revert to his superior status immediately," said Kitty coolly. "You might get away with carnations and chocolates, but Tennyson and tripe? Not in a fit! A local man would probably tell me I'm a grouselooking sheila, and leave the rest to—er—cozier circumstances. You, Dr. Burdum, dislike being laughed at as a figure of fun, so abandon the poetic imagery and silly waffle. Your ideas for the hospital are extra-grouse, sir, so you have a lot of local people on your side. But if they begin to see you as a two-bob Lothario, down you'll come with a crash."

The hideous humiliation was fading. Charles Burdum was big enough spiritually to forgive Kitty the dealing out of that shame; yet in a minute corner of his brain it was filed away with many other slights, injuries, and insults, some done in all innocence, though he didn't interpret them that way, for he was the slighted, injured, insulted one. He had a failing he knew nothing of: the tendency to cherish grudges for a lifetime, their number inexorably increasing. For Charles Burdum was abnormally thin-skinned, and even the smallest of wounds festered.

At this moment, his mortification shrinking because he knew she hadn't really meant her laughter spitefully, Charles gazed past his own lacerated hide to see that Kitty was far from indifferent to him: that she had protected herself from his magnetism with a shield of mirth. And she was so right! How could he have brought personal matters up during a professional interview? No, what he felt was far from one-sided, and what he had to do now was work to establish their relationship on a professional level—no intimate undercurrents! Wooing her would have to be postponed. She had to like him, but not as the wrong Charlie: he was Charles Burdum, not Charlie Chaplin.

Seating himself behind his desk, he regarded her with as much detachment as he could summon, given that he was absolutely mad about her, and always would be. Sybil? A very young chardonnay. Kitty was a vintage champagne, above all rivals. Even with that white-blond hair hidden, the frosty brows and lashes against the dark skin were striking, and on the train he hadn't been able to look into her eyes long enough to see that their piercing blue was shot with lavender, a tiny touch of oriental cat. In fact, the name Kitty suited her, between the domed brow and the wide eyes, the permanent hint of a smile on her exquisite lips. In all his life he had never seen one so fair with skin so dark. Nor, he suddenly realized, had he ever seen eyes so *angry*. But that was ridiculous! What could such a beautiful woman have suffered, to be so angry at a compliment? Not an emotion he had expected to find, certainly. If anything, his fantasies had dwelled on how to satisfy what was bound to be a colossal conceit, queen of all she surveyed. Well, he had seen humor, rage, a scorpion's sting, but no evidence whatsoever of conceit. What *are* you, Kitty?

"Have you a preference for one kind of nursing, Sister?"

"Yes, sir. Children's."

He tapped her file folder. "Yes, I've already noticed that your three years of nurse training have been heavily weighted in pediatrics. Sister Moulton speaks highly of you."

"I can speak highly of her."

"Would you like to continue nursing children?"

"Yes, sir, I would."

"Matron recommends you for the charge position on the two to ten shift in Children's. Would that suit you?"

"Yes, sir."

The film star smile showed; she did not respond.

"Then the position is yours, Sister Treadby."

"Thank you," she said, got up, and left. Outside beyond Cynthia Norman's office she leaned against the wall and sagged in mingled joy and sorrow. Joy, that she had a charge job on Children's; sorrow, that things had gotten off to such a bad start with the new Superintendent.

Throughout the interview she had watched him, hawklike, her initial reaction to that ludicrous display of his peacock's tail stored inside a separate box, its lid firmly closed until she had the leisure to open it and examine it free from other considerations. Somehow she sensed that he was a blend of sincerity and chicanery, though she had no idea what proportions they occupied in his makeup. So enormously attractive! And not too short for her; in high heels he would still top her by an inch or so. But terribly short children if they married! Virtual midgets.

Kitty was very confused, and every word he said only made her state worse. What was he like underneath the words? Intelligent, worldly, experienced. She had become conscious of a furious anger as the interview went on its brief way—because of her wretched face, he had automatically assumed that she was stuck-up, proud! Oh, how dared he do that to her? Another collector of art, it seemed, panting to display her beauty as his property by marriage. No, don't open that box!

But how can I not? He has offered me all the traditional temptations of wealth, power, lifelong comfort—*on no other evidence than my face*! I loathe my face! He waffled on about love, but what can a man who judges a woman by her face possibly know of love? It says he's superficial, a cool man at the core. Cool, not cold; he's not indifferent to the suffering of others, just cool in that he never suffers wholeheartedly himself. A chilly analyst.

Kitty lifted her shoulders off the wall and found out that she could walk. But the contents of this morning's interview she would keep to herself. If Edda and Tufts knew—!

In the meantime, Charles Burdum was coming to grips with the fact that Kitty and Heather—Tufts—were identical save for their coloring. Tufts had diminished the likeness, near-absolute when it came to physique and facial features. The obvious lack was at least one dimple, but the coloring was more than mere difference: it had an essence of the soul about it. Looking at Tufts, any perceptive person understood how profoundly a practical, orderly, and sweet disposition affected the dynamics of attraction. In Kitty the dynamo roared: in Tufts, the dynamo hummed. Never having been exposed to twins, Charles was fascinated. There was the other pair as well, Edda and Grace, who rumor said were more identical than Tufts and Kitty.

What was Kitty's nature? There were mysteries, some of vital importance, but to whom could he turn for solutions?

The image of Edda rose up in Charles's mind. Yes, Edda knew everything, she was the quartet's natural leader according to the gossip grapevine. To Edda he must go, but he had learned from Kitty's lesson. How do I approach Medusa? Never look into her eyes, they'll turn you to stone! She wouldn't like him, either, though that wasn't as important as what she decided he meant to baby sister Kitty. Edda wasn't selfish, she'd put Kitty's wants and needs ahead of her own. Yes, he would have to go to Edda.

I am the victim of my time and my nationality, he thought. I am an Englishman, a bona fide member of the nation that rules the largest empire the world has ever known. Turn the globe of the world in any direction and the land on it blazes with the ruddy pink that is a geographer's code for

British Empire possessions. Only Antartica is without areas of pink, many of them huge, and in the case of the Australian continent, pink in entirety. But these people resent the pink; they would rather be the green of total autonomy, like the USA, I have to forget to be English, just as being English tends to make one forget Scotland, Wales, and Ireland, nominally a part of the ruling Great Britain. Except that everybody secretly has to admit the actual rulers and owners are the English.

He buzzed for his secretary. "Miss Norman, the three Latimer sisters. Do they live in?"

"Yes, sir."

"How do I contact one of them?"

"Usually by letter, sir, which you would give to me to put in the appropriate pigeonhole in the Sisters' Office. If it is urgent, there is the telephone, though undoubtedly Matron would send a porter to fetch whoever is wanted."

"I'll write a letter. Thank you."

He drew notepaper forward, frowning. Flimsy stuff of the cheapest kind. New stationery was on order from W.C. Penfold in Sydney, but until it arrived, he was limited to this—this—lavatory paper. Next week he was summoning the Hospital Board to its first meeting since he had taken over—what a circus that was going to be!

Edda found her letter when she returned to the cottage from her usual ride with Jack Thurlow, physically sated but more restless than she had been in a long time. Oh, what she felt for Jack still had the power to keep her tied to Corunda, but there could be no denying that his idiotic devotion to Grace and Bear annoyed her, even before the quarrel—he *had* been her exclusive friend, no matter what Grace alleged on that memorable day. Edda hadn't spoken of it to Tufts or Kitty, thanking her lucky stars that their shifts hadn't let her tell them what was happening to Grace in her Trelawney isolation—fancy imagining that her fellow housewives thought Jack was her lover! To Edda, so ludicrous it was laughable. Grace didn't live in a vacuum; there were always nosy neighbors calling in to see her while Jack and Edda were working in the garden, and there could be no mistaking which twin was Jack's inamorata, since they arrived and left in the same car and looked into each other's eyes in a certain way. What Edda hadn't begun to understand was the effect two babies and a largely absent husband had had upon her sister, who saw Edda's glamour, clothes, free lifestyle, and easy camaraderie with men as proof that all those qualities of Edda's had been utterly stripped from her, Grace. A sore jealousy had rubbed her so raw that a part of her began to hate the breezy, carefree, *available* Edda.

The fantasy of a Jack–Grace affair had broken on Edda as just that, a fantasy, but to discover that Grace firmly believed it existed in gossiping minds had first amazed Edda, then, after she pondered it, an attack of irritated pity had provoked her into taking the easiest way out—broadcast her affair with Jack for all to know. Jack hadn't minded; Grace could relax, her Trelawney reputation pristine. That *was* how I saw it, ran Edda's thoughts when she had a moment to let them dwell on Grace.

The quarrel itself could never have been foreseen by anyone with logic and good sense—no, that was wrong! It could not have been foreseen by anyone with the tiniest scrap of intelligence, let alone good sense. Wielding the hammer savagely, Grace had brought it down on Edda's head blindly, destructively; the blaze in her eyes hungered to kill as does a mob, without reason. And after her own rage died, Edda found her concept of her sister so shattered that, if she could have found a way, she never wanted to see Grace again. Her fund of logic told her that whatever was wrong with Grace had very little, if anything, to do with her as a sister or even a mere human being, but her anger was so strong, so implacable, that she couldn't forget or forgive. The injustice of Grace's charges corroded and eroded her love to a point where it didn't exist any more.

Which had made this winter finally passing the hardest one of Edda's life, even including Kitty's suicide attempts. Naturally Tufts and Kitty sensed that there had been a quarrel, but various attempts by either as well as both combined, whether addressed to Edda or to Grace, were met with an immovable stone wall. Neither Edda nor Grace wanted to speak about the breach, let alone heal it. And to Edda, the one unjustly accused and judged, the sheer magnitude of Grace's insults eclipsed their relationship.

Kitty went to the Rector, who tackled Edda as the twin with an abiding capacity to see reason—and got nowhere. When he tackled Grace, his only reward was an hysterical outburst of sobs, copious tears, and utter lack of reason. When Maude inserted herself into the act on Grace's side, Edda cut her dead and refused to visit the Rectory until Maude minded her own business.

In the end, Matron Newdigate stepped up to the breach, her trusty battle-axe sharpened, so the spies said, on Liam Finucan's device that did the same for microtome blades; that he had been drawn into the fray was thanks to Tufts, who had seen a faint ray of light at the end of the Edda–Grace tunnel.

"This needs God," she said to Liam, "and a feminine God at that. It has to be Matron."

"But Grace hasn't been a nurse in years," he protested.

"The dragon is etched into Grace's brain with a white-hot poker," Tufts countered, "and Matron is the dragon to end all dragons."

So Grace was summoned to see Matron just as if she were still a trainee nurse, and the moment she was seated, in walked Edda.

Neither twin suspected the ploy; nor was either twin courageous enough to storm out of *Matron's* office in a huff.

"Sit down, Sister Latimer," said Matron with great affability, "and bid your twin a good morning."

An enormous weight fell from Edda's shoulders. "Good morning, Grace," she said, and produced a small stiff smile from paralyzed lips.

Grace's was much larger; she knew whose fault the quarrel was, and hadn't slept well in three months trying to find a way out of her dilemma that let her salvage at least a little pride. The trouble was that no way out could preserve her pride—oh, if only on that awful day Edda hadn't looked so elegant, so—so *soignée*! But she had, and the wounding words had gushed out in a spiteful, petty torrent. How much she rued them! But pride was pride, insatiable.

Matron's office saw Edda in a veil and without an apron, a cool effigy in green and white stripes, while Grace the married woman sat in her Sunday best: a flattering, waisted crepe dress in fuchsia pink, a smart straw hat to match, and navy blue accessories.

"You look *trés chic*, Grace," Edda said.

"And you look like a sister—very intimidating."

"So is this ridiculous spat finally at an end?" Matron asked with a smile.

"It is—if I apologize," said Grace, "and I do, Edda, most sincerely. I put my foot in my mouth."

"Excellent!" said Matron, beaming. "Your causes and effects have become so old they've grown whiskers. Which reminds me, Faulding, that you never did hand in that five-page essay on the fluid balance chart."

The door opened; a wardsmaid wheeled in the tea cart.

"Ah, tea! Now we'll drop formality and use Christian names."

Grace gasped. "Matron! I couldn't do that!"

"Nonsense! Actually I need you, Grace. The hospital under its new administration needs a voice in the Trelawneys, and I hear that yours is a very respected Trelawney voice."

A flattered Grace blushed, eyes shining. "I'm the hospital's to command, Matron."

"Gertie," said Edda, grinning. "The name is Gertie."

The thin letter in a sealed envelope was in her pigeonhole, *Sister Edda Latimer* scrawled across it in near-black ink. Sent by the new Superintendent was Edda's guess—interesting handwriting, very bold and executed with a broad nib. She opened it.

Blunt, yet to the point: an invitation to have a drink with him in the Grand lounge at six, after which, if she so desired, they could repair to the Parthenon to have dinner. She need not reply; if she was interested, he would be where he said at the stated time tonight, tomorrow night, and any other night.

He harbored no man–woman interest, Edda was certain of that; the stare they had exchanged early this morning was of the kind that passed between two warriors from rival tribes. No, he was after Kitty, that day at the train station had told her so, and now he had discovered that Kitty Latimer was Katherine Treadby, nursing sister. A complication, as was the fact that she had taken against him. He was the invading stranger, far too clever not to realize that before he could fix his interest with Kitty, he needed to know a lot about her. And she, Edda Latimer, was his carefully selected informant.

It would have to be tonight; tomorrow she was in theatre, and would remain on duty for seven days before her next leave. He'd known that, too, but not rammed it down her throat.

Having a mere £500 in the bank, Edda made all her own clothes, and lived so thriftily that she funded her wardrobe from her tiny earnings as a nurse. Fabrics, shoes, gloves, and bags had to be bought; dresses and hats she made, so extremely well that Corunda assumed she shopped in Sydney's best fashion stores. She had just sewn the last bead on a dress of purplish grey in the latest style, hem below the knees and a suggestion of a waist, made more interesting at hem and sleeve edges by several thousand tiny purple glass beads; black kid shoes and bag, and a wisp of dark grey tulle sprinkled with the same purple beads on her head. Yes, that would do! Chic.

He was waiting at a secluded low table in the hotel lounge, no drink before him, and rose to his feet the moment he saw her crossing the room.

"A cocktail?" he asked, settling her in a big, low chair.

"Thank you, no. A glass of pilsener," she said, removing her black kid gloves finger by finger, a fastidious task.

"Do many Australian women drink beer?" he asked, seating himself and waving at the waiter.

"Yes, as a matter of fact. It's the climate. We drink thin German-style beers with a relatively high alcohol content, and we drink them icy cold. You'll find no thick English ales served warm out here," she said, finishing with the gloves. "As a bonus, I can tell you that Kitty drinks icy beer, too."

"You're awake on every suit," he said, having given his order. "Did you not wonder if perhaps it were you I was interested in?"

"Not for a second. I'm far too tall."

"Touché. You're very exotic for Corunda, surely?"

"Someone has to be. As you get to know the Latimer sisters better, you'll find that for two sets of identical twins, the similarities in each set are perfectly delineated in the one yet warped in the other, as in a sideshow hall of mirrors."

"Tell me more," he said.

"Take Grace and me. I'm very exotic for Corunda, whereas my sister is absolutely typical—a housewife and mother, always struggling to make ends meet but nonetheless enraptured by her role. With Kitty and Tufts, Kitty is the epitome of modern beauty, from the rosebud mouth to the huge, blind-looking eyes, while Tufts is a born spinster, as down-to-earth and unvarnished as spinsters get." Edda picked up her tall glass of beer, its sides wet with condensation, and inclined it in his direction. "Here's mud in your eye, Charlie."

"Must everyone call me Charlie?" he demanded, irritated.

"Yes, as you're not the Chikker sort. Charles is considered slightly effeminate by *real* men in this Year of Our Lord 1929—at least in this part of the world," she said smoothly.

"Christ Jesus, you're a bitch!"

"In England you'd have thought that, but never said it."

"Triple distilled!"

"And proud of it."

"I really don't need cutting down to size, Edda, but perhaps you can explain why Englishness is so objectionable to almost all Australians, and what the word Pommy means?"

"No one knows why the English are called Pommies, they just are, but they're disliked because this continent was a collection of British colonies until twenty-eight years ago, and we natives were despised. In fact, even now there is a Commonwealth of Australia, a great many Australians feel the country is still owned by the Bank of England and English companies. The plum jobs all go to Pommies, and the more English-inflected an Australian's speech is, the better his or her chances to get ahead socially and financially. Australians educated at state schools are punished for speaking with a low-class accent—yes, you brought the class system with you, and it took root! Whether you wish to consider yourself by your nationality or as an individual, the answer is still Pommy," said Edda, eyes gone white and staring. Then, as if annoyed at betraying so much feeling, she shrugged. "If you want to be liked in Corunda, Charlie, shed the Pommy as fast as you can."

"Cigarette?" he asked, offering her his case.

"I don't smoke. All four of us gave it up after a few weeks on the men's ward."

"The illnesses?" he asked, rather blankly.

A sour smile twisted her mouth, painted very red. "No! One thing a doctor never does is empty and clean the sputum mugs. If he did, he'd understand."

An image of a sputum mug's contents rose in his mind; he put his

Scotch and soda (no ice) down hastily. "What do you want to do with your life?" he asked.

"Travel. Have mad adventures everywhere except Antarctica. That's the continent most people on the top side of the globe always forget. I'm hoping to be classified as a charge sister—more money. My finances are negligible—church mouse poor."

"Well, you are a church mouse, but I'll see what I can do about the charge sister status."

"In return for my feeding you information about Kitty?"

"Exactly," Charles Burdum said, sounding unruffled. "I'd be extremely grateful for any and all information."

The second half of Edda's beer contained no magic; ignoring her glass, she leaned back in her chair, crossed her legs at the knee, and fixed her lupine eyes on the new Superintendent. The mockery had left them, and for some reason she seemed to have revised her original, rather contemptuous estimation of him; he listened intently to a superb raconteur narrating a well-loved story, only interrupting to walk with her two blocks to the Greek café for a steak dinner.

So Kitty was internally scarred, not a stuck-up local belle out to string a series of male scalps on her belt. Very much in love with her, Charles Burdum itched to meet this awful mother Edda so patently loathed. Maude Scobie Latimer. So wrapped in her ravishing child that she couldn't see what adulation was doing to Kitty, too shallow to comprehend that some beautiful females yearned to be esteemed for something more enduring than their faces and figures. A cheese grater, and Kitty just ten years old! It hardly bore thinking of. The attempted suicide that only Edda and the Rector knew about . . .

Oh, my poor, darling Kitty! How much being a registered nurse must mean to you, and how little my declaration of love could possibly have mattered to you! It's a manifestation of what you've spent your life running away from—I must have disgusted you. On no better basis than those looks of yours, I announced myself in love with you. If only I had known! How can I ever persuade you to love me after such a start to our relationship?

"If you love her, you're going to have to convince her that how she looks is the least of your reasons for loving her," Edda said as she and Charles parted. "That means earning her trust a crumb at a time, and don't forget Tufts. You'll have to earn Tufts's trust as well."

Tufts was already conquered, however, thanks to Liam Finucan. The pathologist couldn't speak of the new Superintendent highly enough, especially to Tufts.

"He'll work wonders, Heather, and finally this hospital will fulfill its potential," Liam said to her, repeating the words often.

So when Kitty approached her seeking moral support, Tufts was not prepared to give it. "If he's courting your attentions and you'd rather he didn't, Kits, then use that salty tongue of yours and tell him to piss off. Personally, I deem him a fine man."

"Yes, but that's just it—I don't know what I feel, or what I want!" cried Kitty on a wail. "I've never met such an obnoxious, conceited man in all my life, yet he does have an admirable side, and I sincerely believe he wants to give Corunda Base the chance it's never had. But do I want to be his *wife*? Make his causes and ambitions mine?"

"That's a big deductive jump, Kits, and cart before horse, too. You don't have to become personally embroiled with him to like and admire him for improving Corunda Base, therefore I must conclude from the way you're talking that you secretly hanker a little bit for Dr. Burdum," said Tufts in the voice of reason.

"Should I do an Edda, and go out with him?"

"It would be far different, Kitty. Burdum took Edda out on a fishing expedition about you. Ask her! As she says, he's not interested in her, she's too tall."

"Yes, and that's one reason why I'm not interested in Dr. Burdum—he's too short. The only sight that makes people want to laugh more than a tiny wife with a lanky husband is the sight of Tom Thumb and his wife—ludicrous!"

"Pride goeth before a fall," said Tufts, chuckling. "Good, here's Edda! Edda, tell Kitty about your evening with the Super."

"Delighted to oblige," Edda said, sitting down with a sigh. "One side of me mistrusts him—he's a confidence trickster who could sell the proverbial coals to Newcastle, and it's ineradicable because it's at the core of him. He's driven to big-note himself, blow a loud and brassy trumpet. At the same time I liked other aspects of him—chiefly his affection and concern for you, as well as his ideas about the hospital. If I had as much money in the bank as you do, Kitty, I'd bet it on my certainty that Charlie Burdum the Pommy wonder will be very good for Corunda." She drew in her generous mouth, frowned. "As to whether he'll be as good for you, sweetest little sister, I'm not sure. His intentions are noble, but there's a chance that the most enduring love in Charlie Burdum's life will always be Charlie Burdum."

"You're not helping me, Edda."

"No one else can help, idiot! *Go out with him!* Until you do, you're relying on other people's judgments," Edda said.

"She's right," said Tufts. *"Go out with him!"*

Since Corunda was already buzzing over Dr. Burdum's taking Edda Latimer out for drinks and dinner, the sensation was electric when he took Kitty Latimer out for drinks and dinner. Did he intend to set the sisters up as competitors for his hand in marriage, or did he have more nefarious motives? "Charles" had gone by the wayside to everyone in the district; his name was now the slightly raffish "Charlie" and his image correspondingly reduced.

Kitty, Charles noticed, dressed differently from Edda, though both of them had turned heads when crossing the Grand's lounge to him. Kitty's style was fluffier—no sleek satins or metallic fabrics for Kitty, he concluded. Her chiffon dress was icy green in color, cunningly picked out with details in a darker emerald, and her kid accessories were navy blue; she wore no hat of any kind, the brilliantly flaxen curls cut short in a halo around that bewitching face. By the end of the evening Charles judged Kitty her own arbiter of fashion, and wondered where the Latimer girls got their dress sense, for Corunda definitely had none.

"Why are you the salty one?" he asked over beers.

"The face," she said promptly. "I look as if butter would never melt in my mouth, so being salty takes people aback. I learned that early, and have never wished to unlearn it."

"I hope you're not going to force me to a long courtship."

"I hope you don't intend a courtship at all, Charlie."

"Of course I do!" The gargoyle became the film star. "I have already told you how this must end—you as my wife."

"What precisely gives you that idea? And don't answer love—because that sort of instantaneous love is lust," said Kitty, relishing her pilsener beer. "Using the word in its proper sense, there are only four people in the world whom I love."

"And they are?"

"My three sisters and my father."

"What about your mother?"

The perfect nose wrinkled. "I *love* my mother, but I wouldn't step in front of her to take the bullet aimed at her."

"Why is that, Kitty?"

The large eyes widened even more, giving them a look of wary and startled surprise. Then she laughed, a peal of amusement so infectious that those around them who heard it involuntarily smiled. "Idiot! Because she wouldn't take the bullet meant for me. It's a two-way street, Charlie."

He winced. "Must I be Charlie, even to you?"

"Definitely. It turns you from a ponce into a man."

He swallowed. "I take it that a Charles would never step in front of you to take the bullet?"

"He'd be too busy diving for shelter."

"Whereas a Charlie might face the gunman?"

"He might."

Time to change the subject. "I wish," he said, eyes gone quite gold, "that this benighted town had a decent restaurant! And why the Parthenon over the Olympus, since they're identical twins in all respects from Greekness to decor to menus?"

"Custom. Meaning not tradition, but patrons. The Olympus is closer to the Sydney–Melbourne road, and takes travellers as well as tourists. Haven't you noticed Corunda's tourists? It's September, at the height of the spring flowering. The town is famous for its old world gardens. People flock here to see the azaleas and rhododendrons especially."

"But they bloom consecutively, not together."

"Here, due to some local climatic and soil peculiarities, they bloom together for twice as long. This is the peak week for synchronous flowering. After all, the world *is* upside-down."

"I was wondering why the hotel is so jam-packed," he said, face brightening. "Perhaps I can persuade the Grand to install a first-class restaurant."

"Concentrate on the hospital," was her advice. "You've moved into Burdum House now, so find yourself a chef who suits you. Then you can have poached whosits and braised whatsits as you wish."

Horror was written large on his face. "I can't entertain without a hostess!" he said blankly.

"Of course you can! As long as you have the staff to make sure things go smoothly, no one will find it odd. Posh Pommy punctiliousness isn't practiced here, so the women needn't leave the men alone over their port and cigars. It's more common for the whole table to withdraw together—if there *is* any withdrawing. People here rather like to finish the evening still around the dining table." She gave another of those infectious laughs. "Different places, different customs."

"A man entertaining without a hostess," he said slowly.

"Perfectly permissible in Corunda, though I daresay the Governor-General might object."

He insisted upon returning her to her door at the end of the evening, no matter who saw them on the ramps, but though he took her hand and held it, he didn't try to kiss her.

"You'll be Mrs. Charles Burdum before the winter of 1930," he said in a low voice, shadows filling the cavities of his eyes so that she couldn't see what they held, "but I'll temper my ardor for the time being because I can see that you don't trust me an inch. What it is to be a Pommy! Good night."

The Corunda Base Hospital Board didn't fare nearly as well at Dr. Burdum's hands as did the nurses or the four new sisters, though by the time he convened it a week into September, its members knew they were in for a marathon session and might even be made to feel a trifle—well, *uncomfortable.* That it would turn out to be (metaphorically, at any rate) bloodier and more exhausting than the Anzac attack on Gallipoli during the Great War was not to be credited—until after it was over, that is.

Said the Reverend Thomas Latimer, still gasping, to his wife, "The man stripped us of every last vestige of pride, honor, public approbation, and self-respect! Maude, we stood, shamefully and nakedly exposed, for all Corunda to see—the man insisted the meeting be thrown open to anyone who wanted to attend, so all the medical consultants Frank kept off the Board were there, old Tom Burdum was there—*Monsignor O'Flaherty was there!*"

As seventy-year-old Monsignor O'Flaherty of St. Anthony's Catholic church always called the Hospital Board "Frank Campbell's twelve weasels," this last witness was bitterest of all; Catholics might be poorer, but in Corunda they had the numbers.

The Board was entirely Frank Campbell's creation, that was inarguably true, despite its charter clearly saying that the Mayor, the Town Clerk, and the Church of England Rector must be members of it. If they commenced in a spirit of reform looking and sounding like lions, Frank hammered them into the properly flawless weasels he demanded. Had his daughters only known what went on at a Board meeting, they would have understood why Daddy was as big a weasel as the rest: no one defied Frank Campbell!

The only medical man it contained was Frank Campbell himself; then came the charter-stipulated Mayor, Town Clerk, and Rector, and after them, eight men as thoroughly weasel by nature as conditioning. They were all proprietors of local businesses—butcher, baker, grocer, draper, ironmonger, blacksmith/garageman, produce merchant, and "the egg man," who batteried a shed full of White Orpington hens plus one tired rooster. Weasel reward was exclusively supplying Corunda Base with low cost, low quality goods, from the draper's sheets to the egg man's oldest poultry products. No one made his fortune supplying the hospital, but all the vendors had found the cheapest source, and knew to the last towel or egg what amount Frank would buy.

Examination of the books had convinced Charles Burdum that he could do far better by the hospital's funds than simply letting a bank use them, but it wasn't that which imbued him with an urgent, powerful zeal to wrest control away from the Board. With Dr. Campbell dead, four million pounds sat nakedly at the mercy of a rudderless bunch of weasels. At this moment they were still reeling from the shock of a death considered impossible; even God didn't want Frank Campbell! But the shock would dissipate quickly from now on, and some bolder weasels be tempted to steal the funds. It wasn't hard!

Therefore, Charles had to take the money away from the Board now, at once, before the weasels had even begun to think of rallying and joining together. The funds needed properly looking after, and that was not the duty of a board but of financial managers. No one on the old Board, including Frank Campbell, had honestly known what to do with four million pounds, which had simply sat in various savings banks earning pathetically low rates of interest.

What Charles intended to do was crying out to be done: invest the money in companies and institutions called "blue chip"—a way of saying that if such companies and institutions failed, the race of Man would be so blighted that even the wheel would have to be reinvented. Corunda Base's money *must* be safe and must *earn*!

His primary task was obvious: to rebuild the hospital entirely, and equip it with the most modern diagnostic and maintenance apparatus, then staff it with the best people he could recruit. Despite the long traipses a shed/ramp design meant, it also meant no stairs, steps, or elevator/lifts. For Charles had seen enough hospitals to have learned their greatest lesson: no matter what their design, there was always a huge amount of walking to do.

With all this and much else roiling inside his head, Charles went to battle against the Board, throwing the meeting open, including to the *Corunda Post*, a weekly newspaper not to be sneezed at, and the city's consultant physicians and surgeons, not to mention Dr. Liam Finucan and Matron Newdigate. Among other mysterious trips to Sydney had been one that saw him take the Minister for Health out to dinner after a late afternoon discussion in the Minister's parliamentary chambers. Thus Charles was empowered to fire the present Board and review the hospital's charter; the Minister had been relative putty after he learned of Corunda Base's wealth and was made to see that he couldn't garnish its funds for his own department, in constant need of money. It did mean, however, that Corunda Base could be brought into being as a showcase hospital whose cost to the State would be minimal. A bargain was struck.

One other factor drove Charles to be quick about controlling the funds, but it wasn't anything he could put his finger on; it was purely a feeling (shared by a few London colleagues) telling him that some financial evil was brewing worldwide. Its nature, he couldn't for the life of him divine; but somewhere, in the tangled jungles of money markets and far too many investors, an unspeakable beast was grimly stalking anonymous prey—a shadow, a phantom—yet not, Charles was sure, a figment of his imagination. It was there and it was real, said some few colleagues too, which meant he had to have Corunda Base's money safe in his care.

One metaphorical Gallipoli, and it was accomplished; faced with a knowledge of the financial world they couldn't begin to rival, and understanding that, if necessary, Charles Burdum would take them through the courts all the way to the Privy Council, the Board crumbled in disorder. Eleven weasels found themselves dismissed, and none, including the Rector, was reappointed. It turned out, in an odd way, to benefit Corunda businesses far above expectation, as Charles Burdum informed the locals that he would call for tenders in all matters relating to hospital supply, and that in future supplies would be of good quality rather than the sweepings off the floor. Local firms were encouraged to tender.

There would be no Religious whatsoever on the Board, nor any prejudice, let alone bigotry, against any person on grounds of race, creed, or other. So, much to his astonishment, Bashir Maboud, who ran a general store in the Trelawneys, found himself the only retailer on the new Board, for all that he was a Catholic Lebanese; according to Charles, who (most undemocratically, in which he was just like Frank Campbell) chose the Board members, Bashir was an Australian by right of birth and education, and as a general store-keeper knew a great deal about the people of ordinary Corunda.

Dr. Erich Herzen, Dr. Ian Gordon, Dr. Dennis Faraday, and Dr. Ned Mason, all town medical practitioners, now joined the Board, as did Dr. Liam Finucan and Matron Gertrude Newdigate. The manager of the local branch of the Great Western Stores, the president of the Corunda Pastoralists' Society, the most senior among the stock-and-station agents, and the head of the Corunda Historical Society formed the nonmedical minority, from which it might be deduced that no one on the Board would give the Chairman of the Board, Dr. Charles Burdum, any arguments about how to manage hospital moneys. Totalling twelve members, it was an absolutely local affair whose membership would be reviewed as necessary, at the Chairman's say-so.

The formalities that handed Corunda Base's funds over to this new Board were completed early in October of 1929; Charles Burdum sat back with a sigh of profound relief. The four million was now invested shrewdly, but with extreme conservatism, at the sole dictate of the Chairman, who retained all financial powers. Of his reasons or his reservations he spoke not one word, nor was his wisdom queried; Charles didn't ride roughshod over other opinions; such was not his way. Instead, he explained every decision he made in minute detail, and encouraged a healthy debate he wasn't usually offered. Trust and knowledge said he was right. Paid no membership fees, the new Board received its charter halfway through October.

In mid-October, Charles held a dinner for the medical men, Matron Newdigate and Bashir Maboud, though no spouses were asked. He hired a room of suitable size at the Grand Hotel, but had the meal catered by a firm from Sydney; only the size of the fee reconciled the Grand Hotel to this insult, but as its manager was a pragmatist, he had to admit his own cooks couldn't hope to emulate the menu: Beluga caviar, a sorbet, poached flounder, and a pinkish Chateaubriand with the sauce of the same name that takes three days to make. Since it was high spring, the dessert was perfectly ripe strawberries, lightly whipped cream optional.

He broached the subject over the aperitif drinks, knowing it would carry them through all the leisurely courses and beyond to after-dinner drinks and coffee. As always, Gertie Newdigate thrived on being the only woman, too wise to thrust her sex under a man's nose, but enjoying the chance to wear lipstick and a dress that didn't creak from starch. Liam knew what was in the wind, no one else; they sat in comfortable chairs, eyes fixed on Charles.

"We're going to rebuild the hospital," he said, "and this dinner is my way of introducing all of you to what will be a great undertaking beneath the Board's shield. Understand, however, that it will be a gradual process, not begun next week, perhaps even not next year. I'm bringing all of you in so early because I don't want an architect's idea of a hospital, I want a doctor's. Bashir, you're here because you represent a patient's idea of the hospital. Is everybody with me?"

The exchanged glances and murmurs were joyous; every pair of eyes was shining.

"On the surface it won't be much different—long, single-storied buildings with verandahs so a patient's bed can be wheeled out for some sun, or fresh air, or a look at the gardens—joined by ramps that will be completely covered. The site is level, and we'll always adhere to the rule of no steps. When the level does change, the ramp will slope gently over a long distance. Yes, it means those irritating trudges, but it's healthy and I'm going to have little open cars powered by batteries for those who need transporting, including visitors." He caught Liam's eye. "Liam?"

"Wooden on stone piers, Charlie?"

"No, brick on whatever foundations are to hand—we won't waste the limestone blocks. I want cavity-brick construction to make it easier to heat in winter and cool in summer, so the roofs will be terra-cotta tiles insulated with tar paper and good, well-ventilated attics. Unfortunately the nurses' home is already on its way to completion, but at least Frank Campbell put it at the back of the grounds, and we'll do what we can with it later."

He spied the head waiter standing in the doorway, a signal that dinner was being served, and helped Matron from her chair. "We can continue in our little dining room," he said, leading the way, the rest trooping behind.

"The important thing," he said a long time later, over cognac or liqueurs, coffee or tea, "is to understand that as the building goes on, the hospital continues to function. Which means that it will all take place over time, and that should conserve our assets. Where possible, we'll fund from interest rather than from capital. We shouldn't forget either that we have State moneys as a public hospital, and I see from the hospital's books that Frank Campbell was a ruthless collector of debt. The Almoner had a hard fight to get an impoverished patient cleared of his debts. That, candidly, is a disgrace. Were it not for the efforts of Corunda's churches and private charities, people here would have been denied what I consider a basic right—hospital care. Oh, don't think it doesn't happen in Great Britain! It does."

Listening, Liam Finucan sat grinning from ear to ear. Well done, Charlie! They were all with him, Bashir Maboud most of all.

At midnight, returning to the cottage on hospital grounds he now called home, Liam found Tufts waiting, eager to hear what had gone on, and determined that he wasn't going to escape without today's ration of having his hair brushed.

"How did you know a cuppa was what I needed to settle my belly after so much rich food?" he asked, blowing on his tea, which he took without milk or sugar, and very strong.

"What was the menu?"

"Russian caviar, bland fish, an incredibly delicious filet of beef with a tarragonny sauce, and strawberries."

"My heart bleeds for you," she said, attacking his black hair. "I ate hospital shepherd's pie with watery cabbage."

"Get away with you, Heather, you know Charlie's doing wonders for this place. It was brilliant to drop the news about the new hospital on the medical segment of his Board over a dinner that must have cost him a fortune. St. Patrick and the snakes, how they did enjoy it! I thought Gertie was going to swoon over the beef."

"Bully for Charlie," Tufts said, brushing hard. Liam grabbed at the brush. "No more, Heather, please! My scalp must be lacerated."

"Sook! Your scalp is perfect. What revived Gertie?"

"The strawberries. I do believe she'd die for Charlie. In fact, he has what I believe is called a fan club."

"Yes, he has a fan club." She sighed. "I just wish my silly sister would either join it wholeheartedly, or cut him dead. Her vacillations are driving the rest of us around the bend."

"Luckily she's your problem, not mine." He ran his fingers through his hair. "Now the skin's stopped smarting, I must admit it's wonderful not to be blinded by hair."

"I rejoice for you, you stubborn old Ulsterman."

The door opened on a knock and Dr. Ned Mason walked in. "I knew I could smell a pot of tea! Tufts, delight of my heart, does Liam have another cup to spare for a glutted and slightly nauseated old obstetrician?"

It appeared on the desk in front of him as he sat down. "I had a feeling Tufts would be brewing you a pot of tea. Why do you always call her Heather?"

Liam looked surprised. "Do I? I suppose it's the name my mind thinks of when I think of her. It *was* a rich meal, though."

Ned Mason nodded. "Disturbed your routines, did it, Liam? You and Tufts are two faces on the same clock."

"Why are you here, Ned?"

"Winnie Joe skated on her water at about the time the strawbs were served, and of course Winnie Bert didn't take any notice. But Winnie Jack did, and promptly developed angina pains," Ned Mason said.

"Why are all the Johnston women named Winnie?" Liam asked.

Tufts grimaced. "Daddy says his mind slips into the same old sprocket whenever a girl is born—Silas Johnston, I mean. The name on the sprocket is Winifred. When each girl married, she tacked on her husband's name to distinguish her, as childhood names didn't work any more. Did you sort the Winnies out, Ned?"

"I hope so, given that there's no midwife on duty in the Labor Ward tonight—some domestic disaster befell her. I left Winnie Joe there in a trainee's terrified hands, put Winnie Jack in Casualty and sent Winnie Bert looking in the pubs for Joe."

"I'm a midwife, Ned," said Tufts, getting up. "It's my night for a pedicure, but feet can wait. Babies don't. If you need me, I am yours the minute you finish your tea."

"Bless you, Tufts, I can certainly use you!" He drained his cup. "I feel better already. After Perkins Saline, nothing settles a tummy like hot, black tea. Coal-tar tea, Charlie calls it."

The pair went out into the balmy night, leaving Liam to wash the tea-cups and put away his pedicure kit. Heather was right; feet waited, babies didn't. Why *did* Charlie serve such rich meals?

One aspect of Hospital Board financial doings had forced Charles to postpone certain plans he cherished, and that was the time they gulped so greedily. Until things were properly tidied up, he had neglected Kitty disgracefully. When finally he leafed through his calendar, he was appalled to learn that he hadn't really *seen* her in two weeks. What attentions he had paid her were hurried and perfunctory—a smile in passing, a few words on the hop, two better opportunities missed.

"Have dinner with me at my home, unchaperoned," he said to her.

It came out of the blue, striking her as conceited, cocksure, conquering. "Certainly," she said, a child across her left hip as she stood in the doorway of Children's. "When?"

"Tonight?"

"Thank you, tonight suits me well."

"Then I'll call for you at your door at six tonight."

"Thank you." She turned away, smiling—for the child, not for Charlie.

This time she wore organdy printed in various shades of pink, with pink accessories, and actively displeased him. "You look like fairground spun sugar," he said, his nostrils pinched, his eyes rather dull.

She grimaced. "You've just echoed Edda on my appearance, only she was less polite. She says my mother influences me too much."

"You could do with some of Edda's style," he said clinically.

"Slinkier, you mean?" she asked, unoffended.

"No, just more tailored. Short stature doesn't lend itself to frills and excessive femininity."

Little wonder she said nothing as they drove up Catholic Hill. Finally, and perhaps thinking the evening was getting off to a bad start, he said, "Why on earth is it called Catholic Hill, since St. Anthony's is off the Tre-lawneys?"

"Because our English colonial overlords were violently anti-Catholic, and apportioned the first urban or municipal land grants," said Kitty, glad she could display a little knowledge. "The Church of England always got the best land, and the Catholic Church the worst. But towns have a habit of growing, so the Church of England grants gradually became too small and too slummy, while the Catholic bits, usually on top of hills, grew more valuable. The idea had been to make the Catholics plod up hills to go to church, but what the overlords forgot is that with hills come incomparable views. The best illustration of the phenomenon," she said, warming to her theme, "is in Sydney. St. Andrew's Cathedral, home of the Church of England, cowers on a wee postage stamp of land literally rubbing sandstone shoulders with the far more impressive Town Hall, plus the office towers and traffic, while St. Mary's Catholic Cathedral sits on a glorious natural eminence surrounded by parks and gardens, has a superb view, and relative quiet. When the land was deeded, it was animal pasture and shanties on the outskirts of town."

"A cautionary tale," he said, laughing. "Interesting, how human prejudices can end in biting the bigot on the rear end." He turned into the gates of Burdum House. "The name is Catholic Hill, but I gather the Catholic Church doesn't own it."

"No, it provided the funds to build St. Anthony's, a handsome and roomy edifice, as well as the two Catholic schools. Old Tom Burdum had leased the very top on the understanding that if the Church sold it, he'd have first refusal."

"So you end in knowing more about my house than I do!"

On the imposing but plainly Doric portico Kitty now witnessed for the first time how cannily old Tom Burdum had chosen the site of a house he had, when he built it, looked forward to filling with the magical life children give their home. Oh, poor old man, to have had but one son and one daughter, neither, in his lights, a satisfactory child. The daughter, a wild harum-scarum, had run away with a handsome no-hoper before she turned nineteen, and stuck to him like a burr to a fleece. The son, years older than the girl, had vanished to parts unknown while the girl, Jack Thurlow's mother, was still a toddler. The boy, Henry, had been the child of old Tom's first wife; the girl, Mary, was Hannah's child.

So the house, a Victorian Gothic monstrosity of round towers, huge windows and steeply sloping roofs, had never been a home. It stood in ten acres on the flat top of Catholic Hill's six-hundred-foot bulk, and looked not toward the district of Corunda in its broad and fertile river valley. Instead, it looked north toward the mighty red-cliffed gorges and illimitable forests of the dissected plateau that hemmed Sydney around. Oh, how beautiful! thought Kitty: vast distances coated in thin blue mist, the wind-tossed leaves of a million-million trees a massive sigh from just one throat, the hint of impish mirth in white-water streams, and the groaning crimson weight of so much rock oozing bloodlike, everything delineated by the hand of a master.

"I wish I were a poet," she said, soaking it in. "Now I know why you wanted me here so early. The light is perfect for my first glimpse of this incredible landscape."

"It takes some beating," he said in quiet satisfaction, "and I've done my share of travelling."

Inside, the mansion's Victorian roots showed glaringly, not a prospect that could cheer a homemaker up, she thought wryly.

"The place has to be gutted," he said, leading her to a room he had made into a kind of sitting area, though the furniture was old and uncomfortable and, she suspected, the nearest toilet might be in the backyard. On that, he could cheer her.

"There wasn't any sort of sewerage, so before I moved in, I had one of the new septic systems installed, and put in some good lavatories and bathrooms. There's an oil-burning furnace coming by ship from San Francisco, and a second in case one isn't enough—like the British, I notice that Australians don't central heat, and I imagine that Corunda in winter is cold, from my brief taste of it." Choosing to sit a little distance from her, where he could see her well, he sat with his Scotch of choice—a squirt of soda but no ice—and contrived to make his eyes the same color as his liquor. "I'm not going to batter you with my plans about what I intend to do after we're married, except here and now to say that I would hope you'll make the home of this place old Hannah never did. She's not my grandmother, so much I know, but if you could tell me a little of my family in Corunda, I'd be grateful."

Her dimples leaped into being. "Neatly evaded yet stated!" She settled into her chair. "You need good furniture, sir. As to old Hannah and old

Tom—well, it's said the Burdums have had no luck in making a home any-where, but that's just Corunda legend, a part of the myth. It was the rubies, really. Treadby found the first ones, about seventy-five years ago, and thought he'd inherited the world. The town gets its name from corundum, which is the mineral that yields rubies and sapphires. Here, just rubies, and the very best—pigeon's blood in color, some of them starred, all remarkably free from inclusion bodies." Her face changed. "But you know all this, I should stop."

"Please don't," he said, refilling her sherry glass. "I like the sound of your voice, and you're that rarity, an intelligent woman. There's a whole evening to get through, and you surely can't think I'm so insensitive that I don't understand it's awkward?"

"Women are quite as intelligent as men, but they're reared to think it's a fault, so they hide it. Daddy never did that to us." She sighed. "Mama did, without success."

"Rubies, Kitty," Charles said gently.

"Oh! Oh, yes, rubies . . . Treadby's mistake was the typical one of ig-norance—having made a fortune from rubies, he didn't bone up on them, diminish his ignorance. His rubies were the ones lying about in rubble washed down from the gravel beds where they lurk—caves, stream beds, crevices. They lasted a long time. But old Tom Burdum did his homework, and set out to find the major deposits. When he did, he acquired title to the land. And, in the fullness of time, Treadby's patches dwindled, ran dry, while Burdum rubies continue to be found in regulated quantities. Rumor says £100,000 a year, but you'd know for sure."

"Do you want to know for sure?" he asked, smiling.

"No," she said, surprised that he'd ask. "Money is only worth what it can buy you. I can't conceive of spending a half of that."

They went to the dining room, where the butler hovered and a maidser-vant whose face Kitty didn't know did the actual serving. Lobster quenelles were followed by a sorbet, then roast veal. The presence of staff inhibited Kitty, who enthused about the lobster, then looked at the veal in horror.

"I'm sorry," she said, staring at her plate, "I can't eat that."

"I beg your pardon?"

"I can't eat it. It's oozing *blood.*"

"It's veal," he said blankly.

COLLEEN McCULLOUGH

"It's bloody," she said, pushing her plate away.

"Veal has to be eaten underdone."

"Not by me, it hasn't." She smiled bewitchingly. "Have them take it back to the kitchen, shove it in a frying pan, and *cook* it—please, Charlie. Otherwise I'd sick it up at once."

"My dear child, I couldn't do that! My chef would quit!"

"Then may I have a crispy bacon sandwich instead?"

What a business! Flabbergasted, Charles sat wondering how he could have dismissed all those signals semaphored at him since he arrived, including, now he thought about it, the disgracefully overdone Chateaubriand. While he apologized profusely for its pinkness as evidence of overcooking, he understood now his guests had assumed he was apologizing for undercooking! He knew from many meals in Sydney that this issue of cooked meat was far more civilized in Sydney; but these were rural people, and they knew too much about everything from liver flukes to tapeworms.

He beckoned the butler, a Sydney import. "Darkes, ask the chef to make Sister Treadby a dish of bacon and eggs."

"Make sure the yolks are rock-hard!" she said.

"Name me your favorite meal, or food, Kitty."

"Crisp bacon on a crunchy fresh white bread roll. Fried sausages and chips. Fish and chips. Lamb cutlets all brown and crunchy on the outside. Roast pork with crackling and roast spuds. And Mama's butterfly cream cakes," said Kitty without hesitation. Her eyes shot lavender sparks; she chuckled. "Oh, poor Charlie! Such grand ideas for a marriage, but how can you keep a chef *and* a wife? Never the twain shall meet!"

"On that diet, you'd be a balloon before you were thirty."

"Codswallop! I work my arse off, Charles Burdum. It's not the food that matters, it's how much of what you eat that you burn up."

"Why do I love you?" he asked the ugly old chandelier.

"Because, Dr. Burdum, I don't piss in your pocket like all the other women. You've too high an opinion of yourself."

"Some self-opinions are genuinely earned, and a high one, if based in deeds done and things achieved, is not to be sneered at. You have a low opinion of yourself, the result of too few years on this earth and boundaries far too constricted. In America, they'd call you a hometown girl."

186

"In America, they'd call you Little Caesar."

The eggs and bacon came, but the yolks of her two eggs were runny; she sent it back, with instructions to break the yolks and make sure the whites had browned exteriors. Dismayed and at a loss, Charles witnessed his evening deteriorate into a disaster.

However, she approved of the coffee, taken in the sitting area and without hovering servants.

"You made every mistake possible tonight," Kitty said then in a friendly voice, "and it's part of why, I think, Pommies are so disliked. You never consulted me or did any research into my food preferences because you deemed me a provincial ignoramus in sore need of instruction as to the right things to eat in the proper environment. I was supposed to come, be suitably awed, utterly overwhelmed, and pathetically grateful for this evening's lessons. Your gastronomic judgment was purely financial: if it's rare and/or costly, it must be better in every way. A bacon roll is *so* pedestrian: Q.E.D., it cannot compare with a lobster quenelle. I agree, it cannot. It's far tastier. As for your underdone meats, I see enough blood in the course of my work, I don't need to see my food bleeding, too. The rarer the meat, the more fat it contains. One of the reasons Man started cooking his meat was to melt away the fat and make the gristle more detectable." She shrugged. "At least so I learned in nursing school. Do doctors learn different?"

His face had twisted into its gargoyle image, but the thoughts that fed its expression were not of offended pride or pricked conceit; Charles Burdum was wondering if there were anything in the world he could possibly do to make this glorious, peerless woman see him for what he was: a man eminently worthy to be her husband.

"If I gave you unleavened bread to eat and river water to drink, Kitty, it could be no worse than these—er, rare and costly foods, which I offer not to abash you or point up your lack of sophistication, but to show you how rare and costly you are to me." He kept his voice reasonable and his body relaxed, his eyes telling him that she was still, as the evening neared its end, wary and mistrustful. "Why must you pick and scratch at me?"

She looked suddenly very tired. "I think, Charlie, that it must be my way of trying to get it through your head that I don't want your attentions. You—you annoy me. I can't think of another way to put it. You don't revolt me, or depress me, or any of a thousand strong emotions. You just annoy me, like an eyelash caught and stuck underneath the lid, scratching away," she said.

"If that be true, why did you come tonight?"

"One more attempt to get at the eyelash."

"Would you like to go home?"

"Are you going to leave me alone?"

His hands flew out, a gesture pleading her to understand. "I can't!" he cried. "Kitty, I can't let it go while you dismiss me so lightly! What can I do to prove how much I love you, to prove that we were meant for each other? I don't care if I sound silly to you, I love you desperately, I want you for my wife, my one true mate, and somehow I have to get that eyelash out, make both your eyes see I'm the right man for you—"

The hand on the table was a sharp, angry crack, the purple in those eyes flared up hard and hot. "Don't say silly things to me! Take me home, please. Thank you for an educational meal."

And that was that. In silence they quit the house, walked to the maroon Packard; he opened her door and settled her.

Down the hill, a stony and wordless waste between them; Kitty looked at what the headlights briefly illuminated—a huge tree trunk, a cluster of bushes, mailboxes toward the bottom, then the overhead lamps of George Street, Victoria Street, and, up ahead, the hospital at last.

This time he wasn't quick enough; she was out and fleeing up the ramp away from him at the perfect nursing pace: neither a run nor a walk. No fire or hemorrhage, but elude Charles Burdum.

Who returned to Burdum House and sat amid the ruins of what he had planned as an evening of preliminary seduction, sure that no woman could resist the evidence he presented her of time, care, thought, and love. The most delicious food, the best wines, well-trained servants to inform her that when she was his wife, all the messy and irritating jobs would be done by someone else—even the sight of Burdum House's disarray, crying out for her decorating attention, expense no object.

An annoyance! Someone not important enough to her to dislike—*an eyelash*! Why that, of all metaphors? Driving you crazy, until you finally washed it away or held it up triumphantly on the corner of a screw of gauze. Oh, thank God, the wretched thing is gone! To be dismissed so lightly, so tritely, so inanely . . .

Wounded to the core, Charles bled from what he assumed was his soul because he lacked the one kind of person in his life who might have disillusioned him—a best friend. The peculiarities of his childhood, isolated from an unstable father, deprived by death of a mother, had set him in stone before he was old enough to go to school. At Eton, at Balliol, at Guy's, he formed a band of one—himself. His stature, always that of the smallest boy or man in his class, forbade any sort of intimacy; it also shaped a shell of arrogance, unshakable self-confidence, and iron determination to surpass all his bigger, taller peers. Hand in hand with growing maturity came a realization of his ability to charm and dazzle; rather than a moody loner, the fully rounded Dr. Charles Burdum presented as a smooth, charismatic kind of man, of enviably ready wit atop a steel foundation. Such a pity he was so short! Knowing all who met him thought it, Charles hid his frustration and his anger.

He was very aware that a part of the intensity of his love for Kitty lay in her size; no one would laugh at them when seen as a couple, for they were short, yes, but not midgets, and Kitty was as beautiful as Helen of Troy, a universal love object who could marry anyone she pleased of any height. And no Paris lurked within Corunda, so much was sure. If Kitty chose him, he was vindicated.

This wandering, illogical thought process healed, he found; and so it did tonight as he sat with a Scotch, sipping slowly. He was not drunk by any means, simply bitterly disappointed that his overtures of love were so scornfully spurned. Which led him out of the slough of Kitty's despond, and into another that haunted him even more, since its solution didn't lie in his hands.

There is some sort of disaster looming, I've known it for more than a year, and share it with a very few others. The Bank of England is unsettled, the City of London uneasy. But all of it boils down to rumors. Debt in government is too high and unemployment keeps increasing—in Australia, very much so. The country is economically troubled, and I lay much of that at the door of governmental inexperience. The Commonwealth of Australia is less than thirty years old, and its governments are green as grass.

There are glaring signs. That miners' lockout on the northern coalfields—a fifteen-year-old shot dead! And the federal government passes too much responsibility to the states, which do not have the power to tax income and are given federal moneys for reasons more political than fair.

Are these actually symptoms of Melbourne's stranglehold on the nation? Twenty-five years of federal government in Melbourne, with the biggest, most taxable state, New South Wales, playing host to a Canberra only just beginning to function now? This place is the same size as the United States of America, and equally divided, but not equally populated—its people are squeezed into half a dozen vast cities, and rural areas as densely populated as Corunda are rare. I do not understand! But do Australians understand? Their schools seem to teach more British than Australian history, and I don't know where to go. Corunda is as isolated from central government as Scotland is from London!

A gust of wind blew down the chimney with a roar: Charles jumped, shivered.

How long have I been here, three months? But already Corunda people are looking at me as at a local leader. I have blood links and investments in the area, which is why I chose to come here when I decided on a new world. I wanted to preserve my Englishness, which negated anywhere in North America. The Americans left the Empire in 1776, and the Canadians are plagued by a loud French voice. In South Africa, it's a Dutch voice. Here in Australia I can carve out a political career, and be Prime Minister.

After all, it's only a two-hour drive from Corunda to Canberra. But how do I go about the distance inside my head?

And first, marry Kitty.

The second task will be harder, and hurt far more: abandon my Englishness. To keep it will retard me.

PART FOUR

DISASTER STRIKES

On 30th October the Sydney newspapers reported that on the 29th the New York Stock Exchange, sixteen hours behind in time, had crashed from a record high to a record low, accompanied by lemminglike suicides as men plummeted out of Wall Street skyscrapers. A juicy story! Yet New York was so far away, and the American financial structure something without the power to influence events in Australia the way British and European financial structures did. America was genuinely foreign, its affairs its own business, its politics severely isolationist when it came to the globe.

Charles Burdum saw 29th October in its true light, breathing a sigh of resigned relief. Yes, it had happened, but his funds as well as the hospital's were safe. And better the reality than more months waiting for the unknown axe to fall. In the glare of reality a man could act. Nor would everything occur overnight. As to what its symptoms would be below the level of theoretical abstractions, Charles couldn't in honesty know, beyond the fact that more and more men would be out of work, and that those who kept their jobs would be forced to accept reduced rates of pay. More property would be offered for sale, but fewer Americans would be buying. For no one, it seemed, had yet divined that what happened to the American financial market had the power to shatter every market in the world.

🌀

Dinner at the Rectory with Grace Olsen as his companion completed the Latimer jigsaw puzzle for Charles; Grace was the only twin he hadn't until now encountered. Privately he decided that all she actually did was further obscure the picture's meaning. The same height and build as Edda, she was utterly unlike Edda from face to character. Beautiful but sad grey eyes, a mouth that had a tendency to quiver and turned down at its corners, a stylish dress of mottled grey diagonal stripes, and a propensity for fever-ish chatter that revealed her lack of interest in anything beyond husband, sons, sisters, father—and Jack Thurlow. When she spoke of Jack, her rather mournful face lit up, but Charles noted that from his first mention, the Rector and Maude were not at all perturbed by Jack's presence in Grace's life.

"Bear would have loved to be here," Grace said to Charles on meeting, "but he's in Wagga and not due home for another month. He's a Perkins Man," she added, as if that explained everything.

"He sells ointments, lotions, and the like from door to door," said Maude, simpering slightly.

Grace flushed. "He's Perkins's top salesman," she said sharply, "and he's a very good provider."

"I have no doubt of that," Charles said, giving her his most charming smile. Poor young woman! Very much in love with her commercial travel-ler, and in constant need of him. Jack Thurlow doesn't keep Bear's side of her bed warm, he simply chops the wood and makes sure she doesn't kill herself or a child in some zany domestic accident. Grace is the helpless type.

There was no harm in her, but the same couldn't be said for Maude: a downright, outright bitch with no time for either of the Rector's older twins, and scant time for her own Tufts. A shiver of apprehension rippled down his spine when he beheld her tiny form. Very pretty even at her age, she was a fussily frilly dresser who spent a lot of time and money on appear-ances. And how kind of the Rector to limit this first dinner to the four of them—he had the time and few enough demands on his attention to get the most out of meeting Grace and Maude.

He could see the germ of Kitty in this sickly sweet apology for a mother, but only as far as externals went. Their natures, he concluded, were poles apart. More interesting to Charles was the discovery that the Rector controlled Maude, not the other way around. How had he achieved that?

The dinner was an excellent one, somewhere between his own chef's Parisian delicacies and the Parthenon menu—smoked salmon with thin brown slices of bread and butter, followed by tasty and tender roast turkey, and ending with a cheese board and seedless white table grapes.

"Maude is so clever!" Grace gushed over coffee in the lounge. "She buys baby turkeys and roasts two. I love her stuffing—she puts tart fruit in it and makes a relish as well."

Maude swelled a little at the praise; no doubt Grace had been issued orders to say it. Who whispered that I like my red meats rare? Maude solved the problem by serving turkey.

He heard all about Grace's delightful house as well as far too much about her sons, one eighteen months, the other five months.

"Who is minding the children tonight?" Charles asked politely.

Whatever Grace might have answered was never said; Maude gave a sniff and rushed into speech. "Grace's sister, Edda. I can't say strongly enough and often enough, Grace, that you shouldn't let Edda near your children! She's not a good influence."

Not only Grace, but Thomas Latimer also stiffened in outrage, and Charles couldn't even begin to guess what had provoked Maude into airing a private difference of opinion to a stranger.

"Edda is a Medusa!" Maude said with a spit and a hiss.

The Rector laughed easily, his eyes, grey like Grace's, twinkling. "Medusa the Gorgon! It's a name Edda has borne for many years now, Charlie. She earned it on the day Maude and I gave the four girls an afternoon tea to celebrate their starting nurse training. Calm as you please, without alarming a single soul, Edda drove her chair leg through the head of a seven-foot red-bellied black snake, and kept it there until Kitty managed to hack its head off with the fireplace tomahawk. Edda was covered in shocking bruises as from a man's fist where the snake had crashed into her during its death throes. Maude," the Rector added in the same tone, "was in strong hysterics and occupying all of my attention."

"Was it a lethal snake?" Charles asked, curious.

"Very, especially at that size."

"Then Edda was valiant." Charles smiled at Grace. "A great example for your sons."

"So I think," said Grace.

"And so too does Maude. Sometimes, however, she gets her own daughters confused with her maidservants over the years," Thomas Latimer said, frowning in genuine concern.

"Kitty was involved with the snake, too?"

"Yes. The fireplace tools were on the wrong side, which was why Edda had used her chair leg. Kitty was closest to the tools, and was there very quickly to help."

"While I," said Grace mournfully, "emulated Maude and cried."

"And there's nothing to be ashamed of in that," Charles said warmly. "Tears are a natural reaction. Not, it seems, for either Edda or Kitty. Your girls are brave, Rector."

"Indeed they are," said the Rector proudly.

"I intend to marry Kitty," Charles said, tone conversational, "but I'm having some difficulty persuading her that I'll be a good husband." Downcast one moment, his face blazed into its film star good looks the next. "But I'll win her, never fear!"

His announcement came as a shock—he expected that—but Charles found it illuminating to see what followed the shock. In Grace, a genuine joy that said she was nothing but glad; in Maude, a huge flare of triumph, a final vindication of her policy since the beauty of Kitty emerged, and which he knew about from Edda and that frank dinner some time ago now; and in the Rector, a wary delight that told Charles this was only good news if it was what Kitty wanted—and needed. He wasn't convinced, he had reservations.

"Grace, take your mama over there and chat for a while," the Reverend Latimer ordered. "Charlie and I need privacy." He proffered the decanter. "Another port?"

"Thank you, sir."

"Why won't Kitty have you? You're very eligible."

"As best I can work it out, she doesn't trust me. Or herself, I think. By the way, I know of her difficulties as a child. Edda told me, and at some length as well as honestly."

196

"That's a rare compliment. How old are you?"

"Thirty-three, to Kitty's twenty-two."

"A man should be older than his wife, otherwise women's natural maturity gives them an unfair advantage in a marriage," said the spiritual adviser of a large flock with quiet conviction. "The more traditional customs are flouted, the harder it becomes for a home to maintain its stability. Were you Kitty's age, I would oppose the marriage as demanding too much of an indulged young man—you would be tempted to abandon your responsibilities as husband and father, to the detriment of your children above all. As it is, your extra eleven years endow you with an authority your wife can respect." The Rector sipped his port reflectively. "I must approve of your suit in many ways, but it perturbs me that Kitty doesn't *trust* you. In what way?"

"If I knew that, I could break it down," Charles said.

"Not fear that there will be other women?"

"I doubt it, Tom, given that I've offered not one scrap of evidence of a weakness for philandering. She is my employee, she knows me on a day-to-day basis." He hunched his shoulders and spoke the words. "She deems me conceited and arrogant, and I daresay I am, but not without justification. It seems to me that she would rather I was falsely modest than truthful about my talents and abilities. Whatever I am, I've been honest about it."

"Are you a God-fearing man?"

"I believe in a properly Church of England God, though I'm not a bigot of any sort," Charles declared. "I think it important that any man in the public eye should be seen to attend church on a regular basis, so I will be in the Burdum pew on Sundays." He paused, then asked in a different voice, "Is the Corunda Church of England prosperous, Rector?"

Thomas Latimer blinked. "As a matter of fact, yes. Corunda is wealthier than most districts because it's not very drought-prone, and its more affluent people support their churches. But why ask me that, Charlie?"

"Because times are going to get hard, Tom. I gather that the nation depends heavily on exports for prosperity—wheat and wool in the main. Neither is a Corunda crop. The huge demand for uniforms and blankets during the Great War gave the Australian governments, federal and state, a false sense of export optimism. Well, the Great War has been over for a decade, and now no one wants or needs so much wool. Added to that, drought has greatly reduced the amount of export wheat," Charles said unhappily. "The governments borrowed heavily against what were seen as continued exports. But any financial man can see what's coming, given the American stock market crash. The loans have to be repaid, and where is the money going to come from?"

"The hospital funds? Your own money?"

"Oh, they're safe, though the hospital money will suffer if the Australian pound is devalued, of course. But that's a loss can be absorbed. My own money is based in England." Suddenly Charles laughed, looked wry. "I may be alarming you for nothing, Tom, it's too early to tell how far the cracks in the structure will spread." He sighed. "Yet somehow I feel it's going to be bad."

"I respect your instincts, Charlie, but let us return to my daughter. Do you want me to talk to her?"

"Thank you, no. Except that I would like your blessing."

"My dear chap, you have it, you have it!"

"Now all I have to do," said Charles, "is to persuade Kitty."

Maude had had enough of exile, came sidling back in time to hear this. "Kitty doesn't dislike you, Charles," she said, the only one to accord him his proper name. "If she did, she would have told you—most impolitely!—where to go. Instead, she accepted a dinner invitation. Her defenses will weaken, truly. And when they do—strike!"

He didn't say it sounded rather snaky.

While ever the long-term conservative federal government of Stanley Bruce was in power, its business, by and large, was conducted from Melbourne; a quarter of a century after the Commonwealth of Australia came into being, the national capital of Canberra was spiritually still in the wilderness. Then, a few days before the Wall Street crash, a newly elected Labour federal government under Prime Minister James Scullin decided, amid a big splash of publicity, to sit *permanently* in Canberra. A government of fumbling beginners inherited the aftermath of Wall Street.

Following the horrors of the Great War and the two consecutive outbreaks of influenza that killed even more people than the war, it was perhaps inevitable that the fledgling Commonwealth of Australia would embark upon a spree of public works. Most such public works were undertaken by the state governments for the most obvious of reasons: each state had existed as a separate British colony, and how did one tiny, utterly untutored central government administer three million square miles of mostly desert? Its Constitution had nothing to say about the people who comprised its entity, or gave them a bill of rights; it was a document about the judiciary, the parliaments, the states, the Commonwealth, taxes and tariffs and trade. So between 1901 and the late 1920s, while the new federal government stumbled along in Melbourne, each state, maintaining a government, did the things its people wanted and/or needed—schools, roads, hospitals, railways, bridges, dams, grain elevators. There was also a massive soldier-settlement scheme to put returned soldiers on the land as primary producers, this being the perceived source of the nation's wealth.

Each of the states raised its own loans, chiefly with the capital markets of the City of London, at hefty rates of interest, and the sums borrowed were staggering. Tumbling international prices for Australian grains and wool forced huge cutbacks in industry and agriculture; employment declined and—far worse for the various state governments—revenues fell sharply. Suddenly, right at the moment when the Wall Street crash happened, Australia's state governments realized that they couldn't pay the interest on their City of London loans.

The general consensus of opinion among economists, civil servants, and politicians was that the cure for this disaster lay in stringent control of money, achieved by not spending it. Every penny that could be scraped up must go to pay those foreign debts. Prime Minister Scullin announced that the federal government would cease to spend on public works and reduce its workforce. The only voice that cried against them belonged to Jack Lang, a New South Wales Labour leader, who wanted more money spent, not less, and more men employed, not fewer.

Apart from Charles Burdum, no one in Corunda was much bothered by the immediate aftermath of Wall Street. The townsfolk read what was going on in the nation's big cities and tiny, raw, ivory-towered Canberra; the district was weathering the first convulsions of the Great Depression *almost* unaffected. What jobs were lost belonged to men employed long-distance by Sydney or Melbourne. Within weeks, however, some unknown local put up a sign at the T-junction where the Corunda road met the Sydney–Melbourne highway; it said, in bold and professional letters, NO WORK IN CORUNDA.

Of far greater interest was the relationship between Charles Burdum and Kitty Latimer. If Kitty had known her own mind, it would have been settled one way or the other long since; the trouble was that she didn't know it, and she blamed her bewilderment on a combination of elements, including the fact that no man had ever pursued her so persistently. And he both attracted and repelled her, tugged her in a curiously oblique way rather than head-on. So what she felt as ominous in him was merely sensed, never witnessed, and what she clearly saw without distortion was admirable, worthy of love, tremendously stable, rock-firm. And how could she explain that what she searched for was his pain? Once she could find that, she would *know*. Her own childhood had been one long pain grounded in something she couldn't change: her appearance. Instinct said his childhood must have had similarities as all the boys of his own age grew in height, and he did not. Grounded in appearance! The pain *must* be there! Why then wouldn't he show it to her, why wouldn't he consent to share it? Only by sharing would he admit her into the very heart of him. Hungering to heal his pain, she felt herself forever relegated to a distance.

So when they met, which they did often, she was prickly and defensive, strung up for battle, and never relaxed. They fought like cat and dog, at arm's length or through a fence, for when he said something she took exception to, she lashed back fiercely.

More exposed to them than Grace, Edda and Tufts watched their struggles in helpless dismay.

"They'll each bleed the other to death," Tufts said to Edda.

"But why, when they're made for each other?" Edda asked.

"It's Kitty. I thought perhaps Maude had irritated her by pushing, but Daddy assures me she's behaving quite well. Charlie has some qualities that Kitty can't understand, and she hates the feeling."

"That's shrewd, Tufty." Edda shrugged. "Well, I for one refuse to interfere. I'm just sorry for Charlie."

Though Corunda wasn't to know it, the Great Depression moved faster than Charlie Burdum's siege of Kitty Latimer. He hadn't yet found the courage to kiss her lips when a few Sydney-based shops closed and threw a few more Corunda residents out of a job minus severance pay or benefits of any kind. Nor could the local unemployed find new work; no one was hiring, even the hospital. The federal government announced that a million pounds would be given to the states to dole out to unemployed men, then left it to each state to cut up its portion as it saw fit, as well as distribute the money. This led to municipal fiddling and furious outcries availing no one. South Australia, shockingly beset, was gifted disproportionately because of it, which provoked no anger. However, Western Australia was also disproportionately gifted for a less well-founded reason: the state wanted badly to secede from the Commonwealth, so Canberra deliberately wooed its government with an unduly large portion; Canberra was determined to keep the whole continent within the Commonwealth.

"Two hundred and seventy-six thousand pounds is a lot of money," Kitty said to Charles over a cup of tea in the cottage, "and I imagine that Sydney will get most of it. But will Corunda get any at all?"

"Probably not. Joblessness is low here compared to other country districts, even with the recent closures. No job—what a Christmas present!"

"Father is concentrating on the orphanage. He seems to feel it will inherit child victims of this horrible crisis. But surely no one will take a child from its mother?"

"Suicide, Kitty. It's risen appallingly among men, now some women are taking their lives, too. Besides, some mothers feel that if they abandon their children, their children will at least be fed, clothed, and sheltered in an orphanage."

Kitty shivered. "How cruel the world can be!" Her eyes went to his in anxious query. "I can't bear to talk about mothers deciding to abandon their children, but the subject has given me a little courage. Charlie, don't you carry any pain?"

He stared at her in genuine astonishment. "*Pain?* Why?"

"From your childhood? Not having a mother and father?" Her voice sank to a whisper. "Being—different from the rest?"

His laughter was too spontaneous to doubt. "Oh, Kitty, what a romantic you are! How could I miss two people I never knew? My childhood was splendid, honestly. My aunt and uncle—she was my mother's sister—brought me up to want for nothing. Nothing, Kitty, absolutely nothing! I was loved and well treated."

"But surely your differences?" she persisted, unconvinced.

"My want of height, you imply?"

"Yes, and anything else that gave you pain."

He shifted his chair and took her hands in his, which felt warm, dry, strong. "My uncle was shorter than I, and brought me up to regard lack of height as a challenge, not a cross to bear. I vindicated his faith and his trust in me—what more can I say? As to *pain*—romantic twaddle! Greek tragedies aren't rooted in the physical, but in human nature. I am Charles Henry Burdum, and one day I'll be *Sir* Charles. Women may get a kick out of high drama, it's permissible for women. But not for men. There was no pain as you mean it. I simply rose to combat challenges."

"I don't see it," she said. "Not to suffer is inhuman."

"Nonsense!" he snapped, tired of this conversation. "What would be inhuman would be to feel no sorrow, no grief, no fear. I've soaked my pillow with tears over a dead dog, to this very day grieve at the deaths of my aunt and uncle, and I can assure you that when a thug pointed a revolver at my chest one day, I knew fear." The eyes, gone bronze, looked at her with puzzlement. "You've been a nurse for three and a half years now, my dear, and I have reason to believe you're a very good one. Children are your great love—in which case, why aren't you having your own rather than peering at them through a cloudy window?"

Her breath caught, she stiffened. How brilliantly he could do that, snatch the advantage away from her and use it to crush her! Her quest for his pain derided and belittled, she stared at him in wonder.

"Yes, you're right," she said slowly. "It is a nonsense."

The charm flashed to the surface, together with a wonderful smile. "I'm very sorry," he said gently, "I didn't mean to cut you down so brutally. Oh, but you ask for it! If I had my wishes, I'd choose a soft wooing, full of tenderness and kindness, but you have an unerring instinct for the kill that makes you turn in the doorway of your boudoir and transform like lightning from the world's most seductive woman into a hissing, snarling wildcat. Every time you do it, I have to tame the wildcat all over again, and I am not by nature a hunter." The face changed, became ugly. "What I have to think about, I now understand, is whether I love you enough to put up with more of this. Frankly, I don't know."

"Perhaps," she said, "it's that I sense Corunda is too small for you, that you'll move on, and I don't want to live anywhere in the world except Corunda."

"I do have grand ambitions," he conceded, "but it isn't necessary to leave Corunda to achieve them. I want to enter the political arena, preferably on a federal level, and Corunda is perfect for that. It's a mere two-hour drive from Canberra."

Her face lightened. "I see! Yes, that makes sense."

"So if you married me, my darling Kitty, there would be no need to give up Corunda."

Her eye fell on the clock; she jumped. "I'm late!"

"I'll walk you to Children's, then no one can object."

Even so, he left it until the very last moment to ask her if she would have dinner with him. As always, she accepted.

Kitty didn't like to ask if the chef was still in the Burdum House kitchen, since dinner was meatloaf with gravy and mashed potatoes, but she suspected he was, since the meatloaf was minced lamb with a touch of cumin and no tendency to crumble, the gravy tasted like a sauce, and the mashed potatoes were pureed. She sent the potatoes back as too sloppy, not buttery enough, and devoid of pepper. Charles considered he did well to get two out of three correct, and had asked the chef to have fried potatoes in reserve. Since the chef was an Australian despite his Cordon Bleu training, he was seriously considering asking Con Decopoulos at the Parthenon if the man could observe Corunda-style cuisine.

"I liked the meatloaf," she said artlessly over coffee in the sitting room. "It was a little springy in texture, and it didn't break into chunks. Whatever it was flavored with has a delicious taste, but why turn good old spuds into milky mush?"

"If you marry me, I'll probably lose my chef," he said.

"Definitely! There are heaps of women in this town who can cook brilliantly, according to the natives. For, Charlie, if I marry you, we eat Corunda food, not bleeding meat and milky mush. And on that point there is absolutely no negotiation."

"You actually said, if!"

"So I did. If, not yes."

"It's a huge leap forward. You must love me a little."

"Love isn't really the stumbling block. Do I *like* you?"

"Let me kiss you," he said, coming to kneel before her. "Liking can only come from a degree of ease and companionship you won't permit, and that's my fault for telling you I loved you before I so much as knew your name. I'm not sure I like you, for that matter. What I do know is that we're destined to marry and spend our lives together. Here in Corunda, eating Corunda food. Let your guard down, please! Don't turn at the boudoir door and become a wildcat. Until you let your guard down, we rotate around each other on a fixed orbit."

She smiled. "You follow the ninth planet debate."

"I believe in the laws of Nature, and I also believe that human beings are a part of Nature," he said seriously.

Kitty leaned forward. "Kiss me, Charlie."

Her first consciousness of him was his smell, finding it heady, unexpected: some very expensive soap, a smooth and boyish tang, no hint of sweat. His embrace was enveloping but not alarming, for he had pushed her knees together off to his left, meaning he couldn't grind his groin against her; nor did he when he stood up and brought her with him. She hadn't realized how comfortable it would be to stand at much the same height as his; no stretching and straining. Either he was clever, or his respect was genuine, for he kept his hands above her waist at her back. Oh, Charlie, why do you always have two faces? Lucifer one moment, Satan the next. But both aspects of the Lord of Hell.

He didn't fumble his way across her cheek to her mouth, he hovered near enough to make her close her eyes by reflex, then put his lips on hers slightly at an angle, their pressure feather-light, their skin silky. Oh, yes, it *was* nice! Her body relaxed, nothing thus far having repelled her, especially a thrusting dominance that would have had her breaking free in a second. As if he were content to leave the response to her in her own time, a highly seductive lure for Kitty. When she parted her lips a little, he followed; her arms crept up around his neck.

The kiss went on as if she floated unanchored in a space of air and light until his left hand moved from her back to her side and sank into her flesh so suddenly that, against all reason, her body arched on a moan and fitted itself against him. In the same moment the kiss changed, deepened, became a turmoil of dark and velvety emotions that had her as much his prey as he was hers.

Then she was free; Charles was on the other side of the room, turned away from her and gazing out a window.

"Time to go home," he said after what seemed a long while. She found her gloves and purse and walked out ahead of him.

Grace didn't look at all surprised when Kitty confided in her the next morning.

"Well, you love him, so what are you waiting for?" Grace asked, giving a bowl of green jelly to Brian, then popping the teat of a bottle in John's mouth.

"Why do children love jelly so much?" Kitty asked. "It costs a tenth what baked custard does and has no nourishment except sugar to rot their teeth, but kiddies grab for the jelly and turn their noses up at the baked custard. Insane!"

The mother looked at the children's nurse in scorn. "Honestly, Kits, sometimes you're plain thick! Jelly is sensuous, it's cool rather than cloying—kiddies prefer cool to cloying—and they adore sucking it through their teeth, feel it melt on the tongue. Besides which, the sun shines through jelly yet it's brightly colored. And *don't* try to change the subject, which is whether you intend to marry Charlie Burdum or not. I say, stop all this maidenly quivering and do it."

Kitty departed feeling she had learned more about jelly than marriage—

which had its funny side, but didn't help. The one thing she didn't doubt was that Charlie loved her; what she doubted was whether she loved him, and nothing so far had given her the utter conviction that she couldn't live without him. Grace felt it for Bear, and it sustained silly Grace through all her mistakes.

The kiss had opened Kitty's eyes to pleasures she hadn't experienced when other men had kissed her, and seemed to promise the kind of lover a woman yearned for.

But there was far more to marriage than that, and her father's plight preyed on her. Never once had Daddy spoken of it, but it was there for his daughters to see and sorrow about. A quarter of a century irrevocably tied to a woman he couldn't esteem, whose actions often embarrassed or shamed him, without once coming into the open and admitting it was the unhappiest of unions. To Daddy, his vows were sacred, and could she enter into her marriage on less demanding terms than his? It wasn't a simple question of weakness, it was a horror of taking those vows and waking up to find herself plighted to a man whose charm and outward qualities had fooled her.

If he hadn't been rich, if he didn't have the signs of success written all over him, if he wasn't so self-confident, so sure his was the right way . . . What was it about him that set her back up?

And she was tiring, flagging. Why Kitty felt so strongly that she was fighting for her right to life, she didn't know, save that Charlie was a millstone grinding her into submission, the hunter out to cage his wildcat— she, who wasn't wild or catlike or domineering!

Then Grace invited her to morning tea on her new verandah, with Edda and Tufts to round out the celebration.

"Isn't it wonderful?" she asked, leading her sisters into it with delighted pride. "Bear and Jack did it for my birthday."

What had been a bare verandah was now a glassed-in place of white-painted cane chairs and innumerable pot plants from lush ferns to begonias in full bloom and tubs of Kentia palm trees.

"It faces south, so it never gets direct sun," Grace continued amid sounds of awed approval, "and Bear found a piece of workshop roof glass at the railway yards. Jack helped him fit it into the verandah roof so that the plants get light strong enough to flower. I love it!" She sat in a big planter's chair looking queenly.

"You do have good taste, Grace," said Edda affectionately. "Inside its walls, your house is out of the ordinary."

"Sit down, all of you," Grace said in a commanding voice. "Before we split into gaggles to make the tea, I want us to talk about Kitty's dilemma."

"What is holding you back, Kits?" Tufts asked, sitting.

"The fear of losing my own identity, I think," Kitty said. "How can I explain a feeling, a presentiment?"

"Do you doubt that Charlie loves you?" Grace asked.

"No, not for a second." She sat forward in her white chair, her eyes pleading for their patience and tolerance. "I suppose my fears are based in what I don't know about how Charlie's mind works—no, not that! It's a fear that what I call love isn't what Charlie means by it. Am I a human being, or property?"

"A human being," Tufts said instantly.

The others nodded emphatically.

"Kitty, Charlie would never choose a bride the way a man who collects Russian icons would choose another one," Edda said. "He looked at you and loved you without knowing a single thing about you—I call that choosing with the soul. If I ever met a man who felt like that about me, I might change my mind and marry him." She grinned. "Chemistry rather than biology."

"You're no help," said Kitty.

"As the only expert in the field," said Grace in superior tones, "I can at least offer you this pearl of wisdom, Kitty. Marriage is never what you imagined. It's a joining, and I don't mean that in a physical sense. Both the partners in it wake up married to a stranger—how can it be otherwise? They pool their ideas, dreams, money, minds as well as hearts. I made terrible mistakes early on, mostly thanks to ignorance and listening to the wrong advice. Because there's more than self involved. If you can't put Charlie ahead of yourself, you shouldn't marry him."

Edda was staring at her full twin in surprise. "My word, Grace, you *have* learned!" She turned to Kitty. "Dearest baby sister, none of us can make up your mind for you. That, you must do for yourself. But no matter what you decide, and no matter how things fall out, we'll be here for you."

The tears rolled down Kitty's cheeks. "Thank you, that's as much as I'll ever need," she whispered.

Grace gave her a lacy handkerchief. "What color do you want your bridesmaids to wear?" she asked briskly.

Brian chose that moment to invade his mother's party, both arms wrapped around his brother, who was getting too heavy for him to carry, though he refused to admit it.

They were, thought Edda, the most fetching little chaps, each owning a sweet disposition that would always be there. Flaxen-blond like their father, appealing little faces, both with widely set, pale blue eyes. Hardly anything of Grace.

Gazing at them, Edda spoke. "Kitty, life never meant you to be a children's nurse. Your life means you to have children of your own! Darling heart, you should have a tribe of them! In you I see about as perfect a mother as mothers come—sensible, hard when you have to be hard and soft when you have to be soft, the fount of love, warmth, security. Think of that, too."

"I agree," said Tufts, removing baby John from Brian's hold and cuddling him on her lap. "You have to have my children, too."

"So," said Grace, getting up to go kitchenward, "we're back to the color of the bridesmaids' dresses."

Whatever her sisters assumed, that first Christmas of the Great Depression loomed to find Kitty no closer to accepting Charles Burdum's hand in marriage. They had continued to meet regularly, but a change had crept into their relationship; Kitty was cooler, less prickly, seemed to be moving farther away. Sensitive to the tiniest nuances in her behavior, Charles began to despair without letting her see that he did. He equated success in everything, including love, with unbending strength; let him display weakness and she would think poorly of him. Especially given his lack of stature, he must *never* do anything that made him seem small in her eyes—he was fully the equal of any six-footer!

His actions since the economic difficulties began late in October had been admirable, with the result that his reputation in Corunda was growing rapidly. He had made no secret of his intention to use the hospital's "war chest" to aid unemployment by building a new hospital, though it would inevitably be some time before work was started. In his role as hospital superintendent he had taken to attending every kind of public meeting held in Corunda, and was not afraid to speak his mind from the gallery, even when what he said caused a furor.

All of which Kitty couldn't help but applaud. Charlie was no flash-in-the-pan, he was setting out to become a man of note and influence in Corunda's affairs separate and distinct from its hospital. This definitely indicated that under the charming veneer lay a sterling character, fearless, right-minded, clever, strong.

The Rector and his wife were giving a Christmas night dinner for the family, and all three nursing sisters were off duty until Boxing Day. Grace and Bear, Edda and Jack Thurlow, Tufts and Liam Finucan, and Kitty and Charles were invited.

Charles called at the cottage to collect Kitty, and found her alone; Tufts and Edda had already gone.

He kissed her tenderly and took her right hand, wrapped it around a small leather box. "Merry Christmas, my darling," he said, "and wear this for me. The battle's over, I declare a lifelong truce. There can be neither victory nor defeat."

Even knowing what was inside, Kitty in the Pandora tradition opened the box. It seemed to throw wide a door to the sun, the diamond blazing fiery prisms of every color as it moved in the light. "Ohh!" Kitty breathed, transfixed.

"It's only two carats," he was babbling, "but it's absolutely flawless, of the very first water. I couldn't find another stone half as good, even in Amsterdam."

The indecision rolled away; Kitty held out her left hand. "Put it on, Charlie," she said.

"*Will* you marry me?"

"Yes."

"Am I forgiven for the hubris of choosing your ring alone?"

"Yes, of course. It's your ring that you give to me."

⑤

The wedding took place with suitable pomp in St. Mark's at the end of January of 1930. Charles had made a decision that endeared him to all the male participants; Maude had demanded morning suits or white tie and tails, both of which would have had to be hired from Sydney, but Charles said firmly that three-piece suits were more practical. What a relief!

Kitty wore white satin to the floor and sweeping into a fan-shaped train so cunningly cut that no one needed to carry it; it was trimmed with seed pearls and much plainer than Maude had craved. Kitty had elected to put herself in Edda's hands.

The three bridesmaids wore plummy pink and carried bouquets of pink orchids; Maude had to wear fussy frills, of course, but no one else did, which rather put a dampener on her day.

Corunda packed the church and overflowed outside amid eddies and swirls of multicolored confetti that would linger until winter gales finally blew the last of the paper discs away. Since the Rector couldn't afford a huge reception and refused to let Charles contribute, the actual ceremony was all Corunda managed to see. Yet another disappointment for Maude, whose pink organdy frills should, she felt, have received a better airing.

Due to the hard times, the bridal couple didn't take a honeymoon; they went straight from the small reception at St. Mark's Rectory to Burdum House, there to begin married life.

At first, ordinary people who didn't dabble in stocks and shares thought that the economic disaster had to be a temporary affair, a matter of months at the outside. This attitude was particularly prevalent in Corunda, whose inhabitants were slow to suffer the full onslaught. In Corunda, jobs at first didn't fall like autumn leaves brought down in a violent wind, for all that the newspapers kept saying this was true in cities like Sydney and Melbourne. Protected from the early depredations of the Great Depression by Charles Burdum's liberal use of his own fortune and the hospital, Corundites kept their jobs or else found new ones.

Charles decided to start rebuilding the hospital at once, and at an accelerated pace; it never occurred to him that anyone would see the solution in any other light than of creating new jobs and getting men back into work as quickly as possible, though he should have known better: he was City of London nurtured. Only later did he pause to think that the formal theories of economics dictated otherwise.

Corunda was plentifully endowed with carpenters, plumbers, cabinet-makers, bricklayers, electricians, plasterers, skilled laborers, and gardeners in a town famous for its gardens. When Jack Thurlow told Charles about a deposit of brick clay out at Corbi, he seized on the information eagerly; it meant that the town could furnish the main building material, bricks, from within itself rather than have to import. Extra jobs, too!

Many, especially on the hospital staff, objected strenuously to the old

211

design's being used with so little modification—what griped about it, of course, was walking the same old ramps. Since he had gone to the expense of commissioning a first-class model of the hospital from a Sydney firm that made nothing else, Charles could point to a three-dimensional example and show his various grievance groups how splendid the new ramps would be; but nothing converted those who hated the ramps or the old shoddy design. They wanted a modern multistory block hospital. And at this point a great many inhabitants of Corunda discovered that Charles Burdum was as tough a Burdum as any in history, and had a suavely savage side.

"You can whinge and whine and whimper until Hell freezes over," he said to two hundred indignant anti-ramp protesters in the Town Hall, "but it won't make a scrap of difference to me or the new hospital. Corunda Base Hospital goes up as the model shows. I'll not put my patients at risk of lifts or elevators or whatever you want to call them—this is not Sydney! And if you don't care to exercise voluntarily, I'll oblige you! Construction of a new hospital in this form keeps jobs here rather than see much of the materials imported, even from abroad! Corunda will cut its precious cloth of jobs and prosperity to suit its status and its needs! Whether you like it or not, ladies and gentlemen, I, Charles Burdum, am the guiding light and prime mover of this enterprise! There are many schemes in my head to make this kind of hospital design more tolerable than it seems to those who hate to walk a foot more than they must, but I have no intention of enlightening you today—or tomorrow! You don't deserve it. Be thankful that there are jobs to be had! Now go away!"

"That," said Kitty, tucking her arm through his, "was not very politic, Charlie." She grinned, kissed his cheek. "Oh, but I did enjoy it! Some people are never satisfied."

"Your father will be, when he learns that I'm using some of the hospital's money to set up a ward and clinic at the orphanage."

"Oh, Charlie, that's wonderful! And becoming very needed."

Once a Hospital Board weasel, the Reverend Thomas Latimer had turned into a rabid lion over the orphanage. A late Victorian pile not unlike Burdum House, it had originally been foisted on Corunda as part of a movement that flourished around the 1890s and very early 1900s; orphaned children should be accommodated in rural circumstances where they could learn to farm, produce some of what they ate, and breathe sweet, unsmoky air. As a result, it drew its intake statewide, the fate of a particular orphan decided by clerks in Sydney. Most such institutions were charities run by religious denominations, but Corunda's wasn't. Now, with the axe of retrenchment reducing everything governmental to kindling, the orphanage was in dire straits. Almost every day saw some new child put on the train in Sydney and sent off to live at Corunda orphanage, groaning at the seams.

Thomas Latimer made it his main concern, as he did so displaying a rare talent for interdenominational—could it be called *politics*? Whatever Corundites liked to call it, by March of 1930 the Rector had managed to see the Salvation Army reign supreme in the matter of soup kitchens and other traditional Sally areas, get every single minister, pastor and priest working on the same team for the benefit of the orphanage, deserted mothers, indigent aged, and any others needful of help. Monsignor O'Flaherty possessed one curate, Father Bogan, who had a genius for organization; thanks to the Rector, Father Bogan took over as master-controller of all charitable efforts, thereby saving needless duplication and avoiding religious power plays that would have wasted time.

Maude Latimer found herself put on a far smaller, strictly regulated income, and also found that her complaints fell on deaf ears.

"Cease your grizzling, Maude," the Rector told her firmly. "You want for very little, while these children, through no fault of their own, want for everything. And yes, Billy Marsyk is to practice on the Rectory piano. The lad has a great talent."

"Great talent, humbug!" cried Maude to Tufts, who paid her a duty call the next day. "The dirty little beast wee'd in my cut glass lily vase!"

"Well, Mama, at least he didn't wee on the carpet," Tufts said with twitching lips. "I think it shows Billy has finer feelings."

"Oh, you're as bad as your father!"

"Come, Mama, after all these years you should know Daddy far better than you obviously do. Daddy scrapes to find the money to buy his orphans shoes for winter. They can't go barefoot in a Corunda winter. Don't grizzle, Mama."

Maude drew herself up. "I *never* grizzle!" She gave vent to a sudden, rather eerie giggle. "Have you seen my baby Kitty lately? Isn't she the most beautiful child in the world?"

Caught unaware, Tufts gaped, then strove to look ordinary, terrified her mother might see her reaction. Relieved, Tufts saw that Maude hadn't noticed a thing. What made her say *that*?

On her way out she encountered her father outside the garage. "Daddy," she said when the greetings were over, "is Mama quite all there in the head? I've noticed other things, but just now—!"

The long and handsome face, so reminiscent of Edda, shut in on itself, grey eyes—wary? "Your mama is all right, dear."

"Are you sure?"

"Positive. I take it she said something about Kitty? Yes, I thought as much. Kitty's marriage hit her hard."

"But she always wanted a rich man for Kitty!"

"Wishes are evanescent, Tufts. Reality is a different thing."

"Daddy, to all intents and purposes Kitty has been gone from the Rectory since April of 1926." Tufts put her hand on her father's arm. "Mama's mind is slipping slightly, and I think you know it."

Australian journalists had only one way to estimate unemployment figures, for no one in government kept statistics on things that were seen as insignificant. One group of men with jobs did keep records, however; these were the trade unions, to whom it was important to know employment figures. At first each union wasn't too interested in how many members of a different union were employed, but very quickly in the wake of federation the unions understood how important an overall impression of the unionized was. The central body kept figures released as percentages, and on this slender foundation the jobless in Australia were estimated.

Someone decided that unionized working men comprised half the total workforce, as many with jobs either felt no need to belong to a union, or disliked paying union dues, or had no union to cater for their kind of work. So newspapers and news magazines, devoid of any other alternative, applied a rule of thumb: the total jobless were double the union jobless.

At the end of 1929, perhaps fifteen in every hundred men in jobs no longer had a job.

The unemployment was accompanied by horrific hardship as people were evicted from their homes nationwide. Whole towns of shanties came into being on the fringes of big towns and all cities to shelter the wives and children of jobless men. A jobless man rolled a tiny assortment of essentials in a blanket, called this cylindrical bundle a "swag" and set off on foot to walk sometimes thousands of miles in search of the thing Australia could not give him—work.

According to government and financial men, the key to overcoming all this misery was something known as retrenchment. It meant that no public body at least—and most private bodies followed suit—could spend money on anything from wages to works: no new infrastructure to be built, no new jobs, drastic paring of existing jobs, and big reductions in pay. One or two voices cried in the wilderness that to cure the Great Depression meant public bodies *should* spend money on new infrastructure, but in 1930 no one was prepared to listen.

Employment, not retrenchment, was the answer, said the renegade New South Wales Labour man, Jack Lang, who also advocated that no Australian government should repay its foreign loans until Australians themselves had more to live for. No one of any social stratum wanted to understand that governments hungry to modernize and expand had done so using foreign money, and in the process incurred massive debt the times suddenly rendered unpayable; in effect, they had mortgaged their people rather than real estate.

Ordinary housewives like Grace Olsen weren't sure enough of their facts to judge financial turmoil, and among the Latimer sisters she was the most isolated from informed opinion. In her exquisitely furnished house on Trelawney Way she was gradually acquiring a social status thanks to a combination of qualities not usually seen in the Trelawneys: she knew about women's and children's health, she could write letters or fill in forms aggressively or tenderly or other, she knew about councils and utility bodies, and she wasn't a snob.

Toward the end of December of 1929, Bear had severely limited Grace's spending in ways she couldn't evade; sounding wretched, he had told her that he must put something away against the future, and to do so meant he would have to cut her housekeeping allowance. No new clothes, no new curtains, no expensive cuts of meat, and buy Brian's clothes far too big—John could wear them when outgrown. Caught completely off-guard, Grace had responded meekly.

What Bear didn't have the heart to tell her was that his income had fallen drastically; people weren't buying Perkins products save those they couldn't live without, like the liniment, ointment, and corning mixture.

Half of the sales force had been dispensed with, which for Bear meant a circuit so huge it took weeks to travel; his living allowance had been reduced to subsistence level, so he slept in his car for six nights, with one in seven nights at a hotel to wash his person and his clothes properly.

Something in his eyes silenced Grace's protests. They looked hunted, even a little exhausted, and the merriment that had always lurked in them had vanished. Obviously times were hard for him; she just didn't know how hard, and judged his plight too lightly.

So she turned to Jack Thurlow, as constant as the sun.

"Do you know what's happened to Bear?" she asked him.

Long experience with Grace counselled him to keep his wariness on the inside, not let her see a trace of it. He looked mildly enquiring. "I'm not sure what you mean, Grace."

A shrug. "He's changed. Or do I mean that he's lost his sense of humor? Bear was always laughing, now he never does. He says things are hard—well, they must be, he's cut my housekeeping—but he won't *talk* about things."

"You should take that as a compliment," he said with an easy smile. "Bear's firm is feeling the pinch, it's that simple."

"But he told me to buy clothes for Brian that are far too big—does he want *our son* to look like a West Ender, with his trouser bottoms turned up to his crotch and his coat sleeves turned up to his armpits? Darning the darns on his socks?"

"That's how I was brought up, and my parents were well off. Handsome is as handsome does, Grace," Jack said in a no-nonsense voice. "Brian is a good-looking little chap. Whatever he wears can't change that, and you know Brian himself won't give a tuppenny-bumper about turned-up clothes."

Balked, Grace asked no more questions, but, she said to Edda when Edda paid her a visit, "It goes against the grain to have to squeeze every ha'penny so hard that the copper melts. Brian looks like a West Ender—scandalous! Little John permanently in hand-me-downs! What will people say?"

"In the Trelawneys, that your sons are like everyone else's, I imagine. You sound like Maude," said Edda unsympathetically. "It could be much worse, can't you see that? Bear's got a job as long as Perkins is in business, but he's on a commission as well as a flat wage, and his earnings are down." She took a breath. "Make some tea, Grace. I brought some of the Rectory Anzacs."

"And isn't that a sign of the time?" Grace heaved a sigh. "No more pikelets with jam and cream, just Anzac biscuits." She brightened. "They dunk beautifully, never fall apart."

"Why else do you think I chose them? Brian and John can share the dunking."

Once the tea and Anzacs were consumed and two little frost-fair faces washed, Grace returned to her plaint, lack of money. "How long do you think it's going to be before Bear is back to earning well?" she asked, polishing the kitchen table.

"I'll give you this, Grace, you may be the world's greatest moaner, but you keep an immaculate house without any help at all, which is more than Maude can do."

"To have my scrubwoman back would be heaven, but even I can see those days are over!" Grace answered tartly; she never liked being reminded that she was a moaner. "How long will it be hard?"

"Charlie Burdum says years."

"Huh! He's still swimming in money!"

"True, but he employs many, and Kitty employs, too. You know the rate of deserted wives in the West End, Grace. Everyone forgets women—just as if we didn't exist, or give birth to the masters. In this whole benighted country, there is only one pension for women under sixty—the New South

Wales Government's widow's pension, and it's a pittance. All the other governments *deride* New South Wales for giving it. It's the state that owes the
most money to London, but if it got its fair share of the federal money it
wouldn't have needed to borrow so much. Victoria and Western Australia
always get proportionally more than they should." Edda leaned forward
and shook her sister savagely. "Get that glazed look off your face! This is
important! It may even be personally important to you one day, so *listen*!
Don't switch the light off!"

Edda's frustration at Grace's apathy and density hadn't entirely evaporated
when she met Jack Thurlow for a gallop along the river, though by the time
they entered his bedroom at Corundoobar the cobwebs were sufficiently
blown away to let her enjoy his love-making. After a long liaison his body
was as familiar to her as her own, but it still delighted her. So, apparently,
did she delight him.

"Why do you keep coming back to me?" she asked.

"Oh, that's easy," he said, relishing his cigarette. "You are a fastidious,
highly desirable woman who condones a sexual encounter without demanding that it be legitimized by marriage. It's heaven to have a mistress of
class and respectability. Most men have to settle for a whore, and if you had
a hundred lovers, Edda, you'd still not be a whore."

"Why?" she asked, stretching her naked body.

"Whoredom is a state of mind in which the woman expects to be paid
for her services. Money isn't always the tender—that might be anything
from power to deeds—but there is always a contract to be signed. It's not
the *act* makes a woman a whore, it's purely her mental attitude. Men are
whores, too, but usually sex isn't their weapon."

"That's very odd and perceptive for a mere grazier to come out with. But
it's the quality in you draws me, I freely admit it. Your mind isn't boring. You
plant potatoes magnificently, but potatoes don't enter your thoughts." She
linked her hands together above her head on the pillow. "So I'm desirable?"

"As a buffet to a glutton."

"A little lacking in the bosom department," she said, her grin impish.

"More than a mouthful is wasted."

"Come and scrub my back, you lazy sod."

They were enamored of shared showers, after which the fussy Edda changed into clean clothes to get rid of the horse aroma, and sat with him in the old homestead's venerable kitchen drinking cold bottled beer from Jack's ice chest. A fat lamb grazier, he made his own ice.

"Charles Burdum is the town hero," he said.

"My esteemed brother-in-law. He's rightly a hero, I feel. Rome wasn't built in a day and nor will the new hospital be, but he's started it, and he won't stop until it's finished. The money is there." She gazed at Jack with affection—why wasn't it love? "Thanks to you, even the bricks will be local. No one knew that there was brick clay out at Corbi until you said so."

"Old Henry Burdum knew. Infertile ground, which is why he never spread in Corbi's direction. No one wanted that land."

"Where do you think Charlie's going, Jack?"

"Huh?"

"Corunda is never going to satisfy him. There's a political aspect to all his good works, haven't you noticed? After he found out most West Enders don't have the transport to get to Corbi and make bricks, he went to Sydney and bought an elderly double-decker bus. The local mechanics are happy to keep it running free of charge beyond the cost of the parts—he's shrewd, is Charlie. He could have afforded a new bus and paid a mechanic. But if he were standing for parliament, every West Ender would vote for him no matter what his party," Edda said dreamily. "He gave them a new industry *and* transport to it. Cost, all up? A hundred quid."

"You don't think that's too harsh a judgment?"

She blew a rude noise. "Look at it and him, Jack, do! Sydney is boiling with riots between the police and the workless, the federal idiots palm off their responsibilities onto the states and can do no more for people than to announce that some knight-director of the Bank of England is coming out to advise the nation on its economic strategies—pah! Western Australia is trying to secede again—I wish they would, they couldn't make a worse mess of things than Canberra has. Our Australian pound is being devalued, and now Jimmy Scullin has had to sack his Treasurer because it's said the man is a blatant crook! I ask you, is this government? To me, it's pathetic."

"I love to watch you when you're indignant."

Having had his laugh, Jack took her hand and kissed it. "You're right about the politics, but how *exactly* does Charlie Burdum fit into the picture?"

"Don't be dense, Jack. I've already told you. He has big political aspirations, I think directed at the federal parliament in Canberra. The Right Honourable Charles Burdum, Prime Minister of Australia. What I can't see is which party he'll join. By background and fortune he should be a Tory, but he has a spiritual affinity with the working man that suggests Labor's right wing."

"He can't be prime minister!" Jack exclaimed, aghast. "He's a Pommy, not a dinkum Aussie."

Edda's eyes mocked. "That's not written into the constitution, though it should be, like the American one. Being a Pommy won't stop any ambitious politician."

"You're right. They'll just play the fact down, maybe even sweep it under the rug."

When Bear Olsen returned home at the end of July 1930, he came in on the Sydney day train in a second-class compartment, then walked the three miles from the station to his cream and green house on Trelawney Way, carrying his suitcase as if it weighed a ton. His hat was pulled low over his brow because the eyes its brim hid were red and puffy from weeping. The five-hour trip on this local that stopped at every tiny station had proven a boon, for he could let his tears flow unchecked. What did it matter if anyone saw him? Not that many did; even a second-class ticket on a train was unaffordable for most men and women these days. Unaffordable for him, too, except that he knew he had to get home as soon as possible once he started in home's direction; taking to the dirt roads as a swagman was for the future.

His sons were in the backyard. He could hear their happy yells and chatter as he mounted the front verandah, and shrank from that inevitable meeting. Grace was on her plant verandah, he could hear her humming—how she loved that green haven!

"Grace?" he called from the lounge room, suitcase dropped.

"Bear! Oh, Bear!" she cried, arriving at a run to cast her arms around him, kiss his unshaven chin. "I didn't hear the car—did you park on the street?"

"No car," he managed to say.

The hat came off; Grace looked into her husband's face and began to tremble. "Oh, Bear, what's happened?"

221

"Perkins has gone under," he said tonelessly. "No job, no car, no severance pay, just a glowing reference that calls me the best salesman in Australia. But I didn't have the heart to sell things people can do without when times are so terrible. Not that Mr. Perkins asked me to. It was like a landslide in the end."

One arm about his waist, she led him into the green haven and seated him in the planter's chair, pulled another chair close to him and took his hands in hers.

"You'll get another job," she said, trying to absorb the tragic eyes, measure the volume of tears he must have shed.

"No, Grace, I won't," he said. "I've spent ten days going all over Sydney, my glowing reference in my hand, but there are no sales jobs. None at all. People have stopped buying. Oh, what a shock, Grace! Jobless men everywhere, queues *thousands* long applying for just one job, police wearing revolvers in some places where the rioting is constant, shops boarded up, house after house empty, cut off from everything to keep squatters out—if it weren't for the Sally soup kitchens and a few other religious mobs doling out food, I reckon Sydney would be a city of dead people. At least the parts of it I saw. Some parts are better, but the jobless don't go there because there are no factories or workshops." He began to weep again. "Jeez, I didn't want to cry! I thought I'd be all dried up by now."

She squeezed into the chair alongside him and held him to her breast, amazed to find herself tearless and composed. "You must cheer up, Bear. You're *home*," she said, throwing every ounce of feeling into that lovely little word. "You have family here, helpful contacts—Charlie will find you something to do, he's giving out lots of jobs."

"Not to salesmen," Bear said.

Grace fished out her handkerchief and gave it to him. "It doesn't have to be a job in sales, dear. Not right away, at any rate. Until times improve, it might be—oh, I can't guess!"

"Grace, the only jobs anyone is offering are in hard labor, you know that. I've been a salesman since I was a beardless tyke, so all I can do is talk, walk, and drive. I can't heft bags of wheat or swing a pick and shovel to save my life." He drew himself up, the tears gone again. "Besides, I can't use my relationship to an important man to step into a job that thousands are fighting over. So no, I'm not applying to Charles Burdum for any sort of job—or to Jack Thurlow or your father, for that matter."

Appalled, Grace pulled away to stare at him and saw the humorous mouth turned down implacably, the cheeks fallen in, a faint scrag under his chin—when had he last eaten?

"Let's go into the kitchen and I'll make you lunch," she said, pulling him to his feet. "The boys have already eaten, so we won't tell them you're home until you've had a chance to eat, have a hot bath, and put on clean clothes. Mark my words," she chattered as they crabbed along, "you'll feel a different man."

In the kitchen she put him at her work table and busied herself slicing bread. "See? No ham or tinned salmon, dear!" She laughed, a merry sound. "It's my own homemade jam, fish paste, or Marmite these days, and I put the ice chest into storage in the garage. Edda gave me her little old one out of her quarters—it keeps what I need chilled on a much smaller block of ice."

Now why did that make him cry again? Determined to ignore it, she finished making his fish paste sandwiches, and while he ate them, washed down by a whole pot of tea, she ran him a bath with hot water from the chip heater. Finally, fed, bathed, shaved, and clothed, he was fit to meet his sons. Oh, Bear, don't weep under their eyes, too! Grace prayed.

He did not. As he had sold virtually right around a quarter-million square miles, this last had been a lengthy absence, so to Bear his sons came as a shock. Brian was four months past two years, straight-legged and tall, slender like both his parents; his hair was still very fair, but less flaxen. And John was Brian at nearly fourteen months—walking, talking, busy, curious, adorable. From somewhere Bear managed to summon the strength to behave with them as he always did, tossing them around, laughing, pretend-spanking them—even, from out of his suitcase, to give Brian a jigsaw puzzle and John a humming top. Broke he might be, but how could a father come home to his sons without producing presents?

"Where do I register for work in Corunda?" he asked Grace after the boys settled to play with their presents.

"It's only for hard labor," she said. "They'll give you a dole for government work, which is limited to hard labor. Jobs with skills just don't exist.

Few can do the actual labor, but they take the dole anyway. If they have to report, they just lean on their picks."

"I'll not take a dole! It's something in return for nothing."

"Charlie will find you something honest to do."

"I'm not pulling strings by going to Charlie, that's final."

Luckily his travails over the past two weeks had exhausted him; by five o'clock he was tucked up in their bed asleep, and Grace was free to deal with the boys, settle them for sleep, too.

At six o'clock, in the pitch darkness, Grace lit a hurricane lantern and walked down to the junction of Trelawney Way with Wallace Street, where there was a red, Georgian-paned telephone booth. Their own phone had been disconnected when Bear cut the housekeeping last December.

When the penny dropped, a feminine voice answered.

"Kitty? Thank God!"

"Grace? Is that you, Grace? You sound odd!"

"Can you come and see me at once? I'm in the phone box, but daren't be away too long."

"As soon as I can find a driver, I'll be there."

Life with Charlie, Kitty was discovering, carried compensations for her giving up nursing. Though she loved Charlie very much, it had been a wrench to abandon her sick children, but the regulations were set in stone: *no married nurses!* However, she had Burdum House to renovate, an undertaking that involved many trips to Sydney to choose tiles, wallpapers, fabrics, floor coverings, chandeliers and sconces, furniture, fixtures, and fittings. As she found Edda a great help in guiding her taste, she timed these expeditions to coincide with Edda's days off, and the two of them had a wonderful time in Sydney, staying at the Hotel Australia and dining at places where the chef was willing to cook his meat.

Her own forays into the kitchen were less successful; she found no thrills in watching pot contents boil over or frying pans go up in smoke, so when Charlie proposed a solution, she was ready to listen. They would hire a chef skilled enough to cater for both culinary poles, Charles's north and Kitty's south.

An enchantment Kitty hadn't expected to feel engulfed her entire life. Charlie was a wonderful lover, though why she had assumed he wouldn't be eluded her until she realized that she had transferred her own inferiority at being so small onto him as well. Small was inadequate, small couldn't possibly be the answer to a maiden's prayers. Now, fallen in love with Charlie, Kitty experienced the delights of being with someone just right for her. Her few encounters with men over the years had intimidated her, she now understood. Average height men were still so tall that she was forced to stand on tiptoe for a kiss, while six-footers lifted her clear off the floor; for some reason there were even men who wanted to pick her up and cart her about like a sick dog—her metaphor, and one that had Charlie in paroxysms of mirth.

Whereas Charlie was—Charlie was *perfect*! As if by instinct he knew how to arouse her, and he had a thousand ways of kissing her, all delicious. He put his hands on her with as much reverence as passion, and he let her know that she gave him huge pleasure.

So the Kitty who had to wait for a taxi was bubbling with joy, a joy she genuinely hadn't thought could grow any greater until that very morning, when Dr. Ned Mason had told her she was definitely expecting a baby. A baby! Her own baby!

Grace and Kitty met, and were stupefied.

Grace saw a transfigured Kitty, beautiful and triumphant, a woman free from care, woe, worry.

Kitty saw a shattered Grace, all joy stripped from her, eyes protruding, body trembling, her beauty blighted.

"Grace, darling, what is it? What's the matter?"

In answer Grace walked past her, wringing her hands together, then turned, it seemed gathering herself to dredge up a vanished courage, and said, "Bear has lost his job."

"Grace! How—how *awful*! Let's sit in the kitchen, it's warm with the fuel stove—thank God Jack Thurlow keeps you well supplied with wood," Kitty babbled, pushing the kettle onto the hotter part of the hob. "No, I can make the tea."

"You're too short," said Grace, pushing Kitty into the chair and tipping a little hot water into the teapot to warm it. "Good strong tea, that's what we both need." Her grey gaze, calming, saw clearly at last. "How lovely!" she cried. "There's a baby."

"I only found out this morning, but don't say anything until I've had a chance to tell Charlie."

"Mum's the word, I promise." The tea making proceeded with smooth efficiency. "I'm actually all right, just terrified at the change in Bear," she said, doling out cups and saucers. "I had to be the strong one when he came home today, isn't *that* a turn-up for the books? And do you know what, Kits? I did it! I was strong for Bear and my boys. I—me, myself—didn't seem important somehow. He cried so! He was that proud of being the top Perkins Man! But the firm's gone under, closed its doors." She poured tea. "The trouble is that he's not a physically strong man, he certainly couldn't do hard labor. And he's a proud man too. *Very* proud! I need you to talk to Charlie, explain all that."

"Don't worry, I will. I agree about the hard labor, but Bear has a brain, which is far better. Charlie will know the answer."

"It's not that simple," Grace said, sipping at the very hot tea. "Bear's got it into his head that it would be wrong to pull strings by asking Charlie for help. In fact, he won't hear of it. Honestly, Kits, I'm not exaggerating."

"I see."

"Oh, Kitty, I hope you do!"

Charles Burdum walked in, mouth tight. "At least you left me a message, I can be thankful for that, I suppose," he said, sitting down at the table, one hand out imperiously to Grace. "No, no tea, *please*! How you can all drink coal tar and call it tea I do not know."

"Dear, dear," said Grace mildly, "in a bad mood, are we?"

"A taxi, Kitty?" he asked. "Was it so urgent that you see your sister at this hour?"

"As a matter of fact, yes," she said, a little winded at his displeasure. "Bear has just come home without a job. Perkins is no more. The poor fellow is a cot-case."

The metaphorical slap in his face had its calculated effect; Charles looked horrified, contrite, embarrassed. "Oh, Grace, I'm so sorry!" And, to his wife, "My dear, I apologize. It's been a nasty sort of day, but I had no right to take it out on you."

"More to the point, Charlie," said Kitty, brushing apologies aside, "Bear is being very stubborn and refuses to ask you for a job or pull strings of any kind."

"I understand," he said, meaning it. "Everything Bear is, he won by his own efforts and hard work. A working man's pride is very strong in him, I've always admired his success."

"In the meantime, Charlie, Grace had to walk with a lantern to the phone box to ask me to come, and I refuse to have that worry as well. Grace must have a phone," said Kitty, "but not a party line."

"Grace will have a phone, and not a party line."

Kitty leaned toward Grace, eyes pleading. "You must explain to Bear, Grace, that it's for Daddy's peace of mind. Without a phone, you and the boys are cut off from the family."

"Yes, Kitty, I understand that, and I'm happy to agree. If Daddy weren't a minister, Bear would listen to him, but he hates religion. He says all the wars are fought over differing ideas of God," said Grace, who was beginning to see that her present problems would never matter to anyone else the way they did to her. And it was all her own fault. Were she not an incurable spendthrift, Bear would have met this disaster with £1000 in the bank, if not more. You, Grace Olsen, she told herself, have a lot of grief to answer for, not the least your husband's present devastation.

"Yes, well," she said brightly, "having told my news, there doesn't seem much else to do until tomorrow, when Bear wakes up. Will you see him, Charlie?"

"Of course," he said warmly. "I'll be here at nine." He rose to his feet. "I'll wait in the car for you, Kitty."

"He'll cheer up no end when you tell him about the baby," Grace said, smiling. "As for me, don't think I haven't admitted that were it not for me, we'd have money in the bank."

Astonished, Kitty stared at her. The whining complaints and constant self-pity seemed to have disappeared in the face of this terrible catastrophe. The path to martyrdom she had visualized as Grace's future just wasn't the route she was going to take. "I wish you'd stayed in nursing longer," Kitty said. "You'd have a better chance at finding part-time work."

Grace smiled, shook her head. "No, that was never an option for me. Once I met Bear, I knew where my life was going. I'd have walked on my knees to China to be with Bear. I watched you vacillate for months about Charlie, but I never experienced one twinge of doubt about Bear. Something in me recognized my fate."

A shaft of bitter envy struck Kitty's heart with the force of a warrior's spear—why had silly, empty-headed Grace known her mate so surely, while she, far more intelligent and grounded, had been so blind to Charlie? Did it mean that the love between Grace and Bear was far greater than hers for Charlie? Charlie had known at once. What was the matter with her, that her feelings had needed so much pushing and shoving before they surfaced?

Kitty joined him in the car not long after he had left the Olsen house, her face in the Packard's dim interior light looking oddly pinched. Well, a shock. No denying Grace could be a burden.

"You'll have trouble persuading Bear to take a job," she said.

"A poor man's pride is always hard to overcome."

"Is it wrong to decline to pull strings?"

Charles gave a snort of laughter. "The world capers and cavorts on denser meshes of pulled strings than you'll ever know, Kitty, starting with the politicians. Poor Bear is too proud to pull strings, so he'll never accumulate the power to set up his sons in plum jobs, and I'll be too busy setting up my own sons to help. Now's his chance."

Something in Kitty twisted; she let out a mew of distress. "Oh, Charlie, don't tempt fate!" she cried.

"What is it, my dear?"

"When we get home," she said.

But first there was dinner to be eaten, and Kitty's tongue was anchored as if by leaden weights; she tried to find the mood of the morning vainly, crushed by Grace's news. At a loss, she prattled about the change in Grace without noticing Charlie's increasing exasperation—all this grief over a *half* sister?

"She's talking about growing her own vegetables, and so happy that she planted an apple and a pear two years ago. Huh! Jack Thurlow planted them, she meant—dearest Grace! She also says she's going to keep chooks. Grace, keeping chooks?"

"Keeping what?" he asked blankly, getting a word in.

"Chooks—hens, Charlie! Chickens too old to be chicks."

"Chook. To rhyme with book and hook?"

"The very same."

"I am forever learning."

A silence fell, thick as treacle.

"Charles?"

"Did you just call me by my proper name?"

"Yes, I did."

Eyes sparkling, he sat up straight. "I answer to Charles."

"I'm going to have a baby."

Her words literally knocked all thought out of his brain; he gaped at her, jaw dropped, mouth working, one emotion after another crossing his face, his eyes gone now to pure fire. Suddenly, convulsively, he jumped up, seized her and held her in a hard embrace. "Kitty, my Kitty! A child? Our child? When, my love?"

"Ned Mason thinks December. I saw him this morning for final confirmation, and he says I'm four months gone." Her laugh sounded. To Charles, it was a victory paean. "A decently respectable interval after our marriage, yet, as Daddy would say, we are a fruitful pair."

Still shaking, he sat with his wife on his knee and put one reverent hand on her belly. "He's in there, growing—four months already! Are you well? Is Ned pleased?"

"Delighted. My pelvis is nice and wide, everything is as it ought to be, my basal metabolism is ideal—in short, Charlie dear, I'm bright eyed, bushy tailed, and my nose is moist."

"It's a boy," he said positively.

"Latimer statistics favor a girl."

"Grace has boys."

"That's what I mean. Daddy had four girls, so perhaps Grace has used up the Latimer boy credits already."

"I'll love a girl just as much. I married one."

229

"True." A shudder ran through her. "Still, today hasn't been auspicious. Bear losing his job—pray it's not an omen!"

"Any omens concern Bear and Grace, not us, Kitty."

Grace decided to be frank about her activities, so when Bear woke next morning, she made him toast for breakfast and confessed that she had confided in Kitty.

"In the old days it would have been Edda, but circumstances have changed, Bear. Kitty is the one with the influence these days, so I asked her to see me last night, and she came here. No, no, I didn't beg for a job, that's not my business, any more than it's Kitty's business to beg one from Charlie. I simply wanted to tell my sister what's happened, and ask her to send Charlie to see you here this morning. He'll be here soon. I don't care what you talk about or what you decide. I've done my bit in getting you together."

He was staring at her, puzzled, not understanding how much Grace had changed over the past eight months, a change he had initiated by reducing her housekeeping allowance. The old, moaning Grace was nowhere to be found; instead, Bear encountered a firm and purposeful woman who completely understood her situation.

"What happened to you?" he asked her, confused.

The old Grace would have tried to play dumb; this new Grace didn't. "I grew up in a hurry," she said, pouring him more tea. "No more locomotive puff-puffs, Bear. Our sons can be excused that behavior, but we're adults. We're parents and providers."

"Don't rub it in," he whispered, wincing.

She stroked his bent back. "Bear, I'm not rubbing it in. What's happened to us isn't of our making, though we must do the sufffering. More, I'd bet, than the people who created this mess will ever suffer. I'm trying to make you see that we used to have the prosperity to cherish illusions, but that now the illusions are forbidden. Including pride, which Daddy calls a sin. Take the work Charlie Burdum offers you, for the sake of your sons."

Badly wounded in spirit as well as in mind, adrift in an ocean of unknowns, Bear hardly heard this alien Grace, and failed utterly to grasp what she said about pride. Well, she was sheltered, how could she even begin to know what it had been like in Sydney, watching the crawlers and boot-lickers swarm to get the jobs other men were more entitled to, except they wouldn't beg and grovel. He wanted his sons to grow up *men*, not boot-licking crawlers.

In the meantime, Grace rattled on about Charles Burdum and how he, Bear Olsen, should be very civil . . .

And then the next it seemed second later he was overwhelmed by this charming, dapper, smooth little man in the proper Corunda clothes, with his grand gestures and his carefree manner—not to worry, Bear, it would all be over in no time!

"Meanwhile, Bear," Charles continued, full of enthusiasm, "I have an ideal job for you! I swear, ideal! There's a new field opening up for men with exactly your kind of skills—the gift of the gab, shall we say? The field is called public relations, and it's *fascinating*! As population grows and governments and other kinds of public institutions grow ever more faceless, it's becoming necessary to teach the general populace what's going on. If the general populace isn't educated about the faceless men in real authority or owning real power, trouble will erupt due to ignorance and misinterpretation." The khaki eyes dwelled on Bear's face. "Are you following me?" Charles asked.

"Yes," said Bear.

Warming to his theme, Charles rushed on. "What I'm offering you, in effect," he said, "is a selling job. But instead of selling goods, you'll be selling ideas and services people don't see, can't touch the way they do a tin of ointment or bottle of liniment. Head up the new Corunda Public Relations Enterprise and sell Corunda!"

"Oh!" from Grace, awed.

"Sorry, I can't take a job like that," Bear said.

Charles looked stunned. "What?"

"It's not for me."

"Nonsense! You're a brilliant salesman, it's ideal."

"I'm near enough to illiterate," Bear said.

"Literate enough to have written good reports—I've seen them," said Charles, betraying that he had already been thinking of Bear Olsen for his public relations enterprise.

"Sorry, no. Public relations? Confidence trickstering, more like," Bear said. "I don't want the job, it's a swindle. We'd better get things straight now, Charlie. I don't want *any* job from you because it would mean some poor blighter whose turn it really is would be passed over in favor of your brother-in-law. I'm the lowest man on Corunda's job list, so I'll go to the Town Hall and register for available work, take my proper turn. But I *will not* shame my origins by taking a dole for no work!"

With a sound like a rubber cushion suddenly emptied of air, Grace flopped down and gazed at Bear with tears in her eyes.

Charles swivelled to her. "Grace, make your husband see sense!"

Then Grace surprised Charles and Bear, though not nearly as much as she surprised herself. "No, Charlie, I won't do that," she said. "If Bear prefers not to be helped up the ladder a few rungs, then that's all right by me. He's the head of the household."

"You're cutting off your noses to spite your faces!"

"Then at least we won't be stickybeaks," said Grace valiantly.

Charles Burdum flung his hands in the air and stalked out.

So, head up, hat in hand, Bear Olsen registered for available work at the Town Hall, simultaneously declining the money doled out. Word ran like a blue flash of electric current around the district that Bear Olsen had principles, refused to take help from his powerful brother-in-law. There were those who roundly condemned him for his stupidity, but many more who praised him for his working man's integrity.

His mood flattened into a dreary plain of hopelessness and he drifted around his house on Trelawney Way like a ghost, moving out of the way of wife or children when he encountered them as if he couldn't stand being in their company. A kind of self-hatred forced him to cling to tattered pride as to a buoyant spar in a sea so thin it was more vapor than fluid.

"You can at least build Grace a decent chook run," said Jack Thurlow on an infrequent visit; Grace had asked him to limit his calls after his first one caused Bear's mood to sink noticeably lower.

For Jack, too, the Olsen tragedy had come as a series of rude shocks, not the least of which was Grace's newfound strength. Very bewildered, he was thankful to be asked to stay away, and obeyed, yet when Grace did request a visit, he was there immediately, all else thrust aside. He understood Bear's reaction to Charlie's offers of help, which kept coming as fast as Bear's refusals. That Charlie didn't understand lay in his ignorance of the working man who would choose to starve rather than take charity.

"It's Bear's business if he won't take work from Charlie," said Grace to Jack one day, "but he needs a good kick up the bum to do some work around *this* house. I want to keep good egg-layer chooks, but that means a far better run, and I want to grow the vegetables in season—chokos if I can't grow anything else."

Chokos! Jack visibly gagged. Oh, they grew like weeds and you could bake them, boil them, fry them, make jam or chutney out of them, but—! They were awful, awful, awful! As much taste as weak urine, and no nutritional merit anyone had found.

She was continuing, heedless of dropping dynamite like chokos. "But I can't do everything myself, Jack, and the boys are too little to be much help. Bear should take over the garden and the chooks."

By dint of providing the materials and a strict supervision, Jack saw that a good stout chook run was erected and some of Maude's Rhode Island Red chooks installed, together with a daily bucket of his own homestead pickings. As Bear had no idea how to cultivate potatoes or carrots or turnips, let alone cabbages or green beans or lettuces, Jack had perforce to show him, only to discover that his sons were more apt pupils. The best anyone could hope for from Bear was that he made sure he didn't forget to shut the chook run door or tramp through a row of newly planted vegetables. He couldn't stick with anything; the work devolved upon others while he remained flat and drifting, refusing the hard labor dole because to take it was unfair when he couldn't labor.

The two little boys were made of sterner stuff. After Grace took them aside to explain to them how sick in the soul Daddy was, Brian and John were very good to him. Grace was rising to all sorts of occasions these days, but painting a picture to tiny children that they could grasp about being "sick in the soul" taxed all her descriptive powers. However, what she said sufficed; the boys' conduct toward their father bore that out. They were gentle and unfailingly patient with Bear; it was, thought the awed Jack, as if they were the parent, Bear the child.

And in 1930, that frightful year, no one understood the myriad ways in which a mind could crash, or crack, or splinter, though Bear was luckier than most men in his wife and children, who never flew at him in rage, and rarely reproached him. Feeling it his duty, since no one else would, Charles Burdum railed at him several times; but Bear's only reponse was to stand, face bewildered, and repeat that he was not going to pull strings.

"But this isn't about pulling strings!" Charles cried. "It's about caring for your family. You're no help, Bear, no help!"

A statement that didn't seem to impinge.

Kitty's reaction was more practical. She donated a treadle Singer sewing machine that Grace accepted gladly. With Edda as instructor, she set out to become a dressmaker, making jackets and trousers for the boys from Liam's and Charlie's old suits, as well as all her own clothes. Cast-off dresses from Edda and Kitty were accepted, too. And if her life were impossibly busy, at least that meant that when night came she could sleep like the dead. Her marital relations with Bear had gone after John was born, and now seemed remote as the dreams she was too tired to remember.

s 1930 wore on, Charles Burdum got most of the credit for Corunda's continued relative prosperity. Mayor Nicholas Middlemore and Town Clerk Winfield Treadby, both rather colorless men, wore no laurels on their brows, despite their genuine dedication and occasionally successful efforts to help. As they possessed the sense to see that if they said anything against Charles Burdum, it would be taken as sour grapes, they smiled wordlessly when people sang Charles's praises to their faces, and voted his way on the Council.

Corunda had two members of parliament, one for the State of New South Wales, and one for the Australian federal government in the new pollie-town of Canberra. Everyone knew that the big cities were the only places that politically mattered; there, Capitalism and Socialism squared off against each other and forced their will on the hapless voters, who, probably because of the continent's history of autocratic rule under virtually dictatorial governors, seemed conditioned from the beginning of democratic government to expect broken promises, poor performance, and corruption.

After months of marriage, Kitty knew that Charlie had his heart set on representing Corunda in the federal parliament, but still he hesitated to make his move. In one way the times screamed for a new style of leadership, perhaps even through the workings of a new political party, a party more geared to a wider variety of voters; both Tory and Labour politicians were die-hard, rigid, intransigent, and therefore did not appeal to voters whose thinking was more flexible and whose desires were not catered to by either kind of politician.

He hadn't understood either that his Englishness would be a colossal handicap in seeking a political career; many Labour men came from more Englishly hidebound backgrounds than he did, but they downplayed their nationality by clinging to the pan-global nature of Socialism. Why was being an English gentleman such a stigma? And how could he understand that the original autocratic rulers on this continent had been English gentlemen, hated and despised to this day?

Dismayed and disappointed, Charles had the intelligence to see that his political aspirations would have to be postponed until he had been in Australia far longer, and that he would have to strive to be considered an Australian, not an Englishman. To get to the country halfway through 1929 and on the eve of the world's greatest economic disaster did not bode well, no matter how hard he toiled to keep Corunda on its feet, free of a shanty town, and holding jobs. For of course he had his enemies, local people whom the Burdum charm and liberality had antagonized; not all of these people were of scant account, and a few were powerful. Every political meeting he was permitted to attend, he attended; every meeting of the Council saw him present, as well as various social assistance associations.

Whenever possible he brought his wife, whose increasing girth delighted everybody as much as her natural air of wifely affection did. Committed to him now, Kitty was determined to be the right partner for this dynamic, perpetually busy man. When he went to Sydney or Melbourne or Canberra to hear the more important debates in the parliament, or lobby for Corunda in some way, Kitty was there at his side.

So it was a surprise to her to find Charles packing his suitcases midway through August, when the weather was bitterly cold and Corunda city itself powdered with a crystalline white mantle that refused to melt.

"I'm off to the Premiers' Conference in Melbourne," he said, inspecting his dinner suit. "Will I need white tie and tails?"

"In Melbourne? Probably. They're a snobby lot down there," she said, eyes dancing. "It's just as well you go to these big city chin-wags occasionally, Charlie—they keep the moths out of your formal clothes. I take it you don't want me along?"

"Not this time. Too boringly masculine. The Depression has rather put the kybosh on festivities, I notice from the agenda I was sent. What I want to know is why these confabs always take place in Melbourne?" he demanded, packing white tie and tails on top of his dinner suit.

"You must know why the chin-wags always take place in Melbourne, Charlie," she said, taking over the packing. "*Think!* There are always lots of bigwigs from England present, and they have to sail from England to Australia—ten thousand miles by sea. Perth is out of the question as a meeting venue, and the next port of call is Melbourne. To stay aboard for Sydney means another thousand miles at sea, when they're absolutely dying to disembark. Now if the aviators flew planes holding hundreds of people, then Sydney would be closer to London than Melbourne. Melbourne would decline. While people have to sail to Australia, Melbourne wins."

"You're quite right," Charles said ruefully. "Melbourne is the first important port of call, which is why Sir Otto Niemeyer will stagger down the gangplank to kiss Melbourne soil rather than sail another thousand miles to Sydney. Clever Kitty!"

She waved a pile of handkerchiefs under his nose. "I may be a bit swollen around the middle, but I can still help you pack. Your suits, however, I dare not touch. You should be using one of those stand-up cabin trunks that open out and have little sets of drawers in them as well as space to hang suits."

"I'd look a fool to arrive with a cabin trunk."

"Rubbish. Sir Otto Thingummy will have several, I imagine." Kitty drew a breath. "In fact, Charlie, you need a valet."

"Yes, I do, but classless Corunda would condemn me."

"It's another job, though not for a Corundite, alas, even poor Bear. Hire a valet in Melbourne, Charlie, and bugger Corunda!"

"I suppose I could put a cabin trunk in the guard's van."

"You could indeed. Where are you staying?"

"Menzies, as usual."

"Good, it has valets who unpack. Why you, Charlie? You're not in any parliament."

"Men in my position always have important enough political friends to linger in the immediate vicinity of conferences, though that's not why I'm going. I'm personally invited by Sir Otto."

Kitty sat on the edge of his dressing room chair. "Just who is this Sir Otto? He sounds like a German sausage maker."

"Sir Otto Niemeyer is one of the governors of the Bank of England, and an old friend of mine from City of London days. More than that I do not know, my glorious Kitty, but I'm dying to find out why he's made that dreadful voyage."

"Yes, I see why you're curious. He's an extremely important man, so whatever he's come for must be vital back in England—I mean, four or five weeks in a stiflingly hot cabin, seasickness, *and* boredom? I'm sure he'll be on the highest deck where the wind blows through his cabin, but home it's not. Of course, he will be port out and starboard home, but the sun is relentless."

Charles eyed her in amusement. "Anyone would think you'd done the voyage, Kitty. Port out and starboard home?"

"The sun, silly!" she said, dimples showing. "It shines on the starboard side of the ship going to Australia and the port side going home to England, so those in the know always book a cabin on the shadier side. It's where the word 'posh' comes from."

"My dear, you are a positive mine of information!"

"I don't know about that, but Sir Otto is a worried man."

Every good hotel in Melbourne was jam-packed with politicians and the small army of hangers-on they seemed to drag with them like a comet its tail, Charles Burdum thought as he moved into his usual two-room suite at the Menzies Hotel. He liked its clubby atmosphere, the staff who sported touches of red-and-white Menzies tartan, the existence of valets and ladies' maids, and the excellent cuisine. His prized Miss Cynthia Norman had nipped in ahead of the pack and secured him a Rolls-Royce car and chauffeur for his visit, and Kitty had been right, the cabin trunk worked. It didn't go against him, either, that he was a generous tipper; Australians, he had discovered very early on, were notoriously grudging tippers.

Dropping Sir Otto's name as his patron, Charles found himself invited to all kinds of meetings, but that all paled compared to the fact that he dined alone with Sir Otto on his first evening ashore. It seemed Sir Otto had some bones to pick, and had chosen Charles as his primary confidant—not illogical, given the two things Sir Otto had in common with Charles and no one else in Melbourne: their long City of London ties and their Englishness.

"My dear Charles, the City hasn't been the same since you packed your traps and emigrated," the Bank of England man said over pre-dinner drinks. Both men wore black tie.

"You exaggerate," said Charles, smiling. "I was based more in Manchester than in London."

"Perhaps, but you were close enough to answer our call when needed, as in sticky or intriguing situations. You surely didn't emigrate over Sybil, my dear fellow?"

"Lord, no!" Charles cried, astonished. "Frankly, I was bored, and it seemed a good moment to take up my antipodean inheritance. How amazing! It seems a lifetime, but it's really not yet two years ago." The face went gargoyle. "On the bottom of the globe, Otto, I am convinced the world—and time—turn faster. I am married to a woman who eclipses Sybil as the Hope Diamond does a chunk of glass."

"You didn't bring her to Melbourne?"

"No. She's expecting our child."

"How splendid!" Sir Otto leaned back in his chair. "Do you know why I'm here, Charles?"

"Certainly because of the Depression, but on whose behalf I do not know. I hadn't thought these bumbling fools intelligent enough to call for expert opinion."

"As to their being bumbling fools, it seems all governments are comprised of those in the face of this disaster, but no, you are right. *They* did not summon me. I came at the Bank's behest."

"What are the Bank of England's intentions?"

"To persuade the various governments of this continent that they cannot default on their loan repayments, particularly on the repayment of interest."

The gargoyle look increased; Charles whistled softly. "I have heard the fringe lunatics muttering behind their hands about denying international debt, and some fairly responsible men have muttered about postponing loan interest repayments until local suffering abates, but I didn't give any of it credence. You're implying, I think, that a large part of the political establishment is restive about loan repayments?"

"Oh, yes."

The first course arrived; they ceased to speak of vital subjects while the waiters hovered, then ate in a pleasurable silence that persisted, save for small talk, until the ruby port and Stilton cheese arrived, when the battery of servitors retired, leaving them to private discussion.

"It is clear," said Sir Otto, "that federation and self-government went to Australian heads. Without the strong veto powers of British governors, and flushed by the demand for wool as well as the continued production of gold, both the federal and various state governments went on a spending spree. Do you realize how much Australian wool was gobbled up by the Great War? Home on the sheep's back! I daresay no one saw an end to the prosperity back in 1925, whereas all save fools should have."

"I see," said Charles slowly. "Pray continue, Otto."

"The various state governments have done much of the spending over the last decade, mostly, I believe, because the federal government wanted the glory without the administrative work. Taking the gold and other reported mineral deposits into account, it was decided in Canberra that Western Australia should not be permitted to secede, despite its clamorings. This led to Western Australia's being disproportionately gifted when the federal government disbursed funds."

Sir Otto put the tips of his fingers together and looked solemnly across them at his intent listener; he was enjoying himself. "By far the biggest spender was the most populous state, New South Wales, which, due to huge financial pressures in Perth and Melbourne, was always short-changed in Canberra. So New South Wales took out massive loans in the City of London markets to finance an ambitious program of public works. The state is now dangerously close to defaulting. Other states, though less parlous, are also on thin ice, and my colleagues in the Bank fear the federal government could default."

"You know, Otto, so tell me—how much has been borrowed?" Charles asked, heart sinking.

"Upward of thirty million pounds a year."

"Ye gods! A crippling interest."

"But agreed to when the money was borrowed."

"Yes, of course. Go on, please."

Sir Otto shrugged. "That's why I'm here—what a frightful journey to have to make! Months wasted by the time I get back, though I hope to terrify the politicians into behaving. If I can, then my time will have been well spent."

"What do you think of the country, if you can make any sort of assumption on such short acquaintance? I know some federal people boarded in Fremantle to start the ball rolling."

Sir Otto's mouth went down. "I think Australia has an inflated idea of its own importance, first and foremost. Then, it has a living standard for the general populace that is disgracefully high. The working man lives far too well! His wages are too high and his expectations from life unrealistic. In short, he doesn't know his proper place."

"I see. What measures will you recommend?"

"Imperatively, that there can be no defaulting on repayment of foreign debt, particularly interest. *Absolute* retrenchment. Every government down to municipal level must immediately cease all spending on public works, cut its civil service to the bone, reduce the wages and salaries it does pay, and decrease all social benefits, from monetary doles to pensions. The Australian pound is in the throes of devaluation and will eventually, we feel, sit at around thirty percent less than the pound Sterling. If there must be defaults on interest payments, then let them be on a government's own bonds, which I understand pay Australian owners nine percent. Local debt is not at issue, just foreign."

For a long moment Charles said nothing, just sat frowning at Sir Otto's fingertips; suddenly he gave a shudder, like a dog shaking off an icy bath. "Oh, Otto! Of smiles there will be none save to speed your passage home, I fear. You are the harbinger of apocalyptic suffering, since it's already clear that the Great Depression has hit Australia hardest anyway."

"No, only second hardest," said Sir Otto. "The Germans are doing it the worst. Their war reparations have bankrupted them. The French want their pound of flesh."

"Well, the French and the Germans have been snarling at each other across the Rhine for two thousand years, but what has poor Australia ever done except try to make life kinder for the working man? Not, in City of London eyes, a laudable aspiration."

Disillusioned and depressed, Charles didn't linger in Melbourne. Next morning in darkness he took the day train for Sydney, his mind seething with so many unpalatable facts that he hardly noticed having to change trains at Albury–Wodonga, on the state border. Victorian and New South Wales rail gauges were different. Federation or no, the Australian colonies all behaved like autonomous nations. In fact, thought Charles, detraining at Corunda, the only way the Australian nation could have made its mark was to own a population as vast as its land area, like the United States of America. Whereas its tiny populace was jammed into six cities on a near-illimitable coast, leaving three million square miles of nothingness inside. Corunda was a very big city-town, but had only 50,000 people all told. After the six cities, one of the biggest towns in Australia.

But I am learning, he thought, finding Corunda still under a glaze of snow, and a fresh fall threatening.

"I can't make head or tail of it," he said to Kitty, very surprised and pleased to see him back so soon. His cabin trunk was hardly disturbed, but with him came a suave, impassive individual named Coates; Charles had hired a valet by the simple expedient of poaching one from Menzies Hotel. "Coates can have a staff cottage on Burdum Row and the use of one of the flivvers," he went on, changing the subject. "He seemed delighted at the chance to join me."

"I should think so, dear. It's a private post, he'll live like a lord," said Kitty. "Tell me about Sir Otto Sausagemaker."

"According to Sir Otto, Coates shouldn't be allowed to live like a lord," said Charles, burying his lips gratefully in his Scotch. "Sir Otto is going to insist upon absolute retrenchment at every level of government, though, since Corunda Base has its own money, no government can order me to stop building it. Nor can they cut my state funds discriminately. I'll get whatever the other hospitals get, as health *has* to be funded."

"But government money comes from taxes, and if no one has a job, no one's paying taxes," Kitty objected.

"Oh, some people will pay taxes. Retrenchment is just a way of using every single penny that comes in to send out of the country in loan repayments. Borrow too much, and you're bankrupt. Retrenchment is a euphemism, Kitty, for bankruptcy. The people of the country won't benefit, the foreign moneylenders will."

"Sometimes, Charlie, you're hard to understand."

"Oh, I'm smarting, that's all. I came away from Melbourne with this image in my mind of Otto and me in the Menzies dining room, sipping the finest wines and eating the finest foods, clad in black tie, waited on by obsequious servants—and I know that Otto believes with heart, intellect, and soul that he deserves to live better than some little Jewish tailor sitting cross-legged on a table getting a penny a pair. No matter that they both share the blood of Abraham—class is class. Otto believes in keeping the working class down, he genuinely thinks it criminal to offer them a decent life. To him the social strata are fixed in stone. Well, I don't believe in the rule of the proletariat because it's devoid of individualism and encourages civil servants to think they can run anything when the truth is they can run nothing—but I'm damned if I like Sir Otto Niemeyer's world, either!"

"There must be a happy medium somewhere," said Kitty, out of her depth. "Jack Lang won't favor Sir Otto's measures, will he?"

"Jack Lang is in opposition, he doesn't have executive clout. He has no power, darling, no power. All I see is a huge increase in suffering," said Charles. "Here's hoping the Scullin government isn't completely cowed by Sir Otto."

"Jimmy Scullin," said Kitty scornfully, "can be cowed by a cabbage moth. He's a shallow opportunist."

Yes, it was balm to the soul to have an ardently supportive wife, but it couldn't solve Charles Burdum's political dilemma. Torn between his situation in life, which inclined him to Tory ideals, his innate conviction that the working man was a creature deserving of respect, which inclined him to Socialist views, he kept on wavering, neither one thing nor the other.

What was basically wrong with all the existing political parties, he concluded, was that they had been formulated for the Old World—for tired and war-torn, resource-exhausted Europe.

So it dawned on Charles that what he had to do was create a political party engineered to meet Australia's needs, a credo that wasn't shackled to Old World political ideas and systems. His credo would have to see both Capital and Labour in new and different terms, and above all work to diminish artificial barriers between men. For instance, why, why, *why* had Bear Olsen thrown the public relations job in his face? What was wrong with the man's social attitudes, that he could dismiss public relations as a swindle? What lay at the base of these inexplicable contradictions? Until he found out, he couldn't possibly run for parliament, for he saw himself as an ignoramus and Bear Olsen as a kind of riddling oracle. Well, no more meetings and conferences! Research instead.

He thought, and he wrote. A child's school exercise book, he discovered, was an ideal repository for his observations, deductions, and theories, especially since one could be closed like a filing cabinet, however many necessary could be used at the same time, and they stored upright on a shelf in labelled rows.

But all that was for the future. He began, was all.

"Are you with me, Kitty?" he asked on his return from Melbourne. "Will you be here for me?"

The eyes flashed violet with love and pride. "Always and forever, Charlie."

At first, she spoke the absolute truth. Had Charles continued in the direction of hospital, orphanage, and purely Corunda projects, Kitty's "always" would have endured. But as winter blew itself out, as spring came and went in a perfumed glory of flowers, conversation at the dinner table and wherever else it happened turned more and more inexorably to one sole subject—politics. And Kitty found in herself a rapidly growing dislike of politics, politicians, and Charlie's political aspirations.

At the end of October, fully seven months gone, Kitty Burdum suffered a miscarriage; the child was beautifully formed and male, but dead on birth, and had been since before contractions started.

"I don't understand," she whispered from her hospital bed, face and pillow drenched with tears. "Everything was perfect, I was so well! Then—this!"

Though he was deeply affected, Charles Burdum hid his own devastation better, especially from his wife; his tears, equally bitter, were shed at home, alone in the night. Had he realized it, he would have been wiser to weep with Kitty, a grieving couple united by their loss and each a witness of the other's pain. As it was, Kitty deemed her sorrow far greater than his, and, loving him, laid what she saw as remote self-control at the door of his maleness. After all, a father had no contact with his child *in utero*, so how could he be expected to feel what she, the custodian, felt?

"It's not unheard of," said Dr. Ned Mason, "to lose a first baby, Kitty, though this late is unusual. Possibly you're a wee bit anemic, so eat plenty of spinach, even if you detest it."

"Am I likely to miscarry again?" Kitty asked. "I'm still so shocked by the suddenness—it came out of the blue!"

"There will be plenty of babies, I do assure you."

A verdict echoed by Tufts, very concerned. There was a new look in the lovely eyes, of bewilderment bordering on confusion. Whatever happened, Kitty *mustn't* be let sink too far into the dumps! "Ned Mason's right, women do lose a first child occasionally," Tufts said firmly. "Take a good long rest, eat spinach, and try again. I guarantee you'll sail through."

"Ned says I may have a wee fibroid."

"Oh, all of us have at least one of *those*." Tufts snorted in derision. "You're a registered nurse, Kitty, you know that's true. Fibroids only become a dangerous nuisance much later."

"Charlie took it philosophically." Kitty sounded a trifle critical, even resentful.

"Charlie was broken-hearted, you goose! He just didn't want to upset you more by showing it. Don't sell his grief short because you can't see past your own, Kits. He wept to me."

"Well, he didn't weep to *me*."

"Then I admire his self-control. Of course he didn't weep to you! He thinks too much of you to do that."

"Daddy says he and Charlie gave it a name—Henry—and buried it. I wasn't even there."

"It," thought Tufts. Oh, Kitty! Did Edda and I spare you too much as a child? No, of course we didn't. But somehow things between you and Charlie never seem to go Charlie's way, and it isn't his fault, it's yours.

She left Kitty's bed in Maternity and walked briskly to Charles Burdum's office, her thoughts still dwelling on Kitty. They didn't see much of each other, and Edda was in like case, but the bond between them was no weaker for that, and she knew that Kitty would look to her and Edda for the major part of her comfort during the weeks and months to come. That note of disapproval for Charlie in her voice! This was one of those times when to be a stiff-upper-lipped, aloof Pommy was a terrible handicap.

Behind her worry for Kitty's marriage something else nagged at her: what on earth could Charlie want to see *her* about? It wasn't to do with Kitty; he was too punctilious to discuss his wife with her sister in the public arena of his office. What, therefore, was the matter?

He looks, Tufts thought as he took some care in seating her, like a man whose world has ended. In some ways it has; yesterday he had seen the tiny coffin of his stillborn son put into a grave, with Henry Burdum's aunts, grandfather, and father the sole mourners. And Kitty griped at his lack of tears? What a business!

"I want to talk to you about your future career," Charles said.

Surprised, Tufts blinked. "What is there to talk about? I have eight trainees to care for, next April five more will bring the number up to thirteen, and the year after, if statistics go on as they're heading, will see as many as ten fresh trainees. That means that by 1934, or thereabouts, the Corunda School of Nursing will be significant, with unqualified women being phased out forever. It's the Depression, of course," she went on, "allied to the lack of young men—we are still feeling the effects of the Great War, and jobless young men can't marry. As Sister Tutor, I'm only going to get busier and busier."

"True, but naturally you will have the aid of efficient and Tufts-chosen assistant Sisters Tutor," Charles said mildly.

"I shouldn't need any assistant until the figures go above fifty," said Tufts crisply.

"And in the truth of that statement lies one of the main reasons why I want to deflect your career somewhat."

Tufts stiffened, seizing unerringly on one word. "*Deflect?*"

"Your emotional attachment to Corunda Base makes you very suitable for what I want, but it's also you yourself—who you are, what you are—and who and what you could become."

Her eyes held his sternly. "This sounds ominous."

"It isn't. I have no intention of harming your career, far from it. In fact, I want to enhance it." His private sorrow had vanished from eyes and face, and the film star appeal came out of nowhere; Tufts could feel his charm engulf her. "In spite of the Depression, things are looking up for Corunda Base," Charles said, his assault prepared. "I know that hospitals used to be where sick people went while God made up His mind whether to take life from them or let them keep it. Of treatment there was precious little. But that is changing rapidly. These days we can actually intervene and save many patients who even ten years ago would have died. We can X-ray broken limbs, remove certain diseased organs from the abdomen—why, even routine transfusion of blood from one person to another is just around the corner! I see a modern hospital as a place where people go not only to have their lives saved, but their health preserved. And, Tufts, I know you feel the same way."

"Doesn't everybody?" she asked. "Come on, Charlie, spit it out! You don't need to woo me with patriotic speeches, you're preaching to the already converted."

His face grew brighter, his eyes intense. "Tufts, I need a deputy superintendent, and I want that person to be you. *You!*"

The chair fell over as Tufts scrambled to her feet, shocked; he was there at once, righting the chair, reseating her.

"Charlie Burdum, you're insane! I'm not even qualified as a matron, let alone a superintendent of anything other than nurse studies and hospital domestics," she said, mouth dry, eloquent because eloquence was the only way to shut this steamroller of a man down. "You're utterly deluded!"

"Anything but," he said, back behind his desk. "Consider it, please. You know as well as any other member of our family that I have political aspirations. It's my intention to seek election to the federal parliament as member for Corunda, but not until at least 1933 or 1934, which gives me time. Entry into parliament means I'll have to give up the hospital. Like any other crafty man, I'll be able to preserve my fortune and commercial interests intact if I go about it the right way, but I can't hold two jobs."

"Qualified men are to be found everywhere," she said harshly. "Pick one now and train him up."

"I am picking one now—you. At this moment, and, I predict, for many years to come, there are no academic qualifications stipulated for a person superintending a general hospital—or any other kind of hospital, for that matter. Most of us have a medical degree because we soon learned after graduating that our skills were not directed at healing people, but at juggling money, functions, and staff. Like your skills, Tufts, for all that you were also, apparently, a brilliant hands-on nurse. You will join me immediately as my deputy superintendent, and I'll guarantee to teach you everything I know. I add that you will be able to carry on as Sister Tutor provided you have at least one assistant."

Tufts threw her hands in the air, at a complete loss—how did one reason with a closed mind? "Charlie, I beg you, listen to me! First and foremost, I'm a woman. Apart from Matron, by tradition a woman, women do not administer any kind of organization, from business to health. The opposition will be huge! My sex will be used against me in the corridors of power both in Sydney and in Canberra, with the unelected civil servants my worst and most obdurate enemies. I have no university degrees of any sort—*none*! The state government will dismiss me."

He had listened, yet clearly didn't hear. "Tufts, believe me, I'm well ahead of everyone concerned. I agree that you need tertiary qualifications, so I've arranged with my very good friend Professor Sawley Hartford-Smythe of the Faculty of Science to make sure you obtain those qualifications. You will undergo an intense and compressed course in medico-scientific subjects and graduate two years from when university goes up next February. That's 1931, to graduate in November of 1933. You will also undergo intensive schooling in accountancy, which will equip you better for this job than a degree in medicine, as you well know. I am *loading* you with work, but it isn't as bad as it seems because much of what you have to learn is already learned. You'll breeze through the science! Accountancy will be more foreign, therefore harder. You, Heather Scobie-Latimer, are my investment for the future."

Her breath had gone; Tufts stared at her brother-in-law in wonder. Could it possibly work? And why did this eminently well qualified and practical man assume it *would* work? Even though the core of him was raw and bleeding from the loss of his child, he was forging onward, always toiling for Corunda and its welfare. A university degree! She, a woman, would own a Bachelor's degree in Science and a Charter in Accountancy! Attend conferences as a hospital executive. The joys of tutoring nurses were many, but Tufts had to admit that the vast challenge Charlie was throwing at her was infinitely more alluring.

"Charlie, have you honestly thought this through?"

"I've crossed the t's and dotted the i's, Tufts, you have my word on it," he said. "Come, do it!" He chortled at a private vision. "Imagine being Liam's boss!"

"Old stick-in-the-mud that he is. He'd be more suitable."

"Were he, I'd have given him the job. No, m'dear, Liam is twenty years too old. I need someone young."

"I see that. Liam doesn't like live patients, that's why he chose pathology." She gave a gasp and held out her hand to Charles across the desk.

"Very well, Charlie. If you're so set on a woman deputy, I'll accept. You won't desert me too soon, will you?"

"I'll never desert you, Tufts."

She raced back down the ramp to Pathology and burst into Liam Finucan's office to find him immersed in a set of huge blueprints that outlined his new department, a building two stories high. Charles's scheme of things saw the ancillary medical services as more important than, for instance, rebuilding the wards or starting the new operating theatre block, simply because their current position in Corunda was very much an afterthought, yet their importance as diagnostic tools and treatments was exploding.

So the new radiology department had gone up first; its carefully chosen chief, Dr. Edison Malvie, had gone on the staff before a single brick earmarked for radiology had been laid and the most modern diagnostic X-ray apparatus purchased, together with the latest ideas on lead shielding. Gone were the days of fuzzy films or uncertain readings; when all was up and running, Dr. Malvie vowed, neurosurgeons as august as those at Queens Square would perform no radiological tests Corunda Base did not.

Which led to the bliss of a whole building entirely devoted to pathology, broken into its various disciplines. If Dr. Malvie was happy, his content was as nothing compared to Liam Finucan's. The transfusion of blood from patient to patient, so very close, pointed the way to hematology as a segment of significant size—in fact, every segment of pathology was growing larger and more important. Hence his poring over blueprints for the new Pathology Department, and his blindness to what would ordinarily be so obvious: Tufts was bursting with news. However, she forced herself to listen to today's bright ideas until he ran down, puzzled at Tufts's rather lukewarm reaction.

Once she told him her news, Liam sat back in his chair, the plans forgotten, and gazed at her. "Charlie's trouble," he said then, "is that he can never leave things alone. Status quo is an alien concept to him."

"Does that mean you think I should refuse?" she asked.

"No! You can't possibly refuse, the opportunity is genuinely groundbreaking—you did accept, I hope?"

"Yes, but I can always change my mind. I *am* a woman!"

"Are you still enamored of a lifetime career in hospital work, Heather? You don't plan on marriage?" he asked.

"Definitely not," said Tufts firmly. "Every time I see Grace or Kitty, I realize all over again that marriage would not suit me. And every time I see Edda I realize that I am not cut out for love affairs, either. Too perilous, especially for a superintendent."

"Then you have two choices, Heather. To stick in the well-known mud of Sister Tutor, or jump into the utterly unknown mire of senior hospital administration. Your mind is very high quality—too high for Sister Tutor, I think, but I'm not you, and I do not presume to advise you," Liam Finucan said, oddly formal.

His thoughts were very different. What, he wondered, looking at her sweet face, might have happened had Gertie Newdigate not stuck her oar in, and I not had a wife to shed? Sixteen months of separation, right as the seed was germinating. Oh, Heather, we missed our chance!

Not thoughts Tufts experienced as she stared at him, though a part of her did understand Matron Newdigate's untimeliness. But, never having known any kind of intimacy with Liam before the long divorce exile, she had no idea what might have eventuated had there been no Eris Finucan. They were best friends, and they were also colleagues. In moving her qualifications up, Tufts was moving further into Liam's world. And that was a lovely thought, no more.

Bear Olsen had found himself a routine that kept him out of the way of his wife and sons as much as possible; after trying to eat two slices of toast for his breakfast, he put his hat on his head, shrugged himself into his jacket, and went out the front door, down the path through the front gate and onto the street. There he turned to walk down the slope of Trelawney Way to Wallace Road, crossed it, and kept on going until he came to George Street, the main thoroughfare that bisected all Corunda City.

Though Maboud's general store sat on the corner, he went past it and trudged all the way down George Street to the main shopping center, where some windows were fragmented with brown-paper bands glued across the glass to indicate permanent closure. No matter; he stopped to peer into every shop, open for business or defunct, down the north side as far as the last store, then back up the south side. Finally he arrived again at Maboud's, with its newspapers, comic-cuts, magazines, packets of tea and tins of baking powder, sugar and butter and flour, women's and men's and children's clothing, teapots and kettles and mixing bowls. Bashir Maboud, who liked him, always attempted to strike up a conversation, to which Bear made little or no response; then eventually he would return up the slope of Trelawney Way and let himself into his front yard again, having walked ten miles and spent the best part of the day in doing it.

He had lost a great deal of weight, albeit he wasn't yet emaciated; food didn't interest him any more than his wife or sons did. From the moment he was back after his slow, clockwork progression, he sat in the garden on an old park bench Jack Thurlow had brought home in happier days, his hat on the slats beside him, his chin sunk onto his chest. Not knowing what significance this action might have, Grace had puzzled as to why, from the time he started sitting there, he had reversed the bench so he sat with his back to the house and his family.

After many fruitless attempts to get Bear interested in doing something—*anything!*—Jack had ceased to visit while Bear was at home; it was just too painful to see external events destroy such a good, decent, caring man. Jack visited while Bear walked.

What did the family live on? Teeth clenched, Grace accepted the bare minimum from Charles to let her family subsist. Beg though he did, Charles couldn't persuade her to take more, and she made it clear that what she did accept was for the sake of her sons. In return she insisted on making things for Kitty's larder that a French chef would despise, like Anzac bikkies, lemon-curd butter, and red, green, and orange jellies.

Bear's mind was not a sluggish slough of self-pity; had it been, people like Grace, Edda, Jack, and Charles might have worked to cure it. But what went on in Bear's mind had neither purpose nor logic nor agony of any kind; it was a literal jumble of idle thoughts, stray little snatches of songs or wireless jingles, all run down so badly that even Bear, the owner of the thoughts, had no concept what they meant, how they were relevant to his existence. His image of self—of his body, even—was in the throes of disintegration, so that when Grace, as terrified as exasperated, cried out things to him like "Pull yourself together!" he had no inkling what she meant or why she was so upset. The shop windows with their criss-crossed brown paper bands were something to look at, just as Bashir Maboud was someone who mouthed words; this last, vague, vestigial part of himself seemed a machine that had to be used up and worn out by walking and looking, walking and looking . . . When he sat, his back to the house, on his garden seat, he was so exhausted that of thoughts there were none at all.

Charles Burdum and the Latimer GP, Dr. Dave Harper, came to see Bear several times; each visit saw Grace hanging on their opinions desperately.

"I'm afraid there's nothing we can do," Charles confessed to her. "However, his condition doesn't seem to worsen. It's three weeks since our last time here, but Bear is unchanged."

"He abrogated his responsibilities as a man, a husband, and a father," Grace said bitterly.

"Abrogated is just a word, Grace. Blaming him isn't going to improve anything, you know that. My dear, you're so brave, so staunch! No one can criticize you, even for railing about Bear occasionally." Charles patted her arm. "Chin up, Grace!"

"We eat fish paste and homemade jam, but that's a lot more than many families are eating, for which I thank you, Charlie," said Grace, hating the faint patronization but understanding she had no right to say so. "I also know that if you had your way it would be ham and steak. Well, I won't take them. I'm grateful that you pay Bashir Maboud's bills, but if Bear were in his right mind, he'd deplore *any* charity. I'm no leech."

"I admire your independence," said Charles sincerely.

"Supercilious bastard," Grace muttered to herself. "All the world suffers, but not Charlie Burdum, cock of the walk." A sentiment she repeated to Edda, who slapped her down by reminding her that Charles had seen *his* son stillborn. "Yours mightn't eat ham sandwiches, but they're healthy as cart horses fed on the best mash, so pipe down, Grace."

Edda was looking, thought the deeply unhappy and frustrated Grace, quite superb. They were twenty-five years old now, once considered past the peak of feminine attractiveness—but that was outmoded thinking. The longer, more shaped clothes of late 1930 suited Edda, whose height and suppleness carried them well: she was so—*elegant*! Red always became her, even the rather trying rust red she wore today, a dress of thin, clingy crepe. No petticoat either, yet she contrived not to give the slightest impression of trollop. And she was growing her thick black hair long—why was she doing that?

"Underneath his posturing Charlie's all right," she said to Grace, smoothing one silk-sheathed leg to make sure the seam of her stocking was straight. "He means well, it's just that he can never overcome his Pommyness. To us, he patronizes, but he has no idea it seems that way. Look at what he's doing for Tufts—you have to be glad over that, and it's all his doing."

"Yes, yes, I'm very happy for Tufts!"

Edda's string bag thumped on the table. "You know bloody well I'm not patronizing you, sister, so use what's in there without getting huffy. Some sliced ham, slices of devon sausage, lamb chops, and a piece of corned silverside. You have to eat better meat than sausages occasionally."

Grace flushed, but held her temper. "Thank you, dear, most kind of you." She fished in the bag and put the meat in her ice chest. "Fancy a woman as deputy super!"

"It might have been you if you'd stuck to nursing," Edda said, a little cruelly. "Wrong sex or not, our Tufts will do very well. Charlie's helping her get a degree in science and accountancy qualifications, so the Lords of Creation won't be able to attack her on educational grounds." She gurgled in the back of her throat. "And good luck to any man who fancies taking Tufts down a peg or two! He'll wind up singing soprano."

Grace giggled. "You're right. But wouldn't you have liked the deputy's job, Edda?"

"Not if it were Bart's or Guy's. I want to travel."

"So you keep saying, but when?"

"When I'm good and ready."

On 25th October 1930 the state of New South Wales had gone to the polls to elect a new government. Its people voted Jack Lang in; New South Wales now had a Labour government whose Premier implicitly believed that Sir Otto Niemeyer's drastic program of retrenchment was wrong, wrong, wrong. What Jack Lang wanted was to increase public spending and get as many men back in jobs as humanly possible. The Sydney Harbour Bridge and the underground railway system were suddenly going again, and Lang was adamantly opposed to paying back interest on the state's City of London loans while so many Australians suffered because of those loan interest rates.

Even cranky Grace was lifted out of her perpetual troubles as she pored over the newspapers Bashir Maboud saved for her every day, talking, as had become her habit, to an unresponsive Bear as he sat on his bench after his walk.

"Jack Lang has to be right," she said, waving a broadsheet at him coming on toward Christmas of 1930. "Look at Corunda!" she exclaimed. "Almost everybody has a job, so the Depression hasn't made the inroads here that it has everywhere else. Thanks to the building of the new hospital! Dearest Bear, your misfortune was to have your skills in something first and hardest hit. And after that, you were too proud to take the dole because you can't do the work it calls for. Well, lots take it anyway!"

He made no answer at all, but then he never did; or listened, or seemed to realize that she sat beside him rustling her newspapers and prattling on, forever talking, talking . . .

Done with the first two pages of the *Corunda Post*, a journal with grand pretensions, she turned to page three, more entertaining.

"Fancy that! Suicide rates in Corunda are increasing," she said, her voice still light and breezy. "Why do people hang themselves? It must be an awful death, dangling at the end of a rope slowly choking, which is what people do who hang *themselves*. When the law hangs a criminal, the *Post* writer says here, he or she falls down a trapdoor and the sudden jerk when he or she stops literally breaks the neck. No, I wouldn't choose to hang myself, and I hope I never do anything that sees the law hang me . . ."

Her voice faded to a murmur, then spontaneously rose again. "Women like to put their heads in the gas oven, but men don't. I wonder why? Gas smells horrible, and it's choking again, isn't it? Taking poison isn't popular, I suppose because one always dies in such a frightful mess, and it's certainly not fair to those left behind to have to clean up the mess. No, it always comes back to men hanging themselves and women sticking their heads in the gas oven." She got up, chortling. "Interesting, if macabre! Time for me to start cooking tea, too. Sausages again, I'm afraid, but I'll curry them for a change. Edda brought me a bag of raisins."

Busy in the kitchen chopping up some of the precious raisins finely to add a tinge of sweetness to the curry—very mild anyway, as the boys disliked too-spicy food—Grace boiled the salt out of the sausages before slicing them into thick coins and tipping them into a pot. She mixed melted lard, flour, and curry powder to a paste, worked it with water until it was a thin sauce, poured it over the sausages, and tipped in her shredded raisins. Simmer slowly. There! Brian and John would love it, and maybe even Bear would eat a little of it, especially if she fried some bread as a base to pile the curry on. Rice was horrible stuff if left savory, but stale bread, cut into doorsteps and fried on both sides, always went down well. The only way rice was edible was as pudding.

"Tea, chaps!" she bellowed out the back door to the boys.

Brian and John came at once, Brian half dragging his little brother, faces beaming because they were always starving and they loved everything their mother cooked. They even loved fish paste or Marmite sandwiches, bless them! Oh, for the days when she might have used butter instead of lard, and stock instead of water!

"Bear! Tea!" she yelled out a window on the plant verandah.

He was sitting bolt upright on his garden seat, his jacket pitched on the ground—unusual for Bear to be untidy, even in his state of mind. His shirt sleeves were rolled up and his hands apparently in his lap, for all she could see were his elbows—sharp, bony pyramids covered in callused skin.

"Bear! Tea!" she yelled again.

When he didn't move, her mouth tightened; so he was about to pass into a new phase of his dry horrors, was he? Didn't he understand the effect it had on the boys? She left the house through the back door and so came upon him in profile, hands loosely in his lap, where a great dark red stain had gathered, seeped into the wool of his trousers and the cotton of his shirt, then, saturated, dripped between his legs onto the rusty ground. His penknife was glued to his fingers by jellied blood and his face was serene, eyes three-quarters closed, mouth faintly smiling.

Grace didn't scream. First she ventured close enough to see the deep gashes in his forearms, on their insides and running up from his wrists many inches. Yet for all his thoroughness, he had missed the arteries, at least while there was sufficient blood in them to spurt; his was a slow, steady, venous bleed, and it must have taken him the entire making of a curry to die.

Satisfied as to what had happened, she turned on her heel to walk back to the house. Inside, she went about the routine of feeding her sons their curried sausages. Only when they were eating did she go to the phone and ring the hospital.

"Put me through to Dr. Charles Burdum, and don't you dare tell me he's not there."

"Yes?" came his impatient voice.

"This is Grace, Charlie. Please send an ambulance to my home. Bear has cut his wrists."

"Is he alive?"

"No. But send someone for Brian and John."

"Can you cope until help reaches you?"

"What a stupid question! If I couldn't cope, someone else would be talking to you this minute. Don't dither, Charlie. If Liam is there, send him—he's the coroner, and it's a suicide." She hung up, leaving Charles winded.

For once there were no curtains drawn furtively back on Trelawney Way; people stood outside their houses to watch as the ambulance drew up quietly and was let into the Olsen yard. Charles followed it in his Packard with Edda and Tufts; Liam rode in the ambulance.

Tufts took over the children, getting them ready for bed. Who in the old days would ever have dreamed that Grace could be so sensible, so forward-thinking? The boys weren't perturbed, she had behaved so normally, and they knew nothing of ambulances or inquisitive neighbors as they splashed their way through a bath and dived into their bed, a double one that they shared.

Liam Finucan and the two ambulance men cared reverently for Bear Olsen, one of them even going so far as to hose down the lawn and the garden seat so that it wouldn't fall to Grace to remove her husband's blood; the ambulance departed as quietly as it had arrived. Only busy vocal cords on the party line told various garbled versions far and wide of what had happened to the unfortunate, inoffensive Bear Olsen.

Charles and Edda inherited Grace, whose extraordinary spurt of practical good sense began to flag soon after the ambulance left and she could hear her boys chattering to Tufts from their bed. The worst was over.

"The worst is over," she said.

"You did superbly well," said Edda, holding Grace's hands. "I'm so proud of you I could burst."

"I was taken out of myself," Grace said, face pinched, white, terrified. "How could I let my children see their father like that? Now they have no father, but at least they won't have any nightmares. Having children changes everything, Edda." Her eyes filled. "Oh, and we were having such an interesting tea for a change! Curried sausages flavored with your raisins. The boys ate every scrap, so I gave them Bear's share as well, and they ate that. Which means I'm not keeping up with their growth or their appetites. I'll have to keep on cooking Bear's share." An eerie chuckle sounded. "No food where he's gone now!"

"Was there any warning?" Charles asked.

"None at all, though I did read him bits of the suicide article in today's *Post*. But he doesn't ever hear what I say, honestly!" she cried, a proffered handkerchief taken, used. "Did I give him the idea, Edda? I was only trying to get him interested in something, anything! I read him the papers *every* day, truly!"

"You mustn't blame yourself, Grace," Charles said strongly.

She turned her wide eyes upon him, their depths displaying wonder. "I don't blame myself, Charlie. Why should I? Giving him the idea isn't blaming myself. That's like saying the only way not to get stung by a bee is not to wear perfume. Honestly, you Pommies are a weird mob! You read too much into things. No, the only one to blame is Bear. How much I love him! Even when his stupid pride made me want to cut his throat, I still loved him. Oh, the children! I need Daddy's help with them."

"Tomorrow, Grace, not tonight," Charles said. "Thanks to your magnificent handling of things, they won't suffer repercussions of the kind they might have, and they're too far off school age to be tormented by other children."

"The things you think of!" Edda exclaimed. "The important thing, Grace, is that they'll grieve in a natural way for a daddy who isn't here any more. *You* did that for your boys, no one else."

"But how am I to live?" Grace asked. "I'm going to have to depend on charity." That broke her as nothing else so far had; she bent over and wept desolately.

I hardly know my twin, Edda was thinking: the most bizarre mixture of hardheaded pragmatism and utter lack of foresight! While I have existed insulated from reality, my sister has coped with increasing reality. When life was easy, she was a selfish, empty-headed Little Miss Dainty. Since times grew hard, she's become a downright heroine on a level with other women. The two Graces shift and slide within each other like warring men shut up together in the same cell. But it's this new, tough Grace has won.

Charles opened his black bag, produced an ampoule and hypodermic equipment, and pushed a needle into Grace's arm before she could object. "What you need most of all, Grace, is a dreamless sleep, and I've just ensured that. Edda, get her into bed."

"That was sensible, Charlie," Edda said, returning. "Tufts is reading the boys a story, she said to start without her."

"Well, the only thing we have to discuss is Grace," Charles said with a sigh that became a wince. "I have to tell Kitty—she'll be a cot-case! And I have to tell your father."

"I can't stop your telling Kitty, but *I* will tell Daddy," Edda said, lip lifting in a snarl. "Nor should you tell Kitty on your own. She'll need Tufts."

Even at this time he could feel anger; Charles rounded on Edda fiercely. "Sisters be damned! Kitty does not need a sister there! She is my wife, a mature woman, in no need of sisters!"

The back door banged, and Jack Thurlow walked in. "Is what I heard true?" he demanded. "The party lines are buzzing with it."

Saved by an outsider from a gargantuan fight with that selfish little dictator Charlie Burdum! Edda thought, making a pot of tea while Charles explained—emphasizing his own importance, of course.

But Jack's patience was thinner than Edda's, nor was he prepared to take a back seat of no importance or relevance. His fist thumped the table. "Grace has no need to worry you, Charlie. I intend to look after her and her boys. As soon as they can pack, I'm moving them in with me at Corundoobar. Oh, I'm going to marry her, but not to please the old chooks who run Corunda's morals—she needs a husband right now, or she'll never handle those growing boys. My own silly mother ruined our lives when our dad died, and she a Burdum and all! The minister was one of those real God-botherers, not a bit like Tom Latimer. And he bullied and badgered her into living for what other people were saying. Since when should flapping tongues dictate how a lone woman with children lives her life? So Grace comes to me *now*, you hear? I won't see her go wanting a minute longer! And I'll educate Bear's boys, word of a Thurlow on that. My dad mightn't have been the husband old Tom Burdum wanted for his daughter, but he was a good husband and a good dad. I'll board this place up until times are better, then Grace can sell it to have her own bit of money—"

He gave a great sob and stopped, aghast at his own spate of words, as if the man speaking them were someone he didn't know. His eyes went suddenly to Charles, then flew to Edda; both his shoulders hunched up as if he took an actual weight on them.

Charles was so staggered he simply stood and stared.

Things crawled through Edda's jaws and cheeks, a wormy army on the move: is this the real Jack Thurlow, the man for whose sake I have delayed leaving this town for years? If it were me in Grace's shoes, would he have come rushing to my rescue like Sir Galahad with the Grail in his sights? Jack doesn't love me *or* Grace, he's in love with duty, and at this moment he sees his duty as if God had written it in flaming letters across the sky. For months he's been yearning to take up Bear's burdens and tend Bear's responsibilities as if they belonged to him. He's grabbing at Grace like a madman after the moon's reflection in a pool.

"My dear chap," Charles was saying, rattled into Pommyness, "is all this really necessary right now? I assure you that I am very happy to fund Grace and her children. It is my *duty* to do so, Jack, not yours."

"Bear and I were mates, good mates," Jack answered in hard tones. "You seem to have taken responsibility for all of Corunda—isn't that enough? I have time *and* room for Grace."

Tufts found a spluttering, confounded Charles Burdum when she entered the kitchen; Edda was wrapped in making the tea, as if her segment of the kitchen were on a different continent.

"Sit down, Edda, I'll finish that," Tufts said.

"Jack says he's taking Grace and the boys to Corundoobar."

"Interesting. Sit, Edda, sit! I'll come with you to break the news to Kitty, Charlie," Tufts said. "Edda, I presume you'll tell Daddy? Good! And shut your mouth, Charlie, you're catching a fine crop of flies. They carry germs, you know."

༄

There were other cases of suicide in Corunda, too; things weren't getting better, they were steadily worsening Australia-wide, and that went for Corunda as a part of the nation. As 1930 slipped away, ever-increasing unemployment combined with lower and lower wages for those who did have work. If bank directors and chairmen of boards somehow managed not to suffer from retrenchment, that was simply the way of the world, whose governments everywhere protected the fat cats, even Stalin's U.S.S.R. Though it had held out well early on, Corunda's prosperity was rapidly disintegrating, despite the new hospital. The spectre of retrenchment grew more visible as all the factors creating good economic health occupied more and more space in newspapers and magazines; terms a working man would never have known before 29th October 1929 were now bandied about in pubs and soup kitchens as the Great Depression ground on—and on.

Having connections to the Burdums and the Treadbys, Bear Olsen's death provided a more public forum in which to air a growing problem, even in Corunda: the burial of suicides in consecrated ground. A vocal minority of Corundites wanted to carry the curse of suicide physically into the grave by denying suicides a funeral blessing or hallowed soil. Old Monsignor O'Flaherty could be expected to oppose, argue though his curates did for a kinder interpretation of God's laws, but he was by no means the only Christian minister of religion so inclined. Some Protestant ministers were equally intransigent on the subject. The arguments were heated and nasty, and produced a new array of cracks in Christian institutions: two Corrigan suicides in the West End saw a huge exodus from Catholic St. Anthony's when the Reverend Thomas Latimer offered the Corrigans assurance that the God of Henry VIII was not as inflexible as the Vatican about the state of grace of the dead, though one of the Rector's own curates felt quite as strongly as Monsignor O'Flaherty that self-murder was the only crime God would not forgive. A formidable force in Corunda, Thomas Latimer was generally felt to be in the right of it when he thundered from his pulpit in a memorable sermon that no man or woman or child who took their own life under such conditions as these prevailing at the present time could be deemed sound of mind: madness, too, was in God's gift, and carried self-murder with it as part of the package. His learned yet intensely emotional opinion seemed reasonable, logical, and, as 1931 loomed closer, one people could live with, if not wholeheartedly accept.

Walking behind Grace and her sons, a black-clad Edda turned her head to assess the size of the crowd following the coffin out of St. Mark's and into the small cemetery next door, where families of the rectors were buried alongside Burdums and Treadbys. Black, black, black, a bobbing flow of black. No one in this trying time lacked black clothes for funerals.

Far more people are dying than being born, for the life force is flickering low, and if people don't know of any other way to avoid conceiving a child than to avoid the sexual act entirely, then that is what they do. Who would wish this world on a child? Things just go from bad to worse.

What is happening to us Latimer sisters? What must still happen?

That *fool*, Jack Thurlow! Thanks to Jack's indiscreet, oft-repeated vows to shelter Grace, people are already gossiping that my twin sister has her next husband picked out before she's seen this one put into his grave. How cruel a weapon, the tongue! Look at her, you stupid people! She's devastated by her loss! *No one can help her*, not even bloody Jack Thurlow! A man without a purpose who thinks he's found one. But unless we three can stiffen her backbone, she'll knuckle under to Jack and do as he says. She's a submissive woman who knows no other way to live than lean on someone. Death in life, fear in love, solace in belonging.

We are a legion of black crows. Kitty has come. I knew she would. I drive in the spike, Kitty lops off the head. Each of us is necessary, with Tufts to provide the earth and Grace the water.

It's hard to get Kitty on her own since she married Charlie Burdum—a very possessive man. But then, all men are possessive; it is the nature of the beast. Her isolation atop Catholic Hill is deliberate. Without a car, a difficult place to reach, and I for one can't afford a car. Nor has he taught Kitty to drive. How much marriage changes things! An unknown man enters the equation and the four sisters are fragmented—I *miss* Kitty!

Poor little Brian. Two years old. This plod is about as far as his tiny legs can carry him—trousers hemmed to knee-length because they're turned up to the crutch, coat buttoned to keep it on, it's so big, tie knotted. Black armband, Edda, black armband! His left sock has fallen down, there's a juicy chunk of snot in his right nostril that he's itching to pick out, and his silvery hair is sticking up in a cocky's comb on his crown. Oh, *adorable*! A bit of their blood is me, I am in Brian and John, even if I have no children of my own. The smell of stocks and carnations! Bittersweet. I will always link the perfume of stocks and carnations with this awful funeral.

Though wakes were deemed Papist, the Reverend Thomas Latimer had been moved by an instinct he didn't quite understand to hold a reception after the graveside ceremony was over; about a hundred people gathered inside St. Mark's Parish Hall to partake of the tipple of their choice as well as plenty of finger food. Charles Burdum had insisted on footing the bill.

Tufts got the job of buttonholing Charles while Edda pounced on Kitty and smuggled her to a little room only those from the Rectory knew. Bear's death had blighted Kitty, but not with crushing impact despite the relative recency of her own loss; she would not sink any lower because of it, Edda saw in profound relief. Physically she looked very well.

"Your dress sense has improved, Kits," Edda said, choosing a chair opposite her sister's. "The hat is delicious—where did you find it?"

"I didn't," said Kitty's low, honeyed voice. "Charlie enjoys prowling the better shops looking for things he'd like to see me wear." The voice dropped even lower. "He's a woman's sort of shopper, Edda, and his taste is much better than mine. I have too much frilly Maude in me." She sighed, giggled a true Kitty giggle—how wonderful to hear it! "He's possessive, so much so that he finds it hard to accept the love I feel for my sisters." She shrugged. "Well, how could he comprehend it? He's an only child, and while he was brought up in a family environment, he knew neither mother nor father. The result is that he tends to think my love for my sisters shortchanges my love for him, and I can't seem to get it through his head that they're two different kinds of love, in two separate compartments. How I hate being on top of that wretched hill! With the Depression worsening, there are no more taxis in Corunda. I have to offer someone with a car a sum of money that's actually an illegal transaction."

"I'm sorry," Edda said, careful not to speak through her teeth. The bastard, the *bastard*! "You have several motor cars."

"But I can't drive."

"I know, but you can learn, and you are going to learn—why? Because every Wednesday you're coming to lunch with Tufts and me at the hospital." The uncomfortable eyes bored into Kitty hard. "You're surely not *afraid* of Charlie, are you?"

"No, no!" Kitty cried, flushing. "It's more that he has fixed ideas about me, and one of those concerns the place his wife must have in his life. He polices me! This is too taxing for me, that isn't worth my doing, and sisters should be packed away with the rest of childhood. Just as if I had made such a colossal step upward in marrying him that nothing before I did the deed has any importance any more! One thing I've learned for certain, Edda—Charlie won't let me live in my sisters' pockets."

Edda hadn't really known what Kitty was going to say, or how she would react to the news of Grace's threatened change of fate, but not for a moment had she suspected Kitty harbored so much *conscious* resentment of her husband that thus far Grace hadn't come up. So when Tufts sidled around the door, Edda welcomed her feverishly.

Kitty simply carried on with the same theme once the hugs and kisses were over. "Oh, if you knew how much I hate that house on top of the hill!"

"I seem to remember," said Edda dryly, "that you had a wonderful time tricking it out, because I was with you on your excursions."

"Yes, I had something to do then! Now, how could either of you understand? You're so busy, you do admirable work and you do it well and you get praised and noticed."

"Oh, Kits!" Tufts cried, feeling more tears, but for a far different reason than Grace and two little boys. "Don't tell me that you're not in love with Charlie, please!"

"I must be, because I put up with things. I mean, I don't dream of walking out on him, and I'm not afraid to walk out on him—" She stopped, shivered. "No, I'm not afraid the way many of the women we've seen are—that they might be killed, or so bashed up they'll never be the same again—it isn't like that, honestly. All the same, Charlie expects me to be there for him in a second, at the lift of a finger, and if I'm with a sister,

COLLEEN McCULLOUGH

he—he *sulks* so! It's as if I'm not entitled to have any kind of pleasure in other people if he sees that I love them. He'd never lay a hand on me in anger, but he makes me suffer all the same. Daddy's not involved because Daddy means Maude, and Charlie is nobody's fool—he knows how Maude affects me. My sisters—oh, very different!"

Tufts kissed her full twin very tenderly. "Dearest Kitty, Charlie is plain jealous. Some people are, and there's nothing can be done about it, it's an innate character trait. You have to put up with it, but you also can't give in to it. Start as you intend to go on, and that means you must see as much of Edda, Grace, and me as you want or need. When Charlie whinges, tell him that it's hard cack, you'll see us no matter how he feels. Come on, you can do that!"

And how much of this, Tufts was wondering, lies in the tragedy of a stillborn child? No one knows why it happened, but ignorance is the worst of all private dilemmas. So I suspect he wants to blame her, and she most definitely wants to blame him. Charlie, Charlie, why didn't you show your grief to her? If you had, she wouldn't be busy piling up grudges. And he, of course, thinks she is obtaining all her comfort from her sisters. What a pickle!

Suddenly Kitty's mood changed. The lilac-blue eyes took on a furtive gleam, her face became conspiratorial. "Girls, tell me what's going on under today's surface calm. Something is! Jack Thurlow is involved, and Charlie is acting like a prude with an inexpressible secret. I am too unwell, blah, I mustn't be upset, blah, blah, I can have no interest in vulgar gossip, blah, blah, blah. Tell me, I demand to know!"

Edda's response was to spring catlike to her feet, descend on Kitty, and hug her, kiss her. "Jack Thurlow is the crux of the matter, and I don't know how else to describe it than to say that I think he must be off his head. The man's an alienist's dream come true, riddled with complexes and primal urges, blah, blah—"

They chorused it together: "—blah, blah!"

"Stop laughing, Kitty! Oh, but it's good to hear you roar! So good!" Edda cried, wiping tears of mirth and sorrow away. "Men are possessive, we've just been through that on the subject of Charlie, and the main reason why I shall never marry. I refuse to be owned. Our Jack is a sheep in wolf's

266

clothing, and a snail in a racing car, and an elephant hiding behind a grain of sand. All that you see is contradictions. I should know, we've been lovers for years. Jack walks through a self-made fog."

In the instant that Edda spoke the last sentence, Kitty's face lit up. "Yes, that's it! A fog! Charlie walks around in a self-made fog, too. But Jack's safe because you won't marry him. He gets rid of his dirty water without putting a ring through his nose."

"Lovely metaphors, girls," said Tufts, gurgling.

"What is Jack about to do that has Charlie convinced will sweep me into a seething snakepit of misery and despair?" Kitty asked, finding a thrill of warmth in her for these beloved women, who could even lift the terrible grief inspired by the dead.

"He's moving Grace and the boys out to Corundoobar tomorrow and marrying Grace as quickly as he possibly can," Tufts said as she gave Kitty a saucer of sparkling wine. "Drink up, Kits."

"Not bad," said Kitty, sipping, "though I suspect that today I'd probably find urine drinkable."

"Oh, Kitty, I love you!" from Edda.

"Of course you do," said Kitty on a purr. "Edda, Jack Thurlow has been your excuse for lingering in Corunda since we were in our teens. Do you think that Grace, Tufts, and I don't know he's just an excuse? What really keeps you here is the mystery of the four Latimer twins, not any outsider like a *man*. Until you go—and you will go!—you enrich our lives, which is what Charlie, being a man, can't see. Whether Charlie likes it or not, I'm going to learn to drive, and see as much of my sisters as I choose."

"All well and good," said Tufts practically, "but none of it answers the riddle of Jack Thurlow. What do you think?"

"What do you think?" Kitty riposted.

"That it's insanity. Poor Grace!"

"I agree" from Edda.

A silence fell; they sipped their saucered wine.

"Maude has rather faded from our lives, Kitty. Or at least from mine," Edda said suddenly.

"Oh, having the use of Daddy's car, she flits in and out of Burdum House," Kitty said lightly, setting her glass down with a thud. "The trouble is that Mama lost her joy in living when I married Charlie, who snatched her role from her. They're both Napoleons, but he has the penis to go with the conceit."

"Keep up the salt, Kits! Penis indeed! It isn't a dirty word, but people react as if it were," Edda said, a laugh in her voice. "How do you feel about Maude these days, little one?"

Kitty grimaced. "Oh, Maude! Our Clytemnestra, or do I mean Hecuba? I lost my terror of her as soon as I went nursing, but you know that. After my marriage she vanished into thin air, a part of the insubstantial pageant faded. Sometimes Shakespeare says things so perfectly there can never be another way to say them. Daddy had her to rights all along—she's just—*there*. A part of the Rectory furniture."

A golden head poked around the door, its mobile face impish. "There you are!" Charles flung the door wide. "What is this, a secret confab? Secrets from *me*? I can't have that, girls!"

"Chook secrets," said Edda, rising, "and therefore beneath your notice, Charlie. However, take heed! Kitty is coming to lunch in our hospital cottage every Wednesday, and you are not invited, even to poke your face around the door." She strolled across to tower over him, and punctuated her next speech with an occasional prod of her right index finger in the middle of his chest. "Since you moved her to the top of Catholic Hill, I see hardly anything of my little sister, and that"—poke—"is going to change. You"—poke—"haven't even organized any driving lessons for her, and that"—poke—"is going to change, too."

Charles flushed, lips tightening. "A mere oversight," he said stiffly. "I'll start teaching her tomorrow."

"Oh no, never the husband as instructor!" Edda said quickly. "Bert the ambulance man is Corunda's best driving teacher."

"Then Bert it shall be," Charles said, outmaneuvered. "It's time to join the others, *ladies*."

The reception was at its height, the participants sufficiently soaked in the liquors circulating faster than the food to be on the downward spiral to a soft muzziness that would permit the closing of Bear Olsen's door forever.

Maude had taken Brian and John to the Rectory, where Grace was staying, and the widow, freed from them, seemed to become more visible as a person than she had while tied to her sons.

When it happened, she was standing with the Rector, Dr. Liam Finucan, Dr. Charles Burdum, old Tom Burdum, Jack Thurlow, and Mayor Nicholas Middlewore; her three sisters were some yards off in a clump that included Matron Newdigate, Sister Meg Moulton, Sister Marjorie Bainbridge, and Matron Lena Corrigan. Nurses all.

Grace looks every inch the widow, thought Liam Finucan, from the slight wispiness that had ill become her until now, to the enormous, exhausted eyes, gone near as pale as Edda's.

Her hands, ungloved, were clamped around a glass of white wine, a picture of stilled function; the line of her jaw as she turned her head to follow the conversation sharp, pure. And, Liam noted, intrigued, all of a sudden every one of the hundred people in the hall had decided to stare at her as if at an actress on a stage. Grace, he sensed, was about to step into her starring role.

"*Jack!*" The word came out like the crack of a whip.

He had been gazing at her anyway, but her tone startled him; he blinked, smiled at her tenderly. "Yes, Grace?"

When she spoke it was in a loud, carrying voice with vowels rounded, sibilants bitten off and consonants crisply enunciated, a voice that told its pricking audience that she had thought about what to say before saying it. "There are wild rumors spreading all over Corunda, Jack, and I've racked my brains as to the best way to scotch them. It's being said that today, with the soil not settled on my beloved husband's grave, I already have his successor picked out and ready to go. But I have done nothing to cause these rumors, so now, here in public on my beloved husband's funeral day, I intend to lay the rumors to rest as well."

"Grace, please," said Jack, bewildered, "I don't know what's troubling you, but here and now isn't the right time to speak."

"I beg to differ," she said, and moved away from the group to stand alone, feet planted sturdily; her wine glass was given to Nick Middlemore as if he were a handy waiter. "This is exactly the right forum to make my feelings known, and once they are known, there can be no mistaken ideas about my future, or the future of my two children."

Divining what was coming, her sisters stood tensely, yet made no move to go to her; this was one thing Grace had to do herself, unsupported. "Though plans for my future were made with the best of intentions, they were not made with my knowledge or consent." She pinned an utterly confused Jack on a fiery stare, then smiled at him. "You are very kind, Jack, and I honor you for it, but I am not alone in my present troubles. I have a family, I have many friends, I have very loyal and helpful neighbors. I loved my husband with every part of me, and it will be a long time—if ever—before I can so much as think of any other man. I am a decent woman. My father is the Rector of St. Mark's. How could I fly in the face of convention for the sake of a material comfort I haven't known in years? I would be branded a common trollop—and rightly so!" One long, floating hand went out. "Come, Jack, let us be friends. Simple, ordinary friends. I thank you most sincerely, but let there be no more rumors that I am moving out to Corundoobar. My home is on Trelawney Way."

"Bravo, Grace," said Edda under her breath, eyes meeting those of Tufts and Kitty. Somewhere, deep down, they had all known.

Jack Thurlow stood stunned. He had taken Grace's hand quite automatically, a look in his fine eyes that Liam Finucan thought reminiscent of the awareness that comes a split second ahead of the poleaxe. His mouth worked, quivered; then he shook his head. "I—" he managed, then could manage no more.

Oh, you poor man! thought Kitty, seeing Jack Thurlow for the first time as someone other than Edda's tamed tiger. It isn't the grief of thwarted love, because you don't love Grace; it's the bitter humiliation of public rejection when you haven't deserved such treatment. How to explain that you brought it on yourself?

Charles stepped into the breach easily. "Yes, Jack, so very kind of you, especially when gossip turned one thing into another far different from what was meant, eh?" He put a hand on Jack's arm and guided him away.

"Did we all know she'd refuse?" Matron Newdigate asked.

"To accept wouldn't have been in character," Meg Moulton said. "Grace likes a fairly hard life, it gives her legitimate grounds for complaint."

"Living the life of Lady Muck out at Corundoobar and sending her boys to board at King's wouldn't suit Grace," said Tufts. "She likes the Trelawneys."

"Why wouldn't she?" Lena Corrigan asked, laughing. "Grace is the Queen of the Trelawneys—Way, Road, Street, Lane, Circle, and all the rest—and she's not about to abdicate. It's taken her the years of her marriage to be crowned, but like Victoria, with widowhood she's entrenched."

Edda's brows rose. "Isn't that to exaggerate, Lena?"

"In a pig's eye! You don't see it because you're Grace's twin, but Grace has a gift for the common touch. I mean, because she didn't last as a nurse, you tend to dismiss her as a useless ignoramus, but to the women of the Trelawneys she's a person of superior education and knowledge—she matriculated from C.L.C., so she can reel off history, geography, literature, classical allusions, algebra, you name it. Yet she never, never, *never* rubs anybody else's nose in their far poorer educations. She has pride in her taste, is a brilliant housekeeper, and never cocks a snook at her neighbors. That's miraculous! The women of the Trelawneys aren't a rough lot like us West Enders, but they don't belong on Catholic Hill, either. And Grace is their queen."

"I hear you, Lena," Tufts said. "I'm the sister who visits her at home the most, and she's always immersed in some sort of Trelawney doings. Well, bully for Grace!"

"Nor were her sixteen months of nursing wasted," said Kitty thoughtfully. "A Trelawney woman with a sick child goes first to Grace, and only after that, to the doctor. Times are hard, and the doctor costs ready money. Grace is usually all they need."

"How do you know that, Kits?" Edda asked, surprised.

"Even on top of Catholic Hill there's gossip."

Edda's mind drifted. "Poor Jack!" The words said, she got up and walked to where Charles had abandoned the rejected swain.

"Cheer up," she said in a level voice. "It may not seem so at the moment, but Grace's decision has actually spared you a life of considerable pain. You and she aren't suited in any way, Jack. I don't mean to sound facetious, but I swear that fat and pampered cat of yours would have left home the minute Grace arrived, and before long you'd be itching to follow its example. Grace isn't weak and helpless. She's made of hardened steel.

Corunda will decide that your impulse to take Grace and her boys on was splendid. It's Grace would have incurred the spite and contempt. No one has ever admired anybody poor for marrying someone rich. As it is, Grace's instincts for survival are magnificent, so she did what she had to—refuse your gesture right out in the open."

"Thereby turning me into a fool."

"Rubbish! You look like a knight in shining armor. No one thinks the worse of you for making the offer, and now nobody thinks the worse of Grace, either. You both smell like roses."

His body twisted, a painful-looking movement. "The thing is, Edda, that I was looking forward to settling down with Grace. I've got Corundoobar, I'll weather the Depression, and I'd like to have some heirs. Brian and John would have loved the life."

"Then take the same path, just more slowly," Edda said, at a cost to herself she preferred not to think about. "Court her as a widow must be courted. Her attempts to keep you at a distance won't last a moment longer than it takes for the chook run door to fall off, or the earwigs to hit the potato patch. Grace is already accustomed to turning to you, Jack. Make sure she always can."

His mouth went thin, his eyes flashed fire. "Not in a bloody fit!" he snapped. "As far as I'm concerned, Grace's chook run door can splinter to bits and she can feed her boys on solid mashed earwigs! She made a fool of me!"

"I'm disappointed in you," said Edda.

"Oh, sisters ganging up, eh?"

"Yes, always." The wolf's eyes mocked him. "You've been a mystery to me for years, Jack Thurlow, but no longer. Beneath all that landsman's swagger is a man of straw. No brains, no stomach for life, and absolutely no bloody backbone."

Turning, she stalked back to the group of women, her chest heaving as if she'd run ten miles pursued by a killer.

"Bye-bye, Jack?" Kitty asked.

"I'd sooner sleep with a scarecrow! There's more to it."

The beginning of 1931 brought one dire lesson with it: that economic ills of this intensity would drag the people down for years to come. The ideological splits in the federal Labour government were made worse by James Scullin's junket overseas; when he finally returned to Australia in January 1931, the populace had learned enough about his caretaker, Joe Lyons, to like him increasingly better than Scullin.

For Charles's sake Kitty tried to sustain fascination in the names—and the personalities owning the names—but politics, time was teaching her, lay far from her heart. Those politicians she met she found uninspiring, no different from most men. Generally, she judged, they didn't take special care of their appearance or display beautiful manners; between the dandruff, the blubbery paunches, the bad teeth, the combed-over baldness, the noses empurpled with grog-blossoms, and the soup stains on their ties, they were a dreary lot.

"If only wireless sets had a moving picture attached!" she said to Charles, "politicians would have to smarten up their act because the people who vote for them would actually see them in action, how they look and behave. After setting eyes on them, I wouldn't vote for more than a handful of them—don't their wives see it?"

"*I* don't let you down," Charles said, a trifle complacently.

"True, but outside Corunda, how many voters know that?"

Alas, unanswerable.

He was very aware that since the loss of their child she had changed in her attitude toward him; the business of learning to drive—a genuine oversight on his part—was one symptom of it. Knowing himself unreasonable, still he blamed her sisters, much and all as he liked each one of them, even Grace. Just not as sisters-in-law.

Hardest of all for him to understand was Kitty's reaction to his natural protectiveness—why did it irk her so, and more and more as time went on? By the end of 1930 she had been begging to fall pregnant again, but when he refused, saying it wasn't a long enough rest, she wouldn't accept his reasons as valid. Instead, she began to sneak into his temporary bed, where of course his traitorous body welcomed her, starved for her. She rejoiced, he feared.

"Charlie, I want children!" she said to him fiercely. "I want my own family, I want a reason for living! And don't say you're my reason for living, because you're not! You live for politics, the hospital, and me, in that order. But where are my politics, where is my hospital? I'm shut up in an empty mausoleum on top of a hill, and I want a home filled with children! Not this showcase showplace but a home—hear me? *A home!*"

"It will happen, Kitty, it will happen! But wait, please, I beg of you, wait!"

Toward Easter, she went to see her father and poured out her troubles to him.

"I can't go to my sisters," she said, walking with him in the Rectory garden, a summer glory, "because I need to talk to someone older, wiser, yet still of my blood. Daddy, you've seen everything in your time, it has to be you."

They paced between masses of flowers, roses and fairylike ferny daisies, asters and begonias, while the elderly man tried to plumb the depths of his most pain-filled daughter—oh, what might have been were Maude a different kind of mother! Or her child less beautiful?

"I'm here for you, Kitty," he said. "Tell me."

"I've got an idea in my head that I can't dislodge, Daddy, and I *know* it's a wrong idea, but that doesn't stop me thinking it." Her eyes brimmed with tears that didn't fall. "I shouldn't have married Charlie. Oh, I love him, it isn't that. But I have this idea that Charlie is the reason for my infertility. That Charlie and I can't make babies."

Thomas Latimer led her to a seat and ensconced both of them upon it, then turned toward his daughter, her hands in his.

"Did Maude put this idea in your head, Kitty?" he asked.

"No! Honestly, Daddy, no. I haven't really talked with her since I married, even when she drives up to see me. Her thinking is muddled, haven't you noticed?"

"Yes, dear child, I have noticed."

"No, it's my own idea," Kitty said. "Charlie and I can't make babies together."

"The idea is insidious but false, Kitty," the Rector said sternly, "and you must eradicate it. Your husband is a perfectly made man eminently suited to you as the father of your children. Whatever happened to little Henry Burdum is a mystery, but not one that can be solved by an invalid conclusion like yours—how unfair! Come, Kitty, you know it is unfair. It's groundless, baseless. Has any doctor suggested it?"

"No," she said miserably.

"Because it has no validity, my daughter, none at all. The act of conceiving a child isn't carpentry, where two boards mightn't quite dovetail, or a jigsaw puzzle with a missing piece. It is God-given. And what God gives, only God can take away. The Almighty may use human vectors to work His deeds, but they remain His, and His alone. You're seeking for a victim, Kitty, but to find one in your husband is utterly wrong."

Kitty listened, the tears liberated to roll down her cheeks. "Yes, Daddy, I hear you," she whispered. "But what if I keep on losing them?"

"Then it is God's will, but I fail to see why you should." He took his handkerchief out, patted it over her face, then gave it to her. "Here, blow your nose, silly child."

Chastened yet oddly comforted, Kitty blew her nose, dried the last of her tears, and looked at her father with love. *He's getting old,* she thought, *and something is bothering him. Not me.*

"What's the matter with you, Daddy?" she asked.

"It's your mother. She's not just muddled, her mind is going," he said.

Kitty jumped. "Oh, Daddy!"

His working lips found speech; the Rector took his handkerchief back and used it. "She suffers memory lapses that are growing more frequent and more noticeable. She forgets where she's put things, especially money, which I think she tries to hide on the premise that I don't give her any." His voice wavered; he strove to discipline it. "The worst of it is obvious—I can no longer trust her with money, and dare not give it to her beyond a few shillings if she goes out."

What to say, what to do? "Then let's go to the Rectory and have a cup of tea with her," Kitty said with decision. "I want to see her for myself."

How well she had concealed her dementia during Bear Olsen's funeral! Though Kitty's nursing had mainly been with children, she had seen enough pre–senile dementias to know how cunning they could be at hiding their disorder from the world, and in this, Maude was no different. She was obviously gorging on food; her face had ballooned, and the corseted bulk of her body needed a larger dress size than the one she was wearing, its underarm seams gaping, its placket far apart, its frills stretched. Over three months since Bear died? She had plummeted.

"Darling Kitty!" she cried, turning as if to face a room full of people. "Isn't my daughter the loveliest child you've ever seen?" she shrilled. "That face! Mauve eyes! Helen of Troy! My gorgeous, gorgeous Kitty!"

"A little long in the tooth now for that description, Mama," Kitty said through a constriction in her throat.

"No, never! Not my Kitty!"

And on, and on, until Kitty managed to get herself away, leaving the Rector to deal with his wife, still rhapsodizing about her gorgeous, gorgeous daughter.

It was Tufts whom Kitty found first, looking competently busy in an office lined with books and behind a desk piled high with neat stacks of paper. She wore a uniform of her own design, a simple, severely cut tobacco-brown dress, and had loosely piled her dark gold hair into a bun on the back of her head. The result was as pretty as professional, no mean feat.

"Did you know that Mama's mind is going?" Kitty demanded.

"Yes."

"For how long?"

"Four months."

"Why wasn't I told?"

"Charlie forbade it. The baby, et cetera."

Kitty emitted a thin squeal. "Well, Tufts, no more of that, do you hear? I am not a child! I am not mentally deficient! I am not Charlie Burdum's property mind, body, and soul! To think that for three months I've had lunch every Wednesday with Edda and you, and never known! I could spit chips! How dared Charlie do this to me? Maude is my *mother*!"

"Calm down, Kits, I'm on your side," Tufts said calmly. "You know Charlie—an autocrat. We kept silent, but unwillingly."

"The trouble is that in one way or another, Charlie holds all of us in his power," Kitty said, subsiding into a chair. "You and Edda suffer him as your boss, Grace suffers him as his pensioner. And I, alas, am his wife. Well, it goes against the grain that we Latimers of Corunda are at the mercy of a Pommy Burdum."

"Don't do anything rash, Kitty, please."

"Rash? Certainly not. I merely intend to beard the lion in his den to-night in a reasonably civilized manner."

"That doesn't sound very reassuring. Do please make proper allow-ances," Tufts said.

"I will. Daddy has made me see that what God gives, only God can take away." Kitty swept a hand in the direction of the bookshelves. "Learn-ing lots?"

"I've started university—interesting, if repetitious. The thing I enjoy most is running the ship."

"And to think that once upon a time I hoped you and Liam would make a go of it," Kitty said, dimples showing.

"Liam and I? Not in a thousand years," said Tufts, snorting. "We're best friends, not lovers."

"Can't you be both?"

"Some, perhaps, but not us."

"And why introduce a new flavor into the mixture if it has a superb taste already? You're absolutely right, Tufty."

Charles Burdum was tired. His political career was going nowhere, though the exercise books were filling. Despite his convictions as to how to cure the Depression, he had nothing else in common with Jack Lang, for he deplored Lang's refusal to pay back the due interest on foreign loans—street urchin tactics, immature and irresponsible.

When he married Kitty he had been positive he could turn her into the close political colleague and helper he so desperately needed; politics was a *vocal* medium, its exponents near invisible. It depended on how seductively a man could *talk* to the public. And, the exercise books had informed him with their well-knit, disciplined thought, a man with political aspirations had to start by assembling his inner sanctum. Only after that could he hope for colleagues and the public arena. Yet with 1931 well arrived, he, Charles Burdum, had no inner sanctum. He didn't even have a politically informed or inclined wife. What he had been inflicted with was a woman who hungered for babies. Oh, children were all well and good, a man had to have them for many reasons, but how many masculine hearts deemed children the top priority in life? Precious few, Charles calculated, being of that kind himself. Oh, for someone at home with whom to talk politics!

So terribly, terribly tired. What he really felt like doing, Charles reflected as he left the Packard in the driveway and plodded up the steps to the portico, was to down a couple of stiff Scotches and then go straight to bed, wifeless, dinnerless, a hibernation. Not a Kitty evening, much as he loved her.

One look at her scowling face was enough to dispel that ambition as futile. Charles drew in a breath and mentally girded himself for war. What on earth had he done?

"Today," said Kitty, following him to the sideboard on top of which the decanters lived, "I found out that my mother has been mentally deranged for months, and that you forbade people to tell me. What gave you that right, Charlie?"

He poured a very stiff Scotch and gave it a spurt of soda from the siphon. Until the first gulp had gone down he didn't answer, then, feeling a little energy steal into his aching frame, he frowned. "The right of a husband to spare his wife," he said, and took another gulp.

"You have no right to decide what I can be told and cannot be told, whether to spare me or not," she said through her teeth. "An unconscionable insult! I am a grown woman and make my own decisions, especially when they concern my blood family."

He was feeling better, and refilled his glass. "Actually, my dear, once you're married what you say isn't quite true any more." He sat down, the image of composure. "To some extent, at law you are my chattel. Your money automatically becomes mine, and you need my written consent to incur debt or engage in any sort of business dealings. As my wife, I can compel you to live with me and cohabit with me."

Her skin had lost its color and the eyes were sheened with purple, as of stone; one hand, trembling, went up to press against her mouth. "I see. You're Soames Forsyte," she said.

"I trust not," he said, sipping. "A man who rapes his wife is a contempt-ible bounder who ought to be shot." He leaned forward. "For heaven's sake, Kitty, grow up! As if I would ever behave tyrannically to you, of all people! I love you with every part of my being. If that sometimes means I tend to become high-handed, it's at least excusable. It was solely to spare you fruit-less worry that I asked people not to tell you about Maude. What could you have done except torment yourself over something as inevitable as demen-tia? Once it's a clinical fact, you can't control it, or alter its course. Believe me, not one member of your family made any objection to my asking for silence."

"That still gives you no right to decide for me!" she cried. "I am my own person, I belong to myself. You can witter on about wives being chattels until the cows come home, Charlie, but you'll not make a chattel out of me!"

The well-being was invading every bit of him; Charles put his head back against the squabs of his wing chair and smiled at Kitty with a slightly muzzy rush of adoration. "I always think of Scotch as a warm tartan rug thrown over the bare bony knees of a man's mind," he said, too tired to be angry.

"I'm not going to get any sense out of you."

"Afraid so."

"I'm having another baby," she said.

His eyes snapped open. "Oh, Kitty! That was unwise."

"Grace's second one was closer to her first than this one is to my first attempt."

His eyes closed again, but on tears she didn't see. "Unwise."

"Go to hell, Charlie!"

In the middle of that same night, Kitty miscarried.

It was the bitterest, the most devastating torment of her life, made more so by what had gone before it; she had flouted medical advice to achieve it, including from a doctor-husband who hadn't bothered to hide his opposition.

"Unwise," he had said.

When the cramps woke her, her first thought was to thank God that Charlie had imbibed so freely of the Scotch that he had dossed down on the sofa. Only then did she realize that she was bleeding, and why. Her mouth opened on a silent scream—no, no, no!

"Oh, please God, please not that!" she babbled, over and over. The tears engulfed her, torrents of them turning her face to a running sheet of total despair—my baby, my poor little baby!

Later on, when she was sane again, she could find no reason of any kind, even the flimsiest, to account for what happened in the seconds after it dawned on her that she had miscarried; she panicked, the terrible, guilty panic of a child caught out in a sin too dreadful to contemplate. No one must know! What would they do to her for disobeying, for getting pregnant when it was forbidden?

Oh, I'll be in such trouble if Charlie finds out!

Scrambling from the bed, she ran for towels, rags, a bucket, cold water, ether soap, all the things she'd need to clean up the mess before anyone discovered what a terrible thing she'd done—a sin, a crime, an *awful* disobedience!

The buckets, made of galvanized metal, were stacked one inside each other; they fell clanging and ringing fit to wake the dead. They woke Charles, too.

He found her, bloody and blundering, shrinking from him as if she thought he'd murder her, when all he wanted to do was take her in his arms and heal her pain. But until Ned Mason and Edda got there, the most he could do for his frantic, gibbering wife was to give her an injection that knocked her out.

"I suppose by rights I should have sent for Tufts," Charles said to Edda after Kitty was tucked up in a different bed, still asleep but not in any danger. Ned Mason had gone home, shaking his head at the stubbornness of women, but not unduly alarmed by what had happened; he continued to maintain that physically Kitty was healthy and ought to bear living children in the future.

"No, I'm the sister of things like this," said Edda. "I'm cheese graters and hangman's ropes, all Kitty's sorrows. Tufts is too young to have the memories, so you did the right thing."

He had been weeping, free to do so now the crisis was over. "Why did she look at me as if she genuinely thought I'd be angry with her?" he asked now. "I swear to you on my mother's grave, Edda, that I have never, by word or look, let alone deed, given my wife any reason to fear me!"

And, looking into his eyes, Edda believed him.

When Kitty woke with the morning she was worn out and worn down, but fully aware of what had happened, and apparently understood why it had happened.

"I was greedy," she said to Edda. "I wouldn't wait for things to settle and heal properly. It won't happen again."

Vastly relieved, Charles saw for himself that by the end of the week following her miscarriage, Kitty had returned to normal. The anger and aggression were gone, so too her tendency to blame him for all her woes.

"Patience, my darling," he counselled her. "Wait out a full six months, then we'll try again."

PART FIVE

DRIVING IN THE SPIKE

When an unexpected opportunity to meet Sir Rawson Schiller K.C. presented itself, Charles leaped at it. For a mere forty-year-old, Schiller had gone very far very fast, including earning himself a knighthood at the amazingly early age of thirty-seven after a series of stunning legal victories in the High Court of Australia and the British Privy Council in the service of commerce and finance. He was possessed of life's advantages—birth, wealth, education, an impressive colonial family history; on his father's side he was Prussian *junker*, on his mother's side English gentleman; the "von" had been dropped long since as inappropriate in a society like Australia, where the family owned a lot of Queensland, the Northern Territory, and the north of Western Australia. As pasture much of it was so poor it grazed only one steer per hundred acres, but some was extremely arable or pastoral, and the mineral wealth was, in places, incredible, including places that only the Schillers yet knew about. No rattle of a convict's leg-iron had ever marred the Schiller or the Rawson families: free settler all the way.

Sir Rawson lived and worked in Melbourne, where the Schiller moneys were concentrated; little surprise, then, that his charitable activities were usually confined to Melbourne, including a Lord Mayor's dinner at £50 per plate to benefit spastic children. The moment he heard, Charles bought two plates at the Speaker's Table (they cost £100 each), for Sir Rawson was the guest speaker and star attraction of the evening, which also boasted a famous dance band for those with the stamina to stay up until dawn.

It was to be a glittering affair: white-tie-and-tails for the men, ball gowns for the women, and since Kitty loathed Melbourne, Charles took Edda in her place. By chance Edda had been attending a theatre nursing seminar in Melbourne that week, so when Charles offered her a hotel room-and-bath for her entire visit if she would accompany him to the dinner, Edda leaped to say yes. Her cup overflowed as he gave her a hundred pounds to spend on a ball dress for the Lord Mayor's charity dinner. Because she made all her own clothes, Edda was able to use the money to buy eleven lengths of different fabrics to make eleven different outfits. Not even the fashion journalists who prowled the periphery of these functions suspected that her deceptively simple robe of black-shot burgundy silk was homemade; they were too busy gushing over its obviously Parisian origins. Her only touch of ostentation was a pair of diamond earrings Kitty had lent her.

She went with Charles in a hired Rolls, as always consumed by admiration for his nonchalance—how, for instance, he passed off their disparity in height as if it were the natural order of things. The blue flare of exploding flash bulbs on press cameras he tolerated well; Edda's acute hearing noted that his male press secretary was calling her "*Sister* Edda Latimer" whenever he gave her name. I like it! thought Edda, inwardly gratified, outwardly indifferent. Charlie is telling the world that I am a professional woman, not a gilded society lily or an upper-class trollop, and I thank him for his consideration. Oh, if only my title were "Doctor!" But, for all his liberality, Charlie would never put me through medicine, for the same reason Daddy didn't years ago—it isn't a suitable career for a woman. How I long to be a doctor!

"It should be Kitty here tonight," Charles said as they trod up the staircase. "It's damned awkward having to explain that you're my sister-in-law, not my wife."

So that's why he's in a bad mood! Nothing but complaints and surly looks since we set out. Oh, Kitty! It wouldn't have killed you to make this little sacrifice for your husband—why wouldn't you? All your dreams and energies have turned in one direction, and one direction only—a house full of children. In which case, you have the wrong life's partner. Charlie doesn't mind children, but he'll never live for them. He lives for public activities.

By some quirk of fate, neither Charles nor Edda saw the guest speaker during the forty minutes they spent beforehand sipping sherry and mingling in anterooms; by another quirk of fate they were among the first through the doors into the ballroom where the banquet was to take place. Edda's memory was of walking through a vast room of big round tables toward the focal one on the fringe of a large dance floor and beneath the speaker's podium. The area was deserted save for a man standing behind his chair at the table.

"Stop grizzling, Charlie!" she growled *sotto voce*, her gaze on—Sir Rawson Schiller King's Counsel?

Yes, this had to be Sir Rawson Schiller K.C. Unforgettable. A Charlie over six feet tall? No, that was to compare a diamond with an emerald or a da Vinci with a Velázquez. There was no sort of comparison possible. Not that Edda fell in love: she didn't. It was more that she seemed to recognize the one person who had always been missing from her life, and for the fleeting second during which his eyes met hers, she had a conviction that he was thinking the same thought. Then he looked elsewhere, and the moment and the conviction were both over.

A slim and whippy man, two inches over six feet, narrow-framed, but with a huge, bulbous head whose cranium housed a lot of brain. Striking yet not handsome: iron-grey hair in thick waves brushed straight back from his massive forehead, high cheekbones, a fine mouth, black brows and lashes, but vividly blue eyes. His nose was large and beaked, his lower jaw and chin big, too.

She and Charles were halfway around the table from him, and no handshakes were exchanged; just smiles and nods. Only a team of wild horses could have dragged Charlie close enough to have to look so far upward, Edda knew as she sat down and assessed the table's population, eleven in number: Sir Rawson had come without a companion.

"But he always does," said her nearest feminine neighbor in a long-suffering voice.

"Why?" Edda asked.

"He's working tonight, pet."

Never having been called a pet before, Edda lapsed into silence. Oh, she thought, exasperated, why will important Australian men insist upon marrying undereducated, domestically inclined women? At this table, the men did all the talking, the women confining their chat among themselves. And Charlie was growing more discontented by the minute, probably because he knew no one and the gargoyle had obliterated the film star out of existence. No one was usually more charming, but when the gargoyle ruled alone, he was horrible. The effect of Sir Rawson Schiller, of course. For once in his career, Charlie felt utterly eclipsed.

A mood Sir Rawson's hour-long speech only served to enhance. His subject—could it be anything else?—was the Depression, and it took Edda's breath away many times, for Sir Rawson had that incomparable gift of an eloquence so perfectly honed from voice to phraseology that one moment tears poured down every face, and the next, every face was crumpled in laughter. Privately Edda thought a large number of people who heard him would always remember what he said and how he said it.

It came after a generous portion of first course; after the main course the speaker answered questions from the podium for half an hour. A hard evening's work; he threw everything he had into making his audience feel that £50 was a bargain.

One member of the audience at least felt that he hadn't got his money's worth: Charles Burdum. Who, with a muttered something in Edda's ear, left his chair as the dessert came in. Everybody at the table assumed he had gone to relieve himself, but Edda knew he wouldn't be back, and began explaining to her companions that urgent business had called him away.

More than two-thirds of his fellow diners were dancing when Sir Rawson got up and usurped Charlie's chair, turning it toward Edda.

"And you are?" he asked, smiling.

"Sister Edda Latimer. I came with Charles Burdum."

"*Sister* Latimer, but no nun."

"By profession I'm an operating theatre nurse."

"Could they spare you, Edda? May I call you that?"

"Of course, Sir Rawson."

"Tit for tat. Call me Rawson. Can they spare you?"

"Easily. In fact, I'm so surplus to requirements that I'm toying with the idea of finding a job in Melbourne. I'm extremely well trained and experienced, so even in the Depression I should be able to find work. I've made some contacts here at a seminar."

"I'd hoped to converse with Charles Burdum. Has he gone?"

"Called away by something that wouldn't wait."

"Leaving you to fend for yourself?"

"Oh, he's family, married to my sister. He didn't think." The sunken, hooded eyes gleamed. "Are you married?" she asked.

The baldness of the question startled him into answering.

"Seventeen years ago, a youthful business. We divorced."

"Were you white as snow, or the culpable party?"

"You ask naked personal questions as if you were an American. I was as unsullied as the driven snow."

"The perfect color for a politician."

"The *only* color," he said meaningfully.

"A pity, that. You don't feel it asks too much of a man?"

"Politicians, would-be or otherwise, should never deal in feelings. Only in realities. And realities can be bleak."

"You're Nationalist Party—a Tory?"

"A die-hard Tory, though how much longer there will be a Nationalist Party is on the lap of the gods. Labour is inclining more and more to the right, but not as far right as I."

"When are you planning to enter—federal?—parliament?"

"Definitely federal. The party has a blue-ribbon seat picked out for me in Melbourne that means I don't have to change my place of abode." He grimaced. "Awful business, relocating."

"Especially for something as ephemeral as votes," she said.

Interest piqued, he leaned forward. "You're an unusual woman, Sister Latimer. Well read and well educated, I suspect. You may juggle sharpened steel in a chamber of anesthetized torment, but that is not what you wanted to do, nor did your life start there. In fact, you think it has ended there."

"I am everything an ultra-conservative man deplores in a woman, Counsellor," she said levelly, eyes glowing at his uncanny insight. "I hold myself the equal of any man—I should have been allowed to do medicine and choose to specialize in whatever I wanted—and I will never marry. To marry is to subordinate myself at law to my husband as my superior."

"Oh, bravo!" he exclaimed, smiling and leaning back. "I knew I liked you enormously! So you wanted to be a doctor."

Suddenly Edda's own problems vanished; all kinds of ideas were chasing through her brain—a muddle of mobile brows, facial expressions, something lurking just beyond vision, delicate and supple fingers, a certain wry crease to the fine mouth. Tangled visions that slid and slipped into place to form a certain male entity . . . She caught his blue gaze and held it sternly, pinning him as only her strange eyes could. And he, discomfited, oddly afraid, waited.

"You're homosexual," Edda said softly.

"That's a baseless nonsense could see you in court," he said, managing to control every part of himself save his breathing.

"I have no intention of disseminating the fact. Why on earth should I? So my brother-in-law could crow? He has enough to crow about already."

"Who told you? Who *knows*?" he asked, quite calmly.

"No one told me. In fact, you hide your secret extremely well. But when I first saw you, you stunned me—it was a little like—oh, coming home. And I was endowed with special perceptions about you. It must be that way," she said, smiling at him tenderly.

Capacity for denial gone, he stared at her like an exhausted boxer told he must fight on just one more round, with no idea in him as to how he could. "How much do you want?" he asked tiredly.

"*Blackmail?*" Edda laughed. "No, there is no possibility of blackmail, ever. I can only imagine what you must have gone through over the years—it's a terrible secret, the worst secret a man with public ambitions can have. I want to be your friend, is all. When our eyes met, *that* was what I knew—that I was, and am, your best friend ever." She swallowed. "I don't expect you to understand, though I had rather hoped you would, because I thought the feeling was reciprocated."

The dance band was blaring, its brass drowning out the sweeter sounds of strings and woodwinds, and this table was taking the full brunt of the noise as determined couples capered only feet away.

A saxophone wowed and wailed; he winced. "Would you come home with me for a quiet drink and a talk?" he asked.

She rose at once. "The sooner, the better."

"Burdum?"

"He deserted me first."

Home for Sir Rawson Schiller K.C. was the entire top floor of one of Melbourne's tallest buildings at fifteen stories, and came with a spacious roof garden shielded from traffic noise and voyeurs by a tall, dense hedge. The interior of twelve rooms, all generous in size, had been furnished and decorated by a prominent design firm, and no doubt reflected the owner's tastes: conservative, comfortable, richly autumnal in coloring, understated.

"What would you care to drink?" Rawson asked, seating her in his library, obviously the room he inhabited the most.

"Since I notice the unobtrusive presence of servants, a cup of really good coffee would please me best, but, failing that, a cup of what Charles Burdum calls coal-tar tea will do nicely," she said, settling into a chair upholstered in amber crushed velvet. "I'm glad you didn't choose leather. Sweaty for bare skin."

"Leather can be a sweaty horror for a man, too, when it's in his own home," he said. "Coffee it shall be."

His eyes took her in, a leisurely pleasure. Such an elegant, sophisticated creature! Pure bones, flawless skin, lovely features, and hands to die for, graceful and speaking despite their short-cut nails. Only her eyes told of a brilliant mind handicapped by her sex, a thirst for interest, a hunger for bigger things to do that was always denied. And such eyes! A white wolf, offputting and eerie, framed by long, thick lashes.

They made casual conversation until the coffee was removed.

"That was the best coffee I've ever had," she said then.

"Not exactly a tall order to fill," said he, smiling. "I happen to like good coffee."

A silence fell then, so comfortable and familiar that Edda ended in thinking she had known him for all eternity; why that was, she hadn't the remotest idea. Every scrap of her understood why Charlie had escaped this man's company the minute that manners said he could leave; to Charlie, this relatively young knight was a bigot with no time for the working man. Edda translated this as envy for Sir Rawson's height and properly Australian-type aristocracy. Archconservatism *did* suggest a bigot, but Edda was not convinced Rawson was one. Simple answers couldn't solve the riddle of such a complex man, of that she was sure.

The silence was succeeded by talk about many things, none of them political, some of them pertaining to philosophies, some to sex. Certainly he was starved for a candid friendship with a woman he could trust implicitly, and clearly until now that had been denied him. In her, Edda, he was beginning to feel a little of that implicit trust; she resolved always to say what she felt.

"What prompted you to marry?" she asked.

"Panic, combined with family expectations," he said, and for a moment panic flared in his eyes. His mouth closed, stoppered.

"No, tell me," she said strongly.

An apologetic smile, and he resumed. "I was psychically at my most confused, and I'd known Anne since early childhood—we were neighbors. Whatever I did, wherever I went, Anne was somewhere fairly close. Our schools were partnered in all social events, and we went up to university together. I did Law, she did Arts, then a secretarial course. We went to the same law firm, I as a junior at the bar, she as private secretary to one of the senior partners. Then she proposed marriage to me, I think because she was tired of waiting for me to do it. Our families were delighted. In fact, *I* was the only fly in the ointment! Also, I realized that if I wanted to keep my secret, I would have to marry. So we married. We were both twenty-three."

"And of course it was a disaster," Edda said.

"Frightful! I couldn't manage to make love to her, and the only logical reason I could find was to keep insisting I felt too much her brother to be a husband. It dragged on for two years. Then she met someone else, and I gave her an uncontested divorce."

"I am so sorry!"

"Don't be. I kept my secret, even from Anne."

"Have you a lover?"

This time his smile was rueful. "I dare not, Edda."

"I refuse to believe you avail yourself of rent boys."

"The rent boy. Why not be done with it and call him a prostitute? Have you ever looked into a rent boy's eyes? Dead—so *dead*! One plumbs a pit, and wonders how he ever got started. No, not for me. I go abroad for a month, usually winter and summer."

"I wish you had room in your life for a best friend," she said.

The intensely blue eyes grew brilliant. "Would you work here in Melbourne to be my best friend?"

"In an instant, though I know nothing about the law, which I suppose means I can't be a satisfactory best friend."

That made him laugh. "My dear, the last thing one wants in a best friend is a mind tunnelled by the law." He reached out to take her hands in his, holding her gaze with what she fancied was a kind of love. "For thirty years I've led a very lonely life, Sister Edda Latimer, but now I think I've finally found a friend with whom I can share *all* my secrets. A natural streak of paranoia has protected me from close friendships, but now—how odd! I don't feel it."

"I'll start making enquiries at the bigger hospitals tomorrow," Edda said, wanting to weep, knowing she didn't dare.

"No, not yet!" he said sharply. "Do you believe that I have the influence to postpone the awarding of any hospital job for—say, another two or three weeks?"

Bewildered, she frowned. "Yes, it's Melbourne. You have the influence," she said.

"Then grant me two weeks of your time, starting early on Monday morning. Grant it to me not knowing what I want you for, just believe that at the end of it, the hospital job will be waiting for you," Rawson said.

"You may have your time," Edda said gravely.

He gasped, thumped his fists on his beautifully tailored knees, and squeezed her hands before releasing them. "Oh, well done! The mystery must remain, but I'll explain enough for you to make plans. One floor down I own a guest flat. It's much smaller than this one, but quite spacious for someone not making a home there. You will move into it tomorrow afternoon, and on Monday you will commence two weeks of living in it doing exactly as I bid you. Your sentence will be up on Sunday evening two weeks from tomorrow."

"Well, stone the crows!" she said, feeling some sort of exclamation was called for. "Two weeks of mystery labor for Sir Rawson Schiller coming up. I wonder what it can be?"

"Time will tell," he said, quietly chuckling. "I will only say that I have been visited by an inspiration. We have talked of shoes, ships, sealing wax, medicine, hospitals, courts, music, books, and God knows what tonight, and out of the jumble has come a wonderful, beautiful idea. I do *not* believe that all men were created equal, otherwise why are there so many idiots around? But I do firmly believe that the world contains as many intelligent women as it does intelligent men."

"What do I say to Charles Burdum?" she asked.

He shrugged. "Anything you like that sits well with you. I presume he knows you're applying for a position in Melbourne?"

"As a matter of fact, he doesn't. I've been here attending a seminar, and listening to the chatter over teacups inspired me with the Melbourne idea. I'll tell him something to make him hope."

"Hope? Hope what?"

"That his most disliked, uncomfortable sister-in-law will decide to live four hundred miles away in Melbourne. That would mean he stands a better chance of discouraging his wife from seeking the company of her sisters," she said with a snap.

"Oh, I see. A possessive husband."

"Very much so. And I'm the one who stirs the pot."

"Sometimes it can be more effective to stir the pot from a long distance," he said slyly.

She laughed. "Occasionally I see a glimmer as to why you've won so many court cases. Tell me why you need me for two weeks!"

"No, and picking away at me won't work, either." He changed the subject. "Interesting, that Burdum and I so detested each other. Like pouring water on phosphorus. However, our feelings won't prevent our collaborating in the federal parliament. He's bound to be a Nationalist Party man."

Edda's brows rose. "Charlie, a Tory? Not in a fit! I don't say he'll join the Labour Party, but he'll side with them on lots of issues. To a socialist he may be on the right, but to a conservative he's definitely on the left."

Schiller looked astonished, then huffed in exasperation. "My instincts were correct, then. He's one of those wretched fellows who thirst to tamper with the status quo. He probably thinks Jack Lang's fiscal policy is the answer."

"Lots of people from all walks admire Jack Lang," she said.

"Then more fool they! When one borrows money, one is honor-bound to repay the loan at whatever interest rate was agreed upon."

"I don't know enough to quarrel with you, Rawson," she said, "so let's agree to differ. Despite my complaints about Charlie, I owe him loyalty and support for reasons that have nothing to do with you, or Melbourne, or politics. It's all to do with the love sisters have for each other—do you have sisters?"

"No. I have an older and a younger brother."

She had to suppress a yawn. "Oh, I'm sleepy! May I go back to my hotel now, please?"

"If you tell me what you like about Charles Burdum."

"That's easy! His passion for people as thinking human beings rather than as mere ciphers on pieces of paper," she said instantly. "He turned our district hospital from pathetic to the best in the state, not by massive retrenchment and huge upheavals, but by putting round pegs in round holes and square pegs in square holes. Discrimination on racial or sexual or religious or gender grounds is anathema to him, so Chinese and Catholics and women and homosexuals can find employment as equals with him. He's arrogant and autocratic, yet his blindnesses are confined to the personal, as with his wife, of whom he's overly possessive. He has a curious intellectual dichotomy—the mind of a stockbroker *and* a healer."

"You'd make a good advocate."

"Why, thank you, but hospitals are where my heart is." She got up and began to prowl about the room taking in the titles of his books, while Schiller watched her. Her figure was magnificent—nothing to excess, everything fused together by a grace of movement that contained nothing artificial. That was the nurse training, of course. And where had she bought her dress? No couturier would have cut that rich shot silk in such a way, but it was extremely clever and flattering.

"Your library is heavily weighted in favor of the law," she said, picking up her wrap and holding it out to him, "and you have no novels. That's a shame. Almost all the great books of the world are novels, from *Crime and Punishment* to *Vanity Fair*. Surely you're reading some of the new writers like William Faulkner and the not-so-new like Henry James?"

"Legal minds are narrow, I freely admit it," he said, taking the wrap and examining it. "Has no man given you a fur?"

"I don't take gifts from men."

"Your stole is beautifully made. By whom?"

"By me. I'm too poor to buy the kind of clothes I like, so I make them." She allowed herself to be wrapped up.

"And you wouldn't let me buy them for you?"

"No, though I thank you if that was an offer. I dislike the idea of being kept by a man, including within marriage."

He sighed. "Then I'll escort you home, Sister Latimer."

When Edda moved into Sir Rawson Schiller's guest flat she found out her fate, far from anything she had imagined. Among the possibilities that had flitted through her mind were various kinds of work to do with health, hospitals, nursing, medical lawsuits; it occurred to her that perhaps he was on some charity board committed to a new approach to surgery, and wanted a theatre sister's viewpoint; courses and curricula sprang to her mind, pet projects he might be helping with: round and round went her mind, to no avail.

On Sunday evening she moved in and ate dinner upstairs with him; at the end of the meal he enlightened her.

"I won't see you at all until you're done," he said by way of introducing the subject, "because from tomorrow morning at nine o'clock you're going to be head down, tail up, studying flat out for two weeks."

"*Studying?*"

"Studying. Specifically, studying human anatomy, physiology, and the new science of organic chemistry cum biochemistry. Those three subjects, nothing else. Your doorbell will ring at nine and you will admit your tutor in all three disciplines, a chap you'll call John Smith. It's not his real name, but that doesn't matter. He's the best teacher in the business, I am assured. Today, Sunday, two weeks hence, you will sit an examination in each discipline. After which, we shall see," said her tormentor, leaning back with his cognac balloon and smiling.

"I would never have guessed," she said slowly. "You thought of this last night, is that so?"

"Yes."

"And in the space of less than twenty-four hours you've set all this up, including John Smith the tutor?"

"Yes."

"I quite see why they knighted you. *Anything* to get you off their backs! The knighthood makes you so expensive they've kicked you upstairs to a career in parliament, complete with blue-ribbon seat and the front bench." Edda put her glass down, laughing hard.

"And you, madam, are extremely clever," he said. "Oh, I do hope you pass those examinations and Plan Schiller can proceed!"

"I am Plan Schiller?"

"Yes."

A purring sound erupted from her throat. "Fancy having a plan named in your honor! I'm also looking forward to the study."

Which was just as well; the amount of knowledge Edda was required to absorb was huge, but she was astonished to find how much of it she already knew from her nursing studies and her own driving curiosity to know more than was actually needed. John Smith was the epitome of his name, anonymous and undemanding of personal attention; provided she worked at what he gave her, he asked for nothing. He arrived at nine and went home at five, though she never found out where or to whom he went home. Edda's meals were sent down from Schiller's apartment, including lunch for John Smith.

Every book and chart she needed had been supplied, blackboards and lecterns, models of molecules, brains, hearts, a skeleton. And Edda loved every moment of this strange, apparently purposeless two weeks, especially the last few days, when she felt able to pit her knowledge against John Smith's.

On the two-week Sunday she did three written examinations. The morning was given to biochemistry, the afternoon to physiology, and the evening to anatomy. Some of the questions were difficult, but when she finished anatomy at eight that evening, she felt she had done well at the same kind of examination a second-year medical student would have taken.

A card arrived with her late supper.

"I will leave you in peace until tomorrow evening, Monday, when I would be delighted to see you at my dinner table. R.S."

It took Edda all the intervening hours to come down from the heights to which such a frenzied and passionate fortnight of study had lifted her, though why she decided to wear pillar-box red to dinner escaped her. It was such a triumphant color, perhaps, and she felt as if she had survived some kind of test above and beyond mere examinations.

"Pillar-box red," said Rawson, taking her purse and gloves.

"After post boxes and telephone booths, I imagine," she said composedly, accepting a glass of sherry and sinking into a chair.

"It suits you, but you already know that. You probably have too much red in your wardrobe, but that's a symptom of not having enough money to indulge in things you won't wear as often because they're not your favorite color." He sat down where he could look at her directly. "I'd like to see you in electric blue, jade or emerald green, amber, purple, and a few interesting prints."

"When I'm a deputy matron and can afford to splurge."

"Affording to splurge might be arranged," he murmured, "but I think I'll save what I have to say until after dinner. That way, if you walk out on me, at least your tummy will be full."

"It's a bargain. What are we eating?"

"Crayfish and crabmeat in an oriental sauce to start, then roast baby chicken."

A menu to which Edda did full justice, consumed with curiosity though she was. Afterward, settled in the library, he produced a sheaf of papers and waved them at her. "Congratulations, my dear," Rawson Schiller said. "You passed all three subjects with high distinction."

Stupefied, all she could find to say was "What?"

"I had those papers set and then had them marked by the chaps who set and mark the Medicine II papers at Melbourne University," he said, sounding pleased with himself.

"Medicine II?"

"Yes. I saw no point in going ahead with my idea until I had discovered exactly what standard of knowledge you already possessed from your nursing career, so I entered into a conspiracy of sorts with some friends of mine up at the university in the Faculty of Medicine. Melbourne has an admirable record when it comes to admitting women students into medicine, whereas Sydney, strangled by a Scottish faculty, has always been disgracefully opposed to women. Fascinating to think that senseless national bigotries belonging to the other end of the world should have so marred a whole university faculty as important as medicine, yet that has happened, to Sydney's lasting shame. But I digress."

Edda seemed to have gone beyond listening properly, her eyes fixed on Rawson's face with a look in them he had never seen: of an unbearable pain unexpectedly resurrected, a pain against which she had no defenses.

So he hurried on, anxious to destroy the root cause of that pain, knowing he could—if she consented. "In February of next year, Edda, when university goes up, you have a place as a student in Medicine III allocated to you on the basis of these examinations. Here, in Melbourne. Commencing as a third-year student, you would have only four years of Medicine to graduate, which you would in November of 1935. After a year of internship, you would be given your license to practice at the end of 1936. Think of it! That would make you a qualified doctor at the age of thirty-one, with years and years of fruitful work ahead of you."

Her body twisted convulsively, she began to get up, face a mask of terrified panic.

"No, don't!" he cried. "Hear me out, Edda, please!"

"I can't take charity, especially from a dear friend."

"This is not charity. It comes at a considerable price."

That stilled her, smoothed away the lines of anguish. "It comes at a considerable price? What price?"

"I need a wife," he said flatly. "That's my price. Marry me and you can do medicine, buy an electric blue or a jade green dress, wear furs—there's no limit, I'm a very rich man. But I need a wife. Did I have a wife, I'd already be in parliament. Men my age who are bachelors are suspect, even if their reputations are unsullied. But I couldn't find her, Edda, I just couldn't. Until I met you. Sophisticated, intelligent, educated, understanding—even humane! For what it's worth, you'd be Lady Schiller. Most women would kill for it, but it doesn't impress you, does it?"

Little trills of laughter began, a stream of small bubbles gathering speed and volume until finally Edda howled—or did she cry? Even she wasn't sure.

"It struck me, too," Rawson went on, determined to give voice to all his ideas while he had the courage, "that I find you very alluring. Perhaps at some time in the future, we might try for a child. I don't know whether I could manage, but later on, when we are at peace with each other—and always provided that you were willing, too—I would like to try. Nannies and nursery help would make it easier—" He thumped his brow with his fist. "I'm getting ahead of myself, these are things for the future, not now! Edda, marry me, please!"

What was there to think about, up to and including that child? "Yes, Rawson, I'll marry you," she said huskily.

He came to lift her hand, kiss it reverently.

"A marriage of convenience," she said, clasping his fingers and smiling up at him. "I can't deny, Rawson, that I'm accepting your proposal for one reason only—it gives me the desire of my heart, a degree in medicine."

"I am quite aware of that; but you wouldn't accept were I the sort of man who repels you. Our blossoming friendship counts for much, don't try to deny it," he said, stiffly stilted.

"How strange! We've gone all uncomfortable," Edda said.

"Well, it's not exactly a traditional proposal of marriage. Very bleak and bare!"

"Then let's talk logistics," she said, "and do sit down again. Do we have a grand wedding, or a quiet wedding, or a secret one?"

"I incline to secrecy, for a few reasons." He finally sat. "Would you like to hear them?"

"Please."

"Really, because I doubt a quiet wedding is possible. I have living parents, two brothers, two sisters-in-law, three nieces and three nephews, plus the usual plethora of aunts, uncles and cousins. They would have to come to a *quiet* wedding."

"I'm nearly as bad—three sisters, one brother-in-law, one sane parent, and a parent with presenile dementia, two men who aren't brothers-in-law but would *have* to be invited, and at least a dozen women who couldn't possibly be ignored. That, for me, would be *quiet*, compounded by the fact that my father would insist on marrying us in person in his church," she wailed.

Two pairs of startled eyes locked on each other. "Dearest Edda, this is awful! Your father is a minister of religion?"

"Church of England, an important New South Wales rural parish of huge area, and until the Depression came along, very rich in C of E terms." She giggled. "Archbishops? Bishops? I know them by the score, and they may truthfully be said to have dandled an infant me on their purple-clad knees."

"My God, Edda, I knew you were eligible, but not *this* eligible!"

"The only thing about me that your family will be able to object to, Rawson, is my lack of money. My antecedents and my background are all that they should be." She looked uncomfortable. "As for a grand wedding, dear Rawson, my father *cannot* afford it."

"A grand wedding is not, nor ever would be, a consideration," Rawson said, sweeping grand weddings under the tattiest old carpet his imagination could conjure up. "No, my dearest Edda, given our mature ages, I think we choose a secret wedding. Our families may feel rebuffed, but the scalpel cuts as keenly to either side of the central aisle. Let all the introductions and opinions and spats take place after our wedding, which I suggest occurs in one month's time at a registry office here in Melbourne."

"Mordialloc?" she asked.

He looked blank. "Mordialloc? Why there?"

"I like the name."

"You are allowed to respond to as many names as charm your ear, my quirky friend, but we'll still marry in an obscure office right here in the heart of Melbourne city," Rawson said firmly. "Then we'll take a small ocean liner from Sydney to California, in which legendary place we'll honeymoon until the New Year of 1932. While we're away, let the storm break—private as well as public. Blood relatives, friends, colleagues, and enemies will all hear on the same day. Shock, horror, and consternation will reign. But will we care, cosseted by the same hands as pamper film stars? No! Reality will be postponed until our return." Suddenly he looked naughtily boyish. "Then, it's face the music time! Only our work will sustain us—you at university, I in politics."

"How much you pack into that one word, politics! I hope I'm a satisfactory wife," she said, assailed by qualms.

"Darling Edda, in you, I intend to show this country what the wife of a politician *should* be, and isn't. You're not shy, you have a mine of conversation, your appearance is stunning, and when it's discovered that you have your own professional career, it will frighten the daylights out of my colleagues. When a journalist asks you for an opinion, he'll get it—and be impressed." He drew a breath. "Both my brothers married well in terms of the right background and adequate wifely fortunes, but said wives are dreary, uneducated, and, depending upon the enterprise, sometimes a real handicap to their husbands. You will *never* be that! Even on its periphery, you'll relish the cut-and-thrust of political life. I won't hamper your medical career, but I will ask you for help."

"And I'll give it gladly," she said warmly, smiling. "Oh, to think that in five years I'll be registered to practice medicine! But under my own name. I pity the poor patient whose appointment is to see Lady Schiller! That, I'll keep for your world." A look up. "How long does it take to arrange a secret marriage?"

"A month. You'll continue to stay downstairs until my ring is on your finger—a ruby for your engagement ring?"

"Do you know, I think I'd prefer an emerald? Anyone from Corunda thinks rubies are old hat."

"An emerald it shall be. Tomorrow morning I'll introduce you to George Winyates and Karl Einmann, my secretaries, upon whose discretion you can utterly rely. They'll know our plans, but no one else. They'll arrange accounts for you at all the places you might shop regularly, including bookshops. The accounts will be temporarily in your own name, but after the knot is tied, they'll be for Lady Schiller."

"Lady Edda," she said dreamily, and laughed. "It sounds—oh, I don't know, unreal."

"It is. You're *not* Lady Edda, you're Lady Schiller. Women who tack their Christian name onto the 'Lady' are the daughters of dukes or marquesses. The wives of knights don't have that privilege."

"How extraordinary! I'm learning already."

"You must have fox furs and sables, but never mink," he said, pulling a face. "Mink is coarse to the touch and too Hollywood."

"Medicine!" she exclaimed, telling him where her heart was, and how little she would value furs alongside her profession. "Rawson, I can't thank you enough for this chance, and I say that from the very core of my soul. I'll go for surgery, abdominal and general. I'd like neurosurgery, but I'm a little too old, and it's too demanding a field," A different thought entered her mind. "Will we live in this flat?"

"Have you any objection?"

"Not at all. I'd just like to know."

"There is a suite of four rooms beyond my own bedroom suite, and I thought of turning it over to you." The big nose and chin that saved him for handsomeness endeavored to meet across his mouth; he pursed his lips, then smiled. "I snore notoriously, so I won't ask you to share my bed. You would have a bedroom, dressing room, bathroom, and sitting room, and I would ask you to speak with the interior decorators who do my work, tell them what you want. They will obey your every request. I thought you might like to use the guest flat downstairs as your medical refuge, thus keeping your studies separate from our life together."

"Wouldn't the other tenants object?"

"They'd better not," he said crisply. "I own the building."

Her head was whirling, a combination of tiredness—she had spent a large part of today walking—and shock.

"Downstairs to bed," he instructed, pulling her out of her chair. "Come up for breakfast at eight, then we'll get down to the real business. And, Edda?"

"Yes?" she asked, smiling up at him muzzily.

"I adore you. Perhaps not in the way a man adores his wife of choice, but it's sincere and ardent. I do adore you."

And if only, thought Edda, climbing into bed, he loved me the way a man does love a wife! Well, that cannot be. But so many compensations!

A degree in medicine, and Lady Schiller the political hostess. How very strange and wonderful!

It sounded like a fairy tale, and so everybody would regard it, from her family clear through to his, and the whole world in between. Like Kitty, another fairy-tale romance ending in marriage to a rich, handsome, busy, and successful man. And look at her, with a huge empty house and two miscarriages to show for nearly two years of wedded bliss. Oh, Kitty!

What will my marriage bring? Edda asked herself, certain that its pains would outweigh its pleasures. Except for medicine. *That* was worth any price the gods might ask her to pay. At least she knew Rawson's secret, she had some bargaining power; Kitty had somehow wound up owning no power whatsoever, and Edda was too modern in her thinking to deem that a good thing, even if it was tradition. There was no question of her, Edda, ever using Rawson's secret against him to achieve some desire of her own. He wouldn't renege on his offer to put her through medicine, the only factor that might have tempted her.

Busy-brained Edda, she couldn't leave it alone; her mind alighted on Rawson's expressed wish to produce a child—now when would it be easiest for her to go through a pregnancy? Never, she concluded, sighing—which also meant, any time at all. If he did quicken her, she would carry the child, go right on with her work until her water broke, then be back at work a few days later. Why not? Women used to be expected to do that—what had changed except social attitudes? Yes, thought Edda, I will cross that bridge when I come to it, and take it in my stride. I have to! I am a twentieth-century woman, I have the chances my ancestors only dreamed of. And I will do it comfortably, because I will be married to a wonderful man who carries a terrible burden.

How lovely it would be to tell her sisters! Or, if but one were possible, to tell Grace. How odd! Grace, existing in straitened circumstances, beset by all the worries of a widow from fatherless children to lack of income, yet it was this selfsame Grace she yearned to tell? The full sister, yes, but also the twin. Kitty would oppose the marriage, knowing the pain it was bound to bring; Tufts would consent but never condone it, seeing the element of sale in it; and Grace would deplore it from jealousy and narrowness of mind. Yet she, Edda, hungered to confront them with it *before* it happened. Somehow to hit them in the face with it afterward felt like treachery.

Even taking their reactions into account, Edda wanted Grace and Kitty and Tufts to be there at her wedding. That it could not be, she understood. Grace would blab far and wide, Kitty would tell Charlie, who would blab far and wide, and Tufts—well, Tufts was Tufts, a hard act to follow.

Sir Rawson Schiller K.C. chose to issue an elegant press release on the subject of his marriage timed to reach its recipients while their ship was on the high seas bound for California, and leaving some hundreds of staggered people with no one to talk to. The release included a black-and-white photograph of bride and groom, their first sight of Sister Edda Latimer for the majority. Intriguing, to say the least. The couple stood close together, he in a three-piece suit, she in afternoon clothes, looking not at each other, but directly into the camera. The best photograph colorist in Melbourne had hand-tinted matte sepia versions as per instructions, revealing that the bride had chosen to wear a dark red ensemble of incomparable smartness. Chic, right down to her dark red seven-button kid gloves. A severe beauty, slightly haughty, was the consensus of opinion; Lady Schiller looked to members of the Nationalist Party as if she would be an excellent consort for the man expected to be their future leader.

There was already a Lady Schiller, of course. Rawson's father was a Knight Commander of the Order of St. Michael and St. George thanks to his business and pastoral career. Sir Martin and his Lady Schiller stared at their copy of the press release, softened by the inclusion of a personal letter from their middle son.

"She's not socially brilliant, but she's acceptable," Lady Schiller said. "An exquisite outfit, though the color is perhaps a little adventurous for a bridal gown. Twenty-six years old—she's not an eighteen-year-old bottle-blonde, at any rate, for which we must be thankful. Father a Church of England Rector . . . Mother was an Adelaide Faulding—good family, too, if it's the one I'm taking it for. I doubt Rawson would marry beneath him."

"She has lovely eyes," said Sir Martin. "Very unusual."

"According to Rawson's letter, she's a medical student—I don't care for that," said Rawson's mother.

"Then she's brainy," said Rawson's father, whose wife wasn't.

"Brains should not be what a man looks for in a wife. Medicine is inappropriate, all that vulgar nudity and exposure to disease."

Martin Junior, an amiable and obedient oldest son who had been designated to take over the Schiller business enterprises, declared himself delighted. "Time Rawson put Anne behind him," he said. "Face it, Mother, he's the Schiller who will shine the brightest, and his wife looks an ideal mate. Brains *and* brains."

"I agree," said Rolf, the youngest son, designated to manage the family's pastoral empire. "Too unusual to be a raving beauty, but she rather frightens me."

"She's a designing harpy!" Gillian snapped. Martin Junior's wife, she had turned forty, and knew she hadn't done so gracefully. Four children and an extremely sweet tooth had ruined her figure, and Martin Junior had ruined her disposition.

"I'm with Gilly," said Constance, who was Rolf's wife. "She laid a trap for poor, silly Rawson, I know she did."

The three men guffawed. Lady Schiller Senior smiled. The lines were drawn about where she had imagined they would be. Neither Gilly nor Connie had a particle of dress sense, and dark red would make them look as if they had a terminal illness. Just as Rawson, the middle child of whom nothing much had been expected, had utterly eclipsed his brothers, the new and youthful second Lady Schiller was definitely going to cast her two sisters-in-law permanently into the shade. As for the first Lady Schiller, time would provide the right answer.

In Corunda, where the press release was softened by four letters from Edda to her father and her three sisters, the news caused a sensation. But to no one quite as profoundly as it did to Charles Burdum. When Kitty, waving her letter and the press release, told him on his return to Burdum House that fateful evening in early December of 1931, Charles looked as if he were going to faint. Reeling to a chair, he sank into it awkwardly and held out a hand for the press release, pushing Edda's letter away.

"*Edda?* Edda has married Rawson Schiller?"

Eyes round, Kitty took in his shock and poured him a drink. "Charlie, you look as if it were a disaster! Why, for heaven's sake? It's wonderful news! Look at her letter, do, please! In February she starts Medicine III in Melbourne—her greatest dream, the desire of her heart, and now she has it."

"At what price?" he asked bitterly, angrily.

"That's her affair, Charlie, not yours. How can either of us ever know? Except that Edda isn't to be bought, and I take strong exception to your implication that she can."

"If I'd known she hankered after a medical degree that much, *I* would have paid to put her through!" he snapped.

"Bullshit!" Kitty exploded, losing patience and tolerance. "You've always known, and Lord knows you have the money, but Edda isn't one of your favorite people, I am aware of that. She tells you what she thinks, from petty things like my not having a mode of transport from the top of this hill, all the way to how you're building the hospital. You've enjoyed knowing Edda can't have what she wants, and don't bother trying to deny it. With you, Charlie, it all goes on underneath consciousness so that you can tell yourself what a super chappie you are! Charles Burdum, the rock upon which Corunda stands. Feeding Edda scraps like the promise of her own operating theatre when you know perfectly well one is enough, and it belongs to Dot Marshall. Well, she was applying to some hospital in Melbourne to run an operating theatre there, she says, when she met Rawson Schiller."

The alcohol was having an effect; Charles sat up straighter. "Oh, yes! She met Rawson Schiller through *my* agency, no one else's! Since you, madam, won't come to Melbourne, I took your sister to the Lord Mayor's charity dinner. It cost me a hundred pounds to buy her a plate at that dinner, and this is the thanks I get—she up and marries an ultraconservative bigot who'd see working men on subsistence wages, the Chinese deported, Melanesians back in the sugar fields, and women barred from all employment. If your precious sister has married a man like Rawson Schiller, then she is no better than a common harlot!"

Whack! Whack! Kitty's blows, one to either side of his face, happened faster than lightning. At one moment she was sitting in her chair arguing with him—oh, fiercely, maybe, but in a civilized manner—and the next his ears were ringing, his head hammered. Eyes blazing magenta fire, she stood over him and kept on whacking his ears, eyes, cheekbones, jaw.

"Don't you dare call my sister a harlot, you puffed-up, piggy, pompous, pox-doctor's clerk! You're a gutless, nutless eunuch!"

Fending her off, he managed to wriggle out of the chair and move to the door. "Harlot! Whore! Strumpet! And you, madam, go wash out your mouth with lye soap! Such disgusting vulgarity!"

"Go to hell!" she shrieked. "You don't care about working men, all you really care about is yourself. It was you deserted Edda at that dinner, left her alone at a table full of strangers—she told me! Rawson Schiller *rescued* her. And guess what? He's tall! No one can ever call *him* a Napoleon, eh, Boney?"

Then she pushed past him, ran to the back door, and out. Came the sound of a flivver starting up: afterward, silence.

Charles went first to the sideboard, then returned to his chair, where he sat and shook so badly that it was five minutes before he could lift the glass to his mouth without spilling the drink. It had been so sudden, so convulsive, so spontaneous. No time to think and no time to draw back from voicing aloud what he should have kept to himself. Edda *was* a harlot, but no sister could stomach such a candid insult. The rage still possessed him, fuelled now by the additional uncaged beast of anger at his wife, whose love for him was always marred and diminished by what she felt for those wretched sisters of hers. Kitty was his wife—legally, emotionally, *totally* his! Yet she always held some part of her back to lavish on her sisters. It wasn't right!

Edda was a harlot—an easy, loose woman who gave her sexual favors to men outside of marriage, men like Jack Thurlow. And Kitty *knew*! How could she possibly condone it without admitting Edda was a harlot? Did it mean Kitty was only a virgin by accident when she married? Was she practiced in all sex short of the ultimate act?

Twenty minutes later the Rector rang: Kitty was with him and would be home later, no need to worry.

"I won't go back!" she cried to her father. "Daddy, he called Edda a harlot for marrying Rawson Schiller! As if she'd concocted a plot!"

"Yes, yes, my dear, and quite unfounded, I know. But from what Charlie said when he came back from Melbourne, I gathered that on meeting Schiller he behaved like a small and aggressive dog setting eyes on a large and particularly complacent cat. Think about it, Kitty dear. Under the skin they're so alike, despite the political differences—and those can be assumed or discarded in a trice. We see examples every day. Politics has to be played like a game, and those who throw themselves into it wholeheartedly are bound to be cruelly disillusioned. For it isn't a fair or a clean game. It's a tissue of lies—deceptions—personal ambitions—false hopes. It's devoid of ethics or morality and designed to give victory to the unprincipled. A man with true aspirations to serve mankind will be in social work or medicine or something with visible positive gains." He gulped and looked confused. "Oh, dear! Oh, dear! I'm supposed to be pointing out their likenesses, aren't I? Take it from an old man, they are veritable brothers poles apart."

An astonished Kitty stared at her father. "Daddy, you're a cynic! I had no idea."

The Rector bridled. "I am not a cynic, I'm a realist!"

"Yes, of course. I'm sorry."

"Kitty, our brain is the most remarkable instrument God ever gifted on living creatures. It flowers to greatest glory in human beings, and we are supposed to *use* it, not suffocate it in frivolities and rubbish. So think! Charlie and my new son-in-law have few real differences compared to what they have in common. My instincts say that Charlie isn't as left as Rawson believes, and Rawson isn't as right as Charlie believes. But there is *one* difference."

"And I have another, more important difference," said Kitty, calming down. "Rawson is nearly a foot taller than Charlie." She sighed. "His inferiority over his height will ruin Charlie."

"Get him into parliament. It's an ideal career for short men."

"Nothing can excuse his attitude to Edda," Kitty muttered.

"Oh, Kitty, it was said to hurt *you*, not Edda! He doesn't think her a trollop, even when he spoke his feelings aloud." Thomas Latimer put the kettle on for a pot of tea. "Have a cuppa."

She stifled a giggle. "I fear I've blackened both his eyes."

"My goodness! Someone *was* annoyed! I'm very happy that my girls have so much love and loyalty for each other, but you must remember that your first love and loyalty is to your husband."

The back screen door banged, and Grace erupted into the old kitchen, clutching her letter and press release.

"Oh, Kitty, you beat me here!" The Queen of the Trelawneys sat down. "A cuppa would be lovely, Daddy. What a shock, eh? My twin sister is now Lady Schiller."

"Miffed, Grace?" Kitty asked, lips twitching.

"*Miffed?* Why ever would I be miffed?" Grace asked, astonished. "I can quite see why they did it secretly, though—imagine trying to plan a wedding that size! Half of upper-crust Melbourne would have to be invited, and Daddy could never afford the expense. It's such poor form if the groom has to pay, I always think. Lady Schiller! Good for Edda! *And* she's going to do medicine at last!"

"Yes, it's wonderful," Kitty said warmly. "I'm very happy."

"I bet Charlie isn't," Grace said shrewdly. "Cast in the shade."

"If you can't say something pleasant, Grace, kindly do not say anything at all," the Rector said sternly.

"Oh, pooh, Daddy! He *is* miffed, Kits, isn't he?"

"Not exactly miffed, Grace, just a little sad that Edda will be moving out of Corunda's ken." The two faces looking at Kitty fell.

"Oh, I hadn't stopped to realize that," said Grace.

"Nor I," said the Rector.

But Tufts had, as she confided to Liam Finucan over morning tea in her office the next day.

"One can't replace Edda, that's the saddest part. So steady and logical, so—oh, I don't know, *straight*. I understand why she's married him, it means a medical degree, and she must like him a great deal as well."

"You imply that love isn't in the equation?" Liam asked.

"Oh, yes. I don't think Edda *can* love. At least not in the way Kitty and Grace do. She's a scientist, not a romantic."

"That's pretty sweeping. What about him, Heather?"

She frowned. "Good question, you old wet blanket. I daresay he must love her tremendously, to marry her. After all, he's a man of forty, far wealthier than Charlie, significantly taller than Edda, and famous within the British Empire. Oh, how much I hope it works out! I pray it does! Because she didn't marry him to be Lady Schiller or a social butterfly. Edda is Edda, a law unto herself. I must meet him, Liam! I'll not rest until I do."

The Rector's feelings were akin to Tufts's, though they did not discuss the matter between themselves. All through Kitty's stormy childhood it had been Edda who spotted the warning signs, Edda who rescued the hapless girl from her mother's idiocies, Edda who provided the strength; and all that said Edda was extremely perceptive, sensitive, loving, and protective. But how would she cope with a Rawson Schiller? Why had she tied herself to his star in such an irrevocable way? Naturally Mr. Latimer knew about Jack Thurlow; he wasn't blind, and he certainly wasn't deaf to gossip. Contrary to God's precepts it might be, but to Mr. Latimer the relationship was far preferable to an unhappy marriage, not to be broken asunder. Now here she was, a ladyship, and one day to be a doctor. And try though he did, he couldn't smother his misgivings.

For Maude Latimer the news came too late. Three times she had boiled the kettle dry and set the Rectory kitchen on fire, the last time badly. After a bitter struggle with himself, the Rector had been forced to put her in the old people's hospice, a place she bumbled around, apparently happy, regaling everyone about her gloriously beautiful baby daughter, Kitty. Told of Edda's marriage, it failed utterly to impinge. It was Kitty who would grow up to make a brilliant marriage. *Edda?* A nobody-nothing.

It appeared that Charles Burdum was never going to climb down from his high horse. True to his word, the Rector sent Kitty home two hours after she had left, but her nose was in the air and she wasn't sure she could forgive him, though for her father's sake she was prepared to try. But she discovered an icy husband who declined dinner, then slept in his dressing room, where he instructed Coates to set up a bed. Face impassive, the man did as he was told, but Kitty knew the tale would be all over Corunda tomorrow—Charlie's valet was superb at his job *and* a born gossip. The pubs might be shut and most people asleep, but Coates would find a way. There had been times when Kitty had slept alone for "health reasons," but it had always been she who moved out of the master's bed. This was very different—the master had done the moving. Sensational news!

Kitty interpreted it as evidence that harlotry was contagious and she had caught it from Edda. In the air as well as in the blood. No doubt, thought the fulminating Kitty, Tufts and Grace also wore scarlet As on their foreheads. How dared Charlie carry on like a bourgeois evangelist! On which thought she fell fast asleep.

In the morning she woke to find she'd had the most peaceful sleep in many moons, and leaped out of bed vibrating with energy. She hurried to breakfast. To find no Charlie. He was already at the hospital, said her trusty domestic help, Mrs. Simmons.

"Splendid!" said Kitty cheerfully. "He and I have had the most ding-dong row, Mrs. Simmons, and I'm moving out of our bedroom. I'd appreciate it if you and Beatrix—oh, and Coates!—would put my stuff in the lilac suite. Charlie *hates* the lilac suite!"

Mrs. Simmons ostentatiously closed her mouth by putting her hand on her sagging lower jaw and shoving it upward. "Jeez, Kitty, that's a bit drastic, ain't it?" she asked, with a typical Corundite's attitude toward her boss—no "ma'am"s for Mrs. Simmons!

Accepting Mrs. Simmons's reaction as the norm, Kitty was unfazed. "Yes, it is drastic, but at least it isn't boring," she said. "Do you know what the little twerp did? Called my sister Edda a harlot for marrying a rich man with a knighthood!"

"Stiffen the snakes and use 'em as broom handles! The mauve rooms you mean, Kitty?"

"Yes, the mauve rooms."

Leaving her removal in the capable hands of Mrs. Simmons, Kitty went to the orphanage and volunteered for nursing work there.

"Kitty, you're manna from heaven," said Matron Ida Dervish, the head of an institution that had mushroomed in just two years. "A trained children's nurse! My dear, we can work you nigh to death, but can you spare the time? Dr. Burdum must keep you busy."

"Time," said Kitty, "is something I have acres and acres of, and no wretched government will allow me to utilize my training by giving me a job because I'm married. Well, the latter is debatable. I have had a right royal bust-up with Dr. Charles Burdum, who finds me surplus to his requirements. One glance around as I came in here, Ida, said that here at least I'm really needed. Charlie can rot!"

"*Kitty!*" Matron Dervish exclaimed. "Say things like that, and it will be all over town in a second."

"It already is. Coates, Ida, don't forget Coates," said the indignant wife with a grin. "Oh, he's hurt me, and I'll have his guts for garters!"

"Who, *Coates?*"

"No, idiot! Charlie. Have you anything I can wear until I can have some plain uniforms sent down from Sydney? A pity our local shops have closed their doors in such numbers." She sighed, sobering, her mood beginning to slide. "At heart I'm very hurt, but I'd sooner die than let Charlie see that. Calling Edda, of all people, a harlot!"

"Is *that* what he did?"

"Yes."

"The man's touched in the head. Not to mention jealous."

A judgment many Corundites made as the news flew around, but not a universal one by any means. Charles Burdum had devoted and faithful followers in all walks, and they had no trouble in seeing the justice behind Charles's comment about Edda Latimer, who might be a stuck-up bitch, but was definitely very shady when it came to morals. Though the cause of the Burdum quarrel was irrelevant; its piquancy lay in its participants, until now considered bound as closely as—well, twins.

For a week Charles ignored Kitty, the public nature of his dilemma, and the fact that his wife was now inhabiting an ugly suite of rooms at the far end of *his* house. The gauntlet he had thrown down so thoughtlessly she had picked up with indecent eagerness, and was busy whacking his face with it. Not helped by the fact that he was sporting two black eyes no one would believe were the result of walking into a door.

At the end of a week he was prepared to climb down a little, and seized his opportunity when he heard the front door shut at six in the evening: his wife had returned from her ridiculous job at the orphanage.

"May I have a word, Kitty?" he asked courteously, appearing in the doorway of the small sitting room adjacent to his study.

By rights she should be looking tired, for her work was no sinecure—hard, heavy, remorseless. His spy network had informed him that she was going through every head of hair for lice and nits, scrubbing every orifice mercilessly, all the jobs the understaffed and overcrowded orphanage staff hadn't had time to do properly.

Yet she was blooming, more beautiful than she had been in many months; the lilac-blue eyes blazed with life, the exquisite mouth was set contentedly, and her skin absolutely glowed with good health. This woman, bear stillborn babies? Never!

"Certainly," she said.

"A drink?"

"Cold beer would be lovely, thank you."

Having served her and watched her settle in a chair, he sat. "This has got to stop," he said.

"What's got to stop?" she asked, sipping luxuriously.

"The shenanigans. Proclaiming that you and I have been rowing, that you're bored, that you dislike my attitude to your family."

"My goodness, what a litany of peccadilloes!" she said.

"They have to stop."

"On your say-so, by your order?"

"Yes, of course. I'm your husband."

"And what if I refuse to stop my shenanigans?"

"Then I should be compelled to take steps."

"Steps . . . Do explain, please."

"I can cut off your allowance, decline to honor your debts, use my influence to make it impossible for you to do any kind of unpaid work. You are my *wife*, Kitty," Charles said, strongly and with unflinching authority.

If he had hoped to see her lose her temper, he was disappointed. Kitty stared at him as if he were a new, rather repulsive kind of insect. Then her upper lip curled. "Oh, Charlie, really!" she cried, exasperated but not angered. "Don't be a bigger fool than God made you! Corunda is *my* hometown, not yours. Try to beggar me in Corunda, and you'll reap a whirlwind. I can ruin you in next to no time. Kitty Latimer, sister of that harlot Edda, *both* much beloved of the locals? It can't happen. What's more, you know it can't happen. This is all a bluff, your last-ditch stand to acquire an obedient and subordinate wife. Well, eat shit!"

"You have a harlot's vocabulary," he said, needing to say something yet having no comeback anywhere in the recesses of his mind. How much he loved her! Why were things going so wrong for him? Those wretched sisters of hers, always her sisters . . . It came hard to admit his jealousy, his possessiveness, for he had never experienced their like before Kitty entered his world, and now he realized that, loving her, he would never be free of the Latimer sisters.

"Yes, I was always the salty-tongued twin," she said with a smile, liking the idea. "When one grows up from infancy being hailed as the most beautiful child in creation, it becomes very necessary to develop a quality that can shock, disillusion people. I make no apologies for it, and I have no intention of apologizing to you, Charlie, for having to suffer an insufferable insult. My sister Edda is a woman of total integrity and strong character, always intelligent, always unswerving in her loyalties. You dislike her because you sense a quality in her that declines to be owned. It's a quality I don't have, unfortunately for me. But this much I do know: that Edda would never sell herself, even for the chance to be a doctor. Which means Rawson Schiller must have wanted something from Edda that cancelled out any element of a sale. It's a union of equals, Charlie, whereas our poor effort gives me nothing."

For a long while he made no answer, just sat and stared at his wife, whom he loved but couldn't plumb. Finally he sighed. "Will you come back to my bed?" he asked.

"No, I don't think so."

A huge and empty pit engulfed his belly. "It's *over*?"

"I didn't exactly say that. Like the Tsarina Alexandra, I love my mauve boudoir. To have my own little realm within your palace is greatly to my liking, I've discovered. I'm happy to admit you to my bed for sex, Charlie, if you ask and you'll come to me, but I won't sleep with you. Nor do I want your touch on my realm. It's *mine*. I'm twenty-four years old, and it's high time I had some genuine privacy. I yearn to have children. But I insist on a life of my own, and that means—for the present, at any rate—that I continue at the orphanage."

"You're hard, very hard," he muttered.

"All women are, when it comes down to it," said Kitty, her composure undented. "Men force us to be. Do we have a pact?"

Not knowing whether he loved her more than he hated her, he nodded. "When I want sexual congress with you, I ask, but that does not include sleeping together. How much of living together does it permit?"

"As much or as little as you want. I will run your house, act as your hostess, eat meals with you, sit and talk with you of the day's events or family doings, be a good mother to your children when God pleases to let them live. Have I missed anything, Charlie? If I have, do tell me," said this new Kitty.

"Is there a chance that the magic can come back?"

Kitty laughed, a sound as brittle and sharp-edged as crystal. "For me, Charlie, I don't think it was ever there. But you wanted it—or me—and you pushed until I crumbled. As for throwing my cap over the windmill— no! A harlot I was not." A gleeful look entered her face; she grinned. "You'd better hope, husband dear, that I continue not to be a harlot. According to you, it may well run in the family."

And so much for indiscreet remarks, thought Charles Burdum, retiring to his solitary bed. Until he had married into Clan Latimer, he had never experienced the emotions of siblings, for he had none. How could an only child have known the strength and depth of the ties between sisters, especially twins?

And she had implied that he pushed her too hard—what had she said, that she *crumbled*? Ground down, eaten away, undermined. But that was ridiculous! To think like that was to demean herself, to have a low opinion of herself. Then, out of nowhere, memories of his talk with Edda when he had first arrived in Corunda came back to him. She had said Kitty had a poor opinion of herself, that the mother had all but ruined her. Why did confidences like that seem to have so little significance at the time of telling? He hadn't taken it in as he ought—overwhelmed, probably, by the wealth of information Edda fed to him in one sitting.

No, be fair, Charles, he told himself now; you genuinely heard only what was grist to your mill, and that mill was intent upon winning Kitty. Nothing else. Kitty the perfect partner, whom Edda was trying to make you see—correctly—as imperfect. *No one* is perfect! Least of all you, Charles Henry Burdum. Now you've stuffed it up a treat. Your wife is damaged through no fault of her own, and you're not the right person to cure her. In effect, she has closed the door on her marriage without shirking its duties, but duties are all they can ever be to her. Is that why she miscarries?

It fell to Tufts and Liam Finucan to be the first Corundites who met Sir Rawson and Lady Schiller, docking in Sydney after sailing from San Francisco at the beginning of 1932. Liam had a conference to attend in Sydney and Tufts took leave to go with him; they had adjoining rooms at the Hotel Metropole not far from Circular Quay, spent their days apart, their evenings together, and their nights chastely separated by a hotel wall. Which suited them very well. Then on their very last day, Tufts received a telephone call from Edda.

"Rawson and I are at the Hotel Australia," she said, "and we would dearly like you and Liam to have dinner with us tonight."

"Wild horses wouldn't keep us away!"

Since Liam's unkempt days were in the past, he was clad in a good suit with a Guy's Hospital tie, and tiny Tufts was beautiful in a dinner dress of amber chiffon. The couple waiting for them in the lounge, however, took all eyes; Tufts and Liam forgot their manners and stared. The man was impressive, if on the ugly side, but Edda was magnificent in emerald green silk the exact color of the ring on the third finger of her left hand, a big square emerald surrounded by small diamonds. Around her neck she wore a simple diamond choker, and in each earlobe a large first-water diamond.

"Starve the lizards!" said Tufts, on tiptoe to kiss Edda's cheek. "You look like a million dollars."

"I nearly cost it," said Edda, laughing.

Then Tufts met her new brother-in-law's blue eyes and liked him, which was such a relief she almost buckled at the knees.

One wouldn't think, Edda mused, listening to Rawson and Liam talk, that a lawyer and a pathologist would have much in common, and perhaps they didn't, but they weren't lost for words, which flowed back and forth in an easy comradeship that told Edda this folded-up, precise Irishman approved of her husband.

"You're happy, Edda," Tufts said in the ladies' room.

"I am, very, except for the gifts." Edda grimaced. "The engagement ring

I couldn't avoid, but I fought the diamonds tooth and nail. I may as well have saved my breath."

"They're beautiful, Eds, and in perfect taste. Simple."

"Yes, thank God I don't have to worry about Rawson's taste. We mesh together amazingly well."

"And you start Medicine III in February?"

"Yes, yes, yes! The jewelry goes to the bank for storage then, I refuse to keep it at home." She stopped, smiled. "Home! The whole top floor of a tall building in the City of Melbourne, isn't that odd? I have a whole flat one floor down for studying."

"Lord! It must be like a dream."

"Yes, it is, and I'm terrified I'll wake up."

"The man loves you."

"Do you think so?"

The amber eyes blinked. "It's written all over him."

"He's moved mountains for me."

"I suspect," said Tufts, tucking her arm through her sister's, "that he's a man accustomed to moving mountains." Yet, walking back to the Metropole with Liam at midnight, she voiced some misgivings. "Oh, Liam, pray for her!" she cried.

"Does she need your prayers, Heather?" he asked, surprised.

"I suspect she does. Rawson Schiller is highly likeable, and I like him . . . But there are many sides to him, and I'm not sure how much Edda knows about all of them."

"Well, they'll be on the day train with us tomorrow, so keep your eyes open and your ears tuned. I share your opinion of him."

"At least he's not stingy. Such jewels!"

He snorted a laugh. "You don't fool me, madam! Jewels are not high on your personal list of priorities."

"Nor on Edda's, alas. Therein lies the rub."

"Only if he thinks she values them. I have a feeling he does *not* think she values them. On the other hand, as his wife she must wear them when the occasion calls for it."

Grace decided that her own position as Queen of the Trelawneys saw her rank equally with a knight of the realm, and was gracious when they met; this occurred in her own cream-and-green house on Trelawney Way for morning tea, a repast that a widow with little children found easier to furnish than anything from luncheon onward.

It being the height of summer, the boys were shirtless and barefoot, clad in cotton shorts.

"Brian goes to school next year at the East Corunda Public, and John will go the year after that—they were born quite close together," she said to her visitors, apparently unimpressed by Edda's clothes or emerald ring.

"It must be very hard, Grace," Rawson said warmly, "but it isn't difficult to see that you're a splendid housekeeper."

"I manage. No point in whinging or moaning, is there? One must take the bad with the good, I always say."

"Would you prefer to see your sons privately schooled?"

On the surface nothing rattled Grace, and the shock of Edda's union was by now old enough to have been incorporated into her scheme of things, considered as a possibility, but then discarded—unless, later, things changed, of course.

"Brian and John know only one world, the Trelawneys," said Grace to Rawson, charm and nobility showing. "I am assured East Corunda Public can provide satisfactory matriculation standards. I want my boys to matriculate with high distinctions."

"What great things do you hope for them?" Rawson labored.

"As a victim of the Great Depression, Rawson, my main hope is that whatever they do, their field of work is more secure than that of selling. Their father was a brilliant salesman, but the moment the Depression crunched down, people just stopped buying. They can't go on the land because we don't own any land, but schoolteaching or a career as an army or navy officer would be safe," said Grace sternly.

Rawson eyed her helplessly, knowing himself totally confounded. *This was Edda's full twin?* Extremely alike to look at, but they had nothing in common mentally or spiritually—absolutely nothing!

"If I can ever help, Grace, promise me you'll come to me," he said strongly. "I won't insult you by pressing the matter, but remember what I've said."

"I understand, but we're all right," Grace said. "Perhaps life's greatest lesson is to aim low. Then you're not disappointed."

"Rubbish!" Edda snapped, finding her tongue. "Aim low, and you stay low! You have two splendid boys, and I hope you intend to make sure they gain university degrees, not merely matriculate."

Grace turned to Rawson with a tolerant smile. "Darling Edda!" she cried. "A typical Edda reaction, you know. But how could you know? *I'm* her twin, I know the lot. Ambitious! Oh, lord, she has enough ambition for some sort of world contest. Though I'm really pleased she's finally doing medicine. Not that it will bring her any joy. Women doctors have a very hard time of it."

"Edda will succeed," he said mildly.

"Do have another finger of toast, Rawson. The apple jelly on it is home-made from my own Granny Smith tree. So much better for you than that bought stuff. Those of us on a Depression budget may eat more monotonously, but we also eat more healthily. Homemade!"

"The apple jelly is delicious," he said, meaning it.

"And," said Edda through her teeth as they drove off in the Rector's car, "Grace is absolutely insufferable! I thought no one could be worse than the old complaining Grace, but all-conquering Grace, Queen of the Trelawneys, is beyond imagination. *Insufferable!*"

"But you love her to death," he said, smiling.

She emitted a sound, half a sob, half a laugh. "Yes, I do."

"Water finds its own level, Edda, and Grace is the pool at the bottom of the cascades. *Not* shallow—hidden depths. Whereas you are the falls, always in motion, full of energy, glorious to watch."

She flushed, loving the unexpected compliment. "Kitty is the cascades—sparkling, dancing, a symphony of sound and rainbows."

"What about Tufts?"

"The Pacific Ocean, nothing less."

"She and Kitty have preserved a strong physical likeness, too, yet all of you seem far more different than you are alike," he said.

"I know what you mean. Each of us has been altered by life." She sighed. "I was wrong to encourage Kitty to marry Charlie—but she dithered so, Rawson! Tufts and I became convinced that the only thing that held her back was the stigma of being judged a gold digger. And I genuinely believed she needed a man who idolized her. Charlie did. She struck him like a high voltage wire, he went a little off his head with love for her. What we couldn't know turned out to be their ruination—Charlie's jealousy and possessiveness."

"Yes, he's the sort who'd like to lock his women up."

Edda ran the gauntlet of Rawson's family the night following their arrival back in Melbourne. The only one who had an enjoyable evening was Rawson himself, at liberty to sit back and watch his new wife's effect on a typical three-generations-of-wealth colonial family. The Schillers, he thought, have forgotten everything except how to maintain their social standing and keep increasing their money. My brothers married out of the stud book, women who labor to write a note; my mother is a snob with her own impeccable family tree; my father is a hard, narrow man who'd keep women in the home. There is only one Schiller with a university degree, me—my three nieces will be allowed to leave school before they matriculate, and my three nephews will matriculate, then not go up to university as a matter of course. But the Schillers are important people.

And here, like a shaft of red lightning, I have thrown down the bolt of my wife to shatter their complacence, split their ignorance asunder. Look at her! *Sophisticated* is the word I always think of first, because her beauty is suffused with all the qualities experience allied to intelligence can give; pain has expanded her sense of being, an innate need to assume full responsibility has endowed her with strength, and a passion to know will forever drive her beyond home, kitchen, and nursery. She has such *style*! That's a gift, it cannot be acquired.

Poor, silly Constance, to try to humiliate her by commenting on her unmanicured nails, unworthy of my emerald ring. How charmingly Edda explains that the rubber gloves of a theatre sister wouldn't tolerate long nails, nor the understatement of a hospital condone red polish on them. And Constance, Gillian, maybe even my mother, sit remembering those awesome women smoothly bullying them into using a bedpan or showing them how to cope with the indignities of that drastic leveller, pain.

My father is baffled, he flounders in a mire of conversational inad-
equacy because he's clever enough to understand that *my* wife outstrips
him, could probably outstrip him at making money if such was her desire.
Thank God it isn't! Baby brother Rolf comes closest to liking her—he's the
countryman, nearer the earth and more in tune with the great cycles of Nature. For Edda, he senses, is the Great Goddess who had the power before
men wrested it from her.

"How did it go for the fly on the wall?" she asked him after they returned to their own apartment.

"The fly saw you terrified them," he said, smiling.

"Then if the fly doesn't mind, I'll keep it that way."

"*Mind?* The fly loves it!"

To inhabit the whole top floor of an office building, even including a roof
garden, meant that Sir Rawson Schiller had literal rooms to spare. Nor did
losing his erstwhile guest flat to Edda inconvenience him, as the top three
floors were subdivided into apartments he kept for family guests and staff
on schedules or duties that made living at a distance from him difficult.

A married couple in their late forties, Ivan and Sonia Petrov, had looked
after Sir Rawson for twelve years; together with a cook, Daphne, a cook's
offsider, Betty, and a scrubwoman known as Wanda, they comprised his
domestic staff. The Petrovs and Daphne lived in the building, whereas
Betty and Wanda travelled by tram from some other part of Melbourne.
Working hours, especially for the Petrovs, seemed to be flexible, but Edda
suspected Rawson wasn't the kind of employer who pinched pennies on
matters like wages and perquisites; his staff clearly loved him too much,
including his male secretaries, each of whom lived in. It's like a tiny colony
up here, she thought, amused and touched. As for his secret—none of them
knew it.

Daphne ruled the kitchen, the Petrovs all else. Privy to Kitty's struggles
with Charlie over a chef, Edda saw the difference in attitude immediately.
Charlie saw only a Cordon Bleu man; Rawson took a woman with no formal training and had by far the better, more versatile cook.

Ivan and Sonia had fled the Red Revolution in Russia, but not because they were wealthy aristocrats; they hated Lenin and all he stood for, their reasons too Russian for Edda to comprehend. What she did gather was that Sir Rawson gave them *their* idea of a worker's paradise. A week after Edda moved in as Rawson's wife, Nina appeared to function as her maid. She was the Petrovs' nineteen-year-old daughter, who lived with them, and had been properly trained as a lady's maid, at which she had worked since fifteen.

"Maiding you is ideal!" said Nina in a broad Melbourne accent.

"Isn't it an outmoded sort of career, Nina?" Edda asked. "You could be a teacher, or a nurse, or a secretary—this is *servile*."

"Yeah, but," said Nina, top lip curling. "Proper maids earn terrific wages. Mum *trained* me. I left Lady Maskell-Turvey to maid you, and she would have doubled my wages to keep me. But maiding you is beaut, even if you'd rather I called you Edda."

Remembering the pittance a trainee nurse was paid, Edda shut up. If this bright, fair-haired, and blue-eyed child of refugees didn't mind washing underwear and ironing dresses for an apparently enormous wage, why should she, Edda, complain?

Though it was a tremendous relief to discover that all Rawson's staff seemed genuinely to like her. *Very* glad to see him married at last to Lady Right, for so they regarded her, that was plain to see.

Edda's own suite of rooms was at the far end of the apartment, and was ideal. But somehow she never managed to make full use of them apart from sleeping, bathing, and dressing. Her leisure soon saw her downstairs in the medical flat, readying it for her study, including keeping the bed made up and towels in the bathroom. No doubt the staff gossiped, but half of it at least did so in rapid Russian. Not much danger there; the Petrovs knew which side their bread was buttered on.

Books, books, and more books filled the wall shelving, always being added to; Edda bought a microscope, a stethoscope, glass slides and cover slips, test tubes, basic surgical instruments in Swedish stainless steel, piles of simple cotton dresses that could be laundered and ironed with a minimum of trouble, short white coats, and sturdy nurses' shoes. When Medicine III began, she wanted to have every eventuality catered for so that she did not need to waste time rushing off to acquire things she'd forgotten. The precise, managing mind was in full control.

She also enjoyed the time she spent with Rawson, who was true to his word and utilized her social services. It sounded impressive, but the truth was that he loved to listen to her as she enthused about her "medical flat," as she called it, and felt refreshed at the end of an evening in her company. Her youth, beauty, and power fascinated him, and he found room to regret that his own sexual inclinations would forever set her on an outer orbit of his life. For wife in the full sense she was not, and he felt no stirrings to make her so; perhaps what he felt for her was more by nature fatherly?

His colleagues in law and politics, skeptical about his sudden union, gradually succumbed to Edda's spell, though their wives held out far longer, and some wives never did come around at all. The senior Lady Schiller was well known to detest her, it seemed chiefly because she had no money of her own, and was good at spending Rawson's. That he could afford an expensive wife everybody understood; what nobody understood was that the gowns, the jewels, the furs, and the increasing cost of his lifestyle emanated from his, not her, impulses and wishes. It had to be left to time to teach Sir Rawson Schiller's world that his wife was actually content with very little beyond a medical degree.

As far as Rawson himself was concerned, marriage to Edda got him all the things so long withheld due to his being a bachelor. In every way he had married the right woman, in that no one ever questioned why such a long-settled bachelor had fallen for this woman and no other. She was incredibly stylish as well as beautiful, obviously well-bred, had a fund of conversation of all kinds, was able to flatter those Rawson needed to flatter, could snub someone with wit and aplomb yet remain a lady—yes, Edda was ideal, and no one blamed him for marrying a fascinating and unusual woman. A medical student, for heaven's sake!

But she made no friends among the women of his sphere, for no other reason than that her studies didn't give her the time. On occasion she would meet someone to whom she was strongly drawn, but how could she spare two hours for morning coffee or three hours for lunch? Impossible. The books called like a siren song, and she was enchanted.

PART SIX

CHOPPING OFF THE HEAD

As the Depression went from bad to worse, so too did government, especially the federal government in Canberra. Now Premier of New South Wales, Jack Lang refused to pay the state's interest on loans, forcing Canberra to pay in his stead. Then, when Canberra demanded to be repaid, Lang refused. Federal Labour was in peril, split into irreconcilable factions; Prime Minister Scullin had reappointed his allegedly crooked treasurer, and that led Joe Lyons to resign first from his ministry, then, in March of 1931, from the Labour Party. Tottering anyway, the conservative Nationalist Party finally succumbed, and a new political party was born, the United Australia Party, led by none other than Joe Lyons, who favored the continuance of retrenchment. A new election saw the U.A.P. victorious, and Joe Lyons was Prime Minister of Australia.

No climate in which to launch a new career! So Charles Burdum kept on with his exercise books and his drafting of a constitution for a genuinely new political party. The marriage of his sister-in-law to Sir Rawson Schiller on the cusp of November–December of 1931 sounded a kind of spiritual death knell to Charles, though whether for his own marriage or because Schiller was bigger in every way, he hadn't decided. Who could ever have predicted that Edda would snare a *Schiller*?

Looking like a raccoon (thank God they weren't native to Australia!) had forced Charles to take leave from the hospital for the whole of December; he buried himself in his library filling in exercise books with his politi-

327

cal philosophy. Halfway through her degree, Tufts was eminently capable of running the place unaided. What he refused to admit was the actual insult tipped the scales in favor of self-banishment: if he heard Liam Finucan sing "Two Lovely Black Eyes" one more time, he'd scream!

Marriage in tatters due to his wife's wretched sisters, his mind ran in ever-decreasing circles, at its hub this insane tussle about where a wife's loyalties should lie, but his wife's loyalties didn't. The districtwide gossip inflamed his temper to a point where it definitely became preferable to skulk at home than go out among a forest of clattering, tattling tongues. Of course he blamed the gossip on Grace and the female staff at the orphanage; it never occurred to him for one moment that its real source was his imported manservant Coates, whose mouth was exquisitely cooled to keep butter solid. Oh, galling! He, Charles Burdum, was supposed to go down on his knees to Kitty to beg a night in her bed, just as if legally she hadn't taken solemn vows to be in his bed each and every night. And since by no stretch of the imagination was he a Soames Forsyte, all he could do was to simmer, carefully below boiling point, and make fresh entries on his grudge list. His wife was *his*, her priorities no longer those of childhood.

The Rector tried.

"Charles, my dear fellow, you are a prince among husbands," said Mr. Latimer on a visit to Burdum House, "but I fear your knowledge of women in general and of wives in particular is not up to this present task. We exist in the reign of George V, not of Queen Victoria, and men must alter their thinking in the matter of wives. The old laws either have been or will be repealed to give women equal status in marriage. One symptom of change is the increasing ease of divorce for women plaintiffs and the occasional awarding of a postmarital income, though judges resist it. Whatever your private views, you *can't* voice them to all and sundry. I realize that your words about Edda were the result of nerves, a flash of temper—Edda was an instrument you used to hurt Kitty. However, the bond between my daughters goes back to their birth. What you said was a lie, and Kitty reacted to a lie."

Gone khaki, the eyes dwelled on Thomas Latimer in affection mingled with exasperation. "Tom, you construct a sentence as if you parse and analyze it inside your head before you utter a single word of it, and I hear what you say. But it won't wash. Kitty has got to learn where her loyalties are! Her sisters should be—well, if not a minor aspect of her life, at least a secondary one."

The Rector gave up. "If you're still blind about that, Charlie, you won't win this battle because you can't. Leave Kitty free to enjoy her sisters, and don't expect them—or Kitty!—to behave to please *you*." He put his hat on his head and picked up his stick. "Try to remember that you are the outsider! I don't mean that in a derogatory way, but as a segment of time in her life. There is so much that you don't understand because you weren't here."

He couldn't help it; Charles sneered. "The famous snake at the tea party? Perhaps the real meaning of that incident is that Edda has an affinity for snakes."

The Reverend Mr. Latimer walked to the door. "Politics," he said, opening it, "can divide people just as effectively as can religion. Your intransigence, son-in-law, is based in something as meretricious as it is repellent. Good day."

Feeling as if he had lost this encounter, but equally sure that by rights he should have won it, Charles returned to his work in a sour mood.

Kitty was having Tufts and Grace to tea in the Lilac Suite, quite unaware that her father had invaded Charles's end of the house.

When Tufts walked in, she took Kitty's breath away. In her ordinary clothes Tufts looked extremely well turned out yet not important, but there could be no mistaking the significance of this small, impressive figure in her tailored speckledy tweed dress, hair swept up into a loosely waving bun, every movement considered, subtly deliberate. Her mouth had firmed into a flower that still retained a hint of the bud, and the amber eyes were unflinching, so stern and direct. Kitty felt like weeping—why, she didn't know, save that this full twin had gone so far.

The Widow Olsen breezed in, Queen of the Trelawneys from her stylish homemade black cartwheel hat to her exquisitely darned only pair of silk stockings. In her widowhood she had found her métier, for what had used to seem silly now seemed noble, and her beauty had improved greatly. The black hair had developed several thin white stripes and fell into a natural obedience; she had taken to darkening her thick lashes with mascara to emphasize the greyness of her eyes, and her lovely mouth was carmined a rich red that drew all eyes to it. Edda had given her the makeup, and she hadn't been too proud to accept it. Her thinness was plumper where that helped, and she had become a good enough dressmaker to produce highly flattering clothes. No wonder Jack Thurlow still hung around to fix the chook run door and dig the potatoes!

"A mauve decor suits your eyes, Kits," said Tufts, sitting.

"I wonder why it is," mused Grace, in touch with ordinary folk, "that snobs persist in calling mauve lilac? Mauve is most definitely a working class color, whereas lilac is preferred by the more toffee-nosed. Like dress and frock."

"Bugger that!" said Tufts, thereby proving that superintending encouraged a touch of salt on the tongue. "Has Charlie climbed down at all, Kits?"

"I don't know—and what's more, I don't care."

"He's pea-green jealous," said Grace, gobbling a pikelet loaded with strawberry jam and whipped cream. "Oh, this is good!"

"Eat up, darling girl. Yes, I'm afraid Charlie is jealous."

"Do you love him?" Tufts asked.

"Yes—and no," said Kitty.

"I know what the matter is," said Grace, on another pikelet.

"What?" her sisters chorused.

"You've got it into your head that Charlie can't make you healthy babies."

Neither Kitty nor Tufts answered; then Tufts poured more tea, admiring the Rockingham china as she did so.

Finally Kitty sighed. "Yes, that is what I think," she said.

"What does Ned Mason say?" Tufts asked.

"The same old thing. There's no *physical* reason."

"Are you scrubbing Charlie in your mind?" Grace asked. "He looks terrible, even without the black eyes."

"He knows I prefer being with the orphans to being with him, I imagine," Kitty said.

"There are no tears in your eyes, Kitty."

"I don't know what happened, exactly, except that it's very hard to live with a possessive man. How can he be jealous of my sisters? But he is, and I'm beginning to dislike him for it," Kitty said, tearless but troubled. "The few married friends I have keep telling me that this is just a down, that marriage is a lot of ups and downs—and I'd believe that, were it not for losing my babies. I can't honestly explain it, girls."

"And I daresay she can't explain it," said Grace to Tufts as they drove down Catholic Hill. "However, I can."

Tufts was driving the hospital Model T, and flung a hasty, sideways glance at her sister. "I'm a spinster set in my ways, Grace dear, so you'd better explain it to another ignoramus."

"It's simple," said Grace, out of her fund of knowledge about the married state. "Kitty's taken against Charlie."

"Taken against him?"

"Exactly. It happens. Oh, not often, but it does happen. Intimacy's a funny thing," Grace went on in the voice of experience, "and neither men nor women have any idea what will happen to them when they live intimately together as a couple. I mean, things like personal habits or invasion of certain privacies—will he let you watch him pee, or will you let him suck your nipple? How does either feel at undressing in front of the other? If he has a hemorrhoid, will he let you have a look? Oh, it goes on and on! And that's only the body. Did you forget and leave your bloodstained towel lying there? What about politics, eh? And religion? A fondness for the bottle? Men hate wives who cut them down in front of their cronies. Intimacy is a very sticky wicket, Tufts. And sometimes one half of a couple takes against the other half. Outsiders will never know why. Certainly I've no idea why Kitty has taken against Charlie. All I know is that she has." Her tone dropped to a conspiratorial whisper. "One thing I can tell you, probably even Kitty doesn't honestly know why. Don't fall for her Charlie-can't-make-babies line, it's utter tripe. That's not why she's taken against him."

"Chuck me to the goannas!" said Tufts feebly. "You surprise me, Grace. Isn't there anything we can do?"

"Just be on hand to pick up the pieces, Tufty, that's all."

The federal election called for 19th December 1931 didn't faze Charles, in that he hadn't planned to run. Had he stood, Charles would have declared himself an Independent, at liberty to vote how he pleased on each issue. But Kitty wasn't really a political wife in the full sense, just a loyal help-mate: oh, for a knowledgeable, politically *committed* helpmate!

So, alone and castigating himself as a donkey, he went to the East Co-runda Public School on December 19 to cast his vote.

"Dr. Burdum?"

Halting at the foot of the school steps, he found himself gazing up into a long, faintly horselike face. Its pale eyes were keen to the point of snap-ping and its bones regular apart from a jutting upper jaw that forced her teeth forward enough to give rise to equine images when describing her. Wearing appallingly tasteless clothes, her skinny body was posed in mute inquiry, reinforced by a notepad and pencil.

"I am Charles Burdum," he said with a film star smile.

"My name is Dorcas Chandler, and I'm on the staff of the *Corunda Post*. Would you mind if I asked you a few questions?" she said in a light, lilting voice that sat as oddly on her as her name and those contradictory eyes.

"Are you new with the *Post*, Miss Chandler?"

"Yes, this is my first assignment. I was with the *Telegraph*."

"May I vote first?" he asked, still smiling. "After I've done that, I can give you all my attention."

"Certainly. Shall we meet outside under the blue gum?"

"Certainly!"

The blue gum was a noble tree that had sheltered fifty years of children from the sun in that thin, dappled way Australian trees do, incapable of dense shade; her greenish-black clothes stood out against its sleekly satiny, creamy bark like a lightning scar. An omen? he wondered as he approached Miss Dorcas Chandler. Is she a portent of my future? Because she's going to matter, she will blast a bolt of destruction through some part of my life—ideals, hopes, fears, plans—I do not know.

"You were expected to stand for this seat," she said.

"I did have aspirations, that's true, Miss Chandler, but this year has seen so much political confusion within the major parties that I ended in deciding the time wasn't right," he said easily.

"Oh, I don't think your motive was *that* cut and dried," she said, leaning her meager rump against the tree's huge trunk.

He blinked. "I beg your pardon?"

"You're in search of a new political philosophy that will suit Australia, and it's proving more elusive than you expected," she said, and winced. "Oh, these wretched insects!"

"Then let us find a seat, Dorcas, but not here amid flying ants. May I call you Dorcas? You will be my friend, won't you?" he asked, hand under her elbow and aware that in order to do this he had to lift his arm considerably. Miss Dorcas Chandler was six feet tall in bare feet. "Coffee at the Parthenon?"

She tittered. "Delighted, Dr. Burdum."

"Charles! My name is Charles! Not Charlie, but Charles."

"Dr. Burdum," she said with a tiny hoot, "you are not—and never will be!—a Charlie."

Coffee turned into lunch; Charles didn't care, so absorbed was he in what this extraordinary woman had to say. At last! Here at last was his political adviser, his helpmate.

When he voiced his fears about Sir Rawson Schiller, she snorted. "A civil servant or diplomat type, Charles, not a politician. He's too rich and too wellborn to head a civil service bureau of any kind, even Foreign Affairs, so he has to approach his dilemma from the left hand, so to speak. I mean, become a minister of government. Then he's the civil servant's chief, and can work his changes. But he's also hampered by the fragility of that approach—I mean, the periods when a party is in opposition and impotent."

"Isn't that what I'm implying? That he intends to be the prime minister?" Charles asked blankly.

"Oh, dear me, no," Miss Chandler said. "Schiller is a highly intelligent man, and sees all the pitfalls. Unusual in a lawyer, actually. The man you should be watching is a young chap—also from Melbourne—named Robert Gordon Menzies. A lawyer of precisely the right sort to lead a political party. His leanings are conservative, but not outrageously so, and he's interested in social legislation. At twenty-five years of age he won in the High Court of Australia for the Amalgamated Society of Engineers—a landmark case! He's really never looked back since, and that was 1920. An extremely handsome man, too, except that he sits too long at the dinner table—it shows around his middle."

"Menzies," said Charles, musing. "Yes, of course I've heard of him, but everybody says Schiller."

"Schiller has an Achilles heel. I don't know what it is, but he has one," said Miss Chandler shrewdly.

A scheme was forming in Charles's head, but first he needed to find out more about Miss Dorcas Chandler. By this, the lunchtime rush was over and Con Decopoulos had sufficient leisure to wonder at this peculiar pair—Charlie Burdum with a woman in her thirties who might be a poster girl for some starving children's charity? What on earth could they find to talk about so intently for so long? She had a notepad, but she hadn't written anything in it, and her faded blue eyes were fixed on Charlie as if he were Prince Charming. Well, that was to be expected! A goodly number of Corunda's less tempting ladies looked at Charlie the same way. The difference was that usually Charlie ran a mile, didn't linger talking for hours.

It didn't take that long to learn what Charles needed, either, for Dorcas Chandler was only too eager to tell him her own little tale. From what Charles liked to call a "working class with upward pretensions" background, she was exactly thirty-five years old and had done very well at matriculation; she even topped the whole state in English! she said. Thanks to the Great War's appetite for men, she had been apprenticed in journalism to Ezra Norton's burgeoning news empire, but in the later 1920s her fortunes declined. Men, now fully demobilized, had shunted her off the more interesting desks to the inevitable female journalist's lot—society, stage and film stars, fashion, an occasional sob story. Then, shortly after she started working for the Sydney *Daily Telegraph*, the Great Depression had stripped the Chandler family of everything; Dorcas was the only one who kept her job. The *Telegraph* sent her to flower shows, balls, fashion parades, dog shows, cat shows, and charity functions. Since she was very good at reporting these affairs, she had become a bit of a joke: her colleagues called her "the fright who got it right". So sympathetic was Charles's mien that she even told him about that awful nickname!

Because women were paid far less than men, when Tom Jenner died the *Corunda Post* advertised for a woman to replace him; it didn't care what Miss Dorcas Chandler looked like, as her reportage was excellent, her experience broad. Noting her passion for politics, economics, and business news, the *Post* editor-in-chief decided she was ideal for Corunda, and hired her for a little more than half what he'd paid Tom Jenner. In fact, Dorcas was a genuine all-rounder who could staff any desk—she even knew who played cricket for New South Wales and understood the difference between Rugby Union and Rugby League football.

Thus Charles had listened to Dorcas for hours without grudging her a single minute of them, hardly crediting his luck.

"Are you irrevocably committed to a career in journalism?" he asked when finally she fell silent, her political theories and brief biographical sketch of herself finished.

"Lord, no!" she cried, snorting on the end of her laugh, a habit. "My real obsession is politics, but as a woman, I'm barred."

"Would you work for me as my full-time political adviser?"

Clearly that came as a shock; she sat back as warily as a cat confronted with a puppy. "I beg your pardon?"

"You heard me. Corunda and I both need a lobbyist, too."

A feral gleam stole into her eyes. "Would there be some sort of contract? A time limit? Are there other incentives than a salary, as obviously you don't want a minion on a wage? As a self-supporting spinster, I would have to consider what such a radical change in employment means, Dr. Burdum. As you are not the proprietor of a big commercial or industrial enterprise, how would you compensate me apart from the allurement of a salary? I need to know all the details before I can consider yours a desirable offer," she said, voice steely.

What a deliberate and logical creature! he thought—not given to impulses, either. Thinking on his feet, Charles was ready to answer her. "Your salary would be five hundred and twenty pounds a year—a fabulous sum, I know. Your private office would be inside my home, Burdum House, and you would live in a guest cottage within the grounds, but in an absolutely private way. You would have the permanent use of a good car, and I would pay all your travelling expenses—provided you were on business for me. Use of the car is more flexible, I am prepared to be lenient. If at the end of five years you are still in my employ, I will see to the funding of a good annuity payable upon retirement and depending in amount on the length of your service," Charles said in brisk tones, face courteously interested.

Eyes opaque, she sat with her left ear cocked toward him—was she a little deaf?—and both hands curled around her teacup. What was she thinking? His generosity was stunning and he knew it, but, looking at her, for the life of him he couldn't be sure whether she was overwhelmed by his openhandedness, or secretly convinced she was worth every penny. Gratitude, or rightful due? She was not about to grant him a victory over her by letting him see how she felt.

So he struck back at her, thanks to Kitty. "You'll have to dress much better."

"If I take your job, I'll be able to afford to."

"And are you taking it?"

"If your solicitor draws up a contract of employment."

"Splendid!" he exclaimed, the film star on display. "Now I must go, Miss Chandler. I'll see you in my office at the hospital on the second day of January at ten o'clock. We can sign the papers there, then I'll bring you out to Burdum House and I'll show you the empty shell of your office as well as your home. The cottage comes fully furnished, but the interior is very bland, so I'm sure you'll be able to put your stamp on it. You are the only one who can furnish your office, down to its books."

She opened her battered handbag, put the notepad and pencil inside, and slipped her hands into frayed fabric gloves. "I'll use my spare time to make a list of books, but I won't order any until I know which works you already have."

"No, no, order your own copies," said he, extending his hand to shake hers warmly. "Thank you, Dorcas. Until the second."

His spirits soared for the rest of the day, didn't even sink at the prospect of an evening at home alone with a wife whom he had failed to keep enchanted. Where *had* he gone wrong? Why did she seem to blame him for the loss of their children? Still, it was old hat, and Dorcas Chandler was someone new and different. Someone with whom he could *talk*, especially politics.

Humming some tune the wireless was playing frequently, he entered the sitting room to find Tufts with Kitty. Typical!

"My dear, how nice," he murmured, kissing Tufts's cheek.

"Nice to see you too, Charlie," said Tufts, matter-of-fact.

"Liam couldn't come tonight to balance us?"

"If you spent more time behind your superintendent's desk, Charlie, you'd know Liam is in Brisbane."

Kitty brought him a Scotch. "It's a three-legged dinner, Tufts on your right and me on your left," she said, smiling. "You look like the cat that got the canary—very pleased."

"I am very pleased. Today I found a person vital to my ongoing welfare—a political adviser." The drink tasted smooth. "You alone can make me a drink, Kitty. This is perfect."

"I know about your drinks, but nothing about any adviser," Kitty said, glad of her sister's company. It was so difficult these days, but it seemed he would never retract his statements about Edda, and that meant the war continued.

"It's no secret that I have political aspirations," he said, sipping luxuriously, "and at one time I'd hoped today's elections would see my standing. I abandoned that idea because of my lack of experienced advice—or enthusiasm in those closest to me."

Kitty stiffened. "Actually that's not true," she said in a controlled voice. "I was enthusiastic and I did try."

"No doubt," he said, wanting to get on. "Whatever the cause, I lacked enthusiastic support. Nor had I understood how different Australian politics are from British politics. I needed a shrewd and capable political adviser, and despaired of finding one—it is a rare creature, you see. Those with sufficient knowledge of the field usually have political ambitions of their own." He tried to sound detached, but his happiness was too great to let him. A dazzling smile dawned. "Today I actually encountered the ideal person—a woman, into the bargain, which does rather kill personal ambitions. Her name is Dorcas Chandler, she's thirty-five, single, and a journalist by profession. You don't know her—she's just arrived in Corunda. But if you encounter a six-foot-tall skeleton with a horsey face, pounds to peanuts it's Dorcas. A sad, homely thing, I admit, but a rare political brain, and one I've hired to keep for my own exclusive use."

"You're collecting a harem, Charlie," Tufts said.

He stared. "A harem? *I?*"

"Women to fill your needs. There's Tufts—me—who does your dirty work as Deputy Superintendent at the hospital. Kitty, the ravishingly beautiful wife all men envy you. Until she did the unspeakable and married high above her, Edda to substitute for Kitty on long-distance trips. Cynthia Norman, your slavishly devoted private secretary who can't even begin to separate her hospital from her non-hospital duties. And now Dorcas Chandler, to advise you on federal politics in Australia." Tufts sniffed derisively. "Honestly, Charlie, you're the outside of enough. I'm tempted to call you Pasha Burdum."

Both pairs of eyes were gazing at him unsympathetically, yet he had to have their consent if this was to work—he needed their cooperation! He was proposing to import this new employee into his private home, even house her in its grounds, and while the Lilac Suite was a long way from the master bedroom, it was still a domestic situation. Talk, Charles Burdum, talk!

"Oh, come on, Tufts, where do I differ from any other man with too much to do and insufficient time to do it in? Perhaps to a cynical observer it does look a little like a harem, but that is a body of bodies whose purposes are sexual satiation and plenty of undeniable sons. Certainly I have chosen to elevate women rather than men, simply because I think women are more loyal, work harder, and I treasure their importance greatly. Don't forget that most of the jobs I've given to women are more traditionally held by men, even secretarying." He paused to draw a deep breath and make sure they were still listening—*damn* Tufts! "Passing to Miss Dorcas Chandler, I confess her sex is an accident. Most political advisers are men. That her value in this field hasn't been appreciated is just one more indication that I, Charles Burdum, am a progressive thinker whose attitude to women is ahead of the times. A harem? Rubbish! It is simply that the nucleus of my staff is female. You should be thanking me, not deriding me."

Tufts inclined her head. "I do thank you, Charlie, and you have the right of it." An impish grin spoiled the words, but at least she did say them. "A nucleus of female staff, not a harem. Actually you're born for politics. You can make a heap of shit look like a bouquet of roses. I can't wait to meet Miss Dorcas Chandler."

"A six-foot-tall skeleton with a horsey face," said Kitty. "*That* won't last."

"What do you mean, won't last?" He took the offered Scotch.

"I know you, is what I mean," Kitty said, smiling. "A good wage will fatten her up and enable her to dress better, to start with. You wouldn't condone a laughingstock in any public position, and her job says she'll be fairly public in places like Canberra, Sydney, and Melbourne." Her slender throat curved back, her eyes contemplated the ceiling. "Look at how your taste changed me from an over-frilly fluff to an extremely well-dressed woman. And you'll do it the same way—produce a hat or a dress or a belt that you thought would suit—and no, Miss Dorcas Chandler won't get the wrong idea because gangling horsey skeletons know their limitations. You have an eye for women's clothes, Charlie, and she'll soon see that. If she doesn't, she's a dead Dorcas, no matter how much she knows about politics."

"All right, all right!" Charles held up his hands in surrender. "In the case of Miss Chandler, I fear it will take some time to wave my magic women's wear wand. I've never seen a worse-dressed female—as if she shops at the Salvation Army."

"Perhaps she does," Kitty said thoughtfully. "How many of her family is she supporting?"

"I have no idea."

"You must have some idea," Tufts said.

"According to her, they lost everything in 1929, but there don't seem to be any other children in her personal sphere. She supports her parents, both of whom are alive. They live in—Lawson, I think she said."

"A poor part of the Blue Mountains," said Tufts, nodding. "I suspect they're cuckoos, or someone undisclosed is a cuckoo. She has never been out of work, you say, and while women are paid less, hers is a profession, therefore something rather bigger than old parents must be draining her purse. Lawson is low rents, gardens big enough for chooks and vegetables—it's an artists' colony."

"Blast and damnation!" Charles exploded. "I knew it was too good to be true!"

"Speculation only," Tufts said practically. "If you need her, Charlie, you need her, and must make full use of her. What this means is that forewarned is forearmed. If she's supporting shiftless relatives or a boyfriend—just because you find her unattractive, brother-in-law, doesn't mean all men will—then it won't come as a bolt out of the blue."

"She demanded a contract," he said.

"Then make sure it's craftily worded. If she's as clever as you say, she'll spot the relevant clauses, but she can't very well object, can she?" Kitty said, enjoying herself. "Your ignorance and her knowledge endow her with the ability to play on your weaknesses. It's a pity that you had to wait so long to experience the effect of women at the center of your life, but now that women are in it, be prepared for women's tricks." She laughed. "There! That's sincerely meant, Charlie. *Learn!*"

And the oddest thing about that advice, Charles thought, is that it says Kitty is finished with me in her soul. What *did* I do? It's far more than Edda.

He turned to Tufts. "I'm taking Cynthia Norman out of the hospital, Tufts. From now on she'll be working purely as private secretary to Charles Burdum Esquire, not Dr. Charles Burdum. I am building more office space onto this house. And you're right about doing my dirty work. I couldn't run Corunda Base without you. Therefore you are going to choose the secretary who takes Cynthia's place. She'll be yours far more than mine. By 1934 I won't be attached to the hospital at all. You graduate at the end of this year, and your accountancy qualifications will follow very quickly afterward."

"Thank you," said Tufts, rather winded. Had he come in tonight with all this already decided, or was he thinking on his feet? Liam will be sorry to lose him, but I don't feel a qualm.

"Dinner is ready," said Kitty, rising. "How extraordinary! Burdum House used to be an echoing mausoleum, but I'll grant you this, Charlie, you've devised a way to fill it."

urdum House was becoming something of a village; in front of it and, so to speak, down a level, a row of cottages had appeared. Each stood in plenty of ground, was two-storied, had three bedrooms, a bathroom upstairs and a second toilet down, and its own garage. To Kitty it seemed a long-term project, since four cottages were in existence before the first tenant, Coates, was more than a wistful wish for a valet. Next to move in was Cynthia Norman—two down, two to go, thought Kitty.

Then, hard on Cynthia's heels, came Dorcas Chandler. To live in one of these desirable residences would have suited Mrs. Mary Simmons, who was Kitty's housekeeper, but when she had asked him for this favor well before Coates, Charles had said a firm no. The cottages were for his employees. Mrs. Simmons was dowered with a car to pick her up from her (rented) home and deposit her back there; that was quite generous enough. Had he only paused to set himself aside, Charles would have understood that decisions of this kind contributed greatly to his wife's taking against him, for she saw them as actions aimed at demonstrating her inferior status. He was so rich! An Englishman, he also knew perfectly well that housekeepers lived in. So his valet lived in and his secretary lived in, but his housekeeper, who answered to his wife, lived out. His secretary had a car as Charlie's gift; so, too, it turned out, did Miss Dorcas Chandler.

"You have to stop this, Kitty," said the Reverend Latimer on a visit, and getting an earful of these domestic biases. "I approve of your working at the orphanage because it takes you out of yourself, but I do not approve of manufacturing ills where none should exist. Has Mrs. Simmons complained to you?"

"No," said Kitty, bewildered, "but that doesn't make Charlie's discrimination more praiseworthy."

"Rubbish! It's you who feels discriminated against, not Mrs. Simmons. My child, there is no need for this! Whether you like it or not, Charles is at liberty to spend his income how he pleases. I find his actions sensible— he accommodates those he may need at a moment's notice. Think, Kitty, think! Would you like to be so far in someone's power? When you were a nurse, you lived in for the sake of the hospital, which could summon you back to work without searching the district for you. I suspect Mrs. Simmons is very happy with her present arrangement—she doesn't live under her employer's nose, but she does get driven to and from work, as there is no public transport."

Because in all save Charlie she was a fair and just person, Kitty acknowledged the truth in her father's words, and simmered down. She was also dying to meet the gangling horsey skeleton.

Miss Chandler had been given the best of the four cottages, she had already noticed; on the far end of the row, it alone had its own entrance off the street, and was hidden from its neighbor, still vacant, by a hedge of a fast-growing tree called a fiddle-wood. Its decor was blandly beige, but its furniture was better quality and its rainwater tank that collected from its roof was a ten-thousand gallon one, very generous for a sole occupant. It also had its own septic system, whereas the others were linked together. Hmmm . . . Miss Chandler was very definitely important to Charlie, no doubt about that, thought Kitty.

The proper thing to do, she decided, was to invite the new tenant of Burdum Row to morning tea on a date of her choosing, as Kitty's graceful letter said when Miss Chandler picked it up off the hallway floor. An equally graceful reply named the day after moving in, as Dr. Burdum wouldn't need her until noon.

Naturally Dorcas Chandler knew that her employer's wife was commonly held one of the most beautiful women anywhere, but she hadn't really been ready for Kitty's striking coloring, the flaxen-blond hair too transparent to call gold, the icy brows and lashes, the chiselled bones, the dimples, the amazing eyes, the trim yet voluptuous body. *Of course* he had to have her! She contributed to his myth, and Charles Burdum was a man very busy constructing a history of himself that future chroniclers of Australia would turn into a myth. Beautifully dressed, too, in fine cotton suitable for the time of day, her hair cut shorter than the new fashion because gamine became her, no jewelry save a glorious diamond wedding pair—very interesting grist to Miss Chandler's mill, after so many years of society events. The only thing wrong with Mrs. Burdum was her nature, inclined to domestic retirement, as was true of so many wives of men in politics. No, Mrs. Burdum wasn't a perfect politician's wife.

On Kitty's part, she found herself liking Miss Chandler, who was far from an object of pity. This, Kitty divined, was a brilliant woman of driving ambition who was sensible enough not to kick at the restraints her sex made inevitable; knowing she herself could never be prime minister, she would work with mind, heart, and soul to be the power behind a prime minister. And in Charlie she had found the right man.

They had plenty to talk about.

"If I am to advise Charles properly," Dorcas said once they had abandoned last names and pretenses, "then I must know about his family and personal connections within Corunda. It won't be prurient interest, but it will be probing."

"Probe away," said Kitty blithely, offering pikelets, jam, and cream. "Eat up, we have to get some weight on you—not a lot, about the same as my sister Edda, who is very tall, slender, and graceful. Charlie hates dowdy women, but he's probably told you that already."

The slightly leathery skin went pink. "As a matter of fact, he has. It will be much easier on a good income."

"You don't make your own clothes?"

Dorcas looked blank. "No."

"Edda always did, and magnificently, so she always looked wonderful." Remembering the debate with Tufts as to whether this woman was being drained by a human leech, and anxious to help her, Kitty took a pad from a side table and wrote on it. "This is my dressmaker, Pauline O'Brien. She's in Edda's league, but her charges are quite modest—the Depression means she's lost a lot of clients and is grateful for new ones. She's good on style and she'll shop for materials for you honestly. I used to buy all my clothes in Sydney, but since I married, Pauline is who I need."

The wife's intentions, thought Dorcas, are pristine; she *wants* to see me succeed in this job! Not a scrap of jealousy or self-interest—or is it that she sees herself negated by any public exposure? I can't ask her about the miscarriages, but she has scars, and she *was* a children's nurse. Now she's a volunteer at the orphanage. I can make capital out of that, but she won't like it. A private person, Kitty Burdum.

"I'd love to see Lady Schiller," Dorcas said.

Kitty laughed. "No chance of that! She's a medical student in Melbourne, and about as happy as any human being can be. Her gender denied her medicine, now she can have it thanks to Rawson."

"You like him?"

"Very much. He's made my sister happy. That's all any of the Rector's daughters asks, that her sisters be happy."

"Would Grace mind talking to me? And Heather?"

"Grace would talk the leg off an iron pot. Tufts is harder to get on side, but she'll do it for Charlie."

"Tufts? Is that a nickname?"

"Yes, almost as old as we are."

"How did she get it?" Dorcas asked.

"A nanny who was fascinated by our forwardness when we were about a year old. I think a part of the forwardness was due to Grace and Edda, only twenty months older than us. We worshipped them! But it was so hard to say Heather! Our infant tongues tripped on it constantly. Anyway, the Nanny had the bright idea of bringing in a kitten—Kitty from Katherine—and a sprig of heather. Trying to explain, she said that heather grew in tufts, and went on to describe what a tuft was. I found it much easier to say tufts than heather, and started calling Tufts Tufts. The next thing, everybody was calling her Tufts, even Daddy."

"Unusual," said Dorcas.

"How extraordinary!" Kitty exclaimed with a sigh. "I had quite forgotten how Tufts became Tufts."

"Nicknames usually point up some character trait in their subjects," said Dorcas, veering into politics. "Bismarck was the Iron Chancellor, the Duke of Wellington was Old Hooky, Louis XIV was the Sun King, Queen Elizabeth was the Virgin Queen, and the Roman nobleman actually tacked his nickname onto his family name as a mark of distinction, even if it meant idiotic or crooked."

The big violet-blue eyes were staring at her, slightly glazed. "You're ideal for Charlie," Kitty said. "He'd lap that up." She looked suddenly urgent, intense. "Dorcas, you reported on fashion for newspapers, so you must know a lot about it. Promise me that you'll smarten yourself up for Charlie, please!"

"A good income will make all the difference," Dorcas repeated.

"Have you heavy drains on your purse?"

"My parents."

"No one else?"

The voice sharpened. "What do you mean?"

"A jobless brother? A boyfriend?"

The cheeks were dull crimson. "That is my own business."

"And I should mind mine? But don't you understand, my dear, that in coming on to Charlie's private staff, you've virtually made your business his? I know him, and I can tell you that he's very possessive. The size of your salary and its perquisites should tell you that you've been bought. Charlie is a millionaire. Such men tend to view human beings as property bought and paid for. I'm not decrying his nobility of nature or the fineness of his character—even in 1932, with hundreds of thousands of men out of work, he's managed to keep Corunda more prosperous than most places, and he throws all of himself, including a very big heart, into everything he does. But there is a tiny bit of Soames Forsyte in him for all that—he's a man of property," said Kitty.

To which Dorcas Chandler made no reply.

And that, thought Kitty, is as much as I can do for that poor woman, who *does* harbor a secret, a secret that costs her money. If she can't confide it to Charlie, then it carries the seed of her destruction with it, and she knows that all too well. The contract clauses will have told her that he's hedged himself against embarrassing disclosures, debts incurred without his consent or knowledge, a multitude of vague implications that, if not contractually tackled, might lead to things like blackmail. But she had signed the contract without a murmur. Poor woman!

Kitty's own life had steadied down into a routine that saw her at the orphanage most days, but home in time to spend the evenings with Charles, who hadn't asked to spend a night in her bed. Perhaps, she thought as Dorcas Chandler eased her way into his life, he too had given up the ghost of his marriage? Not that she thought him interested in Dorcas, bought and paid for; just that he was more comfortable conversing with Dorcas. Which, as 1932 pressed on, led to his asking Kitty if she minded Dorcas for dinner some nights.

"An excellent idea!" Kitty said at once. "Who knows? I might learn something, too. Children are a delight, but the level of conversation is pretty basic."

Dorcas's appearance was improving; the black outfits so old they had gone green had vanished, and she had either put on some weight, or the better clothes displayed her figure better. She was wearing face powder, lipstick, and a touch of rouge, and had gone to a salon to have her hair cut and marcelled in the French fashion. No Hollywood film studio would ever offer her a contract, but she now looked more smartly professional.

What amazed Kitty was the degree of Dorcas's and Charlie's passion for politics. Though Charlie had many duties that took him to the hospital or other Corunda destinations, he still managed to spend a lot of his days with Dorcas, yet the moment she arrived for pre-dinner drinks, he was into politics again, and wanted to talk about nothing else until Dorcas went back to Burdum Row; sometimes he was so immersed in a theory that he would escort her just to keep the discussion going.

Admittedly the times provoked political passion, with rival theories for economic recovery fuelling not only the parties, but factions within each party. After the landslide victory of Joe Lyons and the United Australia Party that Christmas of 1931, it might have been expected that the wrangling would cease, but not all U.A.P. parliamentarians were in favor of London's insistence on retrenchment. Lyons and his ruling cadre were, so the misery went on. When Jack Lang refused a second time to pay interest on the state's loans until times were better, Lyons and the federal government paid up. But this time Canberra insisted on being paid back. Jack Lang refused to pay up or permit his funds to be garnished. Feelings ran so high that the situation culminated in Lang's attempting to barricade the New South Wales Treasury—it was states' rights against central power with a vengeance.

On 13th May 1932, Lang's world fell apart when the governor of New South Wales, Sir Philip Game, dismissed J.T. Lang and his party from office as incapable of governing responsibly. Fed up with the turmoil, New South Welshmen and women voted in a conservative government, and resistance to retrenchment perished, though its opponents still hated its every measure.

To this and much more Kitty was forced to listen each time Dorcas came to dinner, more and more often as Charles leaned on her opinions more heavily. It wasn't that Kitty was indifferent, or unconcerned, or shallow; simply, that since her passions were not engaged, she heard the talk the way a sober person hears two drunks—it went around and around in the same eternal rut. If something new happened, she was galvanized, but something new didn't even happen once a week; more likely, once a month, which meant twenty-nine or thirty days of repetition, repetition, repetition. By the end of Jack Lang, Kitty wondered how much more political conversation she could take without jumping up and screaming "Shut up! Shut up! *Shut up!*"

And winter was here again, snow clouds over the Great Divide, the freezing Antarctic winds stripping deciduous trees bare, and a blue misery in Kitty's heart that she couldn't seem to blow an atom of warmth into. Her husband was happy despite his lack of conjugal pleasures because he was, withal, a man who didn't live for those. He lived for politics, and there was no doubt that when the country next went to the federal election booths, he would be standing as an Independent. All he had really needed was a Dorcas.

June arrived, official winter. On its first cloudlessly sunny day Kitty took a car (why did Dorcas have her own, when Kitty had to hope for a spare?)

and drove down to the river out Doobar way, where the land was at its lushest and fat lambs were still finding a market. Not everybody was starving—just the lower classes, which undoubtedly suited Sir Otto Niemeyer down to the ground.

Kitty left the car to walk along the river, suddenly free of everything Burdum, from House to Row to Charlie. So bitter a wind, yet such sweet air! Fascinating, the contradictions. This was where Edda used to ride, have her trysts with Jack Thurlow.

Since Grace had publicly spurned him, Jack had rather faded from sight in Corunda; gossip said he stuck to his property. He continued to do very well with his Arab horses, despite the hard times; in fact, he was more visible in Dubbo and Toowoomba, exhibiting his spectacularly pretty horses.

But here he was, riding down the bridle path toward her on a huge grey charger whose Roman nose said it had no Arab blood. Kitty scuttled off the path and stood well away, hoping he would canter past her without slowing down, let alone stopping.

Fat chance! He stopped, slid off the beast immediately.

"Well, starve the lizards, Kitty Latimer!" he said, smiling.

Immensely tall; she had forgotten that, though Edda would have qualified it as "moderately" thanks to her own height. He was exactly six feet. What age was he now? Forty-odd sounded a little excessive. It was hard to tell the age of men on the land; they looked older when they were young and younger when they were old. His hair was still the corn-gold waves of a Burdum thatch, his skin richly tanned, his eyes very blue. Absolutely nothing of the two-faced Janus here! Handsome in a masculine way, and a beautiful smile.

He led her to a log, first checking that there was no bull-ant nest nearby, then sat her down and loomed over her.

"All bundled up in woollies like that, you look ten years old. Sensible, but," he said. "How is Lady Schiller?"

"Thriving, to the best of my knowledge. Studying medicine in Melbourne. I like her husband."

"I was just going home. Fancy a cuppa and a scone?"

"Please! I can tell you lots about Edda. I'll drive, but where do I go?"

"First cattle-guard on the Doobar road. The homestead's on top of a hill, you can't miss it—too many horses." He swung himself onto the grey gelding and trotted off. Someone different in my life! Not a new face, but it may as well be, for it was never a face filled my eyes before.

Corundoobar was a magnificent homestead, its house of stone, Georgian in simplicity, verandahs held up by Doric pillars all the way around. His flower garden must be a veritable chocolate box in spring and summer, she thought. The view was superb from its vantage point atop the hill and on the river. There was snow on the distant ranges.

It smelled wonderful inside, as a home should smell, Kitty thought: beeswax polish, dried herbs and flowers, clean linen, cologne water, fresh air. Its windows were floor-to-ceiling and could be used as doors, and one was open a crack to allow crosscurrents, while potbellied stoves and open fires kept the rooms warm.

The interior was scrupulously cared for, yet had no woman's touch. Subtle lacks, rather than blatant ones.

"Who keeps house?" she asked, sitting at the kitchen table and watching him work cold butter through salted self-rising flour—he was making the scones himself, from scratch! An amazing man.

"I keep house," he said, adding cold milk. "It's a poor sort of creature can't keep a house clean and tidy."

"Or make a scone."

"My hands are always cold, so I don't melt the butter—the vital requirement for working butter through flour. After I add the milk, I mix with two knife blades—see?"

"I can't boil water," she said lightly.

"You'd soon learn if you had to." He pressed his dough gently on a floured board, took a block of sweaty cheddar cheese and grated some over the top, then cut the slab into two-inch squares. These he transferred to a baking tray, and slid the tray into his wood-fired stove oven. Twenty minutes from starting, the scones were done—risen high, cheese melted, tops browned.

Kitty's mouth was already watering as he piled the steaming scones onto a plate, set out cut glass dishes of butter and jam, and gave her a knife. Somewhere in the midst of this, he had made a pot of tea and produced two Aynsley cups, saucers, and plates.

"You have nice things," she said, splitting her scone and buttering both sides. "Feather light!" she pronounced through a full mouth. "Fine food on fine china—you're a treasure."

He considered her through narrowed eyes. "I suspect you're a treasure, too," he said, "but your trouble is that no one wants your sort of gold. Everyone assumes it's just tissue-thin plating."

Her breath caught; she had to cough not to choke. "How very perceptive you are! People usually dismiss me as a gold digger, though I imagine Edda saw to it that didn't happen."

A slow smile lit his eyes. "Oh, Edda! Yes, thanks to her I do know a lot about the Latimer sisters. Especially you and your face. I wonder why so many people can't seem to get past how other people look. Charlie Burdum wanted a showcase wife to flaunt and prove that very small men can walk off with the best women, then to cap it he fell for you like a ton of bricks. Oh, it was honest on his part, never think it wasn't. He *had* to have you."

"Edda really talked to you, didn't she? I wish she had to me half so frankly. I might have decided differently."

"She said as much as a sister dared. I was on the outside, it didn't matter what I thought or how I reacted."

"You've been around a long time, one way or another," Kitty said, smiling at him. "I'm very glad your plans for Grace fell through, however. You had a lucky escape."

His head went back, he laughed heartily. "Don't think I don't know it! But Corundoobar needs a wife and family as much as its owner does. I'll be forty before I know it," he said seriously.

"Someone will turn up, Jack," she comforted.

"I know, everything in its due time."

She gazed around. "I love this place. It's a *home*."

"That's because at heart you're a farm missus," he said, his voice quite impersonal, "though you don't know what a farm missus is. Well, she's got half a dozen kiddies underfoot, her legs are bare in summer and she wears gumboots in winter, she doesn't own a decent dress, her darning basket overflows with socks—I could go on, but that's enough to give you the idea."

The tears were threatening, but Kitty knew better than to shed them;

Jack wasn't saying these things to *her*, but to her kind of person. "Yes, I see what you mean," she said brightly, with a smile. "Isn't it odd, how our loves aren't given where our natures dictate they should be?"

"The older I get, the odder it seems," he said with an answering smile.

"Are you surviving the Depression?" she asked when he began to clear the morning tea away, wondering if this was his signal for her to take her leave.

But no. Table cleared, he pulled his Windsor chair out from it to sit, turned toward her, and leaned back at leisure.

"I've been lucky," he said, smiling. "My fat lambs barely make a profit, whereas the Arab horses sell as fast as I can breed them. What money there is has risen to form a crust on top, so the wealthy are the only ones buying."

As he spoke a grey animal streaked across the kitchen from what she guessed was the back door, rose effortlessly into the air and landed in Jack's lap, not merely filling it, but overflowing it. An enormous cat! Jack finished speaking without paying any attention to it beyond shifting to enable the cat to lie with its head against his heart.

"Meet Bert," Jack said then. "The minute I finish eating, he's on my knee."

"I didn't think cats came that big," she said, watching his hand cup the cat's face and stroke it back to its ears; the sound of purring filled the room.

"He weighs twenty-one pounds," Jack said proudly, "and he rules the roost—don't you, Bert?"

Kitty reached out a tentative hand. "Hello, Bert."

A pair of bright green eyes surveyed her shrewdly; this was no dumb beast!

"You're in," said Jack, grinning.

"How do you know?"

"He's still here, hasn't budged. If you were Edda, now—poof! He'd have gone."

"Getting back to the Arab horses, I assume you mean that private school princesses still have daddies who gift them with whatever they want. Including mounts for the horse-mad."

"Well, you were a private school princess."

"But Edda was the horse-mad one. Horses frighten me."

"I noticed, but cheer up. Nowadays cars are handier."

It was a long morning tea; they seemed to yarn about everything from Edda through Maude's dementia all the way to the progress of the new hospital; Kitty felt as if they were two old friends meeting again after a decade spent far apart. Jack took her on a tour of the house and introduced her to his two blue cattle dogs, Alf and Daisy, who weren't allowed indoors. He refused to let her wash the dishes.

"Come and have tea and scones again?" he asked, walking her to her car. "I won't stink of horse if I know you're coming, that's a promise."

"Is the same time next week too soon?"

"No, it's good. Best stock up while we can—sometimes I'm away selling horses."

"Next week it is, Jack. And—thank you."

The moment she drove off he turned back into the house, Kitty noticed, and she felt a twinge of regret. Blighted she might be, but it would have done her heart good had he watched her disappear. Well, he hadn't, and why should he?

Many new ideas had come to Kitty as she talked with Jack, who had been on the periphery of Rectory life since the days of Thumbelina, with a big sign pinned on his back: RESERVED FOR EDDA. But Edda hadn't wanted him, she had simply needed him. At first because he gave her Fatima; then because he gave her physical satisfaction. What a fuss that had led to, when Grace wriggled into the situation! Grace hadn't wanted him, either. Like Edda, she had needed him. Not for carnal pleasure, but to repair the chook run door or dig the potatoes. Oh, poor Jack! Mauled and mangled by the elder Latimer twins, neither of whom had any notion what they were doing to him.

We weren't brought up to assume that men would fall in love with us, and that was especially true of Edda, who thought herself cold and would have been incredulous if told a man could love her. But Jack Thurlow had loved her—of course he had loved her! A Burdum, but of opposite sort from my Charlie. A man of the land, content with his lot, whereas Charlie will never be content.

Remembering, she heard Edda's distant voice deploring Jack's lack of ambition—an unavaricious person, how rare! Not knowing Jack loved her, Edda had gone elsewhere, burned for medicine. What Kitty saw, coming away from two hours in Jack Thurlow's company, was a man who communed with the spirits of wind, water, earth, even fire. Afraid of nothing, but asking for nothing, either.

How strange! All my life, thought Kitty, I have been surrounded by people who wanted what they couldn't have and struggled desperately to grab at it. Struck down, they hauled themselves up and started to struggle all over again. Whereas Jack Thurlow would never so demean himself.

Edda would say he was thick, meaning not very clever. Tufts would say he was a sterling character, meaning he had a sense of honor and of duty. Grace would say he was the essence of kindness, meaning he had offered himself on her altar. Daddy would say he was a fine man who didn't go to church, meaning he was a candidate for a lesser heaven. And what would Charlie say of a cousin? At first he would look utterly blank, for he would genuinely have to cogitate before Jack's face emerged from his morass. Then he'd say Jack was a sterling character, meaning he had not seen the politico-commercial light because he was content with life's dreary backwaters, and therefore of no account.

I am feeling pain for him, Kitty thought, the kind of wringing, juiceless pangs that only come out of blind failure; for, like Edda and Grace, I, too, have passed by Jack Thurlow's sorrows as if they didn't exist. How he must have hoped as he waited out the long years from Edda's seventeenth birthday to her marriage. And when he realized he'd probably never get Edda, he tried for her twin. But he didn't complain, and his reaction to Grace's public refusal looked to the world like stung pride. There are different varieties of pity; Jack chose one that Corunda saw as exactly right.

Today he filled my eyes, I seemed to be gifted with a sudden and utterly unexpected insight. Is it that my own troubles were shown up as something less than I imagined? He's cured of Edda now, yet he hasn't emerged from those nine years diminished, or soured, or emasculated. He's what he always was, and always will be—a man wedded to the earth and its creatures.

Whenever he is in Corunda, I will have tea and scones in his kitchen on Wednesday mornings, say hello to Alf and Daisy on the back verandah, and propitiate Bert on his master's knees. He's an island of granite in a quicksand sea.

She stopped the car to gaze across the sullen, rounded mountains, whitewashed by snow against a bruised sky that hung heavy as a sheet of lead. Flakes of snow, fat and wet, idled by her in a random, carefree dance into the arms of an invisible oblivion. Beautiful!

When Charlie came in with Dorcas that evening, he behaved as he always did: gave her a little kiss on the cheek and asked her what she had done with her day. Tonight, unaware what she did, Kitty moved so that his kiss fell short, and did not answer him.

While he went to the sideboard to prepare their drinks, and after Dorcas had settled herself in "her" chair, Kitty spoke—to Dorcas alone. Those keen yet watery eyes had noticed everything, but the body hadn't betrayed this; Dorcas was terrified of offending Charlie, who didn't like her making deductions from Kitty's behavior.

"You look lovely this evening, Dorcas," Kitty said, pitying her.

"Thank you, Kitty!" Dorcas sounded artificial, for the remark had startled her—*why was Kitty ignoring her husband?*

"You've caught the nuances exactly," Kitty went on with a warming smile for Dorcas. "An understated smartness that will surely go down very well in Melbourne, always the place I dreaded. I'm too frilly and fussy to suit Melbourne feminine tastes, but you're perfect, Dorcas. I give it a twelve-month, and all the politicians will be clamoring for a lady assistant half so elegant, intelligent, and yet unobtrusive as Charles Burdum's peerless Dorcas Chandler."

A whole array of emotions had marched at flicker speed through those contradictory eyes as Kitty spoke, the mind under them racing faster than a meteor down the sky, and all the while the woman knew she didn't dare look for guidance to her boss, stranded with his back turned—how to react, how to divine what Kitty was up to? And he was no help, refused to turn back in the women's direction.

"You don't think this blue is too dark?" Dorcas asked anxiously.

"No, it's lovely—ultramarine rather than dour Prussian or martial navy," said Kitty. "You may take it that I'm right—my poor taste is for myself alone. For others, I'm spot-on."

Charles turned at last. "That's absolutely true," he said, giving Dorcas a sherry. "Yes, Dorcas, ultramarine is spot-on."

Kitty took her sherry with a cool smile.

You bitch! he was thinking. What happened today, that your dislike of me is finally manifest before an audience? I think that tonight I might claim my conjugal rights.

But Kitty was ahead of him. Halfway through the main course she complained of a headache's onset and went to bed. He was left with Dorcas on his hands.

"I wondered what was the matter with her," he said after Kitty had gone. "Some headaches are prodromal before the aura arrives."

"One forgets that your degree is in medicine," said Dorcas composedly, putting her knife and fork together tidily. "No, truly, I've had sufficient. Sometimes I feel like a Strasbourg goose."

"A very charming one," he said, lifting his glass to her. "One fears their aggression—geese—but beneath it, they are first cousins to swans."

Time to burn her boats; did she not, the Kitty situation would explode.

"You may slap me down, and I'll deserve it, Charles, but I feel I must say that your wife is an unhappy woman," she said, no note of apology in her voice. "In fact, *very* unhappy."

Her moment was shrewdly chosen; his shoulders slumped. "Yes, I'm well aware of it. She's a woman lives for children and desperate for her own, but she suffers miscarriages."

"Ah! The orphanage."

"And a trained children's nurse, don't forget."

"She's still a young woman."

"The obstetricians can find nothing wrong. Nor can I. Worst of all is that she blames me." There! It was out, he'd said it.

Dorcas kept her face smooth and impassive, though her eyes had a suspiciously moist sparkle. "I can't pretend to wisdom, Charles, as I've never been married, but common sense says that time heals all wounds, even the mental ones. She's a sensible woman at heart."

"Yes, I hope to see her mend, but there are cures and cures. Kitty is a

COLLEEN McCULLOUGH

homebody, whereas I'm drawn to public life—I revel in it! That's a situation will worsen with time, not improve."

"Then don't worry about it," Dorcas said comfortably. "Haven't you noticed that in Australian politics wives have little or nothing to say? Even very often are unseen, too? You can have politics and she Burdum House. Her importance in political circles is negligible. When, two or three times a year, you are obliged to produce a wife, then yours will stun everybody except Sir Rawson Schiller, who married her half sister. It's a legend in the making, Charles, you must *never* forget that! The Latimer double twins will have their part in Australian myth, between Lady Schiller, the future Lady Burdum—you'll be knighted, Charles, nothing surer—hospital superintendent Latimer, and Depression widow Olsen. I'll write it myself when they're older. In the meantime, don't fret about Kitty. She has her orphanage, her sisters, her father, and Corunda. Your own horizons are far wider, you know *that* without my needing to tell you."

He sat galvanized, his eyes gone to the color of a lion's; she must remember to make sure his barber never thinned the leonine mane of his hair or slimed it with brilliantine—he must have his image. Secretly smiling, she thought of Prime Minister Joe Lyons; another fine head of hair not slicked down to patent leather as the fashion dictated. Or, for that matter, Jimmy Scullin. Women *loved* a fine head of hair! What repelled them were bad teeth, paunches, and baldness.

"Dorcas," he almost sang, "what would I do without you?"

Sink like a stone, she answered silently, into the abyss.

Dorcas noticed it first, but felt she could say nothing, so it was Grace who spoke to Charles just after 1933 began. Even then, such had not been her purpose when she sought a formal audience with him: she was there for her boys.

They came with her. Quite old for their years, Charles saw immediately, especially Brian, doomed to wear the mantle of man of the house. Of course she'd done *that* to him! Oh, not through weepy helplessness and constant verbal reminders that he was The Man Nowadays—Grace was too clever for sledgehammer tactics. Simply, she hadn't concealed her widow's plight from him, either. Some would have called that sensible; others, like Charles, deemed it unnecessary at their ages. Brian would shortly turn five; John would turn four on May's last day. Very alike. They would keep their blond coloring from lashes to thatches, the Scandinavian cast of their facial bones. They made Charles think there was more Teuton and Viking in the Latimers than there was Briton or Celt, for clearly their mother's inheritance was closely allied to their father's. The difference lay in their eyes. Both pairs were the blue of the sky, no hint of the sea's greys or the forest's greens. Ah, but the minds that burned behind each pair were very different! Brian's gaze was unflinching and hard to meet—the thinking warrior. John's gaze was otherworldly, a little sad—the seeker after truth. Poor John, he'd have it stony.

I should own two sons of this age, Charles thought, though if they were mine, they'd be as Carrara marble alongside the Parian of this pair. Here all is flawlessly white, no fascinating veins and swirls of myriad colors. Still, what use in complaining? My lot has been two miscarriages, one so late that I buried a *child*.

"How may I help you, Grace?" he asked, concealing his edgy apprehension; she never meant joy, did Grace.

"Here's the potato with all its eyes dug out and whiskers scrubbed off, Charlie. I want to move to Sydney," Grace announced.

Then he looked at *her* for the first time, made aware that his mind and gaze had devoured her sons alone. The Madonna of the Rocks! flew through the archives of his brain—beautiful, remote, above all earthly pleasures, the granite and adamant encompassing her now an integral part of her, every atom of life concentrated in her offspring. Verily they were extraordinary, the four Latimer sisters!

"A huge upheaval," he said noncommittally, and waited.

"Now is the right moment. Brian will start at school next month. But not here." Her voice altered, became more honeyed, a ploy she knew he'd see through in a second, but wanted to use to reinforce her position as his abject supplicant. "I thought of going to Rawson Schiller, another brother-in-law, but he's a Melbourne man, and as far as I'm concerned, Edda is welcome to Melbourne. Too hot in summer, too cold in winter. No, it's Sydney for me." Her voice thinned from warm honey to cold water. "You're

COLLEEN McCULLOUGH

so rich, Charlie, that I have no compunction in asking you for a little gold to grease my machinery. Bear's sons cannot be reared in a place where everyone knows their history, or go to school with the children of people who witnessed their father's dementia and suicide."

His eyes went back instinctively to the little boys, one at each of their mother's knees, like the lions guarding some statue of Magna Mater—how could she speak of such things in front of them? Brian was looking straight ahead, John into a dream.

And her voice was flowing on, inexorable. "You can easily afford to set me up in a decent house in Bellevue Hill, with a car and an income appropriate for a respectable widow who has no intention of making a social splash. I want my sons educated in private schools, though not the same one. Scots will suit Brian, whereas John will do better at Sydney Grammar. You can see that I've thought it all out and made my own enquiries."

"Admirably thought out," he said, not grudging her a penny of the considerable sum she was about to cost him. With Grace at least, he'd beaten Rawson Schiller to the prize. "You won't be lonely, moving to a place where you have no friends or contacts?"

"I'll soon make friends and establish contacts," she said, smiling. "That's what school parent associations are for. One day the Depression will be over, and I want my boys prepared to seize the fruits of its harvest. The best schools, university, a little influence when it comes time to apply for jobs. They'll have no nest egg of capital if they're inclined toward business, but they'll have the status and education to obtain it."

"Time to go out and play, boys," Charles said lightly. A look to their mother, a nod from her, and they left. "You've brought them up beautifully, Grace."

"As far as I can, in Corunda. They'll be day pupils during their prep school years, but at twelve I want them boarding at school—a more expensive affair, but they have no man at home, and they will need greater exposure to a man's world. A woman is no guide for a boy going through puberty and adolescence, I would flounder in an unknown sea. Daddy's children were all girls."

"You perpetually amaze me," Charles said hollowly.

"Because I can see what my children need ahead of what I need my-

358

self?" Grace laughed. "Oh, come, Charlie! It's a poor mother isn't capable of that. Things happen, and we never know why. I certainly don't. As the mother of Bear's children, I want them to surpass him, which is what he would have wanted, too. He was never an envious or bitter person. Just give me enough money to live the kind of life my sons' friends and their parents will expect to see—good food if I am obliged to entertain, plenty of good clothes for them—I can make my own, it's something to do with my time, since I won't be able to work in Sydney, either. I have my own furniture, but I want to be able to buy books to stock a little library—it will be useful for the boys."

Pad under his hand, he started writing busily. "House in Bellevue Hill, looking down to Rose Bay—yes, I think you ought to have a view, it's a poor house in that part of Sydney doesn't have one—and in your name, though I'll pay the rates and taxes. A nice car, easy to have repaired—in—your—name. Good! I'll have my solicitors add the necessary codicils to my will to protect you in the event of my death—I wouldn't want Rawson stepping in there! Twenty pounds a week income, free and clear—raise it with the cost of living. School fees, uniforms, books, and educational et ceteras in a separate account, I think. And a nest egg of capital, properly in-vested—twenty thousand is about right—not to be touched unless in direst emergency." The pen went down; he screwed its cap on and looked at her. "Is that all, Grace? Have I forgotten anything?"

"Nothing. Thank you, Charles, from the bottom of my heart." Came a dazzling smile. "I will never call you Charlie again."

"That's reward enough."

"I suppose Kitty's at the orphanage?"

His face went immediately to gargoyle. "Where else? Can't seem to have any herself, buries her heartbreak in the children other people have all too freely."

"Oh, don't be bitter, Charles, please! She feels it so! In fact, she's sliding downhill."

He stiffened. "She's what?"

"Sliding downhill. You must have noticed."

"I—I haven't seen very much of her lately."

Yes, you're too busy huddled with Horsey Dorcas, Grace said to herself grimly. Aloud she said, "She doesn't change her dress every day, or even every second or third day. Her hair's a mess and she's stopped wearing lipstick. I had a go at her, but I got nowhere. According to Kitty, the children don't mind what she has on, and they hate lipstick because it comes between them and her kisses. Charles, Kitty's sliding downhill, and as a doctor, you should know what I mean."

"That she's in tune with the times, depressed."

"Exactly."

But never on Wednesdays. That was the key piece of the jigsaw, the one piece Grace had no opportunity to see.

Of course Grace misinterpreted a large part of what she saw, given her own, very different personality; what she did was to resurrect Kitty's childhood depression, attach it to her present situation, and come up with the conclusion that Kitty would shortly be joining Maude at the old-age home. Whereas the truth was far from a mid-twenties attack of the dumps. Her work at the orphanage, she had soon discovered, was hampered by any kind of uniform, and ordinary clothes had to look at least a little like the dresses these children's mothers might have worn. So Kitty "broke in" her garb on a non-orphanage day, and if it survived one day fairly well at the orphanage, she wore it again the next day. After all, no one could say that her loss of elegance made her look like a farm missus! Simply, it was more practical, as well as cheaper to maintain. Why wear silk stockings at ten shillings a pair only to see them laddered within minutes of arriving at the orphanage?

Tufts understood; Grace didn't, nor did Dorcas Chandler.

How she looked was the last thing on Kitty's mind, which found itself strangely liberated to run not in its old circles but in straight lines that forked in ways easy to follow, and led back to the branching point lit up like Christmas trees. Her life, illuminated and emblazoned, finally made sense. How terrible, to gaze back across the years and see them shaped and sustained by one overmastering quality—appearance. Her sisters had always understood, but they too were limited by what each was at her core. And oh, how time had splintered them!

Jack Thurlow floated, a disembodied thought, in the back of Kitty's mind, all through that winter and spring, reinforced on the Wednesday mornings when he was at home by two hours of tea and scones and conversation. Never as an intruder, and never unwelcome. She could tell him anything that his man's intellect and emotions would accept, and so skilled was he at setting the boundaries that she had no trouble stopping before she said too much. About the pieces of her heart broken by miscarriages and a possessive husband Jack didn't want to hear, and out of her newfound wisdom she understood why. There were men's things and women's things; they led on from the manifest differences of anatomy into the realms of the intangible soul.

Without ever saying a word, he taught her what Charlie was incapable of knowing: that she had been right to cling to the love of her sisters and her father, right to struggle for babies of her own. They were so delicate, so fragile, the parameters of the relationship he crafted between them, and she could only wonder at Edda's density in not seeing what Jack had offered her—strength, safety, peace, a properly masculine love suffused with passion. Poor Edda! Always burning for other things.

Therefore Kitty couldn't tell herself that Jack stepped into her life and instructed her how to fix it; his refusal to do so was implicit in their every meeting. No, this was her battle; she had to sort things out for herself. In her own way. In her own time. A mighty conflict for a very small warrior.

But she wasn't alone. Somehow, without a word, or a look, or a gesture, he gave her to understand that he was on her side. That he loved her, loved her far more than ever he had loved her sister. If she closed her eyes, Kitty could feel that love enfolding her like a feathery, blissfully warm blanket, neither suffocating nor devoid of sensitivity.

"Listen to me, Kits," said Grace briskly the day before she and the boys left Corunda for their new life in Sydney.

"I'm listening," Kitty said dutifully.

"With Edda and me both gone, you're more alone than I like. If Charles had the sense he was born with—but he doesn't—he would look after you better, but Horsey Dorcas and the politics just obsess him. There'll be a by-election later this year, and Charles is preparing for it already—you must be aware he's leased a shop and is using it as his head-quarters. Oh, Kitty! You *haven't* noticed? What is the matter with you? George Ingersoll is dying of cancer, and once he's shoving up daisies, his seat will become vacant. Hear me?"

"Yes, I hear," Kitty said tiredly.

"With Charles in Canberra, things will change. Luckily he won't need to buy a house there, it's only a two-hour drive, but he'll spend most of his time in Canberra. If you want to try for another baby, do it now. Once he's an M.P., he'll be too worn out." Amid rustling skirts and billows from a scarf, she descended on Kitty and hugged her, kissed her. "Oh, Kits, I fear for you! So would Edda, if she knew what's going on. There's a spare bedroom in my Bellevue Hill house, and you must promise me that you'll come to me if you've no one in Corunda to turn to!"

The lilac flared up in Kitty's eyes. "No one in Corunda?"

"Or go to Edda. Rawson's a gentleman, at least."

Kitty giggled. "Honestly, Grace, you are the dizzy limit! I am perfectly all right, I'm in no danger."

"Just remember the spare bedroom," said Grace.

George Ingersoll's cancer was diagnosed in January of 1933, when he already looked so awful he was given a month at most to live. But George came of exquisitely stubborn stock, and hadn't beaten off all political rivals for forty years just to curl up his toes and die at the bidding of a parcel of doctors, said he; this was merely a temporary setback—and no, he wouldn't be resigning from federal parliament, either. What did kill him late in October was a massive heart attack, apparently unrelated to his thwarted cancer. At his death he was still the sitting member for Corunda in the federal parliament, which meant Corunda voters held a by-election at the end of November.

Charles Burdum had realized very quickly one aspect of political life: subtlety was wasted. So after the news got out of George's cancer, Charles rented an abandoned shop in George Street and opened his campaign headquarters. There he installed Dorcas Chandler, several eager young Burdum partisans, all the fixings for cups of tea and hard bikkies, and excerpts from his exercise books that outlined his policies. Everything about the operation proclaimed clearly that when he entered the parliament, it would be as an Independent, that he had no truck with tired old party platforms.

The long drawn out nature of George's death had had repercussions. First and foremost, everyone took it for granted that when the Unhappy Event did occur, George's replacement was bound to be Dr. Charles Burdum. So the Country Party, which had owned the seat since its inception, decided not to waste its funds by putting up a candidate at all. Had it not been for a Labour candidate out of the railway workshops, Charles would have been unopposed; as it was, most of Labor's votes would go to this impertinent but undeniably important Burdum.

Kitty hadn't suffered any increased attention from Charles as the months went by; indeed, she wondered if he remembered her existence, between his growing excitement at the vision of Canberra looming, and his ever-accelerating campaign in conjunction with his faithful helper Dorcas. Left in a limbo of his neglect, Kitty drifted, her mind on Jack Thurlow and the impossibility of her own situation, the legal property of the wrong man. How to extricate herself? What was the answer? Yet she wasn't miserably unhappy. Somewhere beneath her skin of impotence lay a tensile strap of confidence that reinforced her strength, a confidence that everything did have an answer.

Of course Charles was aware that his wife had lost interest in his activities, but while George Ingersoll lived, Kitty wasn't worth the expenditure of precious energies. Like her, Charles drifted in a limbo, though his was of building an Australia Party.

George's death galvanized him. Overnight he saw Canberra a mere two hours away, and threw off his private inertia. Time to deal with Kitty, who looked as if she belonged in the Trelawneys: not quite a dowd, but definitely a frump. Nothing that couldn't be fixed, but where was he to find the time? Bother the woman! Too busy at the orphanage to hold morning teas and woo wives, was her trouble. Where to find the time to do battle? Then he had a bright idea—let Dorcas tell Kitty! Yes, let Dorcas do it!

"Tell Kitty to smarten herself up," he instructed. "Compared to Kitty, Enid Lyons is as plain as a pikestaff, but I want that fact glaringly obvious from the moment Canberra sets eyes on her. My wife must be a nonpareil. Go on, Dorcas, do as you're told."

"I can't do that, Charles!" Dorcas said on a gasp, plunged into an icy bath of terror. "Kitty is your *wife*! Whatever needs to be said, only you can say. I'm a virtual stranger, not even her chosen friend! Please, Charles, no! I'm an employee!"

For all the good her protests did, he may as well have been carved from granite. Cold and gold, he stared at her with, she fancied, thunderbolts emanating like an aura, and she knew without being told that if she didn't follow his orders, he would find a new political adviser.

Somehow Kitty sensed what was coming. When Dorcas asked to see her for a cup of tea and a chat that Wednesday morning, Kitty shook her head. "No, not today," she said. "Tomorrow. Wednesday mornings I have a cuppa with Jack Thurlow, and I'll not break that appointment for Charlie or you or anybody else."

The pale blue eyes bored into her and found neither guilt nor disobedience: it was a statement of simple fact.

Jack Thurlow? Who was he? Not a friend of Charles's, nor a man who mattered politically or in civic terms. Memories stirred in Dorcas, who dredged up an old story about the fellow who used to be old Tom Burdum's heir before Charles arrived. A boyfriend of Kitty's half sister Edda—yes, of course! Therefore a man Charles's wife must have known long before she met Charles. An old and treasured friend, Dorcas divined, in no way, shape, or form a lover. So, preparing to have a cup of tea with Kitty on Thursday morning, Dorcas found her task unchanged by Wednesday trysts.

But she had lain in wait to see an immaculately turned out Kitty set off for her appointment with Jack Thurlow. A lavender-blue dress whose silky elegance was set off by touches of apricot reflected in shoes, bag, a gorgeous cartwheel hat, face delicately made up, hair artlessly tumbled. Oh, what a *beautiful* woman!

The pain chewed at Dorcas like an old, broken-toothed dog on a festering bone: I could be queen of the world if I looked like that. And she—she doesn't care. If Charles's stories are true, her face drove her to a cheese grater and a hangman's rope because she loathed it, yet on Wednesday mornings she draws aside the veil of cloud and lets her sun shine for a cup of tea with a man who spells the past, and was *her sister's* years-long lover.

It hadn't taken more than a week in Charles Burdum's employ to lift Dorcas Chandler out of her emotional desert and set her down in the midst not of an oasis but *the* oasis, the one Alexander the Great had entered as a man and left as a god. Inside and under the incongruities of gangling skinny height and equine face there existed a woman like all others: longing for love, needing a man's strength, hungering to be wrapped up in a warmth that would never go away. To Dorcas Chandler, Charles Burdum represented all she yearned for, yet knew she couldn't have. Owning nothing else to give him than advice and knowledge of an activity she understood down to its roots, she gave with heartfelt sincerity because her heart was in the task. Dorcas loved Charles Burdum, though he would never know it. The old dog, the stinking bone—but better that, than no bone at all.

She had pride, never forgetting that creatures as unblessed as she were not supposed to own pride; so she went to tea with Kitty burdened by conflicting feelings. The ugly employee ordered to tell the beautiful wife that she wasn't pulling her weight, the proud woman determined to keep her love a secret, thereby safeguarding her self-esteem.

Kitty cut through everything at the very beginning.

"Dorcas, don't sit there with a metaphorical axe poised on the back of your neck," she said, pouring tea. "Have an Anzac bikkie, they dunk a treat in hot tea, never fall apart. There's nothing worse than having to fish bits of soggy bikkie out of a teacup—it just can't be done with elegance."

"I—er—have never dunked a biscuit," said Dorcas stiffly.

"Oh, you poor thing! The fun you've missed! I brought my Anzac recipe from the Rectory—made on golden syrup, not sugar, or it isn't a proper Anzac. You have no sisters, otherwise you'd dunk."

"I have no sisters and I do not dunk, but that's a syllogism."

"Like all cats are grey in the dark? But they aren't."

"You know what a syllogism is," Dorcas said. "Few do."

"And I'm not about to be diverted, Dorcas. Charlie has sent you to instruct me not to dress and act like a farm missus now he's declared his political ambitions publicly. How silly men are! Until Grace told him, I don't think he even noticed my metamorphosis." She chuckled, sighed. "Well, that's Grace, and she's been gone ten months. You can tell Charlie that you obeyed orders, but that I made no comment one way or another. I will talk to him in my own good time, and when I do, he'll understand. No, better to say, he'll hear me and comprehend. He'll never really *understand*, it's not in him. Today, I want to talk about you."

The eyes went wide. "Me?"

"You. I want to know your terrible secret, the one that blights this wonderful dream of a job. You're terrified of losing it."

No answer came; Dorcas sipped her tea and nibbled an Anzac.

Kitty watched her, in complete control. Dorcas was wearing a two-piece suit of rusty tweed speckled in black, and sported a smart, snap-brimmed black felt hat tilted to the left side of her head; her bronze-brown hair was well cut and had been marcelled, and she had improved the way she made up her face, especially around the eyes. Shrewd but vulnerable eyes.

"Come, Dorcas, of course you have a terrible secret," Kitty said, smiling at her with genuine kindness and sympathy. "I want to help you, but I can't until you trust me enough to realize that I am both friend *and* ally. So let me tell you what I think you hide."

"Mrs. Burdum, whatever you say will be pure imagination."

"Oh, no, pokering up won't wash with me! Formality is simply another fence to cower behind." Kitty's voice added real tenderness to its warmth. "When you were a very immature, ignorant girl of about fifteen, some man took cruel and cynical advantage of you. I suspected you have no sisters because sisters would have cared for you in ways mothers never do. Whatever their motives, mothers can be hideously destructive, and about their daughters—*so* blind!"

"You've said nothing to impress me thus far, Kitty."

"There was a baby—a son, I think, whom you love very much. But the real drain on your money is his father, who blackmails you."

The fight went out of Dorcas with almost explosive force, leaving her defenseless. Awful to witness, but how much harder to endure?

"Today the slimy leech goes," Kitty said strongly. "No, he goes! The basis for his blackmail won't exist, because you're telling Charlie all about him. Dorcas, don't do a Grace and start crying! Do the new Grace, who grew a backbone overnight when the wolf started ripping down her door. Did your parents disown you? Surely not!"

"No, they took Andrew so that I could continue my journalism. I was twenty when it happened, not fifteen, but I was so ignorant! Andrew's father cut a swath through the lower Blue Mountains villages—handsome, charming, a dazzling preacher full of evangelical spirit! We gave him every penny we had—religious believers are such easy targets. I even gave him my body—I was so grateful to him, that he found me attractive, but all his son means to him is more money."

"How many children did he father?"

"That's the oddest thing," said Dorcas, musing. "Just Andrew."

"How old is Andrew now?"

"Fourteen. He goes to the public school in Katoomba."

"So nearly all your fat salary goes to your parents, son, and a blackmailing turd. My dressmaker must have saved your bacon."

Dorcas licked her lips. "How did you know?"

The laugh was victorious, merry. "Darling, you walk like a woman who has borne a child, and you're too worldly to be a virgin. That your secret was an illegitimate child was manifest. What else could so blight the job of a lifetime?" The violet died out of Kitty's eyes. "It's not too late to rescue Andrew. Bring him to live with you in Corunda at once—it's not December yet, and when school starts in February, he'll go to Corunda Grammar for a private education. By the time he matriculates, he'll be a part of Corunda, well polished and cozily tucked under Charlie's wing."

A trembling Dorcas stared at her, aghast. "I can't possibly tell Charles!" she cried. "He'd sack me in an instant—*the scandal!*"

Kitty blew a rude noise. "Rubbish! You silly woman, how could you work so long and closely with Charlie, yet know him so little? This is meat and drink to him! Charlie, the champion of lost causes, unmoved by your plight? The father of your son a putrid parasite feeding off the boy's mother, draining her dry for fourteen years? My husband both esteems and likes you—it's his answer! Is Andrew an attractive boy?"

"He's handsome, but he has something better—*character.*"

"Tell Charlie!" Kitty urged. "Tell him right now—today, this minute. He's down at the other end of this great echoing cathedral, a few yards away. Get up, get up! *Get up, woman!* Go and tell him just as you've told me, and ask him to rid you of Andrew's father. Oh, he'll love that! It's been so long since Charlie donned his armor that the shine has worn off, and his warhorse is creaking in every joint. This will put the spring back in his step! Go, go!"

Intimidated by Kitty's bullying, Dorcas fled to bare her sins.

Kitty went to put a trunk-line call through to Lady Schiller II in Melbourne. Christmas of 1933, she had resolved, would be a reunion in Corunda for all four Latimer sisters. Ten days, Christmas through to New Year . . . The only affairs left unsettled were her own.

That thought glowing like blown-on coals, coming on sunset Kitty drove to Corundoobar to find Jack in from the paddocks. She knew because his petrol-drum mailbox by the cattle-guard was empty. Leaving her car at the bottom of the hill, she strolled up through the blooming gardens, pausing to admire a single glorious rose, a bush of weeping Geraldton wax, sweet peas rioting across a trellis. *Where does he find the time?* Yes, he was in; Alf and Daisy came to greet her, a business of grins and tail wags—Jack's dogs were too well-behaved to leap and lick. Then he came out onto the front verandah, hair still damp from the shower, and waited for her.

On the top step, now reduced to smallness by his height, she tilted her chin to look up.

"I'm moving in with you," she said, "right this minute."

"Not before time," he said gravely. "I won't say I was fed up with waiting, but I have grown a few grey hairs on moonless nights." His hand described a wide circle in the air. "Here we are, Kitty. All yours, from me to mine."

"I'll be your mistress, but I can't be your wife. Charlie would never consent to a divorce."

"We live to please ourselves on Corundoobar. We'll take you on any terms with nary a shadow of regret."

No scrap of doubt assailed her, even now the moment was a reality. The embraces, the kisses, the lovemaking would come, but for some little while Kitty felt in no need of them, too exalted by the surge of peace and comfort invading her spirit.

And, understanding what she felt, he stood with her to watch the crimsoned sun swallowed by the messengers of night.

Then he slipped an arm about her and turned her to the door.

"Come inside, it's chilly."

"I have a suitcase in the car, but the car has to be returned to Charlie," she said, one nagging barb. "I want nothing from him, nothing!"

"I know. Don't worry yourself, and don't talk of him."

Bert the cat, filling Jack's chair, was tipped off it so quickly that he landed, half-asleep and hugely indignant, in a heap on the floor. Jack sat down with Kitty on his lap.

When she leaned against him she could feel the steady rhythm of Jack's heart, and nothing else mattered. Would ever matter. Oh, dear God, grant him the gift of a long life! The only fear that will dog me now is the thought of existing without him. Her head went down on his shoulder, her eyes closed on wet lashes. I have come home at last.

As Deputy Superintendent of a hospital whose Superintendent was in the throes of handing his duties over to her, Tufts offered Edda and Rawson a staff cottage on hospital grounds when they came for Christmas of 1933, then did the same for Grace and her boys. As a Member of Parliament, Charles Burdum couldn't run Corunda Base; Tufts was assured and confirmed in her position. She and Liam had bought adjacent houses on Ferguson Street and torn down the dividing fence; they shared meals, garden, leisure, two dogs and three cats, the animals neutered. The Rector thought them the only couple he had ever encountered who in mental attitude went straight from youth to old age; uplifted by some things, moved by all things, defeated by no things.

All Corunda was still reeling from the shock that ripped the district's fabric asunder when Kitty Burdum, without a moment's notice or a by-your-leave, left Charles Burdum and his many millions to move out to Corundoobar, there to live in flagrantly open sin as Jack Thurlow's mistress. No hiding, no skulking, no shrinking from any or all the populace. She had taken nothing with her from Burdum House—none of her jewels, furs, clothes, none of her furniture or ornaments, not even (said she, rather strangely) a cheese grater. With her went her books, papers, letters, and snapshot albums.

What floored everybody was that she looked so *shamelessly* happy! As for Jack—well, he wasn't the sort to make a fuss about anything, including his adulterous union. However, people did notice that there were rather fewer lines on his face than of yore, and that sometimes, when he didn't realize he was under observation, he wore a look of slightly catlike complacence. Like his famously massive grey cat, Bert.

Charles Burdum had been absolutely the first to know. A note from Kitty to Dorcas had asked her to make sure that he was left severely alone until he indicated that he wanted company. An instinct told Dorcas to obey it implicitly.

So on Friday he came alone to breakfast and found a parchment letter lying on his service plate, Kitty's wedding and engagement rings atop it like glittering garnish on a pastry packet. The sight of the rings said it all; chest and belly filled with lead weights, he tore the envelope apart in a frenzy.

Charles, husband,

The rings have already told you, but you will need words to back them up, and I find I am too much the coward to voice them in person. You would hector and harangue me into the old confusion, and things would be delayed. Not avoided, Charlie. The axe is in my hands and I am determined to bring it down hard and clean.

I do not love you. I don't think I ever did, but you bluffed me into belief. Then, once you had me, you never thought of me save as a possession. No, that's not quite right. You thought of the person you needed me to be, but you never stopped to wonder if I really was her, or someone different. You can manage huge enterprises and you can make money, but you can't read character, and you're blind to people's souls. The woman you married was never me, Kitty. I thank God that our children miscarried. Whatever their natures dictated, you would have forced them to be what you wanted, and you would have ruined them. Benevolent you may be, but you're an autocrat just the same.

I say such cruel things because that is the only way you will ever believe I mean it is over. It is over. The woman you want should look like me, but have the brain of a Dorcas. You were tricked by my cover, you had no idea of the contents. I am not a suitable wife for a politician.

Politics bore me to screaming point. Marry the brain half, Dorcas. But you won't. You're too thin-skinned to bear the amusement the sight of such an incongruous couple would provoke.

I'm going to live in adultery with Jack Thurlow, who says I am a farm missus. With Jack, I can disappear into the woodwork and run happily to seed. Please do not *forgive me!*

Kitty.

As sheer incredulity gave gradual way to certainty, Charles's first thoughts were of Sybil, daughter of a duke, and his humiliation then; except that this was way, way down time's road and mattered far, far more. A roaring rage overwhelmed him, a fury that had him retching, the sterling silver fork in one hand a twisted mockery, the howl from his gaping mouth too high and shrill for any ear. He, Charles Burdum, had been dumped like a carcass left too long in the meat safe.

He hungered and thirsted to hurt her—hurt her so badly he all but killed her, spared her by a sliver to exist in a living hell hotter than fire yet colder than ice, crushed and mangled by teeth, barbs, claws, fangs, talons, her beauty obliterated. Hating her, he cursed her, wondering in the abysses of his mind why there wasn't some emotion greater than hate to feed his rage.

The moving picture of hate went on and on, hissing and slithering through his brain until even he could think of no new horrors to inflict on her. That was when he reached the very bottom of his pit, to sprawl there lifeless, no sensations left, just the vacuum of a terrible loss that would never heal, no matter how many splints and bandages he applied.

Crawling up out of the pit was worse, done as it was through sorrow and despair, spasms of grief, a monstrous sadness that saw the tears fall until he felt he bled them, a life force quitting him whom she had found unworthy, inadequate. The love of my life, my Kitty, my Kitty!

On a waste of featureless plain above the pit he waited for animation with no idea in him what form it might assume, wondering if this were death and he transfigured, or if it were life and he blasted to a crisp in the furnaces of the soul. But then he remembered he had crashed, and died yet hadn't died, simply risen from the flames like a phoenix, newborn and alive amid the ashes.

He was Charles Burdum, though not the man who existed before this day. Say it, Charles! *Say it!* Before Kitty dumped you. Yes, a new Charles Burdum. A different Charles Burdum. Who would carry the mark of the pit within him, forever branded; but no one—*no one!*—would ever suspect it. His path was clear, found among the tempests that had consumed him. Oh, Kitty, how I love you! And you dumped me. You dumped *me*! Charles Burdum.

Fortitude, understanding, forgiveness, kindness, generosity—I will radiate all those virtues and many more, because a benign, cheerful, perpetually unself-conscious Charles Burdum will tell the world that his adulterous slut of a wife doesn't have the power to injure such a man in any way. What, *that*? Poof! A nothing, truly—would *I* lie?

An immediate divorce from Kitty, as quiet and unremarked upon as his influence could make it, freeing her to go to her tall, lusty, oafish, bucolic Prince Charming and legitimize their (many, no doubt) children. Not too proud to take her sister's leavings—did they compare notes about how well he performed in bed? For that matter, how many of the four had he bedded?

As for himself, that was easy. The new Charles Burdum was divorced but respectable, an Independent M.P. who kept his feminine relationships light and used his horse-faced political adviser on the few occasions when he needed a hostess—no breath of scandal would linger there! Odd, that she should turn out to have a son. Well, Burdum House was about to undergo yet more rebuilding—a spacious flat for him, and another for Dorcas and Andrew Chandler. Perhaps the lad would turn out to be a greater consolation than a son of his own body might have proved? Certainly, were that son of Latimer stock. Vulgar, common sluts—but that's your *private* opinion, Charles! In public? Merely misguided, poor things.

I fell down because I mistook a slut for a lady, he thought, but I have been raised up again, a phoenix. I still have a life.

The Rector had a hard tussle with his conscience as love for his child and a character big enough to admit his own failings saw him come out in public support of Kitty's socially damned action. To live in open adultery made her many enemies, though few condemned Jack, seen as her dupe. Feeling strangely freed, the Reverend Thomas Latimer doffed surplice and stole to retire; within two days of the scandal's breaking he had packed up what he needed of his property from the Rectory and moved into Grace's cream-and-green cottage on Trelawney Way. His reasoning was straightforward: if God had not made Man and Woman with failings, of the flesh and other, worse kinds, there would be no need for men of religion any more than there would be a need for police. Therefore, to abandon them when they cried out for help was as big a sin as theirs.

Unsanctioned it might now be, but his work at the orphanage, the asylum, the hospital, and relief for those suffering from the Great Depression went on, and was gratefully received. Life in the Trelawneys, he soon discovered, was rich, varied, and stuffed with sin. Just his kind of place, really. Of course he paid Grace rent, grew vegetables, and cosseted the chooks into laying.

His daughters were now a larger part of his life than they had been, but when he was in Corunda he never let a day go by without visiting Maude. It kept him humble, in mind of God's mysteries.

Her sisters were wholeheartedly glad for Kitty. Their guilt at pushing her into marrying Charlie had weighed on them more heavily as time went on. So to see her settled with the right man was as much a relief as a pleasure. Perhaps only Edda understood how long and painful Kitty's journey had been, but Edda was the sister who slew the demons, and had been there to slay all of Kitty's save Charles, the last and most terrible. Him, she had to slay alone.

Even though scant time had elapsed between Kitty's leaving and this gathering of the four sisters and their men, Charles Burdum's attitude was being made plain to all and sundry: he was going to be a martyr heroically enduring the stigma of a cuckold. What, *that*? Poof! A nothing, truly—would *I* lie?

They congregated for Christmas dinner at Corundoobar, including the Rector, who read Charles aright.

"Very shrewd," he said to Rawson, whom he liked far more as a person than he had Charles. "No sign of sour grapes, certainly nothing that would turn his political supporters against him. I rejoice for Kitty's sake. Some, of course, will never forgive her."

"It's also meant that the major newspapers can't dig up enough sordid details to create a widely publicized scandal out of it," said Rawson, loving the Rector as a person who wouldn't turn away in disgust if he knew Rawson's secret. "The inhabitants of Corunda are reluctant to discuss the matter with outsiders."

Liam Finucan laughed. "Corundites may love Charlie, but they also love Jack Thurlow, little as Charlie likes to hear it."

Jack didn't hear it because he was cooking the dinner, and had his head over a baking dish in which reposed a magnificent haunch of baby porker, its skin crackled to perfection. He lifted his head, smiling. "Dinner's not far off," he announced.

"Do you keep your own pigs?" Rawson asked.

The fair brows rose. "I'd not eat butcher's pork. Mine is free, the little blighters run everywhere. Keeps the fat down and the flesh tender. The only thing keeps them in their sty is their swimming pool. They lie in it with their snouts out, blowing bubbles. And right when they're old enough to become a nuisance, it's time to cook roast pork with trimmings."

"Are you going to let Kitty cook?" Liam asked.

"I'm teaching her, but she's such a midget I'll always have to deal with a haunch of pork."

Tufts sat sipping her sherry and enjoying listening to Grace on the subject of living in a posh part of Sydney. Who would ever have guessed that the Widow Olsen would take to it like a bee to an ocean of nectary flowers?

"I make no secret of my Depression troubles," she said, waving her glass around without spilling a drop. "One has to have an aura of glamour, and a husband who suicided over the Depression is exactly right. Not for the boys, though. They love the life!" Her eyes went a darker grey. "When Kitty jumped the fence into a new paddock I did worry a bit that Charlie would go sour, which would have been a shame. Still, I had Rawson up my sleeve, so I didn't stew the way I would have were there no Rawson."

"Would you have traded your new life for Kitty's jump at freedom from Charlie?" Tufts asked.

Grace looked scornful. "That's an unworthy question, and you know it. To see Kitty happy, I'd gladly go back to life on Trelawney Way."

"Put your hackles down, Grace," Tufts said, grinning. "I'm only playing devil's advocate."

Edda and Kitty sat together on the homestead verandah gazing across the three-quarter-circle bend in the river that embraced the house and gardens. From inside came the murmur of voices rising and falling as Tufts caught up with Grace's doings and the men provided a resonant background rumble.

"Are you happy?" Kitty asked Edda, an honest question.

The porcelain face turned in respectful surprise. "You were worth saving, to ask me that."

"Yes, I realize it. But you haven't answered me."

"I *am* happy. Just not ecstatically happy, like you," Edda said. "I'm doing the work I was born to do, and my husband loves me." She sighed, a sound more wistful than sad. "I suppose I wish he loved me more."

"Then it's as well you have your work. Nothing is so sweet that there's no tinge of bitter in it."

Edda laughed. "That's life you mean, Kitty. Bittersweet."